REMEMBER
HER
NAME

BOOKS BY LISA REGAN

REMEMBER HER NAME

LISA REGAN

bookouture

Published by Bookouture in 2024

An imprint of Storyfire Ltd.
Carmelite House
50 Victoria Embankment
London EC4Y 0DZ

www.bookouture.com

Storyfire Ltd's authorised representative in the EEA is Hachette Ireland
8 Castlecourt Centre
Castleknock Road
Castleknock
Dublin 15 D15 YF6A
Ireland

ISBN: 978-1-83525-970-2
eBook ISBN: 978-1-83525-969-6

In loving memory of Sharon Timmer, a treasured reader. You are missed.

PROLOGUE
FIFTEEN YEARS AGO

Hot vomit rocketed up the back of Officer Josie Quinn's throat. Her hands trembled as she tore off her blood-slick vinyl gloves, clutching them in her fist. She clamped her other palm over her mouth and ran out the front door of the large Victorian house in Denton's central district. Sour bile, coffee, and chunks of undigested food spurted through her fingers just as she threw her upper body over the porch railing. Bending at the waist was a challenge with her bulky bulletproof vest strapped around her torso like a steel casing. Eyes watering, she heaved the contents of her stomach onto the grass below. Acid seared the back of her throat.

A large hand clapped her back. Her field training officer, Artie Peluso said, "Come on, kid. Get it together."

Her insides spasmed each time the images from the inside of the house flashed across her mind. Blood was streaked up her forearms and soaked into the knees of her pants. The gloves had been useless. She tried to breathe through the dry heaves, but more undigested food clotted in her throat.

"Kid," Peluso said, more urgency in his voice. "Pull your shit together or go back to the car."

Josie straightened up, sucking air in through her nose, and wiped her slimy hand on her pants. There was no point in asking for a tissue or paper towel. There weren't any and Peluso was not about to find one for her. Only babies get coddled, he always told her.

She used her sleeve to wipe the rest of the throw-up from her mouth and turned to look up at him. His expression was inscrutable. "I'm fine," she said.

Then she made the mistake of turning her head. On the sidewalk, at least a dozen neighbors had gathered, their wide eyes locked on her as they murmured to one another. Several marked Denton PD vehicles clustered behind them in the street. Some of the officers were already canvassing to see if anyone had seen anything, while others lingered, keeping the crowd away from the house. The call that had brought Peluso and Josie here was from a neighbor who'd heard screaming. A few of her colleagues smirked or laughed as they glanced her way. One of them muttered, "Fucking rookie" loud enough for her to hear. Her cheeks flamed. At least Officer Dusty Branson, standing at the bottom of the steps, had the courtesy to avert his eyes. He was her husband Ray's best friend. He had a year on her and Ray, but he was still new.

"Kid," Peluso said, his tone softening. "Look at me."

Josie tore her eyes from the crowd that had just witnessed her humiliation. She stuffed the bloody gloves into her pocket.

"You did good in there. All that blood, what happened to those poor people—well, I would still be puking if I saw that my first year on the job."

So. Much. Blood. Peluso's words sparked the images back to life. It was everywhere. Dripping from the ceilings. It was almost impossible to walk in there without stepping in it, slipping in it. Then there were the bodies. The shredded flesh, the insides spilling out, the mutilation. In the six months she'd been a Denton PD officer, she'd seen a body that fell from a roof, a body smashed inside a car that had been pulverized by a semi-truck, a few bodies ravaged by drugs, killed by overdoses, and one body riddled with gunshots.

None of that prepared her for what they walked in on today.

Peluso slapped her shoulder. "Hey, you held out till the very end, that's what matters."

She had been fine. Mostly. Not really, but she'd been able to stow her emotional and physical responses to the horror, pushing them down deep into the place where the bad things lived. That was until she was kneeling next to a girl so tiny she looked like a doll, and her hands were trying to push the flayed skin of her little chest back together.

"Why did you leave me with the girl?" Josie choked, the foul taste of bile stinging her tongue. "You could've... you have more experience rendering aid. I wasn't—"

Peluso leaned down, invading her personal space, his face inches from hers. A muscle flexed in his jaw. "You think we get to pick and choose on this job, Quinn?"

She tried to step back but the railing bit into her lower back. "No, I—"

His voice was low and menacing. "You signed up for this shitshow. Whatever you get is what you deal with, what you live with. You don't get to walk out. You don't get to decide it's too hard. If you can't handle it, then go be a fucking librarian."

Swallowing, Josie thrust her chin up at him. The truth was that she wasn't sure she could handle it. All her life she'd wanted to be a police officer. She'd wanted to have the power to arrest people like her mother. Cruel, evil, ruthless people who bartered with innocent lives and crushed them without remorse. She'd wanted to be part of a team that fought to make people's lives better. Except that this job was an endless procession of depravity and tragedy, punctuated by long hours of paperwork. No one gave a shit if her intentions were pure or if she wanted to protect people. Other than Peluso, the team she had hoped to join was made up of a bunch of middle-aged men who thought she would be better off shaking her ass for tips at the local strip club or serving them drinks at the bar after their long shifts.

Even the damn uniforms weren't made for women. She had to wear men's shirts and pants, which made her look like a little girl playing dress-up in her daddy's work clothes. For the first time ever, she cursed her slender frame and tiny waist. Fitting all of her equipment onto her duty belt was a pain in the ass, and hauling twenty pounds' worth of gear around on her person for hours at a time was exhausting. Not to mention her back hurt constantly, and most of the time, her hips were completely numb.

And now she knew what it felt like to press her hands against a tiny girl's sternum, bone visible under her fingertips, as her heartbeat faded.

Maybe she *should* become a librarian. Maybe she couldn't handle this.

But she'd be damned if she let anyone know that, especially her field training officer. She sure as hell wasn't going to show any more weakness to the assholes on the sidewalk laughing at her. Mustering as much attitude as she possibly could, she said, "I'm not going anywhere."

Peluso narrowed his eyes, staring until Josie knew he was waiting for her to break. She held eye contact. He was a decent guy but if he thought she was backing down from his challenge, he could go fuck himself.

They were interrupted by the sound of heavy footsteps. Hugh Weaver, one of the Denton PD crime scene techs, trudged up the porch steps, swinging a heavy case. The faint smell of whiskey trailed behind him.

Peluso put a hand on his shoulder, stopping him from entering the house. "Where's the rest of your team?"

Hugh shrugged. "Hell if I know, but I'm not waiting all damn day for them."

Peluso didn't let him pass. "There's a man out back but no one else goes inside until I say."

Hugh grumbled but Peluso ignored him, turning back to Josie. "Quinn, go get the clipboard. You'll be posted here at the door. You'll be responsible for logging in every person who enters and exits the house."

Wordlessly, Josie sprinted down the steps and muscled her way through the throngs of onlookers and Denton PD patrol officers until she reached her cruiser. A few officers quietly jeered her as she returned to the porch, but she ignored them. She was just happy that Peluso let her stay and gave her some responsibility. She quickly signed Weaver in while Peluso went around to check on things at the back of the house.

Her back ached as she stood sentry, watching the crowd of neighbors thin out until only a dozen people remained. From the bottom of the steps, Dusty said, "You know who caught this case, don't you?"

"I don't care," Josie said. "All the detectives are dickheads."

Dusty chuckled. "This guy is the king of dickheads."

"Great," she mumbled. Just what she needed. The perfect topping on this shit sundae of a shift.

As promised, Jimmy "Frisk" Lampson showed up fifteen minutes later. He'd gotten his nickname because he routinely pulled over teenage girls for bogus reasons and then made them get out of their vehicles so he could "frisk" them. In high school, several girls had had encounters with him. He was a pervert and a pedophile. Josie always wondered if he'd done more than grope his victims, but no one ever came forward. He was a police officer, and he was very good at intimidating teenage girls. One girl in Josie's class had tried to report him for touching her inappropriately during a traffic stop and she'd ended up in a juvenile detention center for three months. It was a lesson for all of them: Don't fuck with Frisk Lampson.

Now he sauntered down the sidewalk like he had all day, grinning like he was coming to a backyard barbecue and not a crime scene where multiple people had been savagely slaughtered. He stopped to chat with a couple of the uniformed officers, joking and laughing. Ignoring the male neighbors, he zeroed in on the females, mostly older women. Not his type. Eventually, he spotted a group of teenage girls clustered along the edge of the pavement. Their cheeks were stained with tears, and they held themselves, arms wrapped tightly around their torsos.

Was he really going to pull his bullshit right here? In broad daylight, in front of a bunch of people? At a crime scene?

Josie let out a sigh of relief as he continued to chat with the girls, keeping his distance, jotting down notes on a pad as they talked. Minutes ticked by. A woman in her late thirties approached, joining the group. She curled an arm around one of the girls. Her daughter, probably. They turned to leave and two of the other girls went with them. Only one girl remained.

Scanning the street, Josie realized that the rest of the onlookers had migrated several feet away from Lampson and the girl. Separating the weak from the herd. Lampson subtly moved in on the girl until her back was pressed against a police car. There was a whispered discussion between them, Lampson gesturing toward the other vehicles. The girl shook her head.

"Dusty," said Josie.

"I'm not getting involved."

Josie still couldn't figure out why the hell Ray was friends with him.

"Just go over there. Ask him something."

"I'm not getting involved."

The girl's mouth formed the word no. Lampson stepped closer, dropping his lips to her ear and saying something that made her recoil. Josie took a step forward, the movement drawing the girl's attention. Their eyes locked. Josie knew the "rescue me" look. She was a woman, after all.

Rage ignited inside her, blazing through her veins. Her heart thrashed inside her rib cage. She could barely hear over the roar inside her own head. Through gritted teeth, she said, "*Dusty.*"

He must have recognized the change in her tone because he turned and looked at her. "Aww, shit," he said. "The Chief already talked to you about your temper. How many times now?"

"Only twice." Josie held out the clipboard. "Come up here and take this. You're on the door."

"It's not worth it."

The anger was white-hot now, blistering her insides. "I didn't ask for your opinion, Dusty. Get up here and take this. You're on the door."

With a heavy sigh, he tromped up the steps and took the clipboard. "You're gonna regret this."

ONE

Sweat dampened the nape of Detective Josie Quinn's neck. Lifting her black locks with one hand, she used the other to fan her skin. Even at nine in the morning, the July air felt heavy and cloying. She stood on the sidewalk outside a residence in Central Denton, wishing this particular section of the street was shaded. This neighborhood was one of the oldest in the city, featuring large Victorian homes, most of which had at least one tree out front. Not this one. The prospect of air conditioning called to her like a siren song from her SUV, parked nearby.

"Here." A paper coffee cup appeared in front of her face.

Josie took it and smiled up at FBI Agent Drake Nally. He was off duty, dressed casually in a fitted blue T-shirt and tan cargo shorts. Sunglasses shielded his brown eyes.

"Blonde latte?" she asked him.

"That's what you asked for."

"Thanks." She took a long sip, ignoring the burn across her tongue.

Drake looked from her to her SUV. "Why aren't you sitting in your car? In the AC?"

A smile curved Josie's lips and she used her cup to motion toward the house. "Wait for it..."

Drake studied the property. Behind a wrought-iron fence, a Jack Russell terrier lay on its back, sunbathing on the front lawn. Folding his arms across his chest, Drake said, "Looks like a hotbed of crime."

Anticipatory glee stirred in Josie's heart. "Just wait."

"Shouldn't you be in there? Did you get a call?"

She sipped her latte, not even caring that the hot drink was going to make her sweat more. "We did. Margaret Bonitz. She's an elderly widow. Last year she called 911 a half-dozen times saying that someone was breaking into her house and stealing things—but nothing valuable. Dishes and flatware. The remote control. Weird stuff. Responding officers couldn't find any evidence of a break-in. They started to think she was senile."

Drake turned away from the house and dipped his chin, watching Josie carefully. "She wasn't senile, was she?"

"Nope. Neighborhood kids were messing with her. Gretchen had Mrs. Bonitz order a cheap camera, set it up for her, and caught them. Anyway, now when she calls, we come. Gretchen told her to call the investigative team, not 911."

Drake pursed his lips, looking impatient. He wasn't in Denton in his official capacity as an FBI agent. He only ever came to Denton with his girlfriend, Trinity Payne, who was also Josie's twin sister. Trinity was an accomplished journalist who had moved from anchoring a national network news broadcast to having her own show, *Unsolved Crimes with Trinity Payne*. In fact, she was still in New York City finishing up an episode. It was very unusual for Drake to travel without her, much less for him to request a few minutes of Josie's time in private. Something was up, but right now, Josie was solely focused on Margaret Bonitz's front door.

Realizing this, Drake sighed. He pushed a hand through his dark hair, somehow making his already perfectly tousled mane look even more dashing. He couldn't be a more perfect fit for Josie's sister. She hoped he wasn't in Denton early to tell her that he was about to dump Trinity.

"If you got a call, why are you out here?" he asked.

"I'm waiting for my colleague. The new guy."

He tipped his head back, letting out a long breath. "Oh. Douchebag."

"I'm not supposed to call him that anymore. Out loud. But yeah, that's the one." He was still saved in her phone contacts as Douchebag, though.

Detective Kyle Turner had been hired about a year ago to replace their fallen colleague, Detective Finn Mettner. Denton was a small city in central Pennsylvania. Its central district—where Josie and Drake now stood—straddled the banks of a branch of the Susquehanna River but the city limits extended far beyond that, its rural roads threading through the mountains that surrounded it. Its population was enough to support a decent-sized police department as well as a four-member investigative team which included Josie, her husband, Lieutenant Noah Fraley, Detective Gretchen Palmer, and the newest and most loathsome member of the team, Turner.

"He hasn't gotten any better then?" Drake asked.

Josie took another sip of her latte. "Well, I'm more inclined to throat punch him now than knee him in his balls, if that tells you anything."

Drake snickered. "I'm not sure what that says about him—or you."

"He's still late filing his shitty reports. Half the time we have no idea where he is. One of these days his phone will need to be surgically removed from his hand—if Gretchen doesn't shove it up his ass before then—but we're still working on his inability to call us by our actual names."

The front door of Mrs. Bonitz's house opened and Turner emerged, phone in hand, looking as annoyed as ever. Margaret followed him onto the porch, chattering away, pointing an arthritic finger up at his face. Apparently, he made as good a first impression on her as he did on everyone else. Without looking away from his phone screen, Turner said something to her that made her shake her head in disgust.

Finally noticing the presence of his owner and Turner, the dog flipped onto its feet.

"What are we waiting for?" asked Drake.

"You'll see."

Turner waved Mrs. Bonitz away and started down the walk, head bent to his phone, thumb scrolling. The dog let out a growl. Turner didn't notice. The dog followed him to the gate. Turner fumbled to unlatch it. Mrs. Bonitz's dog took that opportunity to lift his leg and make his displeasure with the large unwelcome human known.

Josie hid her giggle behind her coffee cup.

A stream of expletives burst from Turner's mouth as he watched the dog dart away, back to the safety of the porch. Mrs. Bonitz still stood there, now wearing a satisfied smile. Turner looked down at his soaked pantleg and let out a groan. "You've got to be kidding me."

Finally, he got the gate unlatched and stalked over to Josie, not sparing Drake a glance. Turner towered over her, his deep-set blue eyes flashing with fury as he speared a finger at her face. "You knew that was going to happen, didn't you?"

Josie didn't back away. "I know that when you come here, if you don't leave fast enough, Mrs. Bonitz's dog will piss on your leg. I did not know you would take so long getting the gate open."

Turner looked down at his pantleg again, growling. He wore a suit to work every day, even in the middle of the summer. "Unbelievable," he muttered.

Drake watched, an amused smile on his face.

"What did Mrs. Bonitz say?" Josie asked innocently.

"You don't give two shits what Mrs. Bonitz said."

"Now that's not true—"

Turner thrust a finger in her face again. "Listen, sweetheart—"

A slow grin spread across Josie's face when he froze. She reached up and pushed his arm down. Then she held out a palm. "Come on, Turner."

From her periphery she saw Drake arch a brow.

Shaking his head, Turner jammed his hands into the pockets of his suit jacket. "This is bullshit."

"You agreed to this so hand it over. It's only Monday. At this rate, by the end of the week I'll have enough money to buy the entire department a round of drinks."

Mumbling even more curses, Turner started searching his pants pockets instead. Finally, he came up with a crumpled dollar bill and deposited it into Josie's hand.

"You could make an effort to look a little less smug," he told her.

"Fuck that." She did make an effort not to wrinkle her nose when she closed her fist around the dollar to find that it was damp. Stuffing it into the pocket of her khakis, she slugged down the rest of her latte.

Turner's head swiveled toward Drake, giving him a slow appraisal. Both men were over six feet. Seeing them face to face, Josie would venture to guess they were exactly the same height. Turner said, "Who the hell is this? He looks like a Fed."

Drake stroked his goatee and glanced over at Josie. "Does he always talk about people like they're not standing right in front of him?"

She shrugged. "Sometimes."

Turner rolled his eyes and extended his hand to Drake. "Detective Kyle Turner."

Drake accepted the offering. "Special Agent Drake Nally."

"You are a Fed. I knew it. What are you doing here? Don't

tell me Mrs. Bonitz has a direct line to you, too. I don't think we need the FBI to figure out which neighbor keeps putting their garbage in her cans."

"He's here for me," Josie said.

One of Turner's brows quirked. "Really? Does your husband know?"

Drake sidled over to Josie and slid an arm around her shoulders. Deadpan, he said, "I just told him. We're going to fight to the death later to see who gets to stay."

Josie could see the momentary confusion flash through Turner's eyes. Then he returned Drake's deadpan tone. "May the best man win."

Josie sniffed the air. "You smell like piss."

"Thanks to you, sweet—" He broke off and quickly corrected himself. "Quinn."

"That still counts," Josie said. "Half a 'sweetheart' is fifty cents."

"I'll put it in the jar at the stationhouse later," he grumbled. "I gotta go home and change my pants. Let me know if any other old ladies need help with their chores."

Drake released Josie as they watched Turner walk away, phone back in his hand. "Wow. He's a ray of sunshine, isn't he?"

Josie turned to face him, surprised at just how nervous she felt. A bead of sweat rolled down her spine. "Never mind him. What's going on? Why all the secrecy?"

Drake took off his glasses and grinned. "Relax. It's good news. I'm going to ask Trinity to marry me."

Josie's worry quickly transformed into excitement. She rocked up onto her toes and threw an arm around his neck, squeezing him in a half-hug. "Drake! That's amazing!"

He patted her back. There was an edge of apprehension when he said, "She'll say yes, won't she?"

Releasing him, Josie laughed. "Considering that she thinks you've taken way too long to do it already, yes. I hope you've got something dramatic planned for the proposal because it's 'go big or go home' with Trinity."

Drake ran his hands through his hair again. "Uh, yeah, I've met her. It's going to be hard to beat jumping off a cliff though."

"My husband didn't *jump* off a cliff. That wasn't part of the proposal. I hope you got Trinity a ring you can see from space."

Drake rolled his eyes. "Why do you think it's taken me so long to propose? Government employees don't make that much. I had to save up."

Josie laughed again. "You have my blessing. I won't tell anyone besides Noah. What is your plan?"

He told her.

Josie raised a brow. "Oh, you're doing it this week? Here?"

He nodded and let out a shaky breath. He was nervous, which was kind of sweet. "So, will you guys help me?"

"Of course."

Her ringtone sounded. She took her phone from her pocket and answered dispatch with a curt, "Quinn." As she listened, her pulse fluttered. "On my way," she said, hanging up.

Drake frowned. "Catch a bad one?"

Josie walked around to the driver's side door of her SUV. "I'm not sure. Dispatch said there's a baby sitting in a stroller in the city park with no parent to be found."

TWO

The sound of a baby wailing set Josie's teeth on edge as she jogged along one of Denton City Park's wide asphalt trails. Sweat poured down the sides of her face as much from tension as from the heat. Here in the park, which teemed with foliage, flowers, and shrubbery, it was always significantly cooler, but the humidity added a suffocating type of heat to the mix. As she drew closer, she tried to determine what type of cry they were dealing with. Josie and her husband didn't have children. Unable to have their own, they'd spent the last year wading through a lengthy process in order to be able to adopt. Last month, they'd had a successful home study and been approved. They were in the process of preparing their adoption profile in order to be put on the waiting list to match with a prospective child.

But Josie still knew the different types of cries that infants used to make their needs known. The I'm-hungry cry. The I'm-hungry-and-you-waited-way-too-long-to-feed-me cry that was so intense and scary that it always made her worry the neighbors were going to call 911. The change-my-diaper cry. The I'm-in-pain cry which came with a really fun guessing game as to whether it was due to gas, teething, colic, ear infection, or something more serious. The I'm-too-cold-or-too-hot cry. The I'm-overly-tired cry. The I-just-want-to-be-held cry. One of her best friends, Misty DeRossi, had given birth to Josie's late first husband's son almost eight years ago and Josie had been one of little Harris's primary babysitters since his infancy.

Damp with perspiration, the back of Josie's polo shirt clung to her skin. The trail curved twice in an S shape. The infant's shrieks grew louder. Finally, the stroller came into view. It was the kind with the detachable car seat. Josie was glad to see its hood was extended, giving the infant protection from the sun. One uniformed officer—Dougherty—gripped the handle of the stroller and gently pushed it back and forth while peering down at the baby. His partner, Brennan, stood nearby, talking into his radio.

Josie jogged over to the stroller and muscled Dougherty out of the way.

"This poor kid," he said, raising his voice to be heard over the yowls. "Won't stop crying. I don't know what to do. Brennan said try keeping the stroller in motion but that's not working."

She pushed the hood back. A red-faced infant waved her clenched fists. Her chubby legs flailed angrily. Given the flowered headband and pink onesie that proclaimed, "Mommy's Mini-Me," it was clear that the baby was a girl. The cry definitely had something to do with comfort. Josie unlatched the straps and lifted the baby into her arms. She held her against her chest. From her size and weight, Josie guessed she was about four or five months old.

Josie bounced her lightly until the wails subsided into breathy whimpers. "You didn't try to pick her up?"

Dougherty shook his head. "I don't have kids. I was afraid I'd drop her."

"What's going on?"

Dougherty pointed to the cupholder on the stroller's handle where a cell phone rested. "A 911 call came in from this phone. It belongs to a woman named Cleo Tate. Thirty-three. Lives a few blocks from here."

Brennan walked over. "She didn't say anything on the call. There was nothing but dead air."

But the police would still have been dispatched in case there was an emergency in which the caller was unable to speak. If Denton PD had arrived and found nothing amiss, they'd simply mark the call as unfounded and move on.

Dougherty said, "When we got here, we found the baby in the stroller. No Cleo. Her phone was in the cupholder here on the handle. The diaper bag is there."

Josie followed his gaze to the side of the path where a pink diaper bag was tipped onto its side, onesies, diapers, wipes, and an empty bottle spilling out onto the grass.

All of them were streaked with blood. Ice shot through Josie's veins.

"We called the ERT," said Dougherty.

"We searched the immediate area," Brennan said, waving a hand around them. "Called for her. When we couldn't find her, I called in additional units. They're searching the rest of the park now."

The baby tugged at a lock of Josie's hair, trying to put it into her mouth. Gently, Josie pulled it from her grip. She lifted the baby in the air, checking her over for any wounds. There was a reddish smudge marring the back of the baby's onesie, a bloody Rorschach stretching across her little shoulder blades. Josie pulled at the collar and peered down the back. Relief pulsed through her when she saw the smooth, untouched skin beneath.

"Holy shit," said Brennan. "Is she bleeding?"

Josie shook her head. "It's not from her. We need more

units. A team of officers to canvass. Talk to every person you can find inside the park. I want to know if anyone saw Cleo or anything suspicious. Pull her driver's license photo and get it out to everyone so they can use it in interviews. Send it to me as well."

"On it." Dougherty stepped away and began speaking into his radio.

Brennan took out his phone. As his fingers flew across the screen, he asked, "You want the K-9 unit?"

A slobber-covered hand batted at Josie's cheek. She pretended to try to catch it with her mouth, earning a high-pitched giggle from the baby. Looking into her angelic face and big brown eyes, emotions swarmed Josie. She imagined holding her own child like this one day. Then she was overcome with panic for Cleo Tate. Josie's guess was that she'd been attacked and abducted. Or she'd gone with her attacker willingly in order to spare her child. Josie hated to think how long the baby would have been out here if Cleo hadn't called 911. Chances were that someone would have walked by within an hour, but there was no guarantee.

Then again, they had no inkling of Cleo Tate's personality, mental status or the state of her life. Was it possible she'd been in the midst of some kind of mental health crisis? Had she harmed herself? Had she meant to abandon her baby in public and the 911 call was to ensure that the child would be found quickly?

"Quinn?" Brennan said, shaking Josie from her thoughts. "K-9 unit, or no?"

The baby grabbed another fistful of Josie's hair, pulling more forcefully this time. She tried to stuff it in her mouth, but Josie stopped her. "Let's finish the search of the park. If we don't find Cleo Tate, then I'll call Luke and Blue."

"You got it. How about the baby?"

Josie held her out to Brennan. "First, I want to see if she's got a pacifier somewhere. Then we'll see if we can get in touch with someone in Cleo's family—a spouse, maybe—and get them to meet us here."

Brennan looked at the baby like Josie was trying to hand him a ticking bomb. Did none of these young patrol guys have kids? Or nieces or nephews?

"Just take her," Josie said. "I only need a minute. All you have to do is not drop her."

He hesitated.

"Brennan," Josie said. "Take her."

The moment the baby was in Brennan's arms, she began to fuss. "She doesn't like me," he announced.

"I just need one minute," Josie repeated as she squatted in front of the stroller. If the baby used a pacifier, she likely would have had it while her mother was pushing her around. She might have dropped it. Hopefully it was in the seat. Both Dougherty and Josie had already touched the stroller, unfortunately. Josie pushed the hood as far back as it would go and froze.

The baby whined. Brennan said, "Seriously. She doesn't like me. I think you should take her back. I can find whatever it is you're looking for in there. Quinn? Are you okay?"

A prickle of unease ran up the back of Josie's neck. This case of a missing mother was no longer a garden variety abduction. A quick glance at the baby squirming against Brennan's chest made the fine hairs along her nape stand to attention.

Josie backed away. "Don't touch this again."

The baby's whines turned to full-blown cries. She beat a tiny fist against Brennan's chest. He took a few steps closer, bouncing the screaming infant up and down the way that Josie had, without soothing her. Together, they peered at the seat where a picture rested, its edges stained with blood.

"It was under her back," said Josie. She hadn't seen it because she'd been too intent on comforting the child.

"You sure that's a photo? It looks... weird." He shifted the baby in his arms, bending at the knee to get a better look. "What's wrong with it?"

"Nothing wrong with it," said Josie. "It's a polaroid."

THREE

Josie stood to the side of the trail, under the shade of a maple tree, and watched as Officer Hummel, the unofficial head of the Denton Police Department's Evidence Response Team, took photos of the stroller. With each series, he moved in closer, until the camera was solely focused on the polaroid in the center of the car seat. Shifting the baby in her arms, Josie took out her cell phone, pulled up her photo gallery, and studied the shot of it that she'd snapped earlier. The quality was terrible, almost blurred. The picture itself was barely two inches by two inches. Any smaller and it would be the size of a postage stamp. Its white edges were smeared with a burnished red. A partial bloodied fingerprint was visible in one corner. The image itself appeared to be of mud and rocks—the riverbank, maybe? In one corner was a flash of bright blue but Josie couldn't tell what it was from. An object? A trick of light? A reflection from something? It couldn't be from somewhere inside the park. Although Denton's city park seemed to have everything—even a carousel —it did not have a pond, stream or any other body of water.

At this point, it didn't matter all that much. The 911 call, the abandoned infant, and the blood made it clear that Cleo

Tate was in trouble. The most important thing was locating her. Hummel found more drops of blood along the edge of the path —soaking into the dirt that edged the asphalt and forming beads on the leaves of the shrubbery. Assuming the blood belonged to Cleo Tate, the blood at the scene wasn't enough to infer that she had been grievously wounded but it was a clear sign that she was in imminent danger.

Teams of officers had already been dispatched to search the park. The Denton PD was fully mobilized, and yet Josie felt the seconds slip by like water flooding from a faucet. The process was moving but it just didn't feel fast enough.

It was never fast enough when a life was in jeopardy.

Frustrated, she used her thumb to swipe to the driver's license photo of Cleo Tate that Brennan had texted her. Unlike most people, Cleo had smiled for her driver's license photo, as if she was excited to have it taken. Her brown eyes sparkled. Along her left cheek was a constellation of moles. Shiny dark hair, parted in the middle, hung to her shoulders.

"Where are you?" Josie murmured. Hummel didn't hear her, too engrossed in his work.

The baby was growing heavy. Josie put her phone away and shifted the infant again, drawing a soft sigh. It was considerably cooler beneath the tree and a breeze ruffled Josie's hair, offering even more relief. Someone was supposed to be bringing another stroller. While she'd waited for Hummel to arrive, there had been plenty of additional uniformed officers to hand the baby off to, but Josie was the only person that could keep her calm. If she wasn't so worried about Cleo Tate, she might have taken a little pride in this fact. She was nervous enough as it was about motherhood. When an infant she didn't know felt comfortable enough to fall asleep in her arms, she took that as a good sign. The baby's head rested on Josie's shoulder. It reminded her of the way Harris used to fall asleep for her at this age, always leaving a sizable wet spot of drool on her shirt.

Brennan came around the bend. His dark hair was slick with perspiration. He sounded slightly out of breath as he pushed a stroller toward her. This one was sleek, its seat forward-facing and angled back. At the front was a single large wheel and at the back were two bigger ones, all designed for more challenging terrain than a city sidewalk. "Best I could do," Brennan said. "Conlen lent it to us. He's got kids."

"Great," Josie said, trying to keep the disappointment out of her voice. She wasn't sure that this particular model was appropriate for a four- or five-month-old but it had straps to secure the baby. They had to work with what they had.

Brennan pulled a three-pack of onesies from under his arm, still sealed in their packaging, and handed them to Josie. "Someone else ran to the store and got these. Seems like she shouldn't have to stay in what she's wearing, especially with the blood."

"Thank you," said Josie. The onesies were for babies in the six-to-nine-month age range. Holding the baby close to her chest with one arm, she tore the packaging open and took one out. It would be big but she wasn't about to complain.

Brennan went on, "We made contact with Cleo Tate's husband, Remy. Turner's bringing him to the park."

"Turner?" Josie said, unable to keep the incredulity from her tone. He was notorious for disappearing in the middle of shifts. When he went home to change his pants, Josie figured she wouldn't see him again until their next shift together. She had called him right after finding the polaroid, leaving him a detailed voice message about what was happening, but she hadn't expected him to respond, much less return to work. She had been fully prepared to call Gretchen instead, even though she had been occupied all morning with the body of a man found floating in the Susquehanna River.

Brennan shrugged. "Yeah. Dougherty radioed. Turner told him that he'd call when they get here."

From across the trail, Hummel muttered, "Hell hath frozen over."

Ignoring him, Brennan motioned to the Tate stroller. "Look, I don't want to sound stupid. I didn't have time to google it. What's a polaroid?"

Without looking up from his work, Hummel said, "You really don't know? You're not that much younger than we are."

Brennan swiped a hand over his forehead. "I'm pretty sure you're old enough to be my dad."

This earned him a scowl. "I'm not even forty, dickhead. What are you? Twenty-five?"

"Twenty-seven."

Josie motioned for Brennan to hold the new stroller still while she checked the straps. She had a feeling asking him to find the brakes and put them on would take an inordinate amount of time. "Polaroids are instant photos. You take the picture, and it pops right out of the camera. You have to wait a few minutes for it to develop but it's still very fast. My grandmother had one back in the eighties. Some of the baby pictures she took of me were polaroids."

Hummel let his camera hang around his neck and then went over to his kit to get an evidence bag. "They're making a comeback. Teenagers love them."

"How do you know that?" Brennan asked.

Josie laid the baby in the seat. Her little legs kicked as Josie worked to change the onesie. Hummel took the stained one. Josie tucked the packaging with the remaining clothes into the netting under the seat. The baby began to wriggle as Josie secured her. "Because on several of the cases we've worked the last few years involving teens, polaroids have come up."

Hummel nodded as he used a Sharpie to scribble on the evidence bag. "This one kid convinced his girlfriend to let him take nude photos of her using the polaroid. Claimed that way they couldn't be shared."

Brennan winced. "Let me guess. He took digital photos of the polaroids."

Hummel deposited the bloodied onesie into the evidence bag. "You got it. Total nightmare."

"But with this..." Brennan waved a hand at the stroller. "Why take a polaroid of some muddy rocks and leave it in the stroller?"

"The alternative is to take a digital photo and have it printed somewhere," Josie said, tightening the straps around the baby, who was now gazing up at her with curiosity. "You'd have to leave a name, maybe use a credit card, and if you could get away with walking into a store and having them print it on the spot or letting you print it yourself, there would be surveillance video of you, witnesses."

"Couldn't you just print it at home with one of those color printers?"

Hummel interjected, "You could. We probably couldn't track you down that way—unless you left prints on the photo. It looks like I've got a partial here, though it could be from Cleo Tate. Anyway, if we were able to locate you somehow, we'd likely be able to find the digital photo on one of your electronic devices."

The baby put a fist into her mouth. Still, there was no crying. Josie was certain that she would be hungry soon. She had no idea if Cleo Tate was breastfeeding or using formula but either way, there were no other bottles in the diaper bag. Josie said, "There are so many of these polaroid cameras on the market now that even if we could figure out the brand or manufacturer from the photo, we'd never track down the person who took the photo that way."

"It's old-school," Hummel said. "As long as your prints aren't on the picture, you don't exist. Even if they are, unless you show up in AFIS, we can't actually find you that way. We can only match up prints after you're caught by some other means."

Which meant that whoever left the photo had thought about what they were going to do well ahead of time. Josie would bet a week's pay that the partial print was from Cleo and not the person who'd left it. Even if it wasn't, the quality was likely not good enough for Hummel to run it through the database. The photo was some kind of message and Josie's gut told her that no one was going to be happy once its meaning was made clear.

Brennan's radio squawked. "Turner's here with Cleo Tate's husband. They're at the park office."

Josie pushed the jogging stroller down the path. "Let's go."

FOUR

Cold air cascaded over Josie's face as she pushed the stroller into the park office. The temperature in the tiny brick building was at least twenty degrees cooler than outside. It felt glorious. Just inside the double doors was a large metal desk. A laptop and telephone sat on its surface, but no one manned it. Josie took a quick glance at the baby, now asleep, and shoved past the desk into the short hallway beyond it.

"I thought you said they would be here," said a panicked male voice behind the first door on the left.

Then came Turner's voice. "They'll be here any second."

Josie used the front wheel of the stroller to prod the door. A second later, it opened, Turner's huge form filling the doorway. He now wore a blue suit and even in the mid-morning heat, still had his jacket on. From one of the pockets peeked a can of his beloved energy drink. He stepped aside so that Josie could maneuver the stroller into what was a very small room lined with shelves that held tools, paint, and other outdoor supplies. Another empty desk took up most of the space. A window looked out on a grove of trees. A shorter, thinner man pushed past Turner to get to the stroller. Even in the air conditioning, his light brown hair curled from the humidity. The short-sleeved white button-down shirt he wore clung to him, wet with sweat, making the tank top beneath it visible. His green tie hung loosely around his neck.

He dropped to his knees and began unlatching the straps. "Oh my God. Gracie. My God."

Turner said, "This is Remy Tate. Cleo's husband."

Remy lifted his daughter and cradled her in his arms. She continued to snooze. He looked at the crown of Gracie's head. "Is she okay? Do you think she's okay?"

Josie pulled her polo shirt from her neck, shaking it to cool herself down. "She seems fine, but if you'd like to have her checked out at the hospital, we will be happy to take you both there."

Remy didn't even register her answer. He pressed a kiss onto little Gracie's head and sighed with relief. Then his expression changed to panic. His body went rigid. Meeting Josie's eyes, he said, "Detective Turner told me what happened. The 911 call. Gracie left alone in the park. Cleo missing. Do you know what happened?"

"Unfortunately, no," Josie said. "Not at this time. We've got teams searching the entire park for any sign of her or anyone who might have seen her. When is the last time you spoke to your wife?"

"This morning," he said, shifting Gracie so that her cheek rested against his chest. "I left the house around seven. She was feeding the baby. I kissed them both goodbye and then I went to work. We have one of those Ring cameras. She left with Gracie around eight thirty."

"Mr. Tate here provided me with that footage. I pulled a still from it. We can get that out." Turner perched along the edge of the desk, turning his focus back to Remy. "You guys fight at all recently?"

Remy looked mystified. "What? No. Not recently. I mean,

we're exhausted, but that goes with the territory, having a newborn. Maybe we're snapping at one another more lately but other than that, we're good."

"You sure?" Turner pressed. "Kids can cause a lot of stress."

Remy stared up at Turner, mouth open.

Josie jumped in. "Do you have other children?"

"No. Gracie is our first." Remy smiled down at her sleepy face.

Turner's fingers drummed against the lip of the desk. "Is your wife a full-time mom?"

"No. She's on maternity leave. Somehow, she got six months. Lucky. I only got two weeks—which I know is more than most dads get but I would have loved to have been home with my girls longer. I work for the city, by the way. The clerk of courts. Records department. That's where I met Cleo."

"What does your wife do?" asked Josie. Cleo was indeed lucky. Denton PD only offered six weeks of paid maternity leave and it was even less if they adopted.

"She's an attorney for Harbor Insurance Company. She's due to go back to work in two months."

Which meant that little Gracie was four months old, as Josie had estimated.

Turner took out his phone. Was he really going to start scrolling in the middle of an interview? He must have seen her glare because he put it back into his pocket with a sigh. "Mr. Tate, how's your wife's mood been lately? She seem like she enjoys being stuck at home with a kid?"

So much finesse.

Remy laughed, an edge of nervousness to it. "She's looking forward to going back to work. Her mood has been fine. What are you suggesting? That she had some sort of breakdown and left Gracie in the middle of the park? Cleo would never do that. We have enough support from friends and family that if she needed a break, she could have had one."

Josie was certain that someone had told Turner about the blood found with the diaper bag and the picture. Still, it wasn't outside the realm of possibility that Cleo had harmed herself and staged the scene. Unlikely, in Josie's estimation, but not impossible.

Turner didn't answer Remy's question, instead asking another of his own. "She got postpartum, or what?"

Remy shook his head. Gracie shifted in his arms, one of her tiny fists clutching at his shirt. "No. She's fine. It sounds like you're accusing my wife of abandoning our baby. Cleo wouldn't do that."

Josie shot Turner a warning look. He rolled his eyes and took out his phone again. Remy's face turned red, his features hardening.

"We're not accusing your wife of anything," Josie said quickly. "We're only trying to figure out what happened today so we can find Cleo as quickly as possible. Does Cleo often bring Gracie to the park?"

The baby sighed in her sleep. Remy glanced down at her, expression softening instantly. "Yes. If the weather is nice, she brings her here. She tries to come early before it gets too hot. All the fresh air wears Gracie out and Cleo said it's good exercise for her."

"Did Cleo ever mention having any trouble with anyone here in the park?" asked Josie. "Maybe someone who followed her or made her uncomfortable?"

"What? No." Remy covered Gracie's ear as if he didn't want her to hear this line of questioning.

Turner looked up from his phone. "Your wife ever have any stalkers?"

"No, no."

"How about any exes who couldn't let go?" Turner continued. "Coworkers or neighbors or anyone else that took too much interest in her, or anyone she might have pissed off?"

"No," Remy insisted. "There hasn't been anyone or anything like that in her life. She would have told me."

Turner's gaze drifted back to his phone screen, thumb scrolling rhythmically. Josie wanted to smack it out of his hand. He said, "Is it possible she was stepping out on you?"

Remy's eyes bulged. "You think Cleo was cheating on me?"

Josie edged around Remy and the stroller, putting herself between the two men. "Mr. Tate, I know these are difficult questions, but we have to ask them. We're just trying to figure out if there is anyone in Cleo's life—anyone at all—who might have wanted to harm her."

Behind her, Turner sighed.

Remy shook his head, stroking Gracie's back. "No. Absolutely not."

Turner's breath ruffled the top of Josie's hair. "You sure about that?"

Fury flashed in Remy's blue eyes. He looked up and past Josie, glaring at Turner. "Do we have a problem?"

"I don't know. Do we?"

FIVE

If he hadn't been holding his infant daughter, Josie was certain that Remy would have lunged for Turner. She stepped forward and put a hand behind his elbow, ushering him toward the door. "Just a couple of things before you go, Mr. Tate. Do you or Cleo own a polaroid camera?"

Shock slackened the features of his face. "Wh-what?"

Josie took out her phone and showed him the polaroid found in Gracie's seat. She had taken the time to crop out the bloodied edges. "This was found in your daughter's stroller."

He shook his head. "I don't understand."

"Neither you nor your wife owns a polaroid camera?" she asked again.

"No. We use our phones for everything. I didn't even know they still made those."

"What about the picture itself?" Josie prodded. "Does it seem familiar to you at all?"

Remy looked from the photo to her face. "Do a couple of rocks look familiar to me? No. Shouldn't you be trying to find my wife?"

"That's what we're trying to do, buddy," Turner called,

without looking away from his phone. "Unless you don't want us to."

Red bloomed across Remy's cheeks. His mouth thinned into an angry line. Before he could unleash his wrath on Turner, Josie ushered him quickly through the door. "That's all we have for you right now. Thank you for answering our questions."

He craned his neck to look back at Turner, but Josie guided him down the hall to the first desk, which Brennan now sat atop. He jumped to his feet when he saw them. "This is my colleague, Officer Brennan," Josie said. "He will take it from here. He'll help you with whatever you need. If you'd like to take Gracie to the hospital or you would just like to go home."

Face still flushed with rage, Remy glanced back down the hall, as if waiting for Turner to emerge. Josie held a business card out to him. "We need to get back to trying to locate your wife. Cleo is our priority right now." When he didn't respond, she repeated the words, more slowly this time. Blinking, he took the card.

Discreetly, Josie signaled for Brennan to take over. Then she strode back to the other room, where Turner still leaned against the desk, scrolling on his phone. She slammed the door and advanced on him, snatching the phone from his grasp.

His eyes widened. "What the hell are you doing, sweetheart?"

"You're asking me what the hell I'm doing? Me?" she raged, waving his phone in the air. "What the hell were you doing pushing Remy Tate like that? His four-month-old baby was just found abandoned in the city park in the middle of damn July and his wife is missing!"

Turner folded his arms across his chest. "He doesn't have an alibi."

Josie froze. "What?"

"He wasn't at work when I went there to get him. He had clocked in at the usual time and then left the office at eight thirty—the exact same time his wife left the house with the baby. Told his boss that he forgot his laptop and then he went home. That's where I found him. While Cleo Tate was pushing baby Gracie around the city park, Remy Tate was home—or so he says. Guess where his laptop was?"

Unease prickled over her scalp. "His office."

Turner didn't say anything but his smug look confirmed that she was right.

Josie's hands fell to her sides. She kept hold of Turner's phone. "Was anyone else there with him?"

"Not that I could tell. He only let me into the living room, but I asked to use his bathroom."

Of course he had. Turner used the bathroom everywhere they went. It was his way of doing a plain-view search of any premises they entered.

"Most of the doors in the upper part of the house were open. I didn't see any signs of a struggle. No blood anywhere. Then again, there were rooms I didn't see. Like the basement."

"What did the Ring camera show?"

Turner held out his hand for the phone. "They've only got one. At the front door. He showed me the footage from the morning of him leaving for work and then Cleo taking the baby out. No video of him arriving back home. They have a fairly large portico and a lot of shrubbery. I'm pretty sure the camera doesn't pick up the driveway, and if they don't have cameras out back..."

Josie laid the phone in his hand. "He could sneak into the house without appearing on the camera."

"And while Cleo was here at the park, she wouldn't have gotten a notification from the surveillance app that her husband had come home."

"Which means she wouldn't know what time he came home," Josie said. "When we get a warrant for the contents of her phone, we won't know either. There's the GPS on his car—"

"But the park is within walking distance," Turner filled in. "He could have parked his car there and made it look like he was home but then walked here. The 911 call came in around ten, an hour and a half after he left work. The time frame is tight, but it's not implausible that he could have caught up with her."

"You think he did this?"

"I think he doesn't have an alibi."

A man who would stage his own wife's abduction would certainly not balk at putting his child in danger by leaving her unattended in the park.

"Do you have that still?"

Turner punched a code into the phone, swiped a couple of times, and then turned it to face her. A full-color still of Cleo Tate pushing her stroller out her front door filled the screen. It only showed her in profile but that didn't matter. Now they knew what she'd been wearing when she disappeared. Black yoga pants and a navy blue T-shirt. Her dark hair was covered by a white ballcap. Turner texted Josie the picture.

"If the husband didn't do this," Josie said, "then the only other explanation for him sneaking into his own home when his wife isn't home is that he's having an affair."

Turner pocketed his phone. "In which case, it might clear the husband but then we could have a jealous mistress on our hands. Maybe Cleo didn't know anyone who wanted to harm her, but her husband does."

Josie didn't say anything, moving the pieces around on a puzzle board in her head. "But we can't get warrants for the GPS in his vehicle or any electronic devices, and we can't get a warrant to search the Tate home because we don't have enough probable cause to look at Remy."

"Yet," Turner said.

"We'll have to bring him in for an interview. Get his story locked down. Ask him for consent to look at the contents of his phone and go from there. Do you have someone canvassing his street to see if anyone witnessed him returning home?"

"It's not my first day." He shoved a hand into his pocket and came up with another crumpled dollar bill. "I know you didn't miss me calling you sweetheart just now, in spite of all my brilliant investigative work, so do you want my dollar, or do you want to take a shot at me?"

Josie stared at the bill, nose wrinkling as she remembered the one he'd given her earlier, moist with something she didn't even want to think about.

"You know you want to," he goaded her. "Come on, Quinn. We'll call it even."

Josie took out her own phone and texted the photo of Cleo to Brennan and Dougherty, instructing them to get it out to the rest of the officers searching and canvassing. "We've got work to do," she said. "Keep your dollar, Douchebag."

SIX

Josie trudged along the sidewalk, Turner trailing behind her. She heard a snap of the tab on his energy drink, followed by a fizz and then him guzzling it down. Wishing for another latte, she kept her gaze straight ahead to where Dougherty stood talking with a woman in her thirties. He had texted them that he had a lead. They were only five minutes from the main entrance of the park, striding past the line of houses directly across from the park's tree-lined perimeter.

Josie heard Turner crumple his can. Over her shoulder, she said, "Do not litter."

He huffed. "So bossy. Does your husband—"

She stopped walking and whirled on him, sending him staggering back a step with her glare. He put his hands up. "All right, all right. I didn't even say it."

"You were about to."

"But I didn't, Quinn. I told you I'd work on my"—here he used air quotes—"'inappropriate comments,' and I am."

Rolling her eyes, Josie turned away from him and continued walking. "You should have a jar for those, too."

He caught up to her, shortening his pace to stay at her side. "You and Park— Palmer are already putting me in the poorhouse with these dumbass jars. I'm not doing another one. But hey, I'm open to suggestions. Maybe one of those signs that says, 'It's been forty-seven days without an inappropriate comment from Kyle.'"

Josie scoffed. "As if you could make it forty-seven days without saying something completely inappropriate in the workplace. Now shut up. I want to hear what this witness has to say."

She expected him to come back at her with some kind of scathing barb but instead all he did was sigh. Either that energy drink hadn't kicked in yet or what she liked to think of as the "behavior modification" measures that Noah had put into place were working.

The strong odor of fresh paint coated Josie's throat as they reached Dougherty and the witness. "This is Detective Josie Quinn and Detective Kyle Turner," he told her.

The woman's blonde hair was pushed back with a headband. She wore a yellow tank top under white overalls that were stained with bright blue paint. It was shiny, still wet. That explained the smell. As Dougherty stepped away and started speaking into his radio, Josie and Turner showed her their credentials. She gave them a cursory glance. "I'm Charlotte Thompson," she said. She motioned toward the quaint two-story home behind her, showing off more paint smudged along her wrist and forearm. "I live here. Just bought the place."

Turner eyed the streaks down her front. "What are you? Fifteen? You look young to have your own house."

Josie elbowed him sharply but he ignored her. As usual. "Miss Thompson," she said, unable to let this one slide. "I apologize for my colleague. Since he's not going to do it himself."

Turner eyed Josie with a deep frown. She could practically

read his mind. *What the hell's your problem, sweetheart?* Could she demand a dollar for the silent "sweetheart"?

He must have gotten her mental memo because he sighed again and turned back to Charlotte. "I'm sorry for being rude."

Whether it was sincere or not, Josie couldn't tell, but it satisfied her nonetheless.

Charlotte studied him for a moment. "I accept your apology. Not that it's any of your business, but I'm twenty. My older brother co-signed. He's inside."

Turner decided to move on, gesturing to the paint on her overalls. "Are you some kind of artist or you just fixing this place up?"

"Fixing it up," she answered. "You like the color? Blue is supposed to be soothing."

Turner opened his mouth and Josie just knew he was about to say something like "not really," so she asked Charlotte, "You saw Cleo Tate this morning?"

She pointed across the street to where several cars were parked. "I told the other officer that this morning, there was a white car parked over there. I came out onto my porch to get a package that UPS dropped off and I saw this couple—at least, I thought they were a couple—walking down the street. On that side."

A door slammed and Josie looked up at the porch to see a man in a white T-shirt and painter's pants emerge. Dark hair, broody face. He leaned against the house and crossed his arms, watching them.

"He seems pleasant," Turner muttered.

Josie was grateful that Charlotte seemed not to hear him. "What made you think they were a couple?"

Charlotte scratched her face, smearing blue across her cheek. Her eyes were still fixed on the line of cars across from them. "He was holding her arm. Like this." She sidled up to

Turner and curled a hand around his tricep. He looked down in alarm. Josie knew he was worried about his suit. He was always worried about his suits. Miraculously, he didn't protest. Instead, he said, "Usually couples hold hands, don't they?"

Charlotte released him. Josie wondered if it was wrong that she felt so much satisfaction in the blue fingerprint smudged on Turner's jacket. "Right," said Charlotte. "At first I thought maybe she didn't feel well and he was kind of helping her along. Even from over here, I thought she looked super pale. It wasn't until they got closer that I got a weird vibe. They were walking really fast, and she looked uncomfortable, afraid. Then I thought maybe it was like a domestic violence thing. Her one hand was wrapped up in some kind of white cloth. Like a shirt or something."

A onesie from Gracie's diaper bag?

"Did you see any blood?" asked Josie.

"No blood."

"Did she look over here?" Josie looked from Charlotte's home to the vehicle across the street. "Did she see you?"

Charlotte nodded. "Yeah. We made eye contact and she immediately looked away. He was talking into her ear. She kept her eyes straight ahead. I couldn't hear anything he said. Too far away. Then they stopped at this white car—it was directly across from here—and he kind of pushed her into the passenger's seat. He got in the other side, and they drove off. I was going to call the police but then I thought, 'What would I say?' That the woman's hand was wrapped up? That she looked afraid? Nothing actually happened. I put it out of my mind until this officer showed up asking questions and had me look at that photo. It was the same woman, based on what she was wearing, and her hair color. I'm sure of it."

Dougherty was back. "I showed her the still of Cleo leaving the house."

Cleo had looked afraid but when he put her into the car, she hadn't tried to escape. He must have threatened her with a knife. He'd already drawn blood once. That was likely how he'd gotten her to leave baby Gracie behind. The two of them must have passed more than one person exiting the park and coming down this street and yet, Cleo had made no attempt to run or even to signal for help—not even when she made eye contact with Charlotte Thompson—which meant that she believed she was in mortal danger. Fighting back could result in her being stabbed to death. Going along with him was an act of self-preservation.

Cleo Tate was hoping to survive so she could come home to her baby.

From the corner of her eye, Josie saw Charlotte's brother move from the wall to the railing, resting his forearms against it, leaning his body forward. Watching. It was almost unsettling.

Turner shuffled to the side, blocking Josie from the brother's view. "Could you tell whether or not he was armed? Did you see a knife? Anything that looked like a weapon?"

"No, no. I definitely would have called 911 if he was armed. Although now that you say that..." She wiped sweat from her forehead. "His other arm was crossed over his middle, sort of tucked under her elbow. Like this."

Again, she clutched Turner's tricep. His eyes bulged. He looked at Josie helplessly but all she could do was give a little shrug. Charlotte positioned her other arm over her abdomen like a lap bar, her paint-stained hand disappearing beneath her elbow, between hers and Turner's bodies. "Maybe he had something and was holding it like this." Turner jerked as she poked him in the ribs. Honestly, this was the best shift with him that Josie had ever worked. Charlotte continued, "But I couldn't see it from the way they were walking because they were so close together."

Turner extricated himself, giving her a tight smile. "How about the guy? What did he look like?"

"Definitely not as tall as you," Charlotte said, tipping her head back to meet his eyes. "Maybe a little shorter than this officer, here."

Turner was well over six feet. Dougherty was slightly shorter. "Five foot nine or ten, maybe?" Josie suggested.

"Yeah, I think so. White, not too thin, not overweight. Average, I guess."

"You know who else is average?" Turner said to Josie, and she knew he was referring to Remy Tate.

"Not now," she said. "Go on, Charlotte."

Charlotte looked at Turner, as if waiting to see if he'd say more. When he didn't, she continued, "He had on long pants, like the kind that landscapers wear in the summer? Or, mechanics? Black. A navy-blue T-shirt. He was wearing a hat, just like her, so I couldn't see his hair color."

"What kind of hat?" asked Josie.

"You mean like a logo or something? I couldn't tell from here," Charlotte replied. "Just that it had one of those leafy patterns all the hunters around here usually wear. I'm sorry. I didn't get a good look at his face either."

"That's okay," Josie told her. "This is very helpful. Is there anything else you can tell us about the man? Any tattoos? Scars? Facial hair? Anything distinguishing?"

Charlotte shook her head. "None of those things. At least, I didn't notice. I'm sorry."

"Was he wearing gloves?" Josie asked.

"I don't think so. Unless they were like those clear vinyl ones? They were too far for me to tell. Oh, wait! He had some kind of a bag with him. You know, those weird, one-strap back-packs that go across your body? It was black."

"Was there anything distinguishing about it?" asked Josie.

She'd looked so proud of herself a moment ago, remembering the bag. Now her expression faltered. "No. I'm sorry."

"Don't be. You're doing great. This is all helpful. I'd like to show you something." Josie took out her phone and easily found Cleo Tate's Instagram account. It was private but the profile photo featured her, Remy, and Gracie. It was a professional photo. "One second."

Turner sidled up to her, watching as she cropped Gracie and Cleo out of the picture. If Charlotte didn't recognize Remy, Josie didn't want her potentially telling others that the police were looking at Cleo's husband as a person of interest. As Josie turned the screen toward Charlotte, she asked, "Is this the man you saw?"

Charlotte studied the picture for a long moment and then slowly shook her head. "I don't know. I'm sorry. Maybe? Like I said, I just didn't get a close enough look at him."

Turner tugged at his sleeve, craning his neck to get a look at the paint left on his jacket. "How about Mr. Sunshine up there? He see anything?"

Charlotte shaded her eyes with her palm and looked up at her brother. Apparently not offended by Turner's insult, she said, "No, he was in the house."

"Any idea what kind of car?"

"A Hyundai, maybe? Or a Honda? I'm not really sure. Like I said, it was white. Four doors. I didn't take notice of the license plate. I didn't think it was important."

Dougherty said, "One of the LPRs picked up a white Hyundai about three blocks from here. Registered to Sheila Hampton. She lives on the other side of town."

LPRs, or license plate readers, had been installed on three of Denton PD's patrol vehicles. They scanned the license plates of all moving and parked vehicles nearby and alerted on any that had warrants out on them, had been stolen, or had expired tags. They were lucky that one of the LPR devices had been within the vicinity at the time that Cleo Tate was being abducted. They might have a viable lead.

Josie said, "Do you have units trying to find the car on cameras to see if we can follow it?"

"They're already on it," Dougherty said. "If we get something, you'll be the first to know."

"Guess we're off to meet Sheila Hampton then," Turner said.

SEVEN

She held her hair off her neck, fanning the damp skin with her hand. He sat in the driver's seat, staring at her with dark, unblinking eyes. She'd forgotten how creepy he was, the weight of his unsettling stare making her skin crawl. She should never have let him force her inside, but she'd been too afraid to cause a scene. Now, the urge to fling open the door and throw herself out of the car was so strong that her legs trembled. He wouldn't respond well to that, she was sure. He was, after all, a monster. Plus, they were alone. No one around for miles. Getting into the car with him had been a bad idea.

There was no turning back now.

"You're afraid of me," he said. His upper lip curled into a satisfied sneer.

She hoped he couldn't see the shudder that worked its way through her body. "Why wouldn't I be? We both know what—" The rest of the words died on her tongue as he leaned across the console.

He smelled like coffee and stale sweat. Like an old gym sock that hadn't been washed in months. He must have been working outdoors all morning. It took effort not to gag. The door handle lodged under her rib cage as she backed away from him.

"I remember you," he said.

Her stomach dropped. She didn't think he would. Had counted on it, in fact.

A thick palm clamped down on her thigh. Slapping at his arm with both hands, she tried to twist away but his fingers dug into her flesh. A cry of pain tore from her throat. "Stop! Stop!"

The pressure eased as he loosened his grip, but he didn't let go. Her heart galloped. Dizziness set the world around her spinning. Through heaving breaths, she said, "I don't owe you anything. I'm getting out now. Let me go."

A wolfish grin spread across his face. Releasing her leg, he slid his hand up body until his fingers closed around her throat. Fear fisted her heart. The air in her lungs evaporated.

"You're not going anywhere," he said.

EIGHT

"That's piss and paint in one day," Turner complained as Josie pulled down the street that the Hamptons lived on. Their two-story rancher was located in a development north of Denton University's campus. It was a quaint, peaceful neighborhood populated by working-class homeowners. Teachers, nurses, tradespeople. Many of the Denton PD's patrol officers lived on its tree-lined streets. "I bet old Creepy Creeperson enjoyed watching his little sister get paint all over me."

"I did."

"Glad to be of service, Quinn."

Josie glanced at him, feigning seriousness. "It doesn't sound like you mean that. Moving on, did you get that photo over to Amber?"

"Oh, you mean the press liaison who never actually shows up at work?"

Josie sighed, slowing in front of the address Dougherty had given them. One car was parked in a driveway clearly meant to accommodate two. "You replaced the love of her life, Turner. You sit at his desk."

"And I'm not as good as him," he said.

"You said it, not me."

"Yeah, yeah, I've heard it all. Anyway, must be nice for her to work from home."

Josie found a spot on the street. She could argue that he practically worked from home given how often he disappeared during shifts, but it was a waste of time. "Did you send the photo or not?"

"Of course I did." Turner's phone appeared in his hand. A moment later, he flashed the screen at her. It was a post from one of Denton PD's social media platforms featuring the photo of Cleo Tate and asking for the public's help in locating her. Josie skimmed the rest of the text, absorbing the highlights. Abducted from the city park at approximately ten a.m. Seen with a white male, 5'9" or 5'10" in a white sedan.

Josie hoped that Brennan had updated Remy Tate as she had asked. They hadn't told him about the blood found at the scene and had confirmed the abduction after speaking with him. If all he was hiding was an affair, she didn't want him finding out from social media or the midday news that his wife had been kidnapped.

She turned off the car and hopped out. They walked the small concrete path to the front stoop. Turner reached past her and rang the doorbell. When no one answered, he tried again. There were no home surveillance cameras anywhere around the door. They didn't need one. As a member of the Denton PD, she knew this particular area of the city saw little to no crime.

"Come on," Turner muttered. He tugged at the handle of the screen door. It creaked open.

"Turner," said Josie, but she was too late. He pounded a fist against the main door, making it quake in its frame.

Seconds later, a man opened the door, blinking against the daylight. Josie put him at about five foot nine. Blond wavy hair fell across his forehead. Stubble lined his jaw and dotted his upper lip. Dark circles smudged the skin under his eyes, suggesting he hadn't slept well in some time. Early to mid-thirties, Josie estimated. His black basketball shorts and gray Denton University Alumni T-shirt showed off the lean, well-muscled arms and legs of a runner.

"Can I help you?" he asked, voice raspy as if they had woken him from a nap. He blinked again, eyes dropping to the gun at Josie's waist. "Oh. Right. Come on in."

He ushered them inside. "My wife said she called the police but she's been working all morning. I figured I'd wait until this afternoon and if no one came, I'd call again."

Josie and Turner didn't even have a chance to identify themselves or present their credentials. The living room they stepped into was cool and dark, decorated in a soft gray with white accents. Just inside the door was a narrow table filled with sympathy cards. Across from that, a rumpled blanket lay on the far corner of the couch. A box of tissues peeked from its folds. The end table was filled with orange medication bottles, a remote control, and a novel by S.A. Cosby. Behind all of those things stood a large, framed photo of a young woman. It was a school photo taken from the shoulders up. The girl wore a closed-lip smile. Her brown eyes sparkled with mischief, making her look as though she was holding back laughter. Pale blonde curls tumbled over her shoulders, a stark contrast to the generic blue background.

"I told you I called!" came a woman's voice from elsewhere in the house. "You didn't believe me, did you?"

The man started to roll his eyes but quickly stopped when his wife stepped in from what was presumably the kitchen. Long black hair, shot through with gray, cascaded down her back. A green tank top and a pair of denim shorts hugged her sinewy body. They must both be avid runners. She was easily the same height as her husband, and it looked like she had at least ten years on him. The smile stretched across her face was anything but warm and it was directed at her husband.

He turned back to Josie and Turner, looking them over, as if noticing for the first time that they weren't in uniform. Turner was dressed for church while Josie wore her standard Denton PD polo shirt and khakis. His gaze snagged on Josie's face. "Aren't you that reporter? What are you doing here? With all due respect, we're not up to talking with a—"

His wife cut him off. "Isaac, please. She's got a gun! She's not the reporter."

"You're thinking of my sister. Trinity Payne. We're twins." Josie took out her credentials, holding them out for their perusal.

Turner flashed his as well as he looked around the room. "We're not with the press. We're detectives with Denton PD."

The woman stepped forward as they put their credentials away and extended a hand. "Please excuse my husband's rudeness. Sheila Hampton. This is Isaac."

Turner took her hand first, studying her long elegant fingers as they brushed the sleeve of his jacket. He snatched his hand away as if she'd burned him. He really did have a way with people. If Sheila noticed, she didn't let on.

Isaac didn't offer to shake hands. "I wasn't being rude."

"You didn't mean to be rude," Sheila corrected. "But you were."

Choosing not to engage, Isaac instead addressed Josie and Turner. "I'm confused. Do they normally send detectives to investigate stolen cars?"

"Usually, one of our patrol officers would take the initial report," Josie explained, a sinking feeling in her stomach.

Turner rubbed at something on the cuff of his suit jacket, frowning. "Hey, lady, did you have something on your hand?"

"Turner," Josie admonished under her breath.

"Oh, sorry." Sheila wiped her palms on his shorts. "I thought I washed it all off. It's glue. I'm an industrial designer."

"What the heck is that?" Turner asked.

Sheila scratched at a shiny streak on her forearm. More glue, presumably. "We design and develop products. Anything from furniture to medical equipment. Appliances, electronics, you name it. I specialize mostly in safety equipment. I was working on a prototype of a new kind of hearing band. You know, instead of those clunky headphones. For construction sites, mostly. Just trying to stay busy while I'm here."

"Sheila." Isaac's tone held a warning.

Turner said, "You don't live here?"

"We're separated," Sheila explained. "Have been for about a year now. I took a job in New York City. I couldn't convince him to come with me even though he can do his work from anywhere. He's a support specialist for a banking app—for a bank that has branches in New York City."

"Sheila." This time his voice was a growl.

His wife continued as if he hadn't spoken. "So when I moved, we separated. I'm only here now because..." She left the sentence unfinished, for the first time looking sad and uncertain. Her nails found the shiny streak again, digging into her skin much harder this time.

Josie's eyes were drawn back to the cards, all standing like proud little sentinels, proclaiming their battle cries against grief. *Thinking of you in your time of loss. With Deepest Sympathy. May you find comfort in your loving memories.* The words were as flimsy as the card stock they were printed on.

"You just lost a loved one," she said. "I'm so sorry."

Isaac turned to the photograph on the end table. "Our daughter, Jenna. A month ago. She was about to start college. She had cardiac problems."

Josie's heart fluttered as she studied the photo with new

perspective. No wonder the room, the house, felt so heavy with sadness.

Turner was focused on something else entirely. "You must have been young when you had her. I mean you, not your wife."

Josie resisted the urge to elbow him in the ribs. Isaac ignored the question. "I'd rather not talk about Jenna."

She took the opportunity to redirect the conversation. The clock was ticking for Cleo Tate. Offering Sheila a sympathetic smile, she asked, "Your car was stolen?"

"A white Hyundai sedan?" Turner added. He read off the license plate number that Dougherty had given them.

"That's the one," Sheila said. "It's still registered here."

Cleo Tate's abductor was even smarter than Josie thought, which caused a knot in her stomach. Steal a car that can't be traced to you, abduct a woman in a park with no cameras, and leave a photograph that can never be connected to you. Unless he left prints in the car or on the photograph, they wouldn't have much to work with in terms of identifying him. Given that he'd already taken so many precautions, Josie doubted he was dumb enough to leave prints behind. Or if he did, they wouldn't be in AFIS, which would make them useless unless he committed another crime for which he was arrested and printed.

Turner picked at the dried glue residue on his sleeve. "This is a fucking wild goose chase," he muttered under his breath.

"What's that?" Isaac said.

Josie plastered on a fake smile. "Nothing. My colleague was just saying that we'll need to ask you some questions. There is a chance that your vehicle was used in the abduction of a woman in the city park this morning."

Sheila gasped, one hand flying to her chest. "What? That's terrible! Are you sure?"

Their television was off. Unless Sheila had spent the morning on social media—and if she had been working all morning—then she probably hadn't seen the news about Cleo Tate. Isaac had, though, given the way his face paled.

"We're still investigating," Josie told Sheila.

Turner looked down at Josie, lowering his voice again. "Good lord. This is going to take forever."

"You have somewhere else to be?" she shot back, quietly enough not to be heard by the Hamptons. He always acted like he did. Any second now, his phone would come out and he'd start scrolling. Smiling tightly at Sheila, she said, "Tell me about the car."

NINE

Sheila walked over to the couch and snatched a tissue from the tissue box. She worked it over the stain on her arm, to no avail. "I left my travel mug in the car yesterday. I went out this morning around eight to get it, and the car was gone. I don't know how long it was gone. I parked it in the driveway yesterday around dinner time."

"No cameras?" asked Turner.

"No," said Sheila. "This has always been a safe street. Some of the neighbors might have cameras, though. Can you ask them?"

"Yes," said Josie. "We'll do that. When is the last time you remember seeing the car, Mr. Hampton?"

"I went up to bed around nine. I looked outside before I locked the door. It was still there then."

"Did either of you hear anything during the night?" asked Josie.

Both shook their heads.

Evidently bored with the conversation, Turner took his phone out and punched in his passcode. Josie said, "Call dispatch and tell them we need units out here to help canvass.

Send the car information to Amber so she can get it out to the press."

He was already scrolling. Josie edged closer, trying to see what was on his screen but he moved away from her. Clearly, it was on Josie to complete the interview. "Was the car locked?"

Color rose in Sheila's cheeks. Her forearm was raw now from scrubbing it with the tissue. "I'm embarrassed to say it wasn't. Like I said, this is a safe street. That's why we chose it."

"But the car has GPS." Gently, Isaac took the tissue from Sheila's hand and stuffed it into his pocket. He ran his fingers softly over her angry skin, as if to soothe her. "Can't you track it that way?"

"Yes." Josie's heart went into overdrive. "Thank you for answering our questions. We'll get units over here to see if any neighbors caught anything on camera. One of those officers will take a more detailed report. As soon as your vehicle is located, you'll be notified."

Isaac followed them outside. "You said the car was used to abduct someone today. Are you sure?"

"We're still investigating," said Josie.

He lowered his voice, as if Sheila might hear him from inside. "It's that woman, isn't it? The one all over social media? WYEP posted that she was taken from the city park. Is that true?"

"We're still investigating," Josie repeated. Turner was already on the sidewalk, glued to his phone.

Isaac dragged a hand down his face. Flecks of dried glue, clear and glinting in the sunlight, clung to his cheeks. He took a beat to study his palm. "She gets this shit everywhere. Everywhere." He sounded annoyed but Josie had a feeling that his annoyance masked a much deeper, more painful feeling. "Sorry. I'm easily distracted these days. The woman from the park. Her family must be... I just can't imagine." His voice grew husky, and he took a moment to compose himself, swallowing several times.

Josie felt a strong urge to hug him. Since the loss of her first husband, her beloved grandmother, and her colleague, other people's grief—especially when it was most raw and palpable—had a tendency to pierce right through the professional shell she'd constructed around her heart so that she could do her job. Mentally, she patched the breach, reminding herself that little Gracie Tate needed her mother. That was the only thing that mattered in this moment.

Isaac cleared his throat. "I'm sorry. I've been a mess since Jenna passed. Everything seems like it hits harder now."

"I get it," Josie said. "Again, I'm very sorry for your loss."

The words felt meaningless, as they always did in the face of great tragedy, but they were the best ones. Everything else came out trite or insincere or insulting—sometimes all three at once. Josie had a lot of experience with these things.

"Thank you," Isaac said. "Let us know if there's anything else you need from us."

He trudged back inside, closing the storm door softly.

Josie raced down to the sidewalk. "Turner."

Without looking up from his phone, he waved a dismissive hand at her. "I got it, I got it. Dispatch. Units. Car. Press."

"Let's go," she said. When he didn't move, she took his elbow and started pushing him toward the car.

He snatched his arm away from her. "Hey, watch it, Quinn. You're the one who told me I shouldn't be touching you all the time without your permission."

Josie stalked around to the driver's side of her SUV. "Because you shouldn't. I'm sorry, but sometimes it's really hard to get your attention."

A grin spread across his face. "Did you just say 'sorry?' To me?"

Josie yanked open her door. "I'm leaving right now so I can

get back to the stationhouse and prepare a warrant for the GPS coordinates of Sheila Hampton's car. Hyundai's infotainment system is Bluelink. They'll be able to disable the engine remotely. If you don't get into this vehicle in the next three seconds, I'm leaving you here."

Turner opened the door and folded himself into the passenger's seat. As Josie tore away from the curb, he called dispatch to request units to canvass the Hamptons' street and take a complete stolen vehicle report.

"Since you apologized to me, I'll write the warrant for Bluelink when we get back," he said.

"It will be faster if I do it."

"Are you serious? You know I've been at this longer than you, right?"

"It will be faster if I do it," she repeated.

"Unbelievable. Do you think I'm that slow when it comes to paperwork, or are you just a control freak?"

The answer was probably both, but Josie said, "The truth? You're slow. You take forever to complete paperwork, if you complete it at all. You disappear in the middle of... everything. If I let you prepare the warrant, how do I know you won't wander off in the middle of it and not come back until next week?"

From her periphery, she could see his mouth hanging open. She should have mentioned the phone while she was at it but right now, her brain was only half engaged in this ridiculous conversation. The other half was wondering how fast they could locate the car used to abduct Cleo Tate.

"I'll do the warrant," she said.

"You have a really low opinion of me, don't you?" He sounded insulted.

In spite of the circumstances, Josie laughed. "Did you think I didn't?"

"Listen, I know Park— Palmer hates me, and your hubby

isn't that thrilled with me either—although I gotta admit he's been pretty fair and a hell of a lot nicer than you two chicks—shit, I mean ladies. Women. Whatever."

"Just say detectives," Josie said irritably.

"Fine. Anyway, I thought you and I were getting along."

She took a quick glance at him, nonplussed to find he looked serious. "This is your idea of getting along? You know what? We don't have time for this right now."

There were a few beats of silence. Then Turner said, "Let me do the warrant. I'll be fast and then you can apologize to me again because that is my new favorite thing. Josie Quinn apologizing to Kyle Turner."

She briefly tried to calculate whether it was worth the disciplinary action if she punched him in the face. But Noah had told her repeatedly that they had to learn to work with Turner. "I'll drop you off at the stationhouse and then I'll go get food and coffee. If you're not finished by the time I get back, I'm taking over."

"And if it's done, you'll apologize?"

"No."

She waited for him to continue nagging her, but he was surprisingly silent until she sped up.

"Slow down, Quinn."

But Josie didn't want to slow down. Every moment in the search for Cleo Tate was critical. Josie's instincts and experience told her that every moment they didn't locate Cleo brought her closer to death.

TEN

Saliva pooled in Josie's mouth as she watched the barista at Komorrah's Koffee prepare a blonde latte. The Chief's preferred drink—a Red Eye—waited in a cupholder on the counter. Beside it was a paper bag filled with pastries. All the ones her team liked best. While most of the tables and booths in the café were full, Josie was the only person in line. She was too busy wondering if she should get herself two lattes to register the gust of hot air at her back as a new customer entered. A large presence loomed behind her, unusually close. Warm breath skated across her temple. It couldn't possibly be Turner. There was no way he'd finished the warrant by now. For a split second, she considered the best way to enforce her personal space—use her words or accidentally hit him in the groin when she turned to confront him. Then the scent of her husband's aftershave overtook the smell of coffee and pastries. Relief flooded her system. Noah pressed a hand against her lower back, and she sagged into him. As always, his touch soothed away some of the tension in her body.

He planted a kiss on her cheek. "The Chief called me."

Josie looked up into his hazel eyes. He was freshly show-

ered, his wavy dark hair still damp. She said, "Gretchen's busy
with a body in the river. She's working on the reports now. It's
just me and Turner, but this is definitely an all-hands-on-deck
situation. Turner's working on the warrant for Bluelink as we
speak. I hope."

Noah smiled and tucked a strand of hair behind her ear, his
fingertips grazing her jaw in a way that quieted some of her
frenetic anxiety. "I'm surprised you let him."

The barista handed Josie her latte. Then she took Noah's
order, which included drinks for him and Gretchen as well as a
second blonde latte for Josie. Already, half of the one in her
hand was gone. While they waited for Noah's order to be
completed, he pulled Josie to the side of the counter. "I got the
broad strokes from the Chief. I know about the polaroid. Saw
the social media posts with Cleo Tate's photo. I know the
suspect stole the car that he used to abduct her. What else do I
need to know?"

Josie told him about Remy Tate and Turner's theory that he
could be involved. Then she brought him up to speed on their
interview with the Hamptons.

"When units canvassed their street, they found one
neighbor at the other end of the block who has surveillance
footage of the car driving past—away from the Hampton home
—around three a.m. They followed it on camera about three
blocks west and then lost it. LPRs didn't pick it up anywhere
until this morning when it left the park. Then once it left the
park, Dougherty was able to catch it on camera passing a laun-
dromat a few blocks away but then lost it. Although none of that
will matter once we get the GPS report."

"Let's talk about Cleo Tate's husband," Noah said. "You
said Turner thinks he could be involved. If he stole the car, he
would have had to go to the Hamptons' on foot. Could he have
done that?"

Josie calculated the distance and timing. "It's possible, but it would have been a lot of walking to get to the Hamptons' neighborhood. Also, the Tates have a four-month-old. What are the chances the baby sleeps through the night and Cleo didn't notice her husband wasn't home in the early morning hours?"

Noah gave the barista a smile as she pushed his order across the counter in a cupholder. He put the Chief's Red Eye in the last slot, grabbed the paper bag, and they walked out together. "But Cleo isn't here to tell us if her husband was home or not in the middle of the night. Or maybe he does have a mistress and she helped him so he could get back in enough time that Cleo didn't notice him going out at two or three in the morning."

Josie sipped her latte as they headed down the street toward the stationhouse. "Also possible, but that doesn't explain the polaroid."

"True."

One-handed, she slipped her phone from her back pocket and pulled up the photo to show Noah.

"That's not cryptic at all."

"I don't know what it's supposed to mean or why it was left behind," Josie said. "Are we supposed to look for Cleo outdoors?"

"That picture could be from anywhere outdoors," Noah said. "There's no way to narrow it down. Even if it's some kind of bank, the river goes for miles and there are too many creeks for us to search them all quickly enough. We can't put resources behind the picture unless we have a reasonable expectation that it will lead us to Cleo."

"I agree. Right now, our best bet is locating the car."

The stationhouse came into view, the massive three-story stone structure towering over nearby buildings. Gray, with a bell tower in one corner, and double casement arched windows, it resembled a castle. It used to be the town hall but had been converted to police headquarters almost seventy years ago. It was on the city's historic register, which pretty much prevented the police department from upgrading anything inside. Two WYEP vans were parked nearby. Noah said, "The reporters will be around back in the parking lot waiting for us. Let's go in through the front."

In the lobby, WYEP's newest and most ambitious reporter, Dallas Jones, paced. Pressing a cell phone to his ear, he whisper-shouted angrily. "Vicky, I told you. I'm doing the best I can. They're not saying anything. All I'm getting is 'no comment.' I can't make them give me information."

Behind the glass-encased front desk, Sergeant Dan Lamay shook his head as if to say he couldn't get rid of the kid.

Dallas stopped walking when he saw Josie and Noah. "Detectives!" Lowering the cell phone to his side, he blocked them from walking through the door that led to the rest of the first floor. "Please, wait."

"No comment," Noah said.

Dallas's shoulders slumped. A lock of his dark hair had come loose from his shellacked hairdo, hanging along the side of his face. His white button-down shirt was wrinkled. Sweat stains peeked from beneath his armpits. Josie was glad to see that he wasn't immune to the heat. It always bothered her how reporters looked perfect, no matter what the weather. She still couldn't figure out how Trinity woke up looking camera-ready.

"Please." Dallas lifted his cell phone and told Vicky he'd call her back before hanging up. "Our viewers want to know what you're doing to find Cleo Tate."

"Your viewers? Or your producer?" She pointed to his phone. "That was her, right?"

Dallas pursed his lips. He was young, only a few years out of college, and trying to prove himself. "Yes. She's been breathing down my neck, but that's her job. This is a big story. Our viewers are worried. Is it safe for people to go into the city park?"

"We're aware of the public's concern for safety," said Josie.

"We'll hold a press conference later." She muscled past him to the door with Noah in tow.

"Come on," Dallas pleaded. "Give me something. Do you have any suspects? Any leads? Something I can give the public?"

He was hoping to make a name in Denton so he could get on the national stage. Just like Trinity had done. While Josie respected his drive, she would never compromise an investigation. "No comment."

Noah held the door open for Josie to pass through. "We have work to do. We'll see you at the press conference."

"We did a story on Cleo's husband!" Dallas called.

Josie and Noah froze, partway through the door, waiting for him to go on.

"It was about three months ago."

"We'll watch it on the WYEP website," Noah said.

"You can't. Vicky wouldn't air it." He let his words hang in the air, dangling like bait.

Josie glared at him. "I hope you're not trying to trade for information here, Mr. Jones. If you or your producer know something that may help locate Cleo Tate, you need to tell us now. Otherwise you're looking at obstruction charges."

Dallas tried to push the errant lock of hair back in place, but it wouldn't stay. "I know that. I'm not trying to trade but if you could just give me something—"

Noah shook his head. "That's not how this works."

"I get it."

"I don't think you do," said Josie. "If you know something material to our investigation then just say it. We don't have all day to play this game with you. We're trying to find a missing mother."

Dallas had the sense to look shamed. "I'm sorry. It's just that when I did the story on Remy Tate, he seemed... I don't know. Off. It was a filler story. Boring as hell, but Vicky said they'd save it for a slow news day. He works for the Clerk of Courts. He's in charge of the records. The story was about them finally digitizing all the old files. You know, Denton getting with modern times and stuff. I'm telling you though, there was something just... off about him."

Noah met Josie's eyes briefly. She knew he was thinking the same thing. Dallas Jones was hoping they would slip and give some indication that Remy Tate was a suspect—or at least a person of interest—or a hint that they'd already cleared him.

Noah took a step toward him, the cupholder in his hands practically touching Dallas's chest. "Are you really coming at us with this nonsense? You spent five minutes with a guy for a story, what? A few months ago? And you think your opinion of him is relevant to our investigation? Listen, Jones. 'Off' doesn't mean anything. Maybe you caught him on a bad day. He has a new baby. Maybe he was tired. Maybe he just didn't like you. What I know for certain is that Cleo Tate doesn't have time for your bullshit."

Dallas's phone rang. The screen showed a woman with long blonde hair wearing a grim smile. The name above her photo read Vicky Platt. Dallas sent the call to voicemail. "I didn't know about the baby at the time. We didn't talk about his personal life. But I'm telling you—when I played back the footage for Vicky, even she thought something was up with this guy. It was the reason she didn't run the piece."

"Stop wasting our time," Josie said as she and Noah walked through the door and let it close in Dallas's face.

ELEVEN

They took the stairs to the second-floor great room. It was a large open area crowded with desks, most of which were used by uniformed officers to complete paperwork. One of them was assigned to Amber Watts, their press liaison. The only other assigned desks were pushed together into a rectangle and belonged to their four-person investigative team. The Chief's office was only feet from their little bullpen. As they reached the second-floor landing, they heard a raised male voice.

"Wonder what Turner did to piss off the Chief this time," Noah muttered as he used his back to push open the door.

But the Chief wasn't hollering. Josie watched in shock as an older, white-haired man stabbed an index finger into Chief Chitwood's chest, shouting, "As a professional courtesy, I expect full disclosure when it comes to this investigation."

Chief Chitwood pushed his hand away. Josie had never seen his acne-pitted face so red but his tone was carefully controlled, as calm as Josie had ever heard it. "A professional courtesy? You're retired—and a family member of the victim. With all due respect, I will not allow you to come into my stationhouse and start demanding the details of an open and active investigation. You know I can't do that. Go home. When we have an update, you'll get it."

From her desk, Gretchen watched the exchange. Turner was talking with someone on his desk phone. When he saw Josie, he waved a document at her. Had he really prepared the warrant in the half hour she'd been out? It was certainly possible, but it would still need to be signed by a judge and then forwarded to Bluelink.

"I won't jeopardize the integrity of the investigation," the man insisted, voice still raised. "You're being ridiculous. Do you know how many times I was smack in the middle of cases like this?"

Josie studied the man. There was something familiar about him. He had several years on Chief Chitwood, who was in his sixties. Deep wrinkles lined his face. But he looked out of place in this room with the rest of them wearing either suits or their Denton PD polos. Pressed khaki shorts and a blue golf shirt made it look as though he'd just stepped off the golf course. His crepe-paper skin was deeply tanned as if he spent many hours playing.

Again, Josie was stunned at the way the Chief kept the agitation out of his voice. Normally, he'd be deep into an irrational tirade so caustic, it would raise the blood pressure of every person in the room. Instead, he sounded reasonable, almost compassionate. "That's exactly why you should not be here."

"Just give me the details you haven't released to the press," the man said.

The Chief shook his head. "I cannot do that."

Noah handed Gretchen's drink to her across the desks, along with the pastry bag, and then took his seat. Josie stood next to his chair, watching the scene play out. Turner appeared beside her. Quietly, he said, "Who is this fucking guy?"

Noah said, "Kellan Neal. He's a retired city prosecutor."

That's why he looked familiar.

Kellan's voice lowered only marginally. "I won't leak any information. You have my word, not to mention the fact that the decades I spent serving this city speak for themselves."

Turner glanced down at Josie. "You remember him?"

"I was still on patrol when he retired but yeah, now that I've heard his name, I remember him. He was ruthless. A pain in the ass. Where's my warrant?"

"I respect your time in the DA's office," the Chief said. "And your record, but I cannot and will not give out sensitive details of the case at this time."

Turner lifted one of the lapels of his suit jacket so Josie could see the warrant folded up inside his pocket. "But I already called Bluelink. Given the urgent nature of our request, they're going to run the search on the car immediately. They'll disable the engine, too. I just have to get this signed and over to them at some point today."

Josie felt relief and excitement in equal measure.

"Come on," Kellan said, tone pleading now. "We're talking about my daughter. My daughter! My Cleo."

Cleo Tate was the daughter of a former city prosecutor. It didn't make a difference in terms of how they conducted their investigation, but it had potential ramifications.

"Our suspect pool might have just gotten exponentially bigger," Josie murmured.

"And a lot higher-profile," Turner said.

Noah twisted his coffee cup from the holder. "The Mayor will be breathing down our necks now. Not to mention Kellan Neal will be holding his own press conference probably the moment he leaves here."

Josie sighed. "We can't stop him from doing that."

Chief Chitwood appeared unmoved by Kellan's emotional appeal but said, "No one knows better than me what it's like to be in this situation. I can assure you of that. But I'm sure I don't need to remind you, as a former prosecutor, that *every* victim is someone's daughter or son or loved one. Let us do our jobs. I will tell you what I can when I can, and I'll do it personally if that helps."

"It doesn't," Kellan snapped. "I can't sit on the sidelines. I need to do something."

Turner stepped forward. "You wanna do something?"

Kellan turned, his curiosity piqued. He seemed oblivious to the tension that filled the rest of the room.

Josie looked over at the Chief. He arched a brow in a look Josie knew well. Turner was on thin ice.

When he noticed the Chief's expression, he adjusted his tone to sound less confrontational. "Ask your son-in-law what he was doing this morning while Cleo was being abducted."

The color drained from Kellan's face. "What?"

Turner took a step forward, towering over the former prosecutor. "Ask your son-in-law why he left work right around the time Cleo left for the park. Ask him why he's not on the home surveillance footage even though that's where I found him this morning."

One of the desk phones started ringing.

"Remy?" Kellan said.

Turner nodded. "Ask him for an alibi."

Kellan looked back at the Chief, who folded his arms across his chest. Josie heard Gretchen answer the phone, speaking softly to whoever was on the line. For a moment, Kellan looked lost, as if he'd just awakened to find himself in a room full of detectives and had no idea how he got there. Josie remembered him as a fierce and commanding presence in every room he entered. He conducted press conferences with God-like authority. Now he looked like a frail, addled old man. His gaze dropped to the floor and he nodded, almost to himself.

"I'll be in touch," he said, every last bit of his bluster gone. Then he left.

The moment the door swooshed shut, Gretchen said, "We got the car."

TWELVE

"I recognize this place," said Gretchen.

A light breeze cooled Josie's face. The heat was still cloying and here, in this empty dirt lot, overgrown with weeds, the sun was relentless. Shading her eyes with one palm, Josie watched the ERT circle Sheila Hampton's Hyundai. According to the Bluelink representative, the car had been parked in this lot since ten thirty a.m., six hours ago. Given how soon after Cleo's abduction it had been dumped there and how long it had been sitting in the lot, Josie was certain they weren't going to like what they found. Still, she, Noah, Gretchen, and a half dozen patrol units had nearly broken land speed records to get here. Turner stayed back to prepare the warrants for Cleo Tate's phone.

The car was empty. Everyone had held their breath as the trunk was opened. It held nothing but a spare tire. Their relief was palpable but then came more anxiety. Where was she?

The initial search of the area around the car turned up nothing. Even though they hadn't found Cleo's body, Josie still had the sinking feeling that they were too late to help her. Now, they had to hope that her abductor had left something behind that would enable them to identify him and locate her.

"We've been here before," Josie said. "The West Denton Five case."

Gretchen spun slowly, taking in their surroundings again. The massive tract of land they now stood on was directly across the street from a line of houses. Tall trees blocked the residents' view of the lot. It was accessible only through a narrow opening in the forest, large enough to accommodate a truck. Josie remembered the place as soon as they pulled up and saw the giant sign along the road that read "Land for Sale. Fifty Acres," with a commercial realtor's phone number beneath it. The text was significantly faded from the last time they'd been here.

"Right," Gretchen said. "We found the body of that missing woman and then that kid almost ran us down in her dad's truck. Nothing built here since."

"The developers must still be fighting with the civic association," Josie said.

"You think this could be where the polaroid was taken?"

"Possibly, although the photo looks like it's taken next to water. This has been abandoned long enough that there might be standing water."

"How far are we from the Tate home?" Gretchen asked.

Josie calculated the distance and time in her head. "Five or six miles. You're wondering if this location eliminates Remy's involvement? Depends on what we find here, although to get over here and back to his house by the time Turner showed up? Acting alone, I don't think he could pull it off."

"He could have had help. We shouldn't discount him. Especially if he's not able to provide an alibi." Gretchen turned in the direction of the street. Although the trees blocked most of the view of the residences, there were small breaks in the foliage that gave them glimpses of a driveway or yard. "If I recall, none of those houses across the street have cameras."

"I told the canvassing officers to ask anyway."

"We need a geofence. You want to call the jackass, or should I?"

Josie watched as Noah moved around the scene, speaking with an ERT officer and then giving instructions to a group of uniformed officers. "The jackass is on a roll with warrants today. I'll call."

As the officers dispersed to do a wider search of the lot, Josie called Turner and requested that he prepare a geofence warrant. For once, he didn't complain. Maybe it was just because he got to be in the air-conditioned office while the rest of them sweated their asses off in the field.

A geofence was a relatively new tool available to law enforcement. It allowed police to draw a virtual border around a particular geographic area. Then they could track which smart devices, including cell phones and vehicular infotainment centers, were inside that area during a specific period of time. Law enforcement had first started using geofence warrants in 2016. Many people had protested against the use of them, arguing they constituted an invasion of privacy. In response to that, Google had recently changed the way it stored users' location history, making it more difficult for law enforcement to use geofence warrants. However, the practice was still legal in the Commonwealth of Pennsylvania. It was worth a try.

After hanging up with Turner, Josie called their K-9 unit which consisted of her former fiancé, Luke Creighton, and his bloodhound, Blue. They weren't officially employed by the city of Denton. Luke worked for a nonprofit that provided search-and-rescue dogs to police departments that could not afford their own full-time K-9 units at a nominal cost. Fifty acres was a lot of ground for Denton PD to cover on foot. Blue would be able to scent the passenger's seat and hopefully follow Cleo's trail from there. He'd also be able to track the killer.

She hung up just as Noah approached. "That was Luke. He said they can be here in twenty minutes."

"Great."

Josie could tell by his pinched expression that nothing he'd learned so far was good news. "What is it?"

"No one saw anything. There are no cameras across the street. Canvasses turned up nothing."

"We'll still have the geofence," Josie said. "Turner's working on it now. Anything in the car?"

Noah used his forearm to wipe sweat from his brow. "If you mean blood, signs of a struggle, no. They'll impound it and process it to see if they can pull prints but that's going to take time."

Beyond the Hampton car were piles of dirt, now covered with brush, some as high as a house. The rest of the acreage appeared to be forested. Josie tried to put herself in the abductor's place. He'd successfully kidnapped Cleo Tate and immediately brought her here. He'd managed to do it before her photo or the information about the car went out to the press. He could have lingered here for an hour, maybe two. Josie hated to think what he might have been doing to Cleo during that time. If he'd ultimately decided to kill her, the most logical next step would be to walk her out into the middle of the nearby woods, potentially sexually assault her—if that was his intent—take her life, leave her body, and exit on foot.

Noah, who had an uncanny ability to read her mind, said, "I've already got units out to canvass the streets surrounding the property in case he left on foot. Josie, we're at a standstill. I think you should go home. You've been at this all day. Gretchen and I have it from here. I'll send Turner home, too, once he finishes the warrants."

"Noah."

She didn't need to say it. They both knew that there was a very high probability that Cleo Tate was already dead. It was just a matter of how quickly they found her and whether the killer had left behind enough evidence for them to make him pay for his crime. With or without Josie's presence, the outcome would be the same. As usual, she didn't want to go home. She wanted to see this through, sleep and nourishment be damned. But she knew she'd only hurt the investigation and the entire team if she pushed herself too hard.

"If you find something—"

"I'll call you," he promised. "I'll keep you updated. Your sister and Drake are at the house. Your parents are coming over as well. You should go home and see them."

At some point, she'd have to tell him Drake's news. "I'll see you at home."

THIRTEEN

He dozed in the driver's seat of the car while the air conditioning labored to cool the interior. In the nowhere land between waking and sleeping, his mind drifted to her. She was always there, just beneath the surface of his consciousness. Dark hair, soft lips, perky breasts. First came the fantasies of what he'd wanted to do to her, all the ways he had planned to use her body and make her pretty mouth scream. Then those beautiful thoughts were crushed. His brain replayed the look of disgust on her face when he tried to take what she'd been subtly offering him for weeks. She was nothing but a bitch and a tease. It was okay though because what came next gave him a release like he'd never known. In those frenzied moments, he was a god.

Her god.

Even now, the thought made his dick hard. Sweat beaded along his upper lip. He reached for the nearest AC vent, spinning the dial to try to increase the air flow. Reddish flakes broke away from his nails and fluttered around the interior of the car. There hadn't been time to wash his hands. Now he had to get back or he'd be in trouble. Closing his eyes, he called up her face once more. Those final moments. The way she'd been utterly his, powerless, at his mercy.

An involuntary grunt passed through his lips. His body spasmed. The memory was so potent, he didn't even have to touch himself to get off.

Maybe the whole business with the woman today was a sign. Maybe it was time to stop denying himself, to stop caging what was inside him. He could find someone new. Make her his. Be her god.

FOURTEEN

Josie's driveway was crowded with vehicles. Every first-floor window of her home glowed with welcoming, golden light. Her mind was still with Cleo Tate, but as she trudged up the front steps and heard the muffled sounds of her family's laughter, some of the tension in her body drained away. Once inside, it became clear that everyone had gathered in the kitchen. No one heard her come in. Even their Boston terrier, Trout, didn't come racing into the foyer the way he usually did. That could only mean one thing. Food was at stake. Josie and Noah did their best not to feed him table food, but he always held out hope that someone would drop a delicious morsel on the floor.

Trout gave her a cursory look and a momentary butt-wiggle of excitement when she reached the kitchen doorway and then went right back to staring up at Trinity while she cut vegetables at the counter. Every so often she dropped a slice of carrot which he gobbled right up. Even dressed in jeans and one of Drake's oversized FBI T-shirts, Trinity looked like she'd just stepped from the pages of a magazine. Her black hair had a glossy sheen to it and the light makeup she wore made her look camera-ready.

Over her shoulder, Trinity said, "Mom, show Drake the
house you guys just made an offer on. It's not far from here."

Their parents, Shannon and Christian Payne, sat with
Drake at the kitchen table. Josie leaned against the doorframe
and watched them all. The normalcy of the scene, the happy
presence of her true family still struck her as incredibly surreal.
When she and Trinity were three weeks old, Lila Jensen, a
woman employed by Shannon and Christian's housecleaning
service, had snuck into their home while a nanny cared for
them. She set the house on fire and abducted Josie. The nanny
managed to get Trinity to safety but the authorities in that town
—two hours away—believed that Josie perished in the fire.

Shannon rifled through the purse hanging on the back of
her chair. "Let me find it on my phone. I've got that real estate
app."

Lila had brought Josie back to Denton and used her as a
ploy to get back together with her ex-boyfriend, Eli Matson.
Back then there weren't mail-in DNA tests. Eli didn't even
question Lila when she told him she'd given birth to his
daughter in the year they'd been apart. He'd taken her back and
embraced his role as a father, loving Josie with his whole heart
until the day he died. Josie had only been six years old at the
time. Left alone with Lila, she had faced the most horrific years
of her life. Eli's mother, Lisette—the only grandmother Josie
had ever known—had fought like hell to get custody of Josie and
save her from Lila's abuse. Eventually, she did.

Christian slid on a pair of reading glasses and took out his
own phone. "I've got it here, Shan."

Once Lisette had full custody of Josie, Lila disappeared and
then, when Josie was thirty years old, came back to wreak havoc
on Josie's life once more. In the process, the complicated web of
lies Lila had weaved over so many years unraveled. That was
when Josie and Trinity learned they were sisters. Josie had an
instant family: a twin sister, parents, and even a younger

brother, Patrick. It had been a big adjustment for Josie, learning that everything she thought she knew about her life was wrong, and taking her place as part of the Payne family, but they were one of the best things that had ever happened to her.

Christian handed Drake his phone. "It's a lot smaller than the place we've got now, but we really haven't needed that kind of space since Patrick left for college."

Shannon laughed. "We didn't need that much space even before he left for college."

For as long as Josie had known them, Shannon and Christian lived two hours away. Now they were retiring and moving to Denton. Patrick had settled here, and they were excited to be closer to Josie, especially since she and Noah were trying to adopt.

Trinity dropped another carrot slice onto the floor and Trout ate it greedily. Without looking up from her task, she said, "Josie, are you going to lurk there all night, or are you going to join us?"

It was still weird having a twin.

Josie walked over to the table and leaned down, giving each of her parents a hug. "You look so tired, honey," said Shannon, concern pooling in her eyes.

"We saw the news," Drake said. "No luck finding that mother?"

"Not yet," said Josie. She crossed the room and leaned her hip against the countertop, watching Trinity toss sliced carrots into a huge salad bowl.

"Guess this means Noah won't be joining us," Trinity said as she started slicing a cucumber.

"No," said Josie. She took out her phone to see if there were any updates even though she'd only left the scene an hour ago. The searches would take time.

"I know this great photographer who's willing to come here to Denton to take photos of you and Noah for your adoptive parent profile," said Trinity. "Oh! I got one of my producers and cameramen to agree to come out to help you guys make your video."

Gently, Drake said, "Trin, maybe Josie and Noah should decide how they want to assemble their profile."

She waved the knife at him. "I know. I didn't say they had to use my people. I'm just saying they should."

"Trinity!" Shannon exclaimed while Josie and Christian laughed.

Trout whined for more carrots.

"I appreciate your help, Trin," Josie said. "But Noah and I want our profile and video to reflect... us. It has to. We're asking someone to give us their baby."

Trinity rolled her eyes. "You'll still be you. The presentation will just look..."

"Like Josie's famous journalist sister butt in and made it for her?" said Christian. "Trinity, you should let Josie and Noah do this their way. They've gotten this far."

"Did you know there are actually companies out there who help you create your profile?" Trinity said. "I did a story once, ranking—"

A collective groan went up in the room. There was no end to the topics that Trinity had done a story on in her career.

Trout whined and lifted one of his paws, pleading for more carrots.

Trinity turned away from the counter and brandished the knife at them. "Complain about my encyclopedic knowledge now, but just wait until the next time one of you needs to know something you can't find on Google."

Drake stood and walked over to her, wrapping an arm around her waist and planting a kiss on the top of her head. "I love your encyclopedic knowledge. I haven't used Google once since we met."

A delighted smile spread across Trinity's face.

At their feet, Trout gave a defeated sigh and sauntered off, lying across the threshold of the kitchen.

Josie's cell phone buzzed in her pocket. Before she could take it out to see if there was an update on the Cleo Tate case, Trout jumped up and started barking. He ran toward the front door so fast that his paws slid across the hardwood of the foyer floor. Josie followed, palming her phone and tapping in her passcode as she went. There was a text from Noah. Before she could read it, another notification popped up on her screen, this one from her security camera app. Turner was on her front stoop.

Trout's barks grew in intensity as he waited for her to answer the door. Once she reassured him that there were no assassins outside, he backed down to a low growl. Josie swung the door open and frowned at Turner.

"What are you doing here? And how did you get my home address?"

Turner was on the first step below the landing, bringing them nearly eye to eye. Under the exterior light, his face looked drawn. He tugged at his beard, looking from Josie to his vehicle, which was parked across her driveway, then back again.

From behind the storm door, Trout continued to growl.

"Quinn." For the first time in the months they'd been working together, the annoying sexist bravado she'd grown to know and hate was gone. In its place was a tired man in a rumpled suit, paint on his jacket pocket, shifting his weight nervously from side to side.

"Turner," Josie said. "You didn't answer either of my questions."

Another tug at his beard. "The, uh, K-9 searches didn't turn anything up."

"What?" Josie looked back down at her phone, opening the text from Noah. Blue had followed Cleo Tate's scent across the fifty acres of the lot, onto a residential street, and then lost it.

Which meant that she'd been put into another vehicle.

Josie quickly tapped in, *Geofence?*

She didn't know if Turner saw her text or not but he said, "I already got the warrant for the geofence. We're waiting on the results. But Quinn, listen. I got a..."

His eyes drifted from Josie to the doorway behind her. Trout went quiet. Trinity's voice floated from inside. "What's going on? Is that Misty, by any chance? I wanted to talk to her about— Oh."

Josie turned to see Trinity framed in the doorway, staring at Turner. There was a definite flicker of recognition in her sister's eyes.

Turner said, "Miss Payne."

"Kyle," Trinity replied. "What are you doing here?"

He shook his head, as if to say 'not now' and focused on Josie again. "Quinn, I got a real big problem."

FIFTEEN

Josie's phone vibrated in her palm. A text from Noah, telling her the same thing Turner had just said. She barely registered it, dropping the phone back into her pocket. The only thing she could concentrate on in that moment was the fact that Trinity and Kyle Turner knew each other. How in the hell did they know one another? Wouldn't Trinity have mentioned that at some point in all the months that Josie had complained about him? Except Josie never used his real name. She always referred to him as Douchebag.

"Quinn," Turner said. "Did you hear me? I got a real problem."

"Kyle," Trinity said. "You know my sister?"

He didn't even look at Trinity. Josie's stomach bottomed out at the unwelcome thought that the reason they knew one another was because they'd had some sort of tryst. Was that possible?

"I work with her," Turner answered tersely. "Quinn, are you having a stroke or something? I need your help."

No, no, no. Trinity would never. She had to know him in her capacity as a journalist. That had to be it.

"Oh my God," Trinity gasped. She pushed her way out the door and onto the landing next to Josie. "*This* is Douchebag Detective? Are you kidding me?"

Josie wanted to ask Trinity how she knew Turner. Even more than that, she wanted to know why it was surprising that Kyle Turner was Douchebag Detective. Anyone who spent five minutes in his presence would get the nickname immediately. Drake certainly had.

Josie narrowed her eyes at Turner. Why hadn't he said anything about the fact that she'd been referring to him as Douchebag to her sister? He tugged at his beard again, harder this time. He had a lot of nervous tics but this was not one she'd seen before. "What's wrong with you? What did you do?"

"I didn't do anything." He hooked a thumb toward his car. Now that Josie looked more closely, she could see a figure in the passenger's seat. "Your press liaison is in my car."

"Why is Amber in your car?" said Josie.

"Kellan Neal came back to the stationhouse. I was working on warrants. He said he confronted Remy about this morning. The guy won't admit to an affair. Won't admit to anything. Neal told him that as an act of good faith, and so that we won't waste precious investigative time looking in the wrong direction, he should let us search his vehicle and electronic devices. Remy Tate refused."

They already knew that Remy Tate was hiding something. Whether it was a simple affair or involvement in the abduction of his wife was the question. Even if he was innocent of Cleo's kidnapping, would he admit to his father-in-law, a retired prosecutor, that he was having an affair? Providing an alibi seemed like a no-brainer, but if he thought there was a chance Cleo might come home then maybe he was holding out. Once he admitted to it, the damage was done, and Josie remembered Kellan Neal well enough to know that, in his mind, a mistress would only make Remy more viable as a person of interest.

Josie could feel Trinity's presence beside her. She wasn't sure if Trinity was still there because she knew Turner or because she was interested in the details of the case. Probably both.

The dark outline of Amber's silhouette didn't move. "That doesn't tell me why Amber is in your car."

Turner sighed. "I was talking to Neal when she came in to deal with this Cleo Tate mess. Neal told her he wanted to do a public appeal. Amber said it was a good idea. Highlight this guy's service to the city. Get him to ask the public for help finding his daughter. She set everything up for him and the Chief to have a press conference an hour from now."

Josie brushed past him and started walking toward the car. "Get to the point, Turner."

He followed her. "After Neal left, I was looking for something in Mettner's desk drawer. Then the drawer got stuck. I had to pull the whole thing out."

Amber didn't even look over when Josie reached for the door handle. Turner gently grabbed her wrist, stopping her from opening the door. When Josie glared up at him, he released her. Lowering his voice to a whisper, he said, "The drawer was stuck on this key chain. Couple of keys on it. Not important. It said, 'Uncle Finn,' on it. She saw it and just freaked out. Totally lost her shit, Quinn. I didn't know what to do."

Josie opened her mouth to say something about him only knowing how to make women cry rather than soothing them when they did, but another look at him under the dim glow of the streetlight stopped her. He wore an expression she had never seen before. "Are you... worried?"

Turner rolled his eyes. "This isn't about me, sweetheart. Shit. Just talk to her, would you? I didn't know what the hell to do. I couldn't let her sit in that stationhouse with people coming in and out constantly, you know, seeing her like that."

Wait. Was this Douchebag human, after all? Josie shook off the thought.

Turner said, "I hustled her out of there—and yes, she said it was okay—and into my car. She was still hysterical. Then she said to bring her to see you. Gave me the address."

Josie tapped lightly against the window, but Amber didn't look over. "You could have called me to come get her."

Turner groaned and tugged at his beard again. "And waited for you to show up? While the parking lot was swarmed with press? Come on, Quinn. Do I seem like the kind of guy who could spend that much time with a sobbing woman? It was faster to bring her here."

Josie's phone buzzed again but she ignored it. She opened the door and touched Amber's shoulder. Still no movement. Then Trinity was there, pushing Turner out of the way, and helping Josie coax Amber from the car. Trinity had been there the night they lost Mettner. After the shooting, she'd climbed into Josie's hospital bed and comforted her in a way no one else could, not even Noah. Trinity knew everyone in Josie's world of found family and was well aware of the magnitude of Amber's loss.

Trinity put an arm around Amber's waist. "Sometimes it just hits you like that," she whispered. "You came to the right place."

Amber sagged against her as Trinity helped her into the house. Josie watched them go, an uncharacteristic lump forming in her throat. Grief was a wily thing. It made you think that after a year or more, you could handle your loss. It convinced you that you were making progress, that maybe a day would come when your pain would be manageable enough to take a full breath again.

Then grief reminded you that something as small as a fucking key chain could take you out at the knees.

"I'm gonna go now," Turner said. "You, uh, you've got your hands full, looks like. I'll see you in the morning."

He walked around to the driver's side door. Before he got in, Josie said, "Thank you."

She could count on one hand the number of times she'd thanked him for anything. It always made him absolutely insufferable. The gloating went on for days. Except this time, he only nodded.

"Turner," said Josie. "You said you were looking through Mettner's desk."

His fingers drummed against the roof of the car. "Yeah."

"Not your desk?"

With a sigh, he said, "Quinn, I'm a lot of things but stupid isn't one of them. That desk will be mine when I earn it."

For a moment, Josie's breath hitched in her throat. Then Turner grinned at her and slapped his palm against the car's roof. "Now I gotta go get some sleep, sweetheart, 'cause I know as soon as I get into that stationhouse tomorrow, you're going to be right up my ass making sure I do every single little thing the way the great Josie Quinn thinks it should be done."

Irritation flared in Josie's stomach like acid. She bit back her immediate response, that it wasn't how she thought things should be done, but about how the law and procedure dictated they be done. Instead, she turned away and started walking back up her driveway. Over her shoulder, she called, "I expect two dollars in my jar first thing tomorrow."

As she stepped inside, she thought she heard him laughing. Taking out her phone, she read the latest text from Noah.

I'm thinking this guy might be smart enough to not be caught in the geofence. Or leave prints. Hummel typed the blood found in the park. It matches Cleo Tate's blood type. He's working overtime now to pull everything he can from the car. Chief is having DNA samples expedited.

Josie sighed. They'd already assumed the blood belonged to Cleo Tate. No surprise there. All that told them was what they already knew: she was in big trouble. Expedited DNA results in the Commonwealth of Pennsylvania could sometimes still take weeks or months, depending on the volume of samples the state lab had to test. Even if the DNA results came back in a week or two, if the abductor wasn't in the CODIS database they weren't going to be any closer to finding him. If Noah was right and the next day brought one dead end after another, the only clue they had left was the polaroid.

SIXTEEN

Josie's eyes burned, blurring the text on the pages she'd been reviewing for the last half hour. She'd already consumed one latte. Today she'd been smart enough to buy two at the same time before she reported for her shift. Picking the second one up from her desk, she drank down half of it. Blinking, she snatched up the packet containing Cleo Tate's phone records again. Another half hour went by. There was nothing that could help them find the woman. Josie had been through hundreds of text messages, emails, private messages on social media, and nothing stood out. From what Josie could tell, Cleo genuinely loved being a mother. She was also exhausted from caring for little Gracie primarily on her own. Even when Remy came home from work, evidently, he didn't take on much responsibility or attempt to give Cleo a break.

Momma needs a nap, Cleo had texted her sister, who lived in California just days before the abduction. *How did I not notice before that my husband is completely useless?*

Her photo gallery held well over five hundred photos of baby Gracie. Josie's chest tightened at the thought of the poor infant possibly—probably—growing up without her mother.

Everything in the phone's contents was benign. No evidence that Cleo was being stalked prior to yesterday or that things were horribly awry with her husband.

The geofence results weren't helpful either. Whether Google's new policies had helped the abductor make himself invisible within the virtual perimeter or he'd found some other way to disable the GPS on whatever vehicle he'd escaped in, his identity remained a secret. The canvasses of the areas around the fifty-acre lot where Blue had lost Cleo's scent also turned up nothing. There were no cameras within range of the perimeter of the lot so that was a bust as well. Noah had told her all this when he slid into bed next to her in the early morning hours. She hadn't been able to sleep the entire night between obsessing over Cleo Tate and comforting Amber. Plus, the small, nagging question of how Trinity knew Kyle Turner. Josie hadn't had a chance to ask her once she got back inside. Even after Shannon and Christian left and Drake went to bed, she and Trinity were up late talking with Amber. Then Josie had set her up in their other guest room.

Once Noah got home, wrapping his large, warm body around hers, she'd gotten a couple of hours of sleep but when she woke to get ready for her shift, the rest of the house was still and silent. Even Trout stayed in bed with Noah. Here she was now at the stationhouse, alone. Turner still hadn't arrived even though he had been due in over an hour ago. Josie tossed the report aside and stood up, stretching her arms over her head. She walked over to the rolling corkboard that the Chief had bought over a year ago. They'd started using it with every major case. Gretchen had taken it upon herself to print out and pin up salient items. Before Josie was a map of a large part of Denton that had been pieced together using printouts from Google. Gretchen had marked the Tate household, the area of the park where Cleo was taken, the place where Charlotte Thompson had seen Cleo get into the white car with a man, the Hamptons' home, and now the fifty-acre lot where the car was found.

The only other thing on the corkboard was a copy of the polaroid.

Josie was studying it when Turner finally made his appearance. As usual, he was in a suit with a can of his favorite energy drink poking from one of his jacket pockets. Phone in hand, his thumb scrolled endlessly. "We're back to staring at pictures," he said.

The last major case they'd worked had involved a child's drawing. Josie had spent days trying to figure out what it meant. Turner thought it was useless but, in the end, it had proven crucial to solving the case.

"You have a better idea?" asked Josie.

Turner stopped at her desk and dropped two dollars into her jar. "Real evidence. Like fingerprints or something."

"You still owe me fifty cents, Turner," she reminded him.

He huffed and searched his pockets, coming up with some change, dropping it into her jar. "All I've got is thirty-five cents. That's what you're getting."

She was inclined to forgive him the fifteen cents he still owed her because of what he'd done for Amber last night. Instead, she said, "Hummel couldn't pull prints from the photo. He got a bunch of prints from the car but most of them did not come up in AFIS. There was one set that matched a guy named Edgar Garcia. He's twenty-eight, has a conviction for simple assault. Second-degree misdemeanor. Served almost two years."

Turner sat in his desk chair and picked up the tiny foam basketball next to his computer. He squeezed it in his hand. "Anyone interview this guy yet?"

Josie shook her head. "Hummel just called with the results. I looked him up. He works at an auto repair shop near the university. Schock's Auto Repair."

Turner threw the ball at the tiny net by his blotter. As usual, it missed. "Any chance Sheila Hampton has used Schock's?"

Josie went back around to her desk and took another sip of her latte. "Yes. I already asked Mrs. Hampton. Actually, Hummel and Chan are over at her house now getting elimination prints from her and her husband. But I still think someone should talk with Edgar Garcia."

Turner flipped the tab on his energy drink. "You volunteering me?"

Josie braced her hands on her desk and leaned toward him. "Maybe."

"You don't want to go with me?"

"Not particularly. How do you know Trinity?"

His Adam's apple bobbed as he sucked down his drink, watching her the entire time. When he was done, he crushed the can in his hand and tossed it into his garbage bin. Pushing some papers around on his desk, he said, "She didn't tell you?"

"I didn't have time to ask."

Turner stood up and went to the corkboard. "This guy left us a photo for a reason."

Now that Josie wanted to know something, he was suddenly interested in the polaroid. "No shit."

He tapped a finger over the blue object in the polaroid. "What's this?"

Josie joined him. "I've been trying to figure it out since I saw this damn thing. You didn't answer my question."

He leaned in closer, squinting. "This looks like maybe it's made of wood."

"I thought so, too."

"Part of a building? A step? A shed? What?"

"I don't know." Josie traced her finger over the edge of the blue object. "See the bottom? It looks almost curved. Stop avoiding my question. How do you know my sister?"

With a sigh, he dropped his hand, thrumming his fingers against his thigh. "That's for her to tell you."

The lattes in Josie's stomach sloshed around. "Oh my God. You didn't—you and Trinity weren't—"

He shot her a look, one eyebrow raised. "Relax, swee— Quinn. It was nothing like that. Although, if it had been, could you blame her? I mean, look at me."

Josie rolled her eyes. "You know, if someone has a really annoying personality, that tends to make them unattractive. When did you meet her?"

He chuckled. "You know, you're like one of those little ankle-biting, yappy dogs. It was right after your episodes of *Dateline* aired."

Which meant it was pre-Drake. After Lila was arrested and Josie was reunited with the Payne family, Trinity had talked her into giving interviews to *Dateline* about their unique situation. Josie still kind of hated that those were out there. "You saw those?"

"Hasn't everyone? Man, that Lila chick did a number on pretty much everyone she met, huh? She still alive?"

It always gave Josie a strange sense of peace knowing that Lila was no longer with them, that there was absolutely no chance of her hurting another person, even in prison. "No. She died six years ago. I spread her ashes in Co—"

She broke off, her mind going back to the case she'd worked right around the time Lila died. Her heart thudded in her chest. "Turner," she said. "I think I know where this photo was taken."

His fingertips went still. "Really? Where?"

Josie went over to her desk and snatched up her keys. "Let's go."

SEVENTEEN

Josie expected Turner to protest following her without knowing where they were going. His superpower was giving her shit just for the sake of it. Instead, he trailed her all the way down the stairs, out past the press gathered at the back entrance of the stationhouse and into her SUV. Maybe he wanted to avoid the conversation about Trinity. As Josie floored it out of the parking lot, he asked, "Where we headed?"

"In South Denton, bordering Lenore County, there's a tributary that goes into the river. It's called Cold Heart Creek."

Josie could feel Turner's eyes boring into the side of her face. "Wait. You spread Lila Jensen's ashes in a place called Cold Heart Creek? I didn't think you had a sense of humor."

She came to a stop at a red light. "We worked a case down there right around the time Lila died. There was a commune in Lenore County. The members kept turning up dead. One of the bodies was found in Cold Heart Creek, but there's a smaller stream that flows from it when the water level gets high. Back then, there was this dory boat stuck in the mud near the stream. It was kind of falling apart."

The light changed. As Josie punched the gas, Turner clutched the grab handle. "You found a boat. So what?"

"It was blue, like a faded teal. If it's still there, it could be the object from the photo."

"Seems like a long shot," Turner said.

Josie turned her head long enough to skewer him with a look. "I can drop you off to interview Edgar Garcia while I check this out."

He said nothing, taking out his phone and starting to scroll. It took them a half hour to drive to South Denton. Josie drove past the sprawling business district that made up that area of the city, crossing the narrow, little-used South Bridge into a forested area that went for miles. She found the one-lane road that ran parallel with the river. She'd forgotten just how remote this area was—without residences or businesses. There weren't even fishing areas. No landmarks either. The perfect place to dump a body.

"How the hell do you intend to find this place?" Turner asked.

"There should be a bend in the river up ahead. We can park on the side of the road and walk."

"Through the woods?" he asked incredulously.

Josie ignored him. A few minutes later, the curve she'd described appeared. She found a grassy area along the shoulder of the road and parked there. She got out, waiting for Turner to follow. As he emerged from the car, scanning the wall of trees opposite the riverbank, a grimace stretched across his face. "Is it too late for you to drop me off to talk with Garcia?"

Josie started walking. Over her shoulder, she said, "You really should invest in work wear that's more appropriate to this area."

Twigs snapped under his feet. "Or people could stop disappearing and leaving bodies in the fucking woods."

Josie fully expected Turner to complain the entire time they trudged through the trees searching along the bank of Cold Heart Creek, but he was strangely silent. The sun rose higher in the sky, its rays peeking through the foliage overhead. It wasn't as humid as it had been yesterday, but it wasn't long before they were both soaked in sweat. Mosquitoes swarmed them.

"You sure you know where this thing is?" Turner said after they'd been walking for an hour. Most of the time, he had to slow down to accommodate Josie's shorter strides but today he trailed behind her.

Josie was starting to doubt herself. She hadn't been anywhere near Cold Heart Creek since the day she spread Lila's ashes.

"If this is where he brought Cleo Tate, it seems like an awful lot of effort," Turner said. "How do you know this boat is still even out here?"

She didn't. The longer they were out here, the more she doubted herself. Yet, this was the perfect place to commit a crime. No civilization for miles. No cameras. Not many people came this far into the forest, which meant that if the abductor had brought Cleo Tate here, the chances of anyone seeing them was slim to none.

Turner's hand clamped down on Josie's shoulder. She froze, head swiveling to look up at him. Lifting his hand, he pointed to his right. "There."

Ahead, the creek curved sharply but between the trunks of two maple trees, Josie saw a flash of blue, out of place in the lush green forest and its muddy floor. Turner nodded at her. She led the way, her heart tapping out an erratic rhythm against her rib cage. The unmistakable odor of decomposition wafted through the air as they got closer. Instinctively, Josie had known what they'd find and yet, she couldn't stop the overwhelming sadness that washed over her. All she could see was little Gracie Tate's cherubic face. Before the emotions bubbled too far into her consciousness, she shoved them into her mental vault. The only way she was going to help Gracie Tate now was to keep working this case.

Rounding the bend, Josie saw the boat on the opposite side of the creek. Its stern was still mired in the mud. Deep enough that even rushing water couldn't move it. The rest of it had decayed with time. Its frame was rotted, one side of it sagging into the rocks beneath it. Weeds and brush reached up from the ground, claiming it as part of the forest.

"I don't get it," Turner said, whispering even though they were the only ones out here. "Why leave a photo of this place?"

Josie's heart hammered so fast and hard, she had trouble hearing his words. "Let's cross."

Turner hesitated. "You want me to walk through this?"

"It's only, what? Ten feet across, maybe? Come on." Josie plunged into the stream. At its deepest, the water came to her knees. Although wet boots made it more difficult to walk, the cold of the water soothed her heated skin. Turner splashed behind her, muttering something about his loafers and suit pants. The smell of death was stronger here, invading her nasal passages and coating her tongue and throat. A loud, pervasive buzz filled the air. Josie's heart stuttered as they drew closer. Bloodied fingertips curled over the boat's edge.

"Son of a bitch," Josie said, forcing her feet to keep moving.

Turner trudged alongside her, faster now.

Mud squelched around Josie's boots as they reached the opposite bank. More of the horror cradled inside the boat's crumbling shell came into view. Blood clashed with the faded blue of its hull and the green growth all around them. Cleo Tate lay on her side, legs stretched like she was running. One arm was folded under her body while the other gripped the side of the boat. Dried blood matted her dark hair.

Blowflies buzzed around her, skittering across the pale skin of her face, arms, and calves. They were drawn to corpses, showing up minutes after death. They blended with Cleo's dark blue shirt, dozens of them forming a single roiling mass that undulated across her torso, their metallic blue and green backs winking in the shafts of sunlight that punched through the trees. Little sequins of death. Every few seconds, one or two flies would break away, flitting to her face, looking for any orifice in which to lay their eggs. Adult female blowflies laid as many as two hundred and fifty eggs each. They disappeared into Cleo's ear and then crawled back out, one after another. One perched on her lower lip before scurrying inside her mouth. More followed. Others attacked her eyelids, seeking entry. Several emerged from her nostrils, making way for more blowflies to enter, their movements jerky and frenzied.

A breeze soughed through the trees, skating over Cleo's body. A lock of her hair lifted. The rippling swath of flies covering her middle shifted in response to the disturbance, climbing over one another. A gap formed long enough for Josie to see a large stab wound near Cleo's kidney. It gaped open. The small pearly bodies of maggots wriggled inside it. Dozens upon dozens spilling out until the blowflies' bodies cloaked the gash once more, impervious to anything other than their task.

Over the persistent hum of the insects, Josie heard Turner swear.

There was no point in checking for a pulse. Cleo Tate had been dead for some time.

EIGHTEEN

Josie swatted at the mosquitoes and gnats that assaulted her face. No matter where she positioned herself, they followed like a cloud enveloping her. Finally, she stopped moving. Leaning against the trunk of a large maple tree, she watched the ERT and Dr. Feist work. After Hummel and his team cordoned off the scene, setting a perimeter, they had erected a pop-up tent over the boat. When Josie and Turner made their calls, notifying everyone necessary to process the scene as well as uniformed officers to secure it, they'd kept it off the police scanners that the press and many citizens followed. The longer they could keep this quiet, the better. Remy Tate and Kellan Neal had yet to be notified. Still, there was always the chance of the press finding out and WYEP sending a helicopter out to the scene.

The sound of mud sucking at someone's boots drew Josie's attention. One of the uniformed officers trudged toward her. Conlen. Just like the rest of them, he was sweating profusely. He'd been the one to provide a stroller for little Gracie Tate. He was out here helping them process the body of a mother who'd been savagely ripped away from her child, all while he had little ones at home. For a moment, Josie wanted to ask if it ever bothered him. She was an overachiever when it came to compartmentalizing, but would she be able to do it as well once she and Noah had their own baby? She shook off the thought.

Conlen said, "We've broken up the area into quadrants. We're going to start the line searches. See if this asshole left anything behind."

"If I were marching a kidnapped woman out here to kill her," Josie said, "I'd take the shortest route, which is from the north."

Conlen nodded. "We'll start there."

"Keep me posted." Josie watched him walk off. Turner had gone to interview Edgar Garcia. He had also promised to speak with Cleo Tate's family. A knot of apprehension tightened in the pit of her stomach at the thought of letting Turner notify Cleo's husband and father that they'd found her body, but she let it go. Noah had been drilling it into her head since Turner's arrival that as long as he was there, they had to find a way to work with him. For Josie, that meant not trying to micromanage the aspects of every case to keep Turner on the sidelines.

Officer Jenny Chan ducked under the crime scene tape and worked her way over. Using the sleeve of her Tyvek suit, she wiped perspiration from her brow. A camera rested in her gloved palms. "We found a bunch of partial footprints around the boat," she told Josie. Flipping the screen of the camera so Josie could see it, she clicked through several photos. "We couldn't find one that was complete."

"The treads look like they're from boots," Josie said.

Chan nodded. "We'll likely be able to narrow down the brand through the FBI's footwear database, but I'm not sure how helpful it will be. There's not enough for us to determine his shoe size, unless the search turns up additional impressions."

Josie looked past Chan to where Dr. Feist leaned over Cleo Tate's body. "Anything else?"

"Looks like your killer left the murder weapon behind," Chan said. She clicked through several more photos until she came to one of a large, bloodied knife. "It was in the bottom of the boat, near her feet."

He had stabbed Cleo Tate, likely repeatedly, then dropped the knife at her feet and walked away.

The next photo showed the ruler Chan had put next to it in order to measure the knife's length. The blade was eight inches, the black handle five point six inches. "That's a chef's knife," Josie said. She had one at home in her butcher block.

"Yeah," Chan agreed. "Once we get it cleaned up and processed for prints and DNA, we can try to figure out the brand."

Josie's empty stomach burned at the thought of that blade plunging into Cleo Tate's body. Whoever had stabbed her would have made a colossal mess. There was no way the killer managed it without getting blood spatter all over himself. The search teams would probably find drops of it from where he walked out of these woods.

Josie's eyes were drawn back to the gently flowing water of the stream. Even if he'd washed some of it off here at the scene, he'd still be dripping with Cleo Tate's blood. It would be on his clothes, shoes, hat. Everywhere. Given the remoteness of the area, it was possible he had walked out of this forest covered in blood and gotten into a vehicle without being seen, but that vehicle would have Cleo Tate's DNA all over it.

Behind Chan, Dr. Feist waved at Josie. "Suit up and have a look," she called.

Josie thanked Chan and found the impromptu station that Hummel had set up containing all the equipment the ERT needed to do their jobs. As quickly as she could, she donned her own Tyvek suit. Her hair got tucked up inside a skull cap. She worked her feet into booties and her sweat-damp hands into gloves. The uniformed officer standing sentry outside the scene logged her information on his clipboard before lifting the crime scene tape to allow her to duck under.

She joined Anya at the side of the boat. The smell of decomposition was stronger now, clinging to her, invading her senses. Angry blowflies dived at their heads, their shiny green and blue metallic bodies gleaming. They still teemed over Cleo Tate's body, trying to return immediately after Anya shooed them. Cleo's clothes looked stiff with dried blood. Up close, Josie could see where it flaked along her bare skin.

Anya said, "I'm sure I don't need to tell you by now that everything I'm about to say is based on my initial impressions. I can't give you any definitive answers until after the exam and autopsy."

"Of course," Josie said.

"I'd put her time of death at twenty to twenty-four hours ago, based on the emergence of the maggots alone."

Maggots hatched from the blowflies' eggs within twenty-four hours of being deposited into a body's openings.

"That means she was killed shortly after she was abducted," Josie said, doing the calculations in her head. The killer hadn't wasted time. He'd likely killed Cleo shortly after arriving here. Yet, this did not strike her as an impulsive act on his part. Stealing the Hamptons' car and ditching it at the lot was meant to throw the police off, waste their time and resources, and stretch them thin. It was all distraction.

Which meant that there was more to this case than they knew. Josie had the sinking feeling that they hadn't even scratched the surface.

Anya pointed to a purple lump along Cleo Tate's hairline, near her temple. "She's got a head injury. There's a superficial laceration to her left hand but other than that, if you look at her forearms, there are no defensive wounds."

"He knocked her out," said Josie.

"Or the injury disoriented her enough to make her compliant," Anya suggested.

"There's bruising, so she was alive for some time after he hit her, but she was incapacitated enough not to fight back when he started to stab her."

Anya nodded, swatting at more blowflies, causing a cloud of them to take flight. "So far, I've counted three stab wounds on her body. One here." She pointed to Cleo's chest. "Here." This time, her abdomen. "And here." Her kidney. Maggots writhed inside each of the wounds.

Josie tore her gaze away long enough to see a pair of EMTs approaching with a Stokes basket. She recognized one of them instantly. Sawyer Hayes. Before Josie's grandmother, Lisette Matson, died, Sawyer had come into their lives with a DNA test proving his blood relation to her. Eli Matson had been his father. The woman who abducted Josie had ensured that Sawyer never knew his father. He hadn't even found out about his true parentage until he was an adult.

Anya picked her way down to Cleo's feet, pointing at the backs of the woman's calves. The skin above her white ankle socks was striped in pink and red. "If you look closely, you can see tiny blue paint chips embedded in her skin."

"Which means he could have walked her up to the transom, and then she turned around or he forced her to look at him, at which point she fell back or he knocked her down and then started stabbing," said Josie.

Anya batted more flies away from her face. "I'm not so sure she would have been capable of walking with that head injury."

"Then he carried her, slung over his shoulder, and tossed her onto her back here, scraping her calves against the transom."

Anya made a noise of agreement but it was a long way to carry a grown woman, especially in this heat.

Josie glanced back at Sawyer. He had had precious little time with Lisette, and Josie knew he blamed her for Lisette's death. Josie had done her best to forge a relationship with him, but it was still rocky at times. Today, however, he gave her a wide smile. It sent a shock through her, not only because it was warm but also because every time she saw him, his resemblance to the man she believed was her father for most of her life felt like seeing Eli's ghost. Maybe the few times she and Noah had had him over for dinner in the last couple of months had helped things.

She gave him a wave and turned back to the task at hand. "But she would have been able to move, right?"

Anya brushed a blowfly from her cheek. "I can't say with any degree of certainty. It depends on the severity of her head injury. While I can tell from looking at it that it was likely severe enough to keep her from fighting back and make her more pliable, I can't say whether she was completely unconscious. At least not until I've done the autopsy. Why?"

Josie's eyes swept over Cleo's body, seizing on the way the fingers of her right hand clutched at the hull's edge, as if she were trying to pull herself out. "I'm wondering if she ended up in this position on her own or if he staged her body."

"I'm not sure we'll be able to answer that." Anya waved a hand, indicating the entirety of the scene. "Rigor has already worn off but that's not surprising given this heat. It tends to accelerate decomposition. Here, help me turn her."

Josie knelt beside the boat at Cleo's back. She kept her mouth closed against the flies, praying none tried to climb inside her nose. Small stones bit into her knees. Anya joined her, reaching across the body to peel Cleo's fingers from the boat's edge. Gingerly she pulled the upper portion of the body toward them while Josie turned the lower section. As expected, every inch of skin that had rested along the boat's bottom and its shattered wooden seats was a deep purplish-red. Livor mortis had set in. In the absence of cardiac activity and circulation, gravity made blood pool at the lowest points of the body, causing the discoloration. Twelve hours after death, it became fixed. Josie's gaze was drawn to a slash in the side of her abdomen, above her hip. The curled bodies of larvae spilled out. She pointed out the wound to Anya.

"I see it. Hold her there while I get my camera. I want to—"

She broke off, eyes fixed on something on the rotted floor of the boat, peeking out from under one of the bowed seats. Josie adjusted her stance, craning her neck to see what had caught Anya's attention. There, nestled among the vegetation that had shot up through the splintered planks of the hull, under the board where Cleo Tate's shoulder had just been, was a polaroid photo.

NINETEEN

"He's taunting us," Gretchen said.

Josie turned away from the corkboard and nodded her agreement. The whole stationhouse hummed with activity, uniformed officers coming and going, writing up their reports, checking in with their findings, and heading back out to complete more tasks in the Cleo Tate investigation. Gretchen and Turner sat at their desks while Josie stood beside Noah, studying the enlargement of the polaroid found under Cleo Tate's body. The Chief stalked in and out of his office, grumbling under his breath and occasionally barking questions. Even Amber was there, perched on the edge of her desk, watching all of them with a subdued expression.

"Look at this," Noah said. "There's blood around the frame but not the actual photo."

"He placed it under her body after he killed her," said Josie. "In one of the few places where it wouldn't get soaked with her blood."

"Considering that he clearly wanted us to find this," said Gretchen, "that was a risk. If she'd been out there any longer, the picture could have been damaged by the decomp process, bad weather, or animals. Any number of things."

A chill worked its way up Josie's spine in spite of the frigid air conditioning in the room. Gretchen was right. Any longer and the photo might not have been intact. As it was, the quality wasn't great. Like the first one, it was somewhat blurred in places, as if it had been taken too quickly. From what Josie could tell, the foreground was black asphalt. A horizontal white line cut across it. Part of another white line extended toward the bottom of the photo, the two lines connecting in a stunted T-shape. Above the horizontal line, a spear of light sliced the scene almost in half. In the distance beyond that was what appeared to be part of a building, but all Josie could make out for certain were windows. The section of the building that was visible was slightly out of focus. Something about it seemed vaguely familiar but she wondered if that was just because it might be any parking lot in front of any store or office building.

"You know what it is, Quinn?" asked Turner. "You figured out the last one."

Josie turned to see him throw his foam basketball at the net, missing. "The more important question is where it is," she said.

"There has to be something there that helps us identify it," Gretchen said. "He made sure to include part of the boat when he took the first photo so that one of us would know he'd dumped her near Cold Heart Creek."

"One of us?" said Turner. "You mean Quinn."

Noah shook his head. "I worked the Cold Heart Creek case, too. I was there the day we saw the boat. It just didn't cross my mind when I saw the polaroid."

"The photos are so blurred," Gretchen said. "They only show fragments of places and yet this guy clearly wants us to figure out where they were taken."

For a few seconds, none of them spoke. Josie's stomach

burned at the thought of what they might find if they could figure out the location where the picture had been taken.

Turner drummed his fingers along the edge of his desk. "I'm gonna go ahead and say the shitty thing out loud. If we figure out where this was taken and go there, we're looking at another body. Right?"

"Or if we figure it out quickly enough, would we get there before someone else is killed?" said Noah.

"That would be a hard thing for this guy to pull off," Turner said.

"Not impossible," Noah said. "If the location pictured here is remote enough, he could leave her bound for a certain amount of time and if we don't find her by then, he kills her."

"Then he expects us to play a game he made up when he didn't bother to tell us the rules," Turner complained.

"Even if he's not timing us with the intent to potentially let the next victim live—which wouldn't be smart if she can ID him —if he leaves us another polaroid..." Gretchen drifted off.

"That means he's still killing," Josie filled in. "And he'll keep going until we can stop him. We should start checking for any women who might have gone missing in the last day or so."

Turner tossed his ball again. Missed. "Wouldn't we have been assigned to a case like that?"

"Not if it was something like a welfare check where the responding officers had no compelling reason to enter the home," said Gretchen.

Turner eyed her. "So we're talking about a broad who—"

Gretchen bristled, glaring at him. "No one says 'broad' anymore."

Turner grinned at her. Of all of them, he seemed to enjoy provoking Gretchen the most.

"Okay," he said. "We're talking about some spinster—"

"Turner!" Josie snapped.

His head swiveled in her direction, eyes wide. "What is it now?"

Gretchen's chair squealed as she stood up. A dollar bill appeared in her hand. "I'll tell you what." She leaned over and put the dollar into the jar on Turner's desk. "You're a jackass."

Noah sighed. "Gretchen, that's not how this system works, and you know it."

Gretchen ignored him. Josie could see the satisfaction in every line of her face. Josie was beginning to think she enjoyed calling Turner a jackass to his face more than she enjoyed the pecan croissants she wasn't supposed to be eating anymore.

Turner picked up his jar and swirled it around, the few lonely dollars inside fluttering. "Don't knock her, LT. I don't mind getting back some of the money I've been putting out trying not to offend these two."

Josie looked at the jars on hers and Gretchen's desks, stuffed full of dollars. "Maybe we should get one of those signs you talked about, Turner."

He laughed, a full-throated, genuine laugh. Then he winked at her. Josie tried not to recoil.

With another heavy sigh, Noah said, "We're losing focus here, and the clock is ticking. Since we haven't had any missing persons cases recently, the kinds of reports we're looking for are ones where out-of-town friends or relatives have asked for welfare checks on women who live alone and haven't been heard from in a few days, maybe longer. Employers might also request welfare checks if someone fails to show up for work and doesn't call."

"What if this sicko has some other woman and she hasn't been reported missing yet," Turner asked.

"We can only work with what we have," Noah replied. "Until we can figure out where this photo was taken, or unless the ERT or state lab are able to pull fingerprints or DNA

samples that match someone in one of the databases, this is
what we've got."

Josie said, "The canvasses and line searches near Cold
Heart Creek turned up nothing. I prepared a geofence warrant
for that area, but since we didn't get anything from the one at
the city park or the abandoned lot, I'm guessing we won't find
anything in the latest geofence results. This guy isn't giving us
much."

Gretchen's chair creaked as she turned to her computer.
"I'll check for missing women."

"We should look at reports of stolen cars as well," said
Noah. "This guy stole Sheila Hampton's car and used it to
abduct Cleo Tate. If he's taken another woman or plans to then
he may have stolen another car."

"On it," said Josie, plopping into her chair and booting up
her computer.

Noah said, "What about the auto repair shop guy? The one
whose prints were found in the Hampton car?"

"Edgar Garcia," said Turner. "I talked to him. He doesn't
have an alibi. Says he was home sleeping all morning. It's his
day off. He seemed a little shady. Bad attitude. Said what I
figured he'd say—he worked on the car a few weeks ago after
Sheila hit a deer. That's why his prints are inside. I asked for
consent to search his phone and he shut me down."

Noah sighed. "I looked at the photos Hummel uploaded.
The places where Garcia's prints were found in the car are
exactly where we'd expect to find them given that he worked on
the car. It was a few weeks ago, so still reasonable enough that
his prints would be found."

"We need more than that to get search warrants," Josie said.
"Something that points toward him being involved in the
crime."

"That's a dead end," said Noah.

Turner stood and joined him at the corkboard. "I was thinking."

"That's new," Gretchen muttered.

Turner caught Josie's eye. "Maybe Park— Palmer needs a sign."

Josie ignored him, going back to the stolen car reports for the last week.

Turner continued, "Just about every car has GPS now. They all have infotainment systems we can use to locate a stolen vehicle and even disable it, like with the Hampton car. If this guy wanted us to find his victims, why not just use cars to do it? If he's smart enough to know how not to leave evidence behind, how to avoid cameras, and all that shit, he has to know we have the capabilities to find pretty much any car he steals."

Josie glanced over at the corkboard long enough to see the Chief step up behind Turner and Noah. His hawkish eyes raked over the newest polaroid.

Josie said, "He's trying to make some very specific point with the pictures."

"That he doesn't know how to use a camera?" Turner said.

The Chief held up his phone. "I just talked with Kellan Neal. He's holding a press conference outside the Tate residence in one hour."

Amber cleared her throat. She'd been so quiet that Josie nearly forgot she was still at her desk. Everyone turned toward her. "Is he making another appeal to the public? To help find this killer?"

The Chief nodded and patted down some of the loose white hairs floating above his forehead. "It's not a bad idea given how short we are on clues. He's also gotten several friends, neighbors and old colleagues to put together a reward for information leading to the arrest of the killer."

Noah said, "It can't hurt."

Amber picked up her cell phone. "I'll call him and make sure we coordinate. Work out all the details."

Turner said, "Did you ask him about his son-in-law's alibi?"

One of the Chief's bushy eyebrows kinked upward. "Yep. He told me Remy Tate 'checks out.'"

Gretchen laughed. "That's it? He 'checks out?'"

"I thought you said this guy was a prosecutor," Turner said. "He doesn't know how criminal investigations work?"

"I think he's counting on us giving him a pass because he was an ADA," the Chief said. "But that's not how I run shit, so as soon as the press conference is over, one of you will bring Remy Tate in. I want a recorded interview and written statement from him. Let's lock him into a story. Ask him for consent to search his phone. If he gives a shit about finding his wife's killer, he'll have no problem with it. First thing tomorrow, I want interviews with friends and family members of Remy and Cleo Tate. I don't care if Kellan Neal thinks they were living happily ever after or that his son-in-law 'checks out.' Right now, we've got nothing else, so let's start kicking over every stone in this guy's life."

TWENTY

The dark thumbprint bruises on her thigh throbbed. The pain was deep, like a toothache. Standing in front of the full-length mirror on the door of her bedroom closet, she turned her leg this way and that, grimacing at the way he'd marked her. She'd have to wear pants for the next few days. Otherwise, the bruises would draw too much attention. There was no way to cover them up and she couldn't think of an explanation as to how she'd gotten them that didn't sound like an outright lie. She'd made a grave miscalculation. Again.

He remembered too much. Plus, she hadn't expected him to be so intense. Not now. She definitely hadn't anticipated him assaulting her. The strange glow in his eyes when he wrapped his hand around her throat had nearly made her pee herself. One moment he was just a pathetic excuse for a man, shuffling through life with the weight of the world on his shoulders, and the next, he was a beast begging to be unleashed. It was like a switch being thrown. She hadn't witnessed it before although she'd known it was there. How could she not?

Knowing and experiencing were two very different things.

It had taken some fast talking to extricate herself from that car. Her eyes lingered on her reflection as if to assure herself that she had made it out, that she was safely home, in her own bedroom now. She changed out of her shorts and into a loose pair of linen pants. Then she downed the glass of wine on the dresser. The third of the night. A quick glance out her bedroom window assured her that he wasn't parked outside, thinking about finishing what he started. He didn't know where she lived. Yesterday, she would have thought he was too stupid to find out but now, she wasn't sure. What if he was out there watching? What if he saw how many times she checked for him? He'd see that as an invitation. She knew he would because that was how his mind worked. He was a sicko.

Flicking off her bedroom light, she sank to the floor next to her window. She had to recalibrate. Come up with a new plan.

Or she could forget the whole thing. Go back to normal life. Let the bruises fade and pretend today had never happened.

Except she was afraid she'd awakened the monster in him again, and now that she had, no one was safe.

TWENTY-ONE

For the dozenth time, Josie's gaze drifted away from the CCTV feed to her phone screen and the picture she'd taken of the second polaroid. She blinked, hoping to clear some of the grit from her eyes, and looked back to the large television that showed a haggard Remy Tate still talking to Noah and Gretchen in one of Denton PD's two interview rooms. They'd been at it for hours. The clock on the wall ticked past one a.m. So far, Remy had admitted to having an affair but wouldn't disclose the identity of his mistress.

Early on, Noah had taken on the role of the good guy, easing into the smooth and friendly persona he often donned when interviewing male suspects or persons of interest who knew they'd done something wrong but were afraid to admit it. Now, Noah inched his chair closer to Remy's so that their knees nearly touched. He lowered his voice as if Gretchen wasn't standing over them with her arms crossed, glaring. "Look, Remy, I get it, okay? Your wife's pregnancy was difficult. Then the baby came along, and she wasn't sleeping. Probably pretty crabby, right? Too tired to fool around. Not feeling sexy anymore, not in the mood, blah blah blah. Maybe snapping at you or pushing you away when you tried to touch her."

Josie knew that Noah would never say such things under normal circumstances but right now he was playing a character. A man who understood and shared questionable morals. A man Remy Tate could confide in.

Remy kept his eyes on his lap but nodded.

"Must have been hard," Noah continued. "I know you love your daughter. Fatherhood's amazing, right?"

Another nod.

"But let's be real here. We've got needs, right? Maybe it was a mistake to cheat. I think we can agree on that, can't we?"

"Yes," Remy said. "But listen, I didn't technically cheat."

Noah smiled knowingly. "I know what you're saying. I do. But I'm wondering if your wife would have seen it that way. You know how women are."

Remy nodded. "Right. You're right. Cleo would definitely have seen it the wrong way. Listen, I'm not proud of myself. I wish I could take it back."

Noah shrugged. "But shit happens. You can't undo what you did, but you can give us the name of your mistress so that she can clear your name and we can get on with looking for the real killer. What do you say?"

With a sigh, Remy said, "I... I really can't."

Josie startled at the long groan that sounded behind her. Over her shoulder, she saw the Chief. She hadn't heard him come in even though the viewing room was roughly the size of a walk-in closet. Now he watched the interview, silent and stock-still, one arm crossed over his chest while his other hand rubbed at his chin.

"His mistress is married," he announced.

Josie had been thinking the same thing.

"Or worse," he added.

Josie squirmed in her seat at the thought that Remy might

have been involved in a sexual relationship with an underage girl. Why else would he guard the secret so closely? But Josie couldn't see Kellan Neal covering that up. Maybe he wanted to protect his son-in-law's reputation or, more likely, didn't want the fact that Remy had a mistress to make it into the press and take away from finding Cleo's actual killer, but Josie was certain Neal would never protect his son-in-law if he'd committed a crime.

The Chief said, "We should look at babysitters."

"They didn't have one yet," Josie said. "Cleo did everything."

Gretchen finally stepped forward and snapped, "You can tell us who she is or we can take your entire life apart and find her anyway. First thing tomorrow morning, our team will be interviewing your family, friends, coworkers, everyone you know. We'll get a warrant for the contents of your phone, since you've refused to consent to a search, and we will find her. If you think the press won't notice how closely we're looking at you, you're sorely mistaken. You really don't want to be tried in the court of public opinion. People will think you killed your wife, or that you hired someone to do it for you."

Remy looked stricken. Still, he refused to give them a name. The interview continued. At this rate, they'd be here all night.

Josie went back to studying the polaroid.

The Chief sat down in the folding chair next to her. "You should be home, sleeping. Like Turner."

"Do you honestly think I'd be asleep right now?" she said, without taking her eyes off the picture.

The Chief reached over and tapped a long finger against her phone screen. "Because you know where this is."

Josie laughed. "If I knew where this was, we would have been there hours ago."

"If you didn't know where it was, you wouldn't be obsessing

this hard," he replied. "I've seen you work, Quinn. I know this look."

She sighed and held her phone flat, looking at the polaroid from a different angle. "What look is that?"

"The one you get when the answer is floating around somewhere in the back of your mind, but you just can't catch it."

She met his flinty eyes and smiled. "I didn't know I had a look that went with that."

"Well, you do. So let's get at it. What is this guy showing us?"

On the CCTV, Noah and Gretchen circled round and round with Remy Tate.

Josie pushed her phone across the table so that it was between them. "Asphalt, white line, building in the distance. Windows. This could be anywhere."

"No. It can't be anywhere. If we're right about what's going on here, this guy intends to abduct a woman, get her to this location, and stab her to death. He can't do that just anywhere."

Josie nodded. "Okay, yes. It has to be remote. He's stayed away from cameras thus far, so he'd choose a place where it was not very likely that he'd be caught on surveillance driving there, being there, leaving there."

"That eliminates central Denton or any of the business areas that are densely populated," said the Chief. "Keep going."

"All right. The outskirts of the city. Still a huge area to cover. But it would have to be a place where no people, or at least not many people, would be coming or going. Or at least a place that would be unoccupied long enough for him to commit murder. It might have cameras but maybe they don't cover the entire area—like the parking lot."

"Abandoned buildings, then," said the Chief. "An office building, maybe?"

Josie tapped against the top right of the photo. "A building with lots of glass. Lots of windows."

"An unfinished office building, perhaps."

"Could be."

In the interview room, Gretchen changed topics from the identity of Remy's mistress to how the relationship began.

The Chief pointed to the spear of light that sliced through the center of the photo. Whatever might be between the asphalt and the building—shrubs, parking spaces, anything that might help narrow down the location, was obscured by the flash. "It gets sun though. Look at this glare. Or, I guess this could just be the camera flash reflecting off the windows. Abandoned or unfinished buildings with lots of windows, asphalt parking lot. Outskirts of town."

That still didn't narrow things down. Without driving through the mountains in every remote part of the city—which would take hours, if not days—trying to locate any and all abandoned office buildings with asphalt parking lots, or trying to pull permits for construction projects on the outskirts of the city, which would also be time-consuming, they were not going to find this place.

But the killer wanted them to find it. Josie was certain of that. This was a game. If they didn't figure out where to go from this photo, they couldn't play. Josie didn't think he would give them a clue they couldn't follow, no matter how obscure. She had to look at the scene differently. Why, for example, would he give them a photo with such glare on it? So much glare that the rest of the area could barely be viewed.

Unless it wasn't a glare at all.

"It's a light," Josie blurted out.

"What?"

She picked up the phone and zoomed in on the portion of the photo where the asphalt ended and the streak of light began. "This is from a light that is recessed into the concrete."

The Chief frowned. "Maybe."

Something veiled in Josie's memories screamed to be uncovered. Her heartbeat ticked up. "Not maybe. It's a light."

"What kind of parking lot has recessed lights in the ground?"

Josie's eyes were drawn to the white lines again. The shape of a T. Except maybe not a T. They were missing the larger picture because the killer only showed them what he wanted them to see. "It's not a parking lot."

If not a T shape, then what? Why the recessed lighting?

The glass. Something about the glass. Remote location. Outskirts of the city.

The Chief said, "If it's not a parking lot, what is it?"

The veil in Josie's memory fell away. "It's a helipad."

TWENTY-TWO

Josie's shoulders knotted with tension when she saw the incoming call on her cell phone. Adjusting one of the shoulder straps of her bulletproof vest, she scanned the remote mountain road where over a dozen police vehicles were now parked. It was after two a.m. Inky blackness closed in all around them. The only illumination came from headlights and Josie's ringing cell phone. Once she had figured out where the photo was taken, she'd left a voicemail for the property owner. They couldn't go in until Josie spoke with her. She just hoped that the woman would be up this late. While they waited for the return call, the Chief had assembled as many officers as he could and they'd formed a perimeter around the premises. Not easy considering this place was surrounded by forest. Still, they had to be careful and strategic in their approach in case the killer was still on-site or had set a trap for them. Josie strongly doubted anyone was living or staying in the house, but they had to find out.

Gretchen sauntered over and pointed to the phone. "Want me to take that?"

Honestly, Josie didn't want to talk to Kim Rowland ever

again, but she wasn't going to let her personal feelings affect how she performed her job. She swiped answer.

Kim said, "Has my dad's glass monstrosity finally burned down?"

Josie fought to keep the irritation out of her voice. The only residence in the city with a private helipad was the home of the late Peter Rowland. A Denton native, he had made a fortune developing state-of-the-art security and surveillance systems. He'd kept a home in Denton even though he rarely visited. When he died, his daughter inherited his empire. Kim was every bit the sociopath her father had been. Years ago, Kim had come to town to escape her mobster boyfriend, wreaking havoc wherever she went. Josie's fiancé at the time, Luke, had had an affair with Kim after she convinced him to cover up a double homicide and hide her in his home. He'd destroyed his and Josie's relationship as well as his career. Kim's other machinations had threatened the life of the son of one of Josie's best friends. He was a newborn at the time. The memory of plucking him from a freezing, rushing river—and certain death —still chilled Josie to the bone.

That was the tip of the iceberg.

"It's still standing," Josie told her. "But we might have a body on the premises. We need to search the property and for that, we need your permission."

"Wow," Kim said. "That will bring the property value down, won't it?"

Naturally, she had no concern for the victim. She could have sold the property years ago but didn't. Josie said, "Do we have your permission or not?"

There was a heavy sigh. "Fine. I don't care."

"Thank you. Is anyone living in the house?"

"No," said Kim. "Who would want to live there?"

Josie ignored the question. "Is the security system active?"

"I think so. I can find out. I have a property management

company that does upkeep and lawn care. Their people are only there once a month. That's it."

Depending on what they found, Josie would prepare a warrant for any surveillance footage available from the security system.

"Has the helipad been in use?" Josie asked. "We believe the lights around it may be on."

Kim said, "No one has been using the pad, but the property management company has lights all over the property that are on timers. They go on at a certain time of night and off during the day. It's supposed to deter people from messing with the place since it's basically vacant."

"Great, thanks."

Before Josie could hang up, Kim said, "Do you still see Luke?"

Her tone was bland but the muscles in Josie's shoulder blades pulled so taut, it was painful. Through gritted teeth, Josie said, "I have to go."

She hung up before Kim could utter another word. Gretchen gave a low whistle. "Guess we're lucky she decided to go to New York City instead of settling here."

Josie adjusted her vest again and checked that her radio worked. "Let's go."

With Noah still at the stationhouse speaking to Remy Tate, and Turner at home—or under whatever rock he lived beneath —it was just the two of them and the uniformed officers. The ERT was also there, on standby, as well as an ambulance. Josie and Gretchen led the way down the long driveway, guns drawn, flashlights positioned under their pistols. Several pairs of uniformed officers followed. The driveway was paved but it curved in several places and seemed to go on for miles even though Josie knew it was not that long. It was darker here. The sounds of frogs trilling and crickets chirping was deafening. Every so often, the trees alongside the driveway gave way to small clearings. Flashlight beams swept over the strange sculptures displayed in them. Josie remembered thinking that the place had an almost Alice in Wonderland feel to it when she was last here.

She knew they were nearing the house when LED lanterns appeared on either side of the driveway, lighting the rest of the way. The house rose in the distance, looking as though a giant hand had spilled it from the sky. It was flat but tiered, each level getting smaller and smaller as it rose toward the trees overhead. The first floor was almost entirely glass. Inside, soft lights glowed. White couches that Josie remembered from having visited Peter Rowland here nearly eight years ago still sat in the living room. She wondered if Kim had ever set foot inside. The house seemed trapped in time.

"Car," said one of the officers behind them.

Immediately, Josie's gaze was drawn to the right where an older model Toyota Camry was parked beside a sculpture of several rabbits running across a log. Josie and Gretchen kept watch all around them while the two uniformed officers approached, shining their flashlights inside the car.

"Empty," said one of them.

"Radio to the units on the road," Josie instructed. "Give them the tag number so they can look up the owner."

Once he had done so, they carried on, drawing closer to the house. The glow of LED lights from the driveway and along the front walk to the house was trapped by the canopy of foliage overhead, giving the entire area an otherworldly feel. Goosebumps erupted over Josie's bare arms.

"There," said Gretchen, swinging her flashlight and pistol to the left, toward the small helipad that sat near the front of the house.

This time there was no helicopter parked there. Beams from the recessed lights stretched upward into the darkness. Overhead, a break in the trees revealed hundreds of sparkling stars, breathtaking beauty shining down on a scene of horror. A figure sprawled across the asphalt. Josie's heart sank. She'd known what they were walking into, but again, just like at the Cleo Tate scene, her heart filled with sadness at the loss of life and the knowledge that another family was about to be shattered.

While Josie, Gretchen, and two other officers approached the helipad, the rest of them surged toward the house to clear in and around it. Kim had had the property management company text them a code to get into the house. The four of them remaining out front trod carefully so as not to disturb any potential evidence. The smell of decomposition hit Josie like a slap in the face, far stronger than it had been at Cold Heart Creek. It was a sickening combination of rotting meat, rotting fish, excrement, rotten eggs and oddly, a hint of mothballs. Josie was used to it. One of the uniformed officers behind her gagged. The young one, probably. This might be his first dead body—or at least the first one in which the body had entered the second stage of decomposition. The odor was unmistakable. As the victim came fully into view, the gagging intensified.

From what Josie could tell, the victim was a woman. She lay on her stomach, head turned to the side, long blonde hair fanned out across the blacktop. Either she had been killed shortly after Cleo Tate's murder, or the high heat and humidity of the July weather had significantly sped up the decomp process because her body was bloated. Immediately after death, autolysis occurred. The body's own enzymes destroyed its cells. The bacteria in the gastrointestinal tract began to digest the intestines. Eventually, intestinal bacteria found their way into the rest of the body, causing a buildup of gases and organic compounds: methane, hydrogen sulfide, cadaverine, putrescine, skatole and indole. The gases filled the internal cavities, causing the body to swell, sometimes to twice its size.

Shouts of "Clear!" came from the direction of the house,

again and again, until every last inch of the place was deemed safe.

Josie swept her flashlight along the body. Blood congealed around the woman's torso, blending in with the asphalt. Drops of dried blood were scattered across her marbled cheeks. Her tongue bulged through her parted lips and her eyes protruded from their sockets—the gases building inside her body forcing them outward. Insects teemed in and around her body. They were more plentiful and active than they'd been at the Cleo Tate scene, which meant this woman had been left out in the elements longer.

The young officer behind her dry-heaved. "I'm gonna be sick."

"Not at my crime scene, you're not," Josie told him. "Get out of here."

He didn't hesitate. The next thing Josie heard were his footfalls as he ran back down the driveway. Then, retching. The other officer said, "Fucking rookies."

Gretchen sighed. "Let's not get any closer. I'll radio Hummel and call Dr. Feist."

As she stepped away, Josie continued to sweep her flashlight up and down the body. While the recessed lights along the perimeter of the helipad gave off a dim glow, it wasn't enough to make out details. Clad in a pair of jeans, one of the woman's legs was straight while the other bent at the knee. One of her hands pressed into the asphalt beside her cheek while the other reached over her head, touching the grass that surrounded the helipad. It looked like she had tried to crawl away.

Widening her scan to the area around the body, Josie's torch caught on an object near the woman's feet. A knife. It was similar to the knife found near Cleo Tate's body. The killer had left the murder weapon behind again. Once might have been a mistake born of carelessness and adrenaline. Twice was intentional.

What was he trying to say?

Josie's radio squawked, a unit from outside the perimeter responding. "Car belongs to Stella Townsend, twenty-four, Denton resident."

"Copy," Josie replied.

A glance at her phone told her it was late but not too late to send someone to Stella Townsend's house for a welfare check. Her Camry hadn't been on the list of recently stolen vehicles. Josie radioed her request and units were dispatched. Again, she used her torch to take in the scene until her gaze caught on the next piece in this twisted killer's game.

Gretchen returned. "ERT are on their way. Dr. Feist will be here in a half hour." She pointed her flashlight toward the helipad. "I hope this guy didn't put the next polaroid under her body 'cause it will be destroyed."

"He didn't." Josie focused her light on one of the pockets in the back of the woman's jeans. A square of white peeked out. "It's right there."

"Shit," said Gretchen.

Hours later, after the ERT had meticulously processed most of the scene, Hummel removed the photo from the victim's pocket. He let Josie and Gretchen see it and take pictures of it before putting it into an evidence collection bag.

Another outdoor scene. Another fragmented view of something. Blue sky filled the upper left corner of the polaroid. The rest of it was blurred but looked like the edge of a building, maybe, with white siding. Over the top of it was a darker, distorted shape that cut across the white. The eave of a roof, perhaps.

Whatever it was—wherever it was—Josie was certain it was the place where the killer's next victim had already drawn her last breath.

TWENTY-THREE

A tingle went up Josie's spine where Noah rested his hand on her lower back as he ushered her out of the stairwell and into the basement of Denton Memorial Hospital. They were on their way to the city morgue. Their footsteps echoed along the empty hall. This area of the hospital was always deserted. Besides the suite of rooms presided over by Dr. Anya Feist, all the other rooms were unused. The entire floor was windowless and looked like something out of a horror movie with its grimy yellowed floor tiles and drab white walls, dingy from age and dirt. As they got closer to the exam room, the combined smells of human decomposition and cleaning chemicals filled the air.

She leaned in closer to Noah, her back arching into his hand, and inhaled his aftershave to offset the odor. It was late afternoon but both of them were freshly showered. Josie had stayed at the Rowland house until the body was ready to be moved. Then she'd gone back to the stationhouse to get started on reports. The welfare check on Stella Townsend had turned up nothing. No one at her apartment answered. The door was locked. Denton PD had no compelling reason to force their way in or to request that the landlord let them in.

At least, not yet. Noah had also been at the stationhouse, finishing up paperwork on his interview with Remy Tate, who had given a written statement but still refused to name his mistress.

Noah brushed a quick kiss over her temple while they were still alone. "We should *not* sleep all day more often."

Josie smiled, a shiver of delight working its way down her spine at the memory of his hands and mouth on her skin not even an hour ago. "We should."

Once Josie and Noah had finished their paperwork in the early morning hours after discovering the second body—and spent an inordinate amount of time studying the new polaroid without figuring out where it had been taken—they'd gone home together. Gretchen had stayed. The Chief had agreed to let them change the rotation since Josie and Noah both needed to be present for Drake's proposal to Trinity the next evening. Josie was just relieved she'd get a break from Turner, even if it meant that Gretchen might kill him. She and Noah were supposed to sleep during the day, but they'd come home to an empty house. Drake had taken Trinity to breakfast. Shannon and Christian were meeting with their realtor. They had taken full advantage of their time alone, getting very little rest but making up for the last few weeks during which they'd been busy, occupied with guests, or on opposite shifts and unable to indulge in one another.

At the door to the morgue's exam room, the residual bliss coursing through Josie's body fled. She tried to hold onto its vestiges because once they passed over the threshold, they would be fully immersed in the horror of the case at hand. Her chest tightened at the thought that there was another victim out there already, waiting for them to decipher the polaroid and find her. She took in a steadying breath as Noah pushed the door open, holding it for her.

Turner's voice came from inside the room. "I'm not flirting,

Doc. I swear. I'm just trying to get to know you. We gotta work together."

On the other side of the room, past the two exam tables, which both held shrouded bodies, Turner leaned against the stainless-steel countertop that lined the wall. A few feet away, Anya stood, eyes fixed on her laptop screen. With a sigh, she said, "You don't need to know anything personal about me in order for us to work together."

Noah grumbled something inaudible as they crossed the room. Josie glanced up at him to see his jaw tensed.

"Hey, lovebi— LT, Quinn," Turner said, smiling like they were old friends.

"What's going on?" Noah said.

Turner looked at Anya, but she stayed focused on her laptop. Josie took in her body language. Bored, mildly annoyed, but not afraid or angry. She said, "He came to discuss the autopsy results of your two victims."

Noah eyed Turner. "And then?"

Turner rolled his eyes. "I didn't do anything! I was making small talk."

Anya finally looked at him, one brow arched. "You have a weird way of making small talk."

Josie said, "He's socially inept. It's one of his many gifts."

"Who needs a sign now?" Turner groused. "It's been zero days since Quinn insulted me."

"That's enough," Noah said. "Turner, you should go home and get some rest. We'll take over from here."

Turner took out his phone and punched in a passcode. "You don't want my update first?"

"It's on your phone?" Josie asked.

His thumb tapped and scrolled. Without looking away from the screen, he said, "It is now. My— someone told me about this notes app thing. You ever hear of it?"

A sharp stab of grief pierced Josie's heart. Mettner had

always used his notes app to keep track of the details of investigations. She tried to force words past her lips but none came. Luckily, Turner just kept on talking. "The body recovered at the Rowland place has a forearm tattoo that says, 'I am the storm.' I know that this killer stole a car last time but since the car at the scene belonged to Stella Townsend and she didn't answer her door last night or this morning, I figured it was best to eliminate her as the victim first thing. I checked her social media. Found a photo of her with the tattoo visible."

He turned the screen toward Josie and Noah. An Instagram post showed Stella Townsend as she had been in life. Her eyes were shaded with sunglasses, but a wide smile spread across her heart-shaped face. Wind lifted the ends of her blonde hair. Although she was dressed in a long-sleeved white blouse and fitted black skirt, she held a tiny duckling in her hands. She had tagged the Denton Wildlife Sanctuary and thanked them for the tour. "Story to follow," she'd added. The sleeves of her shirt had been folded to her elbows. Turner zoomed in so that they could see the edge of her right forearm. In black script, the tattoo read, 'I am the storm.' They wouldn't have been able to see the tattoo at the crime scene given the position of the body and all the blood.

"It's the same," Anya said. "He was able to locate her dental records and bring them in. It's a match."

Turner grinned, as if waiting for praise. When none came, he turned the screen back around and started swiping again. "She lived alone. Closest relative is her mother, who lives in Virginia."

"I've asked the coroner's office there to make the death notification," Anya said. "Now, let me give you my findings so the three of you"—she looked pointedly at Turner—"can get out of here. I'm sure you have lots of work to do."

Turner was too busy looking at his phone to notice. Presumably, something that didn't have to do with the case captured his attention. "I already heard all this. I'll meet you guys in the cafeteria after you hear the doc's spiel and give you the rest of my update before I head home."

He didn't wait for a response, sailing out the door without even looking up from the screen.

Noah sighed. "Anya, if he's a problem—"

She held up a hand to silence him, laughing. "He's completely harmless, Noah. He's just... annoying. And odd. But I can handle him."

"What was he asking you?" Josie said. She shouldn't care but part of her was curious.

"He wanted to know if I was trapped on a deserted island but had access to a DVD player and I could only watch three movies for the rest of my life, which movies would I choose?"

"What?" Noah said.

Anya shook her head. "Like I said, odd. I know that's not really personal information, but he claimed that my choice of movies would say a lot about me. I just—I'm tired, and I didn't feel like dealing with him."

"I get it," Josie said.

Noah said, "We won't take up much of your time here because we've got a lot of work ahead of us, so why don't you tell us what you've got?"

TWENTY-FOUR

Beckoning them to follow, Anya walked over to one of the exam tables and folded the sheet down until Cleo Tate's upper body was visible. The constellation of moles on her left cheek stood out against the unnatural pallor of her skin. Her eyes were closed. She looked as if she'd drifted off to sleep—except for the large stab wounds visible on her torso, one on the upper left side of her chest and the other in her abdomen, just below her navel. All the insects had been washed away.

Anya said, "As I told Josie at the scene, there is a superficial laceration on her left hand. There are a total of four stab wounds, but the one here on her chest was likely the one that killed her. The knife pierced her skin, the sternum, the pericardium and punctured the aorta. She would have bled out in minutes. The average amount of time it takes to bleed out from a rupture or tear in the aorta is between two and five minutes. Based on the temperature of her body, taking into account the temperature where she was found, the condition of her body, and accounting for the accelerated decomposition, time of death was between eleven thirty a.m. and one thirty p.m. on Monday."

Noah said, "He killed her within two hours of abducting her."

"Yes." Anya pointed to the lump on Cleo's head. "The head injury was significant. I wasn't able to narrow down the weapon. Only that she was struck with a blunt object. Regardless of what was used, the blow would not have been fatal. However, it likely would have been severe enough to cause a loss of consciousness, a concussion, and disorientation."

"Making it difficult for her to try to escape him or to fight back," Josie said.

Anya nodded. "Yet, there was no sign of sexual assault."

Noah's gaze snapped toward her. "Really?"

"Yes, really. I know. I was surprised, too. Usually, sexual assault is the reason why a man abducts a woman and takes her to a remote location. There was not even evidence that she had had intercourse recently."

Which made sense, given what they knew about Cleo's marriage and Remy's recent extramarital activity.

"He always intended to kill her." Josie stared at the wound on Cleo's chest. "It must have taken a significant amount of force to reach her aorta."

"Yes," Anya agreed. "An extreme amount of force."

"Which means this guy is either very strong or he was very enraged," said Noah. "Or both."

"Given the characteristics of the wounds, it looks like he was standing over her when he stabbed her." Anya's gaze swept over the additional wounds. "She never stood a chance."

The killer had taken Cleo into the woods. He'd either pushed or tossed her into the boat's broken hull and descended on her in a fury strong enough to pierce bone. There was something both precise and incredibly messy about Cleo Tate's murder. The killer had clearly planned the entire thing carefully but then once he had Cleo where he wanted her, he lost control.

Noah pushed a hand through his hair. "How about Stella Townsend?"

Anya repositioned the sheet over Cleo Tate's body and went over to the other autopsy table, uncovering Stella Townsend. Dark purple and red stained the skin of her torso and one of her cheeks where the blood had pooled until the discoloration became fixed.

Anya said, "I estimate her time of death—again taking all factors into account—as Monday between four and six p.m."

Which meant that he had abducted and killed Stella Townsend only hours after Cleo Tate.

Anya motioned toward Stella's head. "You can't see it because of her hair, but she, too, had a significant head injury. This one was at the base of the skull. Again, caused by some sort of blunt object."

The killer had attacked Stella from behind.

"In addition to that, just like Cleo Tate, there was no sign of sexual assault."

Josie exchanged a glance with Noah. If these crimes were sexually motivated and Cleo had been his first attempt, there was always the chance that things hadn't gone the way he fantasized and that he'd ended up killing her before he could assault her. That sometimes happened with sexually motivated killers when they finally decided to try to make their violent, deviant fantasies into reality. However, if his second victim was also not sexually assaulted then that meant the killings were not sexually motivated. It wasn't unheard of, but to a degree, it was unexpected.

Anya continued, "As you know, the weapon was a knife. The knives at both crime scenes were identical. Same brand, same size. Hummel told me you can find them at almost any store that sells butcher block sets."

Josie quickly counted five stab wounds in Stella's chest and stomach as well as another in her throat. "We won't track the killer down through the knives."

Noah said, "These seem like pretty straightforward stabbings. Is there anything else we should know?"

Anya waved a hand across Stella's torso. "Yes. All of the wounds on Stella's body were here, along the front of her body. Torso and neck. Given the characteristics of the wounds, I believe that the killer was standing over her when he stabbed her, just like with Cleo Tate."

"He hit her in the back of the head and knocked her down," Josie said, remembering the way they'd found Stella's body. "She turned over and he stabbed her. Then she flipped back onto her stomach and tried to crawl away but bled out before she could."

Anya held up one finger. "Except she couldn't have crawled away. The stab to her throat was deep. It nicked her cervical spine, severing the nerve that innervates the muscles from the chest down. She would have been paralyzed."

Noah raised a brow. "What if it was the last wound? What if she was trying to crawl away and then he turned her back over and stabbed her in the throat?"

"He still would have had to reposition her," Josie said. "He moved her."

"Yes," Anya said. "Regardless of the order of the stab wounds, Josie's right. Whether he administered the paralyzing wound first or last, before he left her he would have had to put her onto her stomach."

The image of Stella's hand reaching for the grass flashed through Josie's mind. "He staged her to look like she was trying to crawl away."

But why?

"He's trying to tell us something," said Noah.

Anya gently covered Stella Townsend's body. "I sure hope

you figure it out soon. I'd really prefer not to have another one of his victims on my table."

TWENTY-FIVE

It wasn't difficult for him to find out where she lived. She wasn't careful when she fled the car, allowing him to follow her easily. That told him that she was just playing hard to get. Everything was a game to her. She enjoyed playing with him. But she wouldn't have gotten into the car if she didn't want something. Something he was more than happy to give her. It was hard to ignore the way she'd trembled under his touch, the way her eyes had widened. The gasps that slipped from her parted lips. Even now, standing at the edge of the parking lot where her car waited, arousal stirred at the memory of how she'd reacted to him. He hadn't seen her in a long time.

All his prior attempts to find her had failed and he had tried very hard to locate her.

Like a ghost, she'd vanished. Wreaked havoc on his life and disappeared as if she'd never existed. At times, he wondered if she'd been a figment of his imagination. If he was like a character in a movie with multiple personality disorder—or whatever they called it now—and she was just one of his others, whispering lies into his ear. Eventually, he'd given up. But he'd never forgotten.

His eyes swept over her body as she emerged from the building. It wasn't safe for him to take her now, not from her own building—in broad daylight with cameras everywhere—but that didn't stop the exhilaration from pinging through his veins. The encounter in the car had breathed life back into his hollow soul. Fingers twitching, he imagined all the ways he could make her repay her debt to him. He'd finally get to show her what she had done to him, what she had made him. Then he'd find someone new. After all, there was already blood on his hands. Lots of it, and, if the past had taught him one thing, it was that he was untouchable.

TWENTY-SIX

The scents of the hospital cafeteria were welcome after being in the morgue. Josie cataloged each smell as they passed the various kiosks. Grilled chicken, French fries, pizza, stir-fry, pasta drenched in spaghetti sauce. All of it combined to elicit a grumble in her stomach even though she and Noah ate before they reported for their shifts. They were legendary among friends and family for their complete incompetence when it came to making meals—Josie more so than Noah. They'd been taking cooking classes from their friend Misty so that if—hopefully when—they matched with a baby, they would be capable in the kitchen but still, everything not made by them tasted better than their paltry creations. Josie's mouth watered as they came to the coffee counter.

Noah said, "Go find Turner. I'll get us a couple."

She found him at a corner table, a half-eaten slice of pizza in front of him. As usual, he was scrolling on his phone. Josie tried to see what was on the screen as she approached but he sensed her behind him and quickly put his phone face down on the table.

Josie sat across from him. "Want to tell me how you know my sister yet?"

Turner took a bite of his pizza, chewing slowly. Avoiding the topic. Noah slid into the chair next to Josie, pushing a cup of coffee toward her. Looking at Turner, he said, "What do you have?"

Turner took his time swallowing and wiping his fingers on a napkin before picking up his phone and swiping a few times, presumably bringing up his notes app. "Stella Townsend was a student at Denton University, pursuing a degree in communications. She quit school for a while but was re-enrolled for this fall. She was a production assistant at WYEP until recently when she dropped down to part-time. I talked to a couple of her coworkers and neighbors. They all said she has no significant other, no stalky exes, and they weren't aware of her having any trouble with anyone lately. Don't worry—I got assurances from Stella's boss that they wouldn't release anything about her death until we gave them the green light."

It seemed counterintuitive to trust the press, especially after the shakedown from Dallas Jones the other day, but Josie knew WYEP's upper management wouldn't want to burn any bridges with the Denton PD. Not if they hoped to stay on good terms for future stories.

Turner went on, "Warrants are out for her phone records and the GPS from her car. Also there was a messenger bag in the back seat that contained her laptop. Got a warrant out for that. Waiting on that information to come back."

Josie said, "Did you find out when she was last seen? Where she might have gone missing from?"

Turner grinned again, smugly, thumb flying across his phone screen. "Oh honey, wait till you see this."

Josie held out her palm. Without even looking at her, Turner's free hand disappeared beneath the table as he searched his jacket pocket. He came up with a dollar bill, pushing it across the table to her. At least this one wasn't moist. He turned his phone screen toward them. "This is footage from the parking lot of Stella Townsend's apartment complex from three thirty p.m. on Monday."

It was the same time that almost all of Denton's police resources were focused on searching the fifty-acre lot where Sheila Hampton's car had been left, trying to find Cleo Tate. The footage was in color, but the camera was angled downward, from a substantial height. Maybe from a light pole. It made it difficult to see the face of the man who weaved his way through the parking lot until he found Stella's Camry, especially since he wore the same hat that Charlotte Thompson had described. It was too far away to make out the logo on the front of it. The strap of his cross-body backpack was visible. He leaned against the driver's side door. Arms folded, he waited.

Turner said, "I tried following him on surveillance cameras. Found him walking past a few businesses nearby but lost him after that. Didn't get a clearer look at his face."

"He's too careful," Noah said.

In the upper right of the video, the seconds ticked by. Finally, Stella came into view, wearing the clothes she'd been found in, and carrying a knit purse and the messenger bag Turner had mentioned. She paused a few feet from the man, motioning to her vehicle.

"There's no audio, unfortunately," Turner said.

The man spoke. Josie only knew that because she could see his jaw moving. The camera angle didn't allow for them to see his lips, which was unfortunate since Noah was a very good lip-reader. As he talked, Stella moved closer. The conversation lasted a minute and seventeen seconds and then Stella directed him toward the passenger's side. They both got into the car, and she drove off.

"That's odd," said Noah.

"He didn't appear to threaten her," Josie added. A fluttering sensation filled her chest. "But she got into the car willingly, from what it looks like. She might have known him."

"That's what I thought," Turner said. "None of the coworkers or neighbors I spoke with seemed shady. We'll need to take a deeper dive into Townsend's life. She hasn't been enrolled in any classes at the university for about two years, but I could always talk with some of her professors there and see if they remember her having any problems with anyone. Whatever we can get from her phone and laptop might help. Her social media accounts aren't very active. She doesn't give out much personal information there."

Josie took a sip of her coffee. "Rowland's property is remote. If Stella drove them there and he left her car behind—"

Turner interrupted her. "Then he either hoofed it out of there or he had help—someone to pick him up. Rowland's property management company turned over their surveillance footage from the premises but there's no clear shot of the helipad. You can see figures moving but they're too far from the camera to be of any use. Already did the geofence warrant for the area surrounding Rowland's property. The Chief had everyone and their brother over there at first light doing a line search in case he did walk home. Found nothing. We've also got a warrant out for the GPS from Stella's car to see if she stopped anywhere on the way to Rowland's. That'll be in any time now."

Nothing. That's all this case had to give. Nothing, nothing, and more nothing. Josie tried not to feel defeated and yet, the image of that third polaroid sat front and center in her mind, taunting her. Reminding her another woman was out there somewhere, probably already dead.

"Maybe Hummel will have something for us. There's still prints and DNA to be pulled from the car, the knife, the polaroid. Stella's clothes."

Even as she said it, she had a feeling Hummel would find nothing of use.

Noah said, "Hopefully the DNA profiles from the Cleo Tate homicide will come back sooner rather than later. If there's a match in CODIS, we can get this guy."

"Sure, LT," Turner said, without enthusiasm. "If you say so."

Josie said, "How about Remy Tate's phone records?"

"Waiting on those, too." Turner's fingers drummed on top of the table. He wouldn't be there much longer. "Waiting on everything. By the time I see you two again, you'll be up to your eyeballs in reports."

Turner was right. By the end of their shift, Josie's eyes burned with exhaustion, irritated from hours of sifting through thousands of pages. She could barely keep them open. She never thought she'd look forward to seeing Turner, but he was due to relieve them at midnight and she couldn't wait for him to get there.

She wasn't even annoyed when he showed up a half hour late, guzzling down one of his disgusting energy drinks, and belching a hello. He took one look at her and grinned. "Wow. You look like you got dragged behind a car for the last eight hours."

Noah lifted his head from the documents he was reviewing. "Turner. Don't start."

Josie sighed and stretched her arms over her head. "And yet, I still look better than you."

Turner dropped into his chair and started emptying the pockets of his suit jacket. Three more energy drinks, his phone, a charger, and some crumpled pieces of paper. "You find anything good? Actual evidence we can use?"

The update from Hummel hadn't been encouraging. The DNA profile from the knife used to kill Cleo Tate and from her car hadn't come back yet. The DNA from Stella Townsend's crime scene had been sent to the lab, but the results would take time. He had pulled a couple of sets of unknown prints from inside Townsend's car but nothing from the knife or the polaroid.

In addition to that, the geofence around Rowland's property had turned up nothing. Josie was certain that the killer had an accomplice, given the remoteness of the murder scenes, unless he'd thought far enough ahead to plant an additional vehicle nearby. If so, he had to have used an older vehicle that didn't have an infotainment center or GPS in it or, if he had used a newer vehicle, he'd somehow managed to disable the GPS or block it. Doing so would be fairly sophisticated—and illegal—but it wasn't impossible.

"Nothing we can use yet," Noah answered.

Josie shuffled the pages from Stella Townsend's phone records around until she found a series of texts she had flagged earlier. She handed them across the desks to Turner. "When you interviewed Stella Townsend's coworkers at WYEP, did you talk to a producer named Vicky Platt?"

Turner skimmed over the messages. "Blonde chick—I mean, woman? Yeah. Stella was her PA. She was pretty upset. Didn't stop her from flirting with me."

Josie rolled her eyes. "Not every woman you speak with is flirting with you."

He didn't look up from the pages in his hand. "Don't worry, I shut it down."

"How'd you do that? By being yourself?"

In an amazing display of maturity, or maybe self-restraint, Turner ignored her. "These text messages aren't cryptic at all."

"I left Vicky Platt a voicemail asking her to come to the stationhouse in the morning to discuss them," Josie said.

Turner took one last look at the exchange before handing it back to her. "Yeah. Good luck with that. You're telling me between Stella Townsend and Remy Tate's phone records, you got nothing else."

Noah turned another page. "You're welcome to try. We'll leave the last of them for you."

"Great," muttered Turner.

Josie was about to call it a night when a new set of text messages in Stella Townsend's phone records caught her eye. For a moment, she was confused, wondering if she and Noah had gotten their reports mixed up, but as she read on, adrenaline hit, clearing away every last vestige of her fatigue. "Holy shit."

Noah yawned. "What is it?"

"Remy Tate's mistress was Stella Townsend."

TWENTY-SEVEN

Gracie Tate's wails cut right through Josie. Even through the wall separating the interview room from the CCTV room, with the sound turned down on the monitor, she could hear them. Every cell in her body wanted to race next door to soothe the infant. Josie looked behind her to where Gretchen leaned against the wall, sucking down another pecan frappé. By the furrow in her brow, she, too, was bothered by the cries.

It had been just over six hours since Josie had found the lengthy records of Stella's texts with Remy over the last month. Josie and Noah had gone home to sleep while Turner went over them with a fine-toothed comb, looking for anything and everything Noah could use when they brought Remy back in for questioning. He gave Noah a surprisingly thorough report when they came back on shift.

When Josie and Noah had gone to the Tate home to bring Remy in for an interview, he had insisted on bringing Gracie with him, claiming he had no one to call to watch her, even for an hour or two. Josie had run through a number of suggestions: his parents, Cleo's mother, a neighbor, Cleo's closest friend.

Finally, he had agreed to call his mother. She lived outside of Denton but promised to meet Remy at the police station to take Gracie off his hands. Until then, he waited in the interview room with his very unhappy infant.

Noah sailed through the door, a stack of printouts from Remy Tate's text messages in his hands. With a grimace, he said, "You can hear her in the hall. What's going on with this guy?"

On camera, Remy sat hunched in one of the chairs, elbows on knees. He alternated between sinking his face into his hands and half-heartedly pushing Gracie's stroller back and forth. He made no attempt to pick her up. It was a far cry from the concerned father he'd been the day Cleo was abducted. Josie guessed four days of full-time solo parenting was wearing on him.

Gretchen tossed her empty cup into the trash bin under the desk. "I'd like to give him the benefit of the doubt since his wife was just murdered but given Cleo's phone records, I don't think he ever had much interest in being a hands-on dad."

Given his lack of paternal instinct, Josie found it odd that although Cleo had just been killed, Remy was caring for his daughter alone. It was times like these that loved ones tended to surround a grieving spouse, trying to help in any way they could. Had no one close to the couple offered to help, or had he kept everyone away? Did he think people would ask too many questions? Or were people already suspicious of him?

If they weren't, they would be soon. Josie wasn't sure they would be able to keep a lid on his affair after today. They were going to release the news about Stella's murder once they spoke with Kellan and Remy. Josie had no interest in stirring up a press frenzy, but with practically zero leads other than a blurred polaroid, they had no choice but to turn to the public for help. It wouldn't be long before Stella's relationship with Remy spread like wildfire. At least one of Stella's old college friends had known about it. That friend, Abbie Roads, had moved to Oregon a couple of years ago after graduation, but she continued to text back and forth with Stella, most recently about the affair. Mostly because it was hardly an affair at all.

Of course, the press wouldn't cover that part.

Josie had tracked down a number for Abbie Roads and left a message for her, although she wasn't sure how much more Abbie could offer them that might help the investigation. The last exchange, from a week ago, was both curious and instructive given that Noah was about to question Remy.

Stella: *I really screwed this up. R is coming on strong now. Too strong. I should never have let him kiss me.*

Abbie: *You should never have let things get this far.*

Stella: *I know!!!! He's married.* Several crying emojis followed. *What does it say about me that I'm actually attracted to him? I mean, I'm both attracted and repulsed.*

Abbie: *Cheating on his wife is repulsive. Period.*

Stella: *He didn't really cheat. We never slept together.*

Abbie: *Girl, he's a cheater. Not only did you do other things, but the way he was coming on to you from day one, no spouse would put up with that shit. Maybe it's not technically physically cheating but it's emotional cheating and that's worse.*

Stella: *He wants to see me again. Alone at his house while his wife is out. God, why am I like this? How can I be attracted to this guy? R is no better than HE was or my dad.*

Abbie: *Absolutely not. Public place only. You cannot do this.
It's not just unprofessional. It's unethical and immoral. Your
credibility will be tainted and once that happens, you can kiss a
career in journalism goodbye. You can kiss it all goodbye—even
a book deal.*

Stella: *Even if I have a big gun backing me?*

Abbie: *Yes. Even then.*

Gracie Tate went from wailing to shrieking. She was
hungry. Couldn't Remy tell? Had he even brought bottles?

Gretchen paced. "Where is Kellan Neal?"

"The Chief is bringing him up in a few minutes," Noah
said. "He took exception to being put into an interview room."

"I bet," Gretchen muttered.

Josie stood up. "That's a hungry cry."

Noah blocked the door. "I'll go. I've already got a rapport
with him. Maybe if I can get Gracie to stop crying, he'll be more
inclined to talk to me once his mother picks her up."

Josie sat back down. Seconds later, Noah appeared on the
CCTV monitor. He put the printouts on the table and said
something to Remy, who motioned toward the stroller. Noah
lifted the baby, cradling her in his arms. Her cries quieted a bit
until she realized that no bottle was forthcoming.

Noah pointed at the diaper bag stuffed in the stroller's
storage area. Remy pulled it out, prepared a bottle and handed
it to Noah. Seconds later, blessed silence descended over the
floor as Gracie eagerly downed her formula. For a moment,
Josie was transfixed by the sight of her husband holding an
infant in his arms, giving her a bottle.

"Oh God," she whispered. "This is going to make my
ovaries explode."

Gretchen laughed.

Josie had seen Noah with Harris when he was small and with his own niece when she was an infant, but that was long before either of them had considered having children of their own. Now, everything was different. Moments later, Noah was patting Gracie's back, burping her. A small amount of spit-up dribbled onto his polo shirt. The whole thing gave Josie big feelings that had no place in this building. She needed to focus.

Lucky for her, Remy's mother arrived to take Gracie. Noah handed her over and then helped Mrs. Tate get the stroller down the steps. When he returned to the interview room, Josie turned the sound up. Noah read Remy his Miranda rights. He didn't ask for an attorney. With a heavy sigh, Noah sat down as close to Remy as possible. He made a point of asking Remy how he was holding up, expressing sympathy. With each word, Remy's posture relaxed.

Then Noah turned the conversation to Stella Townsend. "I'm sure you know why you're here."

Remy picked a piece of lint from his sweatpants. "Because you went through my phone. You, uh, know about Stella."

Noah spread the printouts across the table. "What I know is that Stella was very reluctant to enter into a physical relationship with you in spite of your... efforts."

Gretchen snorted. "Noah is really good at speaking this guy's language. 'Efforts.' Is that what lying sacks of shit call grooming young women these days?"

Although Remy clearly trusted him, Noah wasn't acting quite as smooth and sexist as he had during the last interview. Probably because it wasn't necessary. Remy's text exchanges with Stella Townsend were pretty damning. They didn't prove his involvement in either murder but they sure as hell didn't paint a pretty picture.

Remy put his head in his hands. "You don't understand.

Stella is beautiful and she was interested in me. Really interested. If I wasn't married, she would have gone for me right away."

Given the texts between Stella and her college friend, Abbie, Josie wasn't sure that Stella would have gone for him 'right away.' There was something else at play here. She just didn't know what. Yet.

Noah said, "You met Stella about a month after Gracie was born. WYEP was doing a story about you?"

Remy tipped his head back, knocking it against the wall. "Not about me specifically. About the overhaul of the city and court records. The cost of digitizing the older ones and what we'd do with the paper copies once that was completed. Stella was there. The reporter didn't seem that interested in the story, to be honest, even though he was the one who approached me. Afterward, it was Stella doing all the follow-up, calling to clarify things and ask more questions. We just kind of started talking and texting. I know it's not cool, but I like her, okay? I didn't mean for it to happen. It just did."

Gretchen laughed again. "I'm pretty sure 'it just happened' is the catchphrase of cheaters everywhere."

But it hadn't just happened. Stella's initial texts to Remy had been nothing but professional, but there had been so many follow-up questions, he'd suggested meeting for lunch. There was no way to know what transpired during that meal—Josie would never believe Remy's version—but after that, the texts changed to Stella peppering him with personal questions. It was almost as if she was interviewing him. Josie wasn't sure what Stella's ulterior motives were or what 'story' she was after. Josie also didn't know why Abbie had mentioned a book deal—but Remy clearly mistook her attention for sexual advances.

Remy said, "Listen, I know this makes me look like an asshole but I don't see how this helps you find my wife's killer."

The landline in the CCTV room rang, startling both Josie and Gretchen. Snatching up the receiver, Josie said, "Quinn."

Their desk sergeant, Dan Lamay, answered. "There's a woman here to see you. She says you asked her to come in. Vicky Platt."

"Yes," said Josie. "Put her in the conference room. I'll be right down."

TWENTY-EIGHT

Vicky Platt sat at the head of the first-floor conference room table with the confidence of a CEO overseeing a board meeting. She even stood when Josie entered, striding over to shake hands. She was striking and far more attractive than the thumbnail photo on Dallas Jones's phone. With her long, glossy blonde hair, silk blouse and fitted skirt, she looked more like a news anchor than a producer. She looked even younger than Trinity. Early thirties maybe. Josie was envious of the ease with which she walked in six-inch heels. Josie would have rolled her ankle just getting across the room.

"Thank you for coming," Josie said. "Please, sit."

Vicky smiled as she took her seat again at the head of the table. A closer look at her face revealed red-rimmed eyes. "Your colleague stopped by the station yesterday. The news about Stella is just shocking. Everyone is quite upset. He wouldn't say what happened but the fact that he was there, asking so many questions, implies foul play."

Already, Vicky was trying to control the interview. It wasn't surprising though. Josie would expect nothing less. Journalists were always looking for a story. She had had years of experience dealing with Trinity.

"I can't give out any details of the investigation." Josie took a seat diagonal from Vicky and placed the papers she'd brought from the second-floor printer face down on the table. "There will be another press conference later today. I'm sure Dallas will be there to gather all the pertinent information."

Vicky nodded solemnly and then went right back in for more. "Is it related to the Cleo Tate case?"

Josie opened her mouth to repeat the same answer but Vicky stopped her, holding up a hand. "I'm sorry." She laughed but it had an edge to it. It was the bitter, lost, almost hysterical laughter of a grieving person. Josie knew it well.

"It's fine, Ms. Platt."

Tears glistened in Vicky's eyes. She took a deep breath. "It's really not. I'm sorry to be acting like, well, like a producer. It's just force of habit. I also tend to fall deeper into that habit when I'm upset or stressed and quite frankly, I'm devastated by Stella's death. Work is a good distraction, you know?"

Josie smiled. "Yes. I do."

Vicky wiped away a rogue tear. "Thank you. Let's start over. You asked me to come in because you had questions. How can I help?"

Josie stood and retrieved a box of tissues from the other end of the table. She handed them to Vicky. "My colleague covered most everything when he spoke with you the other day. I'm interested in a particular exchange you and Stella had by text approximately a month ago."

Vicky used a tissue to wipe more tears from her cheeks. Her brows lifted. "Really? Well, if you refresh my memory, I'll be happy to add whatever clarification that I can."

Josie turned over the pages in front of her and angled them so that Vicky could see them. She reread them at the same time that Vicky did.

Vicky: *I'm going to green-light the records story with Remy Tate.*

Stella: *I just need a little more time. Please.*

Vicky: *This has gone on too long and I've given you more than enough time and leeway to come up with something. If you get a story later and it's as juicy as discussed, then we'll run it separately.*

Stella: *He'll be less inclined to keep talking to me if you run that story. It puts him in the public eye. He won't want to risk his reputation or getting fired then.*

Vicky: *Fine. I'll give you till the end of the month but that is absolutely it. Do whatever you have to do.*

Josie said, "What story was Stella working on?"

Vicky looked up from the pages, a pained smile crossing her pale face. "I don't know."

"You don't know? You held a piece about digitizing records so she could find something 'juicy' and you don't know what she was after?"

With a sigh, Vicky pushed the pages back toward Josie. "It's not really what it sounds like. I didn't exactly hold the story. It was in the queue. We were going to run it when we needed something light or something to fill in time. Then I found out that Stella had been... well, having a lot of conversations with Remy Tate that went far beyond the necessary follow-up for the story we did. I was concerned because I was pretty sure he was married. Dallas didn't get personal with him but in the video, he's wearing a wedding band. Stella is really bright. Brilliant, really, and she has a big future—oh—"

Vicky broke off and covered her mouth. A muffled, "Oh God," came from behind her palm.

"It's okay," Josie said softly.

Vicky lowered her hand and snatched up another tissue, swiping at the tears that spilled freely down her cheeks. "I'm talking about her like she's still here. I just—it's so hard to—"

"I get it," Josie said. "It's a shock. Please, go on."

Vicky closed her fist around the damp tissue. "Stella was smart and driven. She had a very bright future in television journalism. I saw a lot of my younger self in her, so I may have indulged her a little. Okay, a lot. She said she was talking to Remy because he had access to court records. She said that there was a story she'd been working on independently for a long time, but she'd never been able to get the records she needed to break it wide open. She said the records she needed were sealed."

"But she thought that Remy Tate would access them for her." Josie frowned. "Which would have been illegal. It would have been illegal for you to use them. The story would have been a non-starter."

Vicky shook her head. "No, no. It's not what you think. I mean, it is, but I never intended to use illegally obtained sealed court records for a story. I know that's what it sounds like, but I promise you, that's not what I discussed with Stella. In fact, as soon as she brought up asking Remy to access them, I told her that if this big juicy story she was supposedly working on involved illegal activity, I'd fire her instantly. I told her I didn't want to talk about the matter ever again."

"But you did."

Vicky gave a long shuddery sigh. "Yes."

Josie tapped the pages in front of her. "Ms. Platt, from these texts, it looks like you encouraged Stella to manipulate Remy Tate into illegally accessing sealed court records for a story."

"No," Vicky insisted. "I didn't. The next time Stella brought it up, she claimed that she didn't actually need the records themselves, only key pieces of information. A couple of names. Dates. Then she could do her own research—without the court records. I have no idea if she was telling the truth or not but she swore that whatever she brought to me in support of this 'big' story would not consist of any illegally obtained records."

"But she still thought Remy Tate could help her."

Vicky nodded. "Yes. The story was going to air soon and she asked me if we could delay it a bit longer while she continued talking with Remy. Digitizing records isn't the story of the century, so I agreed."

"We're talking about a technicality here, is that right?" Josie asked. "Stella uses Remy to access the sealed records and give her the information she needs which she uses to develop her own sources so technically, it wouldn't be illegal for you to run with the story."

Vicky offered a sheepish smile.

Josie didn't know why she was surprised. She'd seen how ruthless reporters could be in pursuit of a story they believed would change the course of their careers. "But what was Stella working on?"

They hadn't found anything on Stella's laptop although they hadn't been looking for some big, scandalous story. There had been dozens of files filled with hundreds of Word documents on it. No one on the team had taken the time to read through all of them. They had been looking for any recent activity via email or social media that would indicate whether Stella was being stalked or if she'd been in contact with someone who might have wanted to harm her.

"I really don't know, Detective," said Vicky. "Like I said, I indulged Stella because I adored her and hey, if someone says they can deliver a huge story, I'm not going to turn my nose up. She wasn't doing it on WYEP time. She wasn't using WYEP resources. It didn't hurt anyone for me to keep Remy out of the public eye for a couple of weeks by not running the story."

"Did Stella ever indicate that her relationship with Remy Tate was anything more than professional?"

Vicky's spine straightened. Her eyes went wide. She reminded Josie of a predator on high alert. "No. Why? Did something happen between them?"

"I'm asking you," Josie said.

Vicky's posture softened slightly. "Oh. No. She never gave any indication that anything was going on between them other than her trying to get information from him."

"We spoke with Dallas Jones the other day and he indicated that both you and him felt there was something 'off' about Remy Tate and that's why you didn't run the story."

Vicky laughed. "Dallas thought something was 'off' about him. I didn't disagree. Whatever he made of my silence and then the story not running is on him."

"Did he know Stella was working on some mystery story that involved Remy Tate's access to sealed court records?" asked Josie.

"No. You've met Dallas. Do you think he would have allowed a PA to upstage him? Even if I told him that I was simply indulging her?"

"No. I can't see him stepping aside to let Stella grab a big story."

"Now he doesn't have to worry about that." Vicky sighed. "Because Stella *is* the story."

TWENTY-NINE

Back in the CCTV room, Gretchen sat with her feet up on the table, watching the monitor with a bored expression. "They're still going round and round," she told Josie.

Josie glanced at the clock. "It's been twenty minutes."

"Yep, and for twenty minutes, Remy has insisted that his affair with Stella isn't relevant to Cleo's murder. At all."

Josie plopped into the chair next to Gretchen. "'My affair has nothing to do with my wife's murder' sounds like the catch-phrase of cheating men whose wives are found murdered everywhere."

Gretchen snorted.

"Noah didn't tell him that Stella was murdered yet?" Josie asked.

"Nope."

He'd save it for when it would have the most impact, and try to get as much information about the affair from Remy as possible before dropping that bomb. Once Remy knew, it wouldn't take long for him to realize how much worse he came off in the situation and that he was a suspect, at which point he might ask for an attorney.

"What'd the producer say?"

Josie filled her in.

"Hmmm," Gretchen said. "You believe her? That she didn't know what story Stella was after?"

Josie leaned forward, eyes on the CCTV monitor. From Remy's defeated posture, it appeared that Noah was wearing him down. "I don't know, but I can't see how she benefits by lying about it. I mean, she admitted to having discussed illegally obtaining sealed court records with Stella. Why put that out there but lie about the story?"

Gretchen stretched her arms over her head, yawning. "True. I suppose the real question is how relevant this mystery story is to these murders, if at all."

Josie rubbed at her eyes. It hadn't even been that long since her last coffee, but she felt like she hadn't had one in days. "You're right. Maybe it's completely irrelevant—it probably is— but one of us should start going through the Word documents on her laptop to see if we can find anything that might tell us what she was working on."

On the monitor, Noah leaned back in his chair, tapping a finger against one of the pages on the table. "Listen, Remy. We can keep doing this whole back-and-forth thing all day but that's not going to help anyone, and it's definitely not going to get us closer to finding Cleo's killer. I get why you don't want to talk about the woman you were low-key seeing behind your wife's back. Especially now that Cleo's gone. I do. But it's my job to ask questions. Even questions that seem completely off-the-wall. This will go a hell of a lot faster and be a lot less painful for you if you just talk to me. The sooner you do, the sooner you can get back to your daughter. She needs you right now, doesn't she?"

Remy didn't seem very excited about the prospect of being reunited with Gracie but went along with it anyway. Maybe he realized how bad he'd look if he didn't want to get back to his daughter at a time like this. "Okay. What else do you want to know?"

"You and Stella started talking a lot. Met for lunch. You said you liked her. A lot. Did she like you back?"

"Yeah, yeah. Of course she did."

Noah canted his head to the side, regarding Remy skeptically. Then he picked up one of the pages. "Really? 'Cause in a lot of these texts to you, she's saying things like, 'I'm really not comfortable with this becoming more than a friendship.' 'You're coming on really strong.' 'Please don't say sexual things like that.' Oh, and here's a good one: 'You absolutely cannot touch me like that anymore.'"

Remy shook his head vigorously. "Because I'm married! Not because she doesn't want to be with me."

That sort of lined up with what Josie knew from Stella's version of events but Stella hadn't been after Remy as a romantic interest. She'd been after him for some big mystery story that she felt was important enough to try to illegally access sealed court records. The attraction—and whatever they'd done as a result of it—was an unfortunate consequence.

Noah shuffled more pages around. "But then when you contacted her the morning that Cleo went missing—after you spoke with Detectives Turner and Quinn—she told you, 'I will not, under any circumstances whatsoever, give you an alibi. I cannot be involved in this. We didn't see each other this morning.'"

"But we did!"

Noah nodded slowly. "Okay, okay. I believe you. I'm sure that if we check location monitoring on Stella's phone, we can prove she was with you, but Remy, why wouldn't she give you an alibi?"

He banged the back of his head lightly against the wall. "I don't know. Maybe she didn't want anyone to find out about us. Because I'm married."

Noah kept nodding. "But you could have both lied and just said she'd stopped by to follow up on the WYEP story. Sure, it was old, but it might have been believable since it hadn't aired yet. Worth a shot, right?"

Remy didn't answer.

On the other CCTV feed that monitored the second interview room, Kellan Neal appeared, followed by Chief Chitwood. The sound was down so Josie couldn't hear their brief conversation.

"Stella was what? Sixteen years younger than you?" Noah asked.

"She's not a minor," Remy said quickly. "She's a grown woman. We're consenting adults."

"No argument there," said Noah. "I'm just wondering if there was something else, some other reason that Stella was so interested in you and why she refused to give you an alibi."

Noah didn't yet know about what Vicky had told Josie. He only knew about the texts between Stella and her friend, Abbie, in which Stella had only referenced a 'story.'

Three horizontal lines appeared across Remy's forehead. "What are you talking about? What other reason?"

"That's what I'm asking you. Are you sure that Stella wasn't angling to do some kind of story about you or someone you know?"

Josie's gaze flitted back to the other screen. The Chief left Kellan alone inside the room.

"What the hell are you talking about?" Remy asked.

If Stella had been using Remy for a story she was developing, he had no idea.

As if thinking the same thing, Gretchen muttered, "Blinded by all that youth and beauty and lack of stretch marks. What a dumbass."

Noah came to the same conclusion, changing the subject abruptly. "Remy, the day that Cleo was abducted, after you went home with Gracie, maybe got in touch with your family, Cleo's parents, where were you?"

Remy's body went very still. "What?"

"Where were you in the late afternoon of the day that Cleo was abducted?"

He scratched his scalp. "I was home with my daughter."

Noah sat up straighter in his chair. "No one came over to be with you? To help with Gracie?"

"I mean Kellan came by for a little while and then he left. People offered but I just—I just wanted to be alone." More quietly, he added, "I felt fucking guilty, man, okay?"

"Yeah," Noah said. "I get it. Of course you did. But Remy, we've got a much bigger problem now than your affair."

Remy scoffed. "Bigger than my fucking wife being murdered?"

"Well, you tell me," said Noah, calmly lacing his fingers behind his head and leaning back in his chair again. "Because a few hours after your wife was killed, Stella Townsend was also murdered."

All the color drained from Remy's face. "Wh-what?"

"Stella's dead, Remy. Someone killed her."

Remy lurched forward, nearly coming out of his seat, and vomited all over the floor.

THIRTY

For the first time, meeting in a sleazy motel room didn't annoy her. She didn't question it and he didn't offer all his usual excuses. They couldn't be seen together. There was less chance of them getting caught here. It was for her own good. That was usually the point where she tuned him out and shut him up using her body. Now, she was happy to be hidden here, tangled in the scratchy sheets, her cheek against his sweaty chest. The sound of his heartbeat soothed her, blotting out the ever-present fear she'd been carrying around since that day in the car with the monster. She was pretty sure he had figured out where she lived. She hadn't actually seen him. It was just a sense, the hairs on the back of her neck rising each time she left her apartment. Sometimes she felt it in the supermarket or in the parking lot at work. His intrusive, evil gaze caressing her against her will.

"Hey." Her lover's hand grazed her spine. She shivered when he pressed a kiss to the top of her head. "I wanted to ask you something."

Her heart leapt. She hated that the first thing she thought was that he might propose. They were so far from that, it wasn't even funny, but it couldn't be helped. "What is it?"

"I saw bruises on your thigh."

Stiffening, she nestled deeper into his embrace, mind racing to come up with any other explanation than the truth.

"Tell me," he said, an edge to his voice. "Who did that to you?"

"It was just this witness. At work. Things got out of hand, but everything is fine. I handled it."

He lifted her chin with his index finger. Intensity burned in his eyes, setting her heart aflutter. "If you tell me who he is, I'll kill him."

A breath caught in her throat. She willed her body to keep breathing. God, how she loved it when he was like this. But he couldn't know the truth. Licking her dry lips, she said, "What if I told you it was a woman?"

"Do you honestly think that would stop me?"

A shiver ran the length of her body, goosebumps erupting on her bare arms. "You wouldn't really kill someone."

"How do you know I haven't?"

She was going to laugh it off but something about the way his expression darkened stopped her. "Who?"

"I can't say. You already know too much."

Pressing a hand to his heart, she promised, "I would never tell. I hope you know that."

"It doesn't matter. Now I know what I'm capable of and nobody's going to stop me."

THIRTY-ONE

By the time Josie and Gretchen entered the second interview room, Kellan Neal was seated at the scarred table, looking cool and unflappable. Like any prosecutor worth his salt. Josie and Gretchen joined him, sitting as close to him as possible. Gretchen read his Miranda rights, stopping midway through when he scoffed at her. Josie felt a little burst of appreciation for her colleague when Neal visibly reacted to the intimidating look Gretchen directed at him. Swallowing hard, he told her to continue.

Once that task was out of the way, he sat up straighter and smoothed his hands over his slacks. "The Chief would not tell me what was going on but you know who I am. You know what I've lost. I don't appreciate being put into an interrogation room like a criminal."

"We know about Stella Townsend," Josie said. "I don't appreciate you withholding information from us. The Chief is talking with the DA now to see if an obstruction charge can be brought against you."

Kellan smiled. "Don't insult my intelligence. I was a prosecutor longer than you've been alive. I found out information about my son-in-law that was not relevant to Cleo's abduction or murder. I didn't want his... indiscretion to distract from finding Cleo, at least not in those critical first forty-eight hours. As a professional courtesy, I expected your department to trust my judgment on this."

"That's not how this works," said Josie. "You know that."

"Isn't it?" Kellan shot back. "I remember you, you know. We worked together all the time on cases. You were still in uniform. Of all people, you should be able to vouch for my integrity."

It was true that Kellan Neal's professional conduct while his and Josie's careers overlapped was unimpeachable. "I could vouch for the man I worked with back then. Not the man who walked into this building and tried to interfere in the investigation of his own daughter's abduction and murder. The man who expected a *favor*." She put extra emphasis on the word favor. Kellan Neal had always considered it a dirty word in their professions. The law was the law. Procedures were to be followed. Every box had to be checked. No shortcuts. No fudging details. Aboveboard was his watchword.

Josie watched as her jab landed.

The crepey skin around Kellan's eyes tightened. "It wasn't interference. You wanted Remy's alibi so you could eliminate him as a suspect and move on. I gave that to you. My aim was to streamline the process for you so that you could put all your resources into finding my daughter."

Gretchen said, "You want to tell us what's really going on here, Mr. Neal?"

Ignoring her, he kept his focus on Josie. "Whether you consider what I did interference or aid, it really doesn't matter now, does it? You know about Stella. You have Remy's alibi. All I would ask is that you keep this out of the press."

"That's not going to be possible." Gretchen rested her elbows on the table, leaning toward him.

"It is," Kellan insisted, still locked in on Josie. "There is no reason to put her name out there."

Josie narrowed her eyes at him. He wasn't worried about his son-in-law's reputation. He was worried about Stella's name being attached to his family. Why?

Flatly, Gretchen said, "Stella Townsend is dead."

Kellan did a good job of not reacting. Again, not surprising considering how many years he'd spent as a trial lawyer. But Josie could see his pulse fluttering wildly at the base of his throat.

When he didn't say anything, Gretchen added, "Murdered. Just like Cleo."

"Your son-in-law, by the way, does not have an alibi for Stella's murder," said Josie.

Among the team, they'd been trying to figure out what Remy might have done with Gracie while he stalked and killed Stella, assuming he was the one who had killed her. Josie didn't think it was outside the realm of possibility that he could have simply left her at home in her crib. She was too tiny to try to climb out of it or to hurt herself in any way, as long as he knew enough not to leave any blankets or other suffocation risks with her. He could have had a video monitor and taken it with him. Or he had help, which was the predominant theory. Even if it wasn't Remy, this killer had help. Josie wasn't sure any of them were entirely sold on Remy as the murderer. He just didn't seem smart enough. The man they were looking for was operating at a level of sophistication that required more forethought than Remy Tate seemed capable of. Plus, Josie was positive that the same man had killed both Cleo and Stella, and Remy had an alibi for Cleo's slaying.

Still, Josie wanted to rattle Kellan Neal. He was hiding something.

"I remember you, too," Josie told him. "You were a huge pain in the ass but you were never a liar. Why don't you want

Stella's name attached to your daughter's case? Is it because she was so much younger than your son-in-law? Is it because he was carrying on with a much younger woman while Cleo was home with their new baby? Is it to protect Gracie from reading all these sordid details in the press when she's older?"

"You know damn well I've never cared about things like that. People do stupid things, incomprehensible, morally repugnant things. You think I don't know what kind of man my son-in-law is? I never approved of their marriage. It was never going to last anyway. If it wasn't Stella Townsend, it would have been some other woman stupid enough to fall for his pathetic martyr routine."

"But it was Stella," Gretchen said. "And here we sit. Every minute that ticks by is a minute we could be looking for your daughter's killer. Stop insulting our intelligence and tell us the truth."

Kellan's flinty gaze shifted to Josie. "You don't know yet, do you?"

"Know what?"

"Stella Townsend was James Lampson's granddaughter."

THIRTY-TWO

Goosebumps rose along Josie's arms as she stood in front of the corkboard in the Denton PD great room once again. Someone had added crime scene photos of Cleo Tate and Stella Townsend, pinning them over the makeshift map of Denton and next to the third polaroid, which still taunted them. The air conditioning labored to fight the cloying heat outside, but she hadn't been able to shake the chill enveloping her since Kellan Neal said James "Frisk" Lampson's name.

Glancing over her shoulder, she saw that the rest of the team were still at their desks. Even Turner, who had come in for the afternoon and evening shift so that Josie and Noah could be there for Drake's proposal to Trinity. They'd updated him but he hadn't yet started the barrage of questions Josie had come to expect from him. The room was strangely silent, the only sounds Noah and Gretchen typing away at their keyboards.

Turner eyed Josie, expression inscrutable. "You're saying this Lampson guy was dirty."

"As dirty as they come," Noah muttered without looking away from his monitor.

Josie had gone from trying to avoid Lampson in high school to having to work with him on the police force. He was every bit as lecherous and disgusting as the rumors around the city painted him. She and Lampson had gotten into many arguments, especially since Josie reported his misconduct and inappropriate behavior often and vociferously. But the deck was always stacked in his favor. The old boys' club kept him insulated from disciplinary action. The DA at the time was Lampson's biggest ally. In fact, when Chief Wayland Harris took over running the police department and started taking Josie's reports seriously, Lampson suddenly got a swanky new position in the DA's office as an investigator.

Harassing and groping teenage girls wasn't even the worst of Lampson's sins.

"Where is he now?" Turner asked.

"Prison," said Josie. "He was part of the human trafficking ring we uncovered here."

"The big one," said Noah.

Turner squeezed his foam basketball in his hand, clenching and unclenching his fist. "The one with the serial killers? Yeah, I remember seeing the news coverage about that, and the *Dateline*, and the documentary."

Josie grimaced. "There's a documentary?"

None of the officers who had worked that case and lived to tell about it had been approached by a documentary filmmaker. Not that anyone would want to relive it.

"It's mostly about the families whose loved ones were victims. You know, how their remains were found and returned. Closure and all that. It doesn't even mention you guys, or most of the pieces of shit who were arrested for their participation—although I guess there were too many to cover. Lampson's name never came up."

Josie wasn't surprised. His name had always been like a

curse in the city of Denton. Lampson was one of the vilest human beings Josie had ever encountered. Who would want to give him airtime? Though she was surprised there had never been more than a couple of episodes of *Dateline* delving into the network of men who'd been involved in trafficking and who had protected Lampson for years.

"He shot Luke Creighton," Josie added. "Almost killed him."

Turner leaned forward in his chair, eyes wide with surprise. "Luke Creighton, our K-9 guy?"

"Yes," Josie said. She didn't offer any details of her prior relationship with Luke. Turner only knew that Luke meant something to her because she'd asked him to be respectful of Luke the first time they met. It was one of the few times Turner hadn't been a complete asshole. In fact, he always treated Luke with respect.

"This guy sounds like a true-crime buff's wet dream. What's Kellan Neal's problem? That all his convictions that involved Lampson's work were tainted?"

Noah spun his chair around. "Not just Neal's convictions. Any ADA whose cases relied on Lampson's testimony. A lot of them were overturned. It was a shitshow."

Turner tossed the ball toward the net. Missed. "I bet. But who cares if Neal's son-in-law had something going with Lampson's granddaughter?"

Gretchen's chair squeaked. She took off her reading glasses and rubbed her eyes. "Neal probably doesn't want his daughter's name tarnished by the association with Lampson, even though it's a weak connection."

"But who cares about Lampson?" Turner said. "Remy Tate is the connection between our two victims."

It was a good point. Who would want to kill Remy Tate's wife and his mistress and why? Another mistress? There hadn't been any evidence that Remy had been involved with anyone other than Stella, according to his phone records. Maybe there had been someone in his life before Stella? Before Cleo?

Where did the polaroids fit in?

Gretchen stood up, massaging her lower back, and joined Josie at the board. "No, I don't think that's the connection."

"You just like to disagree with me for the sake of it, don't you?" Turner stood up, fished a dollar out of his jacket pocket and leaned across the desks, dangling it over the jar next to Gretchen's keyboard. "Parker."

Gretchen scowled at him. "Keep it, jackass."

With a smirk, Turner curled his fist around the bill and stuffed it back into his pocket.

Noah sighed loudly. "Focus, please. Both of you."

"Gretchen might be right," Josie said. "Maybe it's not about Remy Tate but about Neal and Lampson."

"We should at least consider it," Noah agreed. "The killer targeted Neal's daughter and Lampson's granddaughter."

Gretchen said, "Neal and Lampson both worked for the DA's office, right?"

Josie nodded. "Yes, but Neal had retired before Lampson moved over there."

"So we're looking at someone who wants to get revenge on ADAs and their investigators?" Turner asked.

"Possibly," said Noah.

"Maybe for a case gone wrong?" Gretchen said, almost to herself. "Except that they never worked together in the DA's office."

"But they did work together when Lampson was with the police department," Noah said. "Lampson testified in plenty of Neal's cases. Maybe these killings are revenge for a conviction Neal won but that got overturned once Lampson's corruption was uncovered."

"We're talking about hundreds of cases," Josie said. "Maybe even thousands."

Gretchen walked back to her desk and plopped into her chair. "But we're only talking about the ones where the convictions were overturned. I can get in touch with the DA's office and see if they've got records."

Josie turned her attention to the third polaroid. Either theory sounded reasonable—that the killings had something to do with Remy Tate or that they were connected to Neal and Lampson—but that still didn't account for the photos. What point was this killer trying to make?

"Stabbings," Josie said. "Cases that involved stabbings. He left the knives at both crime scenes."

Gretchen nodded. "That should help narrow it down."

"We should also check our own databases for cases that weren't overturned," Noah suggested. "Stabbings where Lampson was the lead detective and Neal prosecuted."

"On it," Gretchen said, sliding on her reading glasses and turning to her computer.

Turner stood and walked up beside Josie. One of his long fingers traced a circle around the aerial view of Peter Rowland's property. "Is there any significance to the locations? Both had to do with previous cases, from what you guys have said."

"Fairly recent cases, though," Gretchen said, fingers flying over her keyboard. "Neal was long retired, and Lampson was in prison before either of those crossed our desks."

Turner nudged Josie with his elbow. "That makes you the connection between Lampson and Neal. You worked with both of them."

"So did I," said Noah.

"Yeah, but Quinn figured out the locations in the photos. What's that mean, LT? She's smarter than you?"

Turner wasn't looking at Noah, too fixated on the map, but

Josie caught the grin on his face, meant for her. "Why do you think I married her?"

He was going to get very lucky later.

Not getting the response he'd hoped for—annoyance, irritation, and possibly a reprimand—Turner moved on. "Palmer can search up cases but that could take forever. We're back to pictures. We gotta figure out where this guy wants us to go next."

THIRTY-THREE

Josie's knuckles blanched as she gripped the steering wheel. The drive through the campus of Denton University wasn't exactly fraught with difficulty, but her mind was still on the Cleo Tate and Stella Townsend murders. The Polaroid Killings, Turner had called them before she and Noah left for the day. She just hoped the press didn't get wind of the photos—or the name. It would put them into even more of a frenzy than they were already.

"Are you even listening to me?" Trinity's voice broke through Josie's thoughts.

Glancing over at the passenger's seat, Josie saw her sister's perfectly plucked brows knit in annoyance.

"I knew it," Trinity said. "I can tell when you're not listening. Josie, I know how dedicated you are to your work, but you need to be able to shut it out and be present sometimes."

"I know," Josie mumbled even as her brain went right back to the last photo. She had spent the time left on her shift puzzling over it to no avail.

"Really, Josie," said Trinity. "Being present is a skill, like anything else. You have to work on it."

"I know, I know," Josie replied. Turner was convinced that she could figure it out but his supposed confidence in her felt more like pressure. He'd hovered until she snapped at him to give her some space.

Turner.

Josie had been so fixated on the case that she'd been with Trinity all afternoon and hadn't asked her the question that had been burning a hole in her brain since the night Turner brought Amber to her house.

"Trin," she said. "How do you know Kyle Turner?"

"This is you being present? Josie, really."

"I'm not asking because of work. I'm asking because I'm curious. You're on a first-name basis with him."

Trinity looked out the window as they passed the university library. "He solved that escort case. Did you know that?"

"Yeah," Josie said. "Gretchen looked him up when he started. I've read the articles. He got a lot of press for solving that case."

Trinity nodded, eyes still fixed on the campus buildings rolling slowly by. "Yes. National coverage. I had returned to the morning show by that time, and he was a guest. A bunch of cold cases? A serial killer? A determined detective? It was gold. I interviewed him live and then afterward we went to lunch. Whenever he was in town after that, which wasn't that often, we would get together."

Josie's stomach roiled. "Oh God. You had a thing, didn't you?"

"No," Trinity said firmly. "We did not have a 'thing,' although I certainly thought about it."

Her last cup of coffee threatened to come back up. "You've got to be kidding me."

Trinity flipped down the sun visor and checked her makeup in the mirror. "That's the thing, Josie. The Kyle I knew was nothing like the douchebag you've been complaining about for the last year."

"Did you spend more than five minutes at a time with him when you got together?" Josie asked pointedly.

Trinity laughed. "Yes, we spent a lot of time together. There were other cold cases he was looking into, and given my reporting background and everything we'd just uncovered here, he thought my input was valuable."

"I don't understand," said Josie.

Her sister was many things, but attracted to douchebags was not one of them. She had always been intensely focused on her career. Dating was lowest on her list of priorities. Turner had to have made a good impression if Trinity had even considered becoming romantically involved with him.

There was that coffee trying to come back up again. It wasn't that Turner was repulsive. He was fairly handsome, though a bit older than Josie and Trinity, but his personality made him completely unattractive.

"You're telling me that the man I've described to you from working with Turner for more than a year doesn't at all sound like the Kyle Turner you knew?" Josie asked, even though Trinity had already answered her. "He never even called you 'honey' or 'sweetheart?' Or got your name wrong? Or said something so sexist that it made you want to stomp on his kneecap?"

"None of those things." Trinity shrugged. "He was… normal."

"He was definitely faking it," said Josie.

"I don't think that he was."

"If he wanted to get into your pants, he would fake it."

"He didn't try to get into my pants," Trinity scoffed. "I'm telling you, he was normal."

Josie wasn't convinced, although if Trinity was right, then what had happened to Kyle Turner in the last seven years to turn him into someone completely different? What would make

a man go from "normal" and worthy of her sister's attention to a
raging asshole?

Josie didn't have time to press the issue further. Trinity
gasped when the university's new Butterfly Garden came into
view. Josie could see by her awed expression that she was
impressed. Josie mentally put a check in the win column for
Drake. The building was tremendous. Above its tall, arched
windows, colorful butterfly murals had been painted on the
sandstone-colored concrete walls. Flowerbeds ran the length of
the front of the building, teeming with colorful blooms. A bright
blue portico shaded the main entrance. Perhaps the most
impressive sight, though, was the glass pyramid that rose from
the center of its roof, spearing into the sky.

"This place is gorgeous," Trinity said as Josie parked in
front of the atrium. She counted vehicles belonging to Noah,
Shannon and Christian, and Patrick. Josie knew that Drake was
parked nearby where Trinity would not see his car. Everyone
was there, as planned. Check two in the win column for Drake.
He'd managed to get all of them assembled at once, despite their
ridiculous schedules and the fact that they were scattered across
two states.

Trinity had no idea what was about to happen. She knew
there was going to be a proposal, but she had no idea it was
going to be hers. With a sigh, she said, "Don't you think Patrick
is too young to get married? I mean, I know he's been with
Brenna for a while, and they're both college grads with good
jobs now, but this seems too soon, doesn't it?"

Josie stepped out of the car and met Trinity near the passenger's side. "Well, when you know, you know, right?"

"I guess." Trinity smoothed her sundress down over her
hips. Josie had gone to great lengths to manipulate her into
wearing something that she knew Trinity would be happy with
in photos later. Given that Josie was on the opposite end of the
glamour spectrum from her sister, it had been more exhausting

than interrogating a murder suspect. In return, Trinity had chosen Josie's dress for the occasion and insisted on doing her makeup as well. Glancing back at the vehicle, Josie caught sight of her reflection in the window. She hardly recognized herself. Trinity had transformed her from a sweaty, frizzy-haired police officer in a rumpled polo and khakis into something luminous. Her hair was actually silky for once, and she liked the way her own simple blue dress swished around her thighs when she moved. It was perfect for the heat.

"Ready?" asked Josie.

"Just a sec." Trinity fished her phone out of her purse. "Drake's not here yet. I'll just text him."

Trinity fired off a text and then waited for a response, lips pursed as she stared at the screen. Josie heard the ding of a notification. Then another. "He'll be here in a few minutes," Trinity mumbled. "He said to go inside and he'll find us."

"Okay," said Josie. "Let's go."

Trinity's index finger swiped along the phone screen. "Holy shit!" she gasped.

THIRTY-FOUR

A tiny bud of panic bloomed in Josie's stomach. Her entire family had been texting like crazy the last few days, trying to work out all the details of Drake's plan. It had been so chaotic that at one point, Josie had inadvertently sent Gretchen a text meant for Patrick. Had someone done the same thing with Trinity? Josie hoped the surprise wasn't ruined.

Trinity kept swiping, a frown on her cherry-red lips. "Frisk Lampson's granddaughter was murdered? That's the case you guys have been working on?"

Josie snatched Trinity's phone from her hands. "No shop, remember? That means you can't scroll news apps while we're here—or look at the notifications."

Trinity put a hand on her hip. "Look who's talking. You can't go five seconds without talking shop."

"I haven't talked shop all afternoon."

Trinity rolled her eyes and stalked past Josie toward the building. "You were thinking about it, which is pretty much the same thing."

As Josie caught up to her, she heard Trinity mumble something. "What did you say?"

Trinity stopped and turned toward Josie. "I said, 'Poor Stella.' I promise that's all I'll say about it tonight. You're right, no shop talk."

"Wait. You knew Stella Townsend?"

"Josie!"

"No shop talk once we get inside." Josie held out Trinity's phone.

Taking it, Trinity huffed. "I didn't know her well, but she approached me a couple of years ago when I was here for the Jana Melburn case. She worked at WYEP. She was trying to put together a story about her grandfather."

"Why?"

Trinity glanced at the door to the Atrium. The heat was starting to overwhelm them both. "I'm really not sure, to be honest. I think she was trying to reconcile the fact that she came from someone like him. Frisk Lampson's entire family was basically run out of town after he was arrested. Stella's mom hated him and hated Denton—too many bad memories. She didn't want Stella coming back here but Stella was drawn back. She pitched me this idea for a story about her grandfather, like an exposé of all of his crimes, even ones he hadn't been convicted of, but it was too much, too extensive. Fragmented. There was no hook, you know?"

Josie thought about the text exchange between Stella and her friend, Abbie. Was Trinity the "big gun" that she'd hoped to have in her corner?

Trinity went on, "She talked about doing a book, like the kind the children of serial killers write. You know, all about how their dad was so sweet and loving and no one had any idea he was savagely murdering people in his spare time?"

"Yeah," said Josie. "I know the type."

"She wanted to talk with people who knew Frisk and worked with him to figure out how he managed to get away with so much for so long. People who protected him and people who knew he was a creep but couldn't stop him. No one wanted to talk about Frisk Lampson, as I'm sure you can imagine. She asked me for tips on how to get people to talk to her. I didn't know what to say. I don't know if she ever got the book off the ground, but I told her if she wanted to do a story, to come back when she had a hook. She never did."

No wonder Stella hadn't told Vicky Platt the topic of her story. Kicking over those rocks was downright dangerous. While most of the men who protected Lampson throughout his career had also gone to prison for their part in the human trafficking case, Josie was certain that others were still out there. They wouldn't take kindly to the press, even Lampson's own grand-daughter, knocking on their doors to confront them about their misdeeds—all of which were probably illegal. On the other hand, if she chose to go the opposite way and do a story on his victims, that might have provided her with a better, and less dangerous hook.

Regardless, Vicky Platt didn't seem like the type to shy away from a big story, but if Stella had already met with a lot of resistance from other journalists, including someone as influential as Trinity, then maybe she had thought it wise to be discreet until she had everything she needed. If Vicky had been willing to entertain the story, then maybe Stella had wanted to make sure it was cohesive and thorough before presenting it. Josie wondered what specifically she'd been hoping to find in sealed court records though. Or was it possible that Stella had no idea what she was looking for and the records search was a fishing expedition? Unless, over the years, she'd managed to gather bits and pieces of her grandfather's offenses and hoped that the records would put them into context.

Before Josie could give it any more thought, Noah emerged from the Atrium with Trout on a leash. Her breath hitched. He looked so gorgeous in his black slacks and his button-down dress shirt—blue to match her dress, an unintentional choice but adorable, nonetheless. His sleeves were rolled up, revealing muscular forearms.

Trinity shrieked with delight. "Trout is part of the proposal?"

Trout relieved himself on a shrub outside the entrance and then stood waiting for them to get closer, his little butt wiggling furiously. Someone had gotten him a bow tie. Trinity reached him first, kneeling to scratch behind his ears. "How did Patrick get permission to bring him inside?"

Josie and Noah exchanged a look.

"I don't know," Josie told her sister. "But you know Patrick's best friend runs this place, so he probably got special permission or something."

That was somewhat true. They'd been given permission to bring Trout inside after Drake and Noah had brought him to the atrium at least three times to reassure Patrick's friend that he was well-behaved, well-trained, and that they were efficient handlers. Noah had told her that if Trout disturbed anything or even so much as peed inside, Drake would be making a very sizable donation to the university.

Trinity stood up. "You know, I wanted to make Trout part of Noah's proposal. But then this one had to go and throw himself off a cliff. So dramatic, by the way."

"I didn't throw myself off a cliff," Noah said.

"Okay, sure, but you still went over a cliff. What's more memorable than that?"

Josie bent to give Trout some pets before they went inside. As they approached the doors, Trinity said, "I don't love that our little brother is getting married before me but maybe after this, he could give Drake some pointers on proposing."

Josie and Noah let Trinity go through the doors first and grinned at one another behind her back.

THIRTY-FIVE

The inside of the atrium was a humid eighty-five degrees, but it was still somehow cooler than outside. Concrete paths wound through beds of colorful flowers and exotic plants, some of which reached almost to the glass ceiling. Vibrant greens and striking purple, pink, and blood-orange hues surrounded them. Butterflies flitted around their heads. Josie instantly recognized the yellow and orange monarchs. The rest she identified as they slow-walked past signs that named each one. Tiger swallowtails, great purple hairstreaks, and brush-footed butterflies. Among the plants and flowers were small dishes that held slices of orange, lemon, and watermelon. Many of the butterflies flocked there for food. Josie had to tear herself away from the informational placards that explained everything from their life cycles to their feeding habits to take in Trinity's reaction.

She put a third check in the win column for Drake. Trinity was in awe. "This place is amazing," she whispered to Josie, as if they were in some sacred place where they needed to be quietly respectful. In a way, it did feel sacred, teeming with life and lush vegetation, its beautiful and delicate inhabitants living

peacefully. If only human beings treated one another with such
care.

Noah tapped Josie's shoulder and handed Trout's leash off.
He gave his rehearsed excuse for leaving—to use the restroom—
but Trinity was too busy looking around in wonder. A bright
blue butterfly landed on the waistline of her dress, and she
laughed with delight. "Look!" she whisper-shouted. "Brenna is
so lucky."

Josie looked down at Trout so that Trinity wouldn't see her
smile. Her twin could read her expressions perfectly. Trout
walked slowly ahead of them, stopping every so often to look up
at Josie, his soulful brown eyes uncertain. The butterflies didn't
interest him one bit. Josie wasn't surprised. He'd never shown
interest in anything but humans and food. He never chased
squirrels or any other critters they came across whenever Josie
and Noah took him out for walks or hikes. Other than Misty's
chiweiner, Pepper, he didn't even care about other dogs.

But then, as they got deeper into the garden, Trout began to
pull Josie, his very accurate nose picking up on one of the strategically placed treats that Noah and Drake had planted along the
paths. Trinity saw him straining against his leash and frowned.
"What's gotten into him?"

"Not sure," said Josie. "I think he smells something."

Trinity automatically kept pace with them as Trout frantically sniffed the ground and air, moving with purpose, until
they came to a paper lantern on top of one of the walls that
hemmed in the many garden beds. Light from an artificial
candle flickered inside of it, illuminating a photo printed on
white vellum paper that replaced one of the panes. Trout
gobbled up a milkbone left on the ground while Trinity stared
at the photo, lips pursed in confusion. It was a picture of the
outside of a restaurant. "I don't get it," she said finally.

Carefully, Josie said, "The lanterns are supposed to spell
out a story."

Trinity stared at the photo of the restaurant for a couple of beats until Trout had pulled Josie several feet ahead. As she caught up to them, she said, "That restaurant is in New York. Have Patrick and Brenna ever been there?"

"Not sure," Josie said. She'd been sure that Trinity would figure out what was going on the moment she saw the first lantern. Drake had explained the significance of each lantern to all of them. The restaurant was where they'd gone on their first date. Watching Trinity, Josie knew she suspected that tonight wasn't about Patrick and Brenna at all, but the spark of doubt in her blue eyes told Josie that she was afraid to even think it, afraid to hope for it, so she said nothing.

"Trout's on to the next lantern," Josie said softly. "Let's go."

Trinity followed as Trout stopped at each lantern. Josie knew what the photos represented. The place they first kissed; their first trip together; the first piece of furniture they bought together; the first gift Trinity had given Drake; their first joint Christmas ornament; and the first time they'd said 'I love you' to one another.

Trinity took in each one with a look of consternation and from what Josie could tell, fear. All the signs were there that this night was about her and Drake, but Trinity was afraid that when they reached the end of the journey, her hopes would be dashed. Beneath all of Trinity's confidence and sass was still a great deal of insecurity. Probably from the horrendous bullying she'd experienced as a girl. She'd spent her entire adult life building a successful career like a suit of armor so that she'd be impervious to the cruelty of others. The problem with that was that even with Drake, who was deeply, stupidly in love with her, Trinity had a hard time believing he wouldn't betray her.

Josie knew a little something about emotional armor and betrayal. They'd led very different lives, but they had that in common.

At the last lantern, while Trout wolfed down his treat,

Trinity clutched Josie's arm. She opened her mouth to speak but then the first strains of orchestral music drifted through the air, rich and mellifluous. Trinity cocked her head, listening intently. Tears glistened in her eyes.

Josie said, "Everything you want is waiting just around that corner."

Trinity let go of her arm and started to run. Trout, thinking it was a race, yanked on his leash to keep up. Josie was only an arm's length behind her sister when she pulled up short. Drake stood in the center of a large open area in front of a fountain. Surrounding him was a small contingent of the university's orchestra as well as Josie and Trinity's family: Shannon, Christian, Patrick, Brenna, and Noah. Shannon was already crying. Everyone else was beaming. Josie tugged Trout over to Noah. He gripped her free hand, squeezing lightly.

Trinity walked slowly toward Drake. "You look beautiful," he said.

She pointed to the orchestra. "This is..."

"An orchestral cover of the first song we ever danced to—remember? At my colleague's wedding?"

Trinity took in a shaky breath. "'Beyond' by Leon Bridges."

When Drake knelt in front of her and took out the ring, Trinity gasped. Fourth check in the win column. The rock was huge.

Josie couldn't hear much of what he said after that over Shannon and Brenna bawling, but it didn't matter. Trinity's answer was yes. The music swelled and Noah slid an arm around Josie's waist. His lips brushed her temple. "Drake's really making me look bad. I'm sorry I didn't give you something like this."

Josie laughed. "Don't be. The way it happened couldn't be more 'us.' Plans are stupid, remember?"

It was practically his catchphrase. "So stupid," he said.

They all went to dinner afterward, everyone laughing and

glowing, especially Trinity, who started planning their wedding on the drive to the restaurant. It was one of the best nights of Josie's life. She went to sleep with visions of butterflies, lanterns, sentimental photos, and weddings dancing in her head and woke up in a cold sweat, just as dawn was breaking.

Blinking away sleep, her brain latched onto a thought that had threaded itself through her dreams, trying to fight its way from her subconscious into the light. She took a moment to let her body wake and her mind clear. Then she followed the thought, running through the possibilities, testing theories until she was sure that her logic was sound.

She shook Noah awake. "I think I know where the most recent polaroid was taken."

THIRTY-SIX

Josie punched the gas pedal. The SUV roared, picking up speed as she and Noah drove up the winding mountain road that led to Harper's Peak. It was a homestead from the 1800s that had been turned into a modern-day resort. The grounds spanned two mountaintops and hundreds of acres. A glance in her rearview mirror revealed that Gretchen was keeping pace. Josie could just make out Turner in the passenger's seat, his hand gripping the 'oh shit' handle above the door. He didn't like when they drove fast. Behind Gretchen's vehicle were marked units. No lights, no sirens. The press was already so rabid for any little nugget of information about the murders of Cleo Tate and Stella Townsend, they were keeping close tabs on all police activity.

Noah pressed the end call icon on his phone. "Celeste wasn't thrilled, but she gave us permission to search the premises. She's sending Tom Booth, the managing director, over to the church to make sure no guests wander up that way. However, that area hasn't been used or open to guests since..."

He trailed off.

"I know," said Josie.

They hardly ever talked about their failed wedding. The one they had planned meticulously for months. The one that had cost a fortune. The one where a young girl had been murdered and staged outside the tiny church where their ceremony was supposed to take place. That case had not only delayed their wedding, but it had resulted in the death of Josie's beloved grandmother, Lisette. It had also uncovered Harper family secrets that nearly destroyed the resort. Celeste Harper had been trying to rebuild their reputation for years now.

When Josie had told Noah that she thought the third polaroid was taken at Harper's Peak, he hadn't questioned her. His faith in her was unshakable. Now, probably hoping to steer the conversation away from that horrible day, he asked, "Was it the proposal and all the talk of weddings that made you think of Harper's Peak?"

"That was part of it." She told him what Trinity had said about Stella Townsend before they went inside the atrium the evening before. She hadn't had a chance to discuss it with him in the rush to get to Harper's Peak, even though Josie was certain that it would be too late for the victim they found there. "I kept thinking about Drake's lanterns and how they were meant to tell a story. Photos. Just like this killer is leaving at each scene. Noah, he's trying to tell us something. He's telling a story. If he wasn't—"

"Then he'd just kill his victims and leave it at that."

Josie noted the nearly hidden driveway closed off by a metal gate as they flew past. The driveway led to a property owned by some of the Harpers, though, as far as Josie knew, it had been abandoned since the Harper's Peak case. The gate had been installed afterward to make it more difficult for curious citizens and mischievous teenagers to access the property—by car anyway. Briefly, she wondered if she'd made a mistake. That residence was extremely remote. It would be an even safer place to commit a murder than the church on the main resort grounds. But no, nothing in the polaroid resembled any part of that house. The image resembled the church.

Noah's voice drew her out of her thoughts. "What story is he trying to tell?"

"I don't know yet," Josie admitted. "But it has to do with us."

"You and me?" His voice took on a note of dismay.

She took a quick glance at him. "Us as in the police department. Law enforcement. The justice system. Neal was an ADA. Lampson was a police officer. The locations of the bodies and even where this guy dumped Sheila Hampton's car have all been the sites of previous cases. The lot. The creek. Rowland's house."

"Those cases were well-known."

"Exactly. They all got a lot of press coverage. The killer wants us to find each victim. He wants us to play his game. What better way to keep us chasing after him, always too late, than to reference our earlier, well-known cases? Ones he could easily find in news reports."

She took another quick look at Noah in time to see him pushing a hand through his thick, dark hair. "Is that why he's using more recent cases in the polaroids as opposed to clues from fifteen years ago when Lampson and Neal were active?"

Josie slowed as the entrance to the resort came into view. A sign as big as her vehicle sat in the middle of the large driveway, separating the entrance and exit lanes. Flowers of almost every color surrounded it. Such a beautiful place to have been the site of so much pain and violence. Her stomach did a somersault as she turned onto the drive leading to the main buildings. The Harpers were about to get another dose of bad luck, of that Josie was certain.

"I'm not sure," she told Noah.

"Maybe this whole thing isn't about a specific case then, but about law enforcement in general?" he suggested.

At this juncture, that seemed the most plausible explanation, but Josie couldn't shake the feeling that it was something more. Something personal. But to her or to Noah? Or both? He'd joined Denton PD two years after her. He'd had to deal with both Lampson and Neal just as often as she had. Every one of the recent cases that the killer had drawn attention to so far were cases both of them had worked.

"I know what you're thinking," Noah said quietly.

She pulled up in the rear parking lot of the main building, where many of the employees parked. The line of cars behind her stopped as well. Celeste hadn't asked them to attempt to be discreet, but Josie knew that was what she'd want and right now, they needed Celeste's cooperation just as much as they needed as few guests as possible to post on social media about the heavy police presence here.

"We'll talk about it later," Josie said. "Let's go."

THIRTY-SEVEN

Dark clouds hung low and heavy over the peak where the church sat. Josie adjusted her vest for the third time, but no air was getting between it and her soaked polo shirt. The humidity was worse today than it had been in weeks. Although rain never made processing a crime scene easy, she found herself wishing for it as fat drops of sweat slid down her spine and between her breasts. Next to her, Noah, Gretchen, and Turner all trudged along, looking just as drenched and exhausted as she felt. No one spoke. Even the uniformed officers behind them were silent.

They'd parked near Griffin Hall, the more intimate bed and breakfast that sat apart from the main resort buildings. The path from there to the church wasn't that long, but it was on an incline and there was no breeze. They'd decided not to wait for a staff member to bring one of the golf carts. Josie didn't want to waste a single second. Even once they passed through the hedgerow that surrounded the church, at the very top of the mountain, the air didn't move at all. It felt dense and thick. Breathing it in felt like hard work. Noah conferred with the Harper's Peak managing director, Tom Booth, while the uniformed officers circled the church. Josie watched as a few of them cupped their hands around their faces and tried to peer through the gauzy curtains covering the windows.

She approached the stone steps at the front, pausing at the bottom step. A shudder worked through her as she recalled the body they'd found here on the day she and Noah were supposed to get married.

Something bumped her shoulder. Turner stared down at her, sweat beading along his forehead. In a low voice, he said, "You okay, Quinn?"

He actually sounded concerned, which was odd. Flashing back to her conversation with Trinity, Josie wondered if he was really human under all his horrid, sexist, inappropriate behavior. Was it some kind of act? It was awfully damn convincing. She'd still bet money he had been acting for Trinity's benefit and that the douchebag was his real personality.

"Fine," she mumbled.

Gretchen joined them, a set of keys in her hand. "Tom said someone definitely broke in through the back door. The padlock looked like someone took a hammer to it. These are for the front door."

The last time Josie had been here, she'd snuck in through that back door which a killer had already broken into. History repeating. The sweat causing her shirt to cling to her back suddenly felt cold.

Gretchen looked at the ground, at the same spot that Josie had been fixated on. "For some reason, I thought we would find something outside the church."

"Is that what happened when you worked the case here?" Turner asked.

He hadn't asked a lot of questions, still. Josie had given him the broad strokes of the Harper's Peak case but left out all the parts about the failed wedding and Lisette's murder.

Gretchen didn't answer him. Instead, she directed her next

statement at Josie. "Cleo Tate and Stella Townsend were found outdoors."

Here on the ridge of a mountain, the swollen clouds seemed close enough that Josie could reach up and touch them. A sudden gust of air shook the leaves of the nearby azalea bushes. "Maybe he's tracking the weather. Maybe with Cleo and Stella, he depended on us to find the outdoor locations in the photos before it rained. But here..."

Another gust shook the shrubbery, this one stronger. When the wind batted at Josie's face, all she felt was relief at the air caressing her cheeks.

Noah jogged over. "We're all set. Before we arrived, Tom checked the security footage from the last couple of days."

Gretchen sifted through the keys in her hand. "That's a lot of footage. This place is huge."

"Right," Noah replied. "Which is probably why he didn't find anything, but one of his employees says that there's a vehicle in the Griffin Hall parking lot that doesn't belong to anyone in the wedding party currently staying in that part of the resort, so he's going to zero in on that parking lot. One of our guys will run the tags while he's doing that. See who comes up as owner in case it's connected to whatever we find in this church."

What he really meant was "whoever." If the killer had driven here with a victim—and he would have been a fool not to do so—then Griffin Hall's parking lot was the closest he'd be able to get to the church in a vehicle. Unless he'd stolen one of the resort's golf carts, but Josie knew Celeste kept a close watch on those.

Their radios squawked. Uniformed officers were stationed at the rear of the church in case anyone ran out the back door. An ambulance was on its way to the ridge, only two minutes out.

"Let's go," said Gretchen, stepping up to the door and

sliding the key into the lock. They pulled their weapons and held them in a low ready position. The door creaked as it swung open. Heat pulsed from inside the church, washing over them like a wave, bringing with it a mixture of unpleasant smells. Something musty. The unmistakable coppery scent of blood—a lot of it. Human decomposition.

Turner mumbled, "Guess we're in the right place."

Squashing the sadness that bloomed inside her, Josie focused on the task at hand. She entered first, a fresh sheen of perspiration instantly covering her body. "Police!" she called. "Denton Police. If anyone is inside, show yourself!"

Her eyes and the barrel of her pistol moved in tandem, taking an initial sweep of the place. The windows let very little light through. It was a one-room church, with a handful of pews bisected by a short aisle. The altar was straight ahead, its pulpit overturned and shrouded in shadow. A figure lay in a heap in the center aisle.

"Denton Police!" Josie said again, loudly enough to carry through the entire building. "Come out where we can see you!"

She didn't think the killer had stuck around but she was still required to announce their entry.

Turner moved at Josie's back. A light switch flicked. The dull yellow glow of overhead bulbs chased the darkness away. Gretchen and Noah's boots sounded behind her, their weight causing the rough wooden floor to groan. They fanned out, threading between the walls and the pews while she and Turner headed down the main aisle, clearing rows of pews as they went to ensure no one was ducked down among them. The heap resolved into a woman face-up in a pool of dark, congealed blood that touched the edges of the pews on either side of her as well as the step up to the altar near her head. Her right arm extended out, parallel with her shoulder, while the other one was slung across her chest. Her blood-soaked shirt was torn in multiple places. She had the most stab wounds of all the victims so far, from what Josie could see. Several blowflies buzzed lazily around her head and torso but it was nothing like what they'd seen at the Tate or Townsend scenes. Judging by her appearance—no bloating and no marbling even given the temperature inside the church, Josie guessed she hadn't been dead that long.

"We've got our knife," said Turner.

At the victim's feet was a chef's knife. Just like the ones left at the feet of Cleo Tate and Stella Townsend.

Turner said, "There's no polaroid."

He was right. At least, not where they could see it. Then again, if it was beneath her or in one of her pockets, it had likely been ruined by soaking in blood for so long. With all the killer's careful planning, it seemed odd that he hadn't accounted for that. Unless this was the last body. The ending to whatever story he was trying to tell.

Josie knew they'd never be that lucky.

Noah and Gretchen met at the altar, quickly circling the fallen pulpit. It was made of red oak, simple but solid. It would have taken considerable force to overturn it. Just like it had taken considerable force for the killer to stab his victims.

"Son of a bitch," Gretchen said. "We've got another one."

Josie felt the words like a jolt of electricity. Looking away from the altar, her eyes traveled up until they found Turner's. One of his brows arched. "That's new."

She and Turner moved quickly through the nearest row and followed the aisle near the wall to the altar, leaving the female body undisturbed. The only thing visible beneath the massive wooden structure was a large hand, palm-down, with blood dried across the knuckles. Beneath the index finger was a polaroid.

THIRTY-EIGHT

It took all four of them to lift the pulpit and set it aside. Sweat poured into Josie's eyes, stinging them. Her shoulders ached as she knelt to press her fingers against the man's carotid artery. She didn't feel anything, but his skin wasn't the kind of cold she would expect of a dead body—even one left in the oppressive heat of the church. His curly blond hair was matted to his head, slick with moisture. If he was perspiring, he was still alive. There wasn't as much blood pooled around his body, though stab wounds left ugly gaping gashes along his forearms—what Josie could see of them. She adjusted her fingers, searching again for a pulse. A closer look at his face revealed that he was probably a teenager. Sixteen or seventeen, most likely.

"Anything?" asked Gretchen.

Relief surged through Josie's veins as the faint, thready beats of the boy's heart thumped against her fingertips. "He's alive."

Noah spoke into his radio, calling for EMS to come through the front door. Josie lowered her face and spoke into the boy's ear. "Can you hear me? I'm with the Denton Police. We're here to help you."

No response.

Turner dropped to his knees on the other side of the boy, lowering his head toward the floor. His voice boomed through the church. "Hey, kid, wake up. We're gonna take you to the hospital."

Shouting only inches from the boy's ear wasn't the approach Josie would have taken but it worked. His eyelids fluttered. A low, deep moan escaped his parted lips.

Turner kept going. "That's it, kid. Can you open your eyes? Talk to us?"

One of his arms shifted, his finger coming off the polaroid. Josie touched his shoulder. "Try not to move. The paramedics are on their way. Can you talk?"

An indecipherable sound came from his mouth.

"Come on, kid," said Turner. "You can do it."

"He—he—"

Every syllable took tremendous effort. A bead of sweat rolled from his hairline, across his temple and over his forehead.

"He who?" Josie asked, keeping a light touch against his shoulder. "Who did this to you?"

He continued to struggle but his eyes blinked open, a startling shade of blue. Josie bent until her face was nearly parallel to his, the blood-smeared floor only an inch from her cheek. "That's it," she said. "That's good. We're here to help. Can you tell us who did this to you?"

"Don't know... dark. He—he was covered."

"What about the woman?" Turner asked.

The boy's eyes went glassy. Josie's stomach plummeted. His whispered words were inaudible.

A series of bangs came from the front door. EMS trying to maneuver the gurney up the steps and inside.

"That's my mom." The boy blinked slowly. A single tear slid from his eye. "He killed my—my mom."

THIRTY-NINE

He stood under the cover of the trees, waiting for her. It wasn't lost on him that she'd chosen to run through the city park alone. He was certain that she knew he'd been following her. It was obvious in the way she occasionally stopped and tilted her head, as if she was listening to a melody only the two of them could hear. He'd given her time, waiting for the perfect moment to claim her, but she'd stayed too close to other people and cameras. Even when she parked her car, she chose the spot nearest the building she was entering.

Until today.

Once he knew which path she was jogging along, he raced ahead, cutting across through dense woods so that he could meet her in a more remote spot.

The sound of sneakers pounding against the asphalt trail startled him from his thoughts. Seconds later, she appeared, her sprint slowed by exertion and the heat. He stepped out in front of her. She screamed, one hand flying to her chest. His fingers tingled with the compulsion to touch her. The girl he loved was only a memory now but this one—she was here in front of him. There was no way she would have gotten into his car last week, then led him to her apartment after she got out unless she wanted him. Jogging alone was a clear invitation.

"Come here," he said.

She shook her head. "No."

He smiled and she shrank back. Still playing hard to get. It must have been her favorite game. "No?"

"I don't want to... be with you. I *never* wanted to be with you."

He didn't believe her, but he could see by the way she shifted from foot to foot that she would run at his first advance. It only turned him on more. He let his fists hang loosely at his sides. "You found me," he reminded her.

She glanced around but no one was going to ruin this moment. "That was a mistake. I just—I don't want to see you again."

Anger flared hot in his chest. He flexed his fists. "Don't lie to me, bitch."

Eyes wide, she reminded him of a deer caught in headlights. Except when he took a step toward her, she turned and ran.

FORTY

Denton Memorial Hospital's emergency department was bustling despite the fact that it was early afternoon, though Fridays tended to be very busy. Josie waited near the nurses' station, a rapidly cooling coffee in her hand. She couldn't bring herself to drink it. Everything tasted like death and decomposition. She could still smell it on her clothes and in her hair. Closed-in homicide scenes tended to do that. For the third time in less than ten minutes, a patient walked past her, nostrils flaring, face crumpling in disgust. She was definitely going to have to throw this entire outfit away.

Gretchen appeared from a long hall that led to the emergency department's main entrance. Everyone she passed gave her a wide berth. Every single person who'd been inside the church carried the odor of death with them like a cloud. No one had time to go home and shower. Not yet. There was too much to be done. Too many leads to run down, and now they had a potential witness.

Gretchen stopped in front of Josie. "Anything?"

Everything had been a blur once they'd realized the boy was

still alive. Josie had left the rest of the team at the scene to accompany the victim in the ambulance. "He didn't speak on the ride over here. They're working on him now. Running some tests. Dr. Nashat should be out soon. Officer Chan is collecting his clothes, shoes, and any items on his person for processing. The good news is that he had his wallet on him. I checked for it on the way over. His name is Jared Rowe, seventeen. Denton resident. His house is about twenty minutes from here. I texted the address to Noah."

An officer would be dispatched to Jared's residence. They knew his mother was the victim in the church but if his father also lived in the household, they'd need to contact him right away. With the address, they could also find out his mother's name and begin investigating her last known whereabouts.

"Was he at least conscious?"

"Barely." Josie pictured the boy's pale face, his drooping eyelids. She could still hear his incoherent moans. "Sawyer thinks he was in shock. Most of the stab wounds are on his forearms. The hand that was trapped under the pulpit has a pretty large wound straight through. Nothing on his body, but Sawyer was certain he's got some broken ribs. He may have internal injuries."

A man with his arm in a sling walked toward them, slowing as he passed, sniffing the air with a pinched expression. "It's us," Gretchen told him. When he opened his mouth to speak, she added, "You really don't want to know."

Josie watched him until he turned a corner into the waiting room. "What about the polaroid?"

There had been no chance for her to get a closer look at it. They'd left it exactly where they found it. Gretchen slid on her reading glasses and took out her phone. "Hang on. Hummel sent me a picture of it."

The ERT would be processing the church now. Dr. Feist was likely en route. It would be hours before they learned any details about the body or the scene that could help them further their investigation.

Gretchen handed Josie her phone. Just like the previous polaroids, this one was slightly blurred but appeared to be nothing but the tops of trees as far as the eye could see. The top of the photo was distorted but from what Josie could tell, it was just blue sky. From the angle, the camera had been almost level with the treetops when the photo was taken. "This wasn't taken above some valley," Josie said.

"Right," said Gretchen. "It's like he climbed to the top of a tree and took it."

"Great," Josie sighed, giving the phone back. "Now we just have to search every place in the city where there are trees."

Gretchen texted the photo to Josie before pocketing her phone. "Every place in the city where there are trees that we worked a case."

Josie laughed. "That could be anywhere. It's literally every case. Sure, it would have been a significant case. That's his pattern, but this?"

She let the question hang in the air, wondering if the killer really wanted them to find the next victim. Every new piece he shifted in his sick game only made it harder for police to know where to go next. If he stumped them, did that mean he won? Or would he give them a free turn, and leave them a new victim in a more obvious place with a new polaroid that was easier to figure out?

Their cell phones chirped at the same time, interrupting Josie's thoughts. She got to hers first, reading off the texts from Noah before Gretchen had a chance to put her glasses back on. "They found the footage from the parking lot. Around midnight last night, a man drove up with a woman in the passenger's seat. Dragged her out by her upper arm and marched her away, out of camera range."

"Last night." Gretchen looked over her reading glasses at

Josie. "He left the polaroid with Stella Townsend on Monday. Five days ago. We found it two days ago."

Josie's heart thudded painfully in her chest. "He waited. Shit."

Gretchen didn't say it out loud but Josie knew they were both thinking it. If they'd found Stella Townsend and the polaroid sooner, and been able to identify the location in the photo more quickly, they could have put surveillance on the church. They could have caught the killer and prevented the murder of Jared Rowe's mother.

Josie's chest felt tight. Had he done it on purpose? Given them time? Or had he simply not been able to pull off the abduction until last night?

"Josie." Gretchen's tone held both solace and a gentle warning. "Don't get too far down that rabbit hole. Chances are he might have figured out we were waiting for him and changed the location."

Josie paced, pinching the bridge of her nose with her thumb and forefinger. Her other hand squeezed her phone so hard, her knuckles blanched. "That kid lost his mother because we couldn't figure out where the picture had been taken."

Gretchen stepped in front of Josie. "No. That kid lost his mother because some depraved piece of shit murdered her. You know that. It's what you tell family members who think they could have done something to change the outcome of their tragedies."

Josie dropped into the box breathing she'd learned in therapy, trying to calm her body. "Killers kill," she murmured.

"Yes," Gretchen said. "Killers kill, and we put them away. The best—and only—thing we can do right now is focus."

Josie nodded, lifting her phone to read the rest of the messages. There was no way to identify the killer from the Harper's Peak footage, given the position of the camera and the fact that he was wearing a hat. It was nighttime, so it was very likely no one saw them, though Noah had sent units to discreetly speak with the Griffin Hall guests.

"The kid wasn't with them." Gretchen scrolled through her own messages.

"It might have been hard for the killer to control both of them, even with a gun, given the distance they'd have to travel on foot, in the dark, from Griffin Hall to the church."

More texts from Noah populated her screen and Josie read through them as quickly as they came. "The car he used to drive to Harper's Peak is registered to a man named Greg Downey, Denton resident. Sent someone to his home. Should have word any minute."

In the meantime, the ERT would impound Downey's vehicle to see if DNA, fingerprints, or any other evidence could be collected that might help their investigation. More waiting.

"Excuse me. Detectives?"

Dr. Nashat, the emergency department's attending physician, stood behind them smiling politely.

Josie said, "How is he?"

"He's stable." Dr. Nashat folded his hands at his waist. "He has some broken ribs and a fracture to his pelvis, but no internal injuries. The wounds on his forearms are superficial. The one to his hand is quite serious. I'm not sure if he'll regain full function or not. They've already taken him up for surgery."

A barbed spike of sadness lodged itself in Josie's heart. Seventeen, and facing the possibility that he could lose some function in one of his hands.

Josie's phone chirped again. She took it out, quickly reading the latest text from Noah.

Brennan made contact with Greg Downey. Forty years old. Tax attorney. Resides with his mother. Says his car was in the shop. Owner of the shop confirms it was stolen from their lot during the night.

Something in the back of her mind crept forward, a connection asking to be made.

Gretchen said, "How long will he be in surgery?"

Josie fired off a response to Noah. *Which shop?*

"It's very difficult to say. If you check back in an hour from now, I'll know more," Dr. Nashat offered.

Gretchen thanked him for his time just as Noah's response came back. Schock's Auto Repair. Same one Sheila Hampton used.

As the doctor walked away, Josie tapped in a reply. *We're headed there now.*

FORTY-ONE

A plume of cold air shot down the back of Josie's neck as she and Gretchen walked into Schock's Auto Repair. The guy at the front desk didn't even look up from his phone when they asked whether the owner was present or not, though his nose wrinkled as if he'd smelled something foul. "Nah," he said. "He's at lunch."

"How about Edgar Garcia?" asked Gretchen. "He here?"

"In the back," he mumbled, pointing to a glass door on their right. Neither Josie nor Gretchen questioned him. Instead, they pushed through the door and made their way down a hallway that smelled like old tires and motor oil.

"What are you thinking?" asked Gretchen. "We can't put Garcia at any of the crime scenes. His prints inside Sheila Hampton's car aren't a surprise. If they're in Greg Downey's that won't be shocking either since he works here."

"I'm not trying to put him at any of the scenes," Josie said. She hadn't been able to stop thinking about the possible accomplice. That was the only angle they truly hadn't explored, mostly because it had seemed like they couldn't figure out who it was unless they figured out the identity of the killer. But that wasn't true. All they had to do was put themselves in the killer's shoes. What would he need help with? Getting away from his remote crime scenes. What would be the best way for a helper to go about doing that without getting caught, particularly in a geofence? The killer didn't need to know what a geofence was to be able to avoid it. He only needed to understand that electronic devices were ubiquitous and that whether you consented or not, you were trackable at all times while in possession of any one of them.

"Well, since two of the stolen cars left at the crime scenes were worked on here," Gretchen said, "maybe we should be trying to put him at the scenes."

Josie hadn't met Garcia before but he hadn't gotten so much as a parking ticket since he got out of prison. She'd checked his social media before they left the hospital. It was locked down pretty tight, but she was able to view a few posts of him with his daughter. Josie guessed she was about four or five years old. She had the same black hair as her father except hers was curly whereas his was straight. The same eyes, too, and when she looked at her father, they brimmed with adoration.

"I don't think Garcia would knowingly get involved with murder," Josie said. "There's nothing in it for him, but he might be helping the killer some other way."

"I hope your hunch is right," Gretchen said as she pushed open the door to the repair bays. "Because right now all we have is speculation and another shitty polaroid—at least until Jared Rowe is out of surgery and can tell us something helpful."

Somehow, Josie didn't think the boy was going to have anything to tell them that might help them find the killer.

The air inside the large bay area felt at least ten degrees hotter than the rest of the building. Music filtered through Bluetooth speakers mounted in the four corners, playing a song Josie didn't recognize. Someone whistled along with it. There were three vehicles lined up. One of them was on a lift, its tires at eye level as Josie and Gretchen passed. A Jeep sat in the next slot, its hood open. In the last bay, a pair of heavy boots stuck out from beneath an old Pontiac. Their owner stopped whistling and started singing along with the radio.

His feet jerked when Josie said, "Edgar Garcia?"

There was the loud clank of metal, a muttered curse, and Garcia began to emerge, dark blue pants and then a lighter blue shirt, both splotched with stains. A slick of grease ran down one of his forearms as he slid completely out from beneath the car on his creeper. Dark eyes glittered with suspicion as he eyed them. Josie watched his gaze catch on their pistols for a beat longer than necessary.

"I already talked with someone earlier this week. I told him my prints were in that car because I work here. Just because I got a record don't give you the right to keep harassing me." His face twisted in disgust. "What's that smell?"

"It's us," Josie said. "Occupational hazard."

He waved a hand in front of his face. "Damn."

Gretchen said, "We're not here about that car or your prints."

He sat up, keeping the creeper still using the heels of his boots. He produced a rag from one of his pockets and wiped the grease from his arm. "I know you ain't here for my sparkling personality."

A new song filled the bays, up-tempo with a heavy bass. "A car was stolen from your lot last night," Josie said. "You know anything about that?"

He rested his forearms across his knees, the rag dangling from his fingers. "Sure. I usually lock up at the end of the day. You see out back?"

"The fence," Gretchen said. "Yeah. Chains and padlocks?"

"Old-school, yeah, but my boss isn't trying to afford something more high-tech than that. Asshole cut right through the chain. I told my boss. He said he was handling it, so why are you here talking to me?"

Edgar's boss had made a report while they were pulling the pulpit off Jared Rowe. It just hadn't made its way up the chain to the investigative team.

Instead of answering his question, Josie walked around to the front of the Pontiac, trailing a finger along its hood. "How old is this thing?"

Edgar laughed softly. He knew what she was doing. "It's a 2003 GTO. What do you really want to know?"

"You guys work on a lot of these kinds of cars," she said, pressing her index finger into the red Pontiac symbol in the center of the grille.

"Older cars, yeah. I got a few on the lot right now. You wanna hear something crazy? Cars from the nineties are considered classic now."

Changing the subject, just like Josie.

Gretchen laughed. "Were you even alive in the nineties?"

He arched a brow at her and used the rag to swipe at a stain between his knuckles. "Like you didn't check my sheet before you came in here. Yeah, I was alive in the nineties."

"Barely," Josie said. "Whose car is this?"

"No one's," Edgar said. "My boss buys old junkers and I restore them so he can sell them. He gives me a cut. As long as I get the regular work done on time."

"You stay late to work on these," Gretchen said.

He glanced at the clock on the wall. "Yeah. Or I work during my lunch, which is now. I only got another half hour, so whatever you got to say, just say it. I don't think I can stand that smell much longer."

"You're a single dad, aren't you?" Josie asked.

"Yeah, and it ain't easy. Never thought I'd be having tea parties with stuffed unicorns and shit, but I do what I gotta do."

"Including taking on after-hours projects to make extra money," said Gretchen.

Edgar hauled himself to his feet and took a step back, likely trying to avoid their odor. "Yeah. I'd do anything for my kid. I ain't ashamed of that. What do you want to ask me?"

Josie walked back over to him. "You said you lock up at night. Are you the only one with the key to the lot? Besides your boss?"

He didn't answer.

"Do you ever leave the padlock open? In case someone needs to borrow a car?"

Something flared in his eyes. It looked a lot like fear. "I told you. The chain was cut. I had nothing to do with that dude's car getting stolen."

"I'm not talking about his car." Josie pointed to the Pontiac. "I'm talking about cars like this. Older cars with no GPS, and I'm not talking about ones that have been stolen. I'm talking about ones that get borrowed. For a price."

FORTY-TWO

Garcia licked his lips. Josie could tell by the way his breathing picked up, the slight increase in speed in the way his chest expanded and contracted, that her shot had hit true. She let the moment stretch on until, finally, he said, "I don't want to get fired. This is a good job. A good gig."

"But you still needed more," Gretchen pointed out.

Now the spark in his eye was from anger. "Hell yes. I always need more. Kids are expensive as fuck. Even sending my baby to public school, I still got a shit-ton of expenses. Food, doctor's visits, fucking playdates and little kid birthday parties. Clothes and shoes. She outgrows them as soon as I buy them. I bought two new pairs of shoes in the last three months, and I got a girl, so it's not just some pair of sneakers. She wants pretty shoes and boots, too."

Josie said, "Edgar, we're not trying to get you fired. We just need to know who pays you to leave the lot open so they can 'borrow' the cars."

He shook his head, twisting the rag in his hands. "You think I don't know how this works? If I tell you, my boss will find out.

Don't even try to tell me he won't. Cops don't keep shit a secret."

"The person 'borrowing' these cars?" said Gretchen. "They're an accessory to murder—if not an actual murderer—so regardless of whether your boss finds out or not, getting fired is going to be the least of your worries."

He turned away, pacing a short path before them, pressing the rag against his forehead. "Holy shit. I didn't know that. I never would have agreed to it if I knew that. Oh, man. I'm so fucked."

Josie said, "Edgar, cooperate with us, fully, and we'll do what we can to work with the DA to make sure you don't face charges."

"My job!" he said. "What about my job?"

"We can't help you with that," Gretchen said honestly. "But it seems to me that whether you try keeping this one or try getting a new one, it will look better if you cooperated with police."

"Regardless," Josie said, "we already know about your arrangement, about the cars. Whether you cooperate or not, we're going to have every older-model car without GPS impounded and processed for evidence in three homicides. You can take control of who finds out what and when as well as your role going forward, or you can get out of our way and let things play out however they're going to."

He paced for another few minutes, fisting the rag and hitting himself lightly in the head with it. Muttered curses spilled from his lips.

Josie let him go as long as possible, but the clock was ticking. Another victim waited and with her, another polaroid.

"Edgar," Josie said. "I know this is hard. We really didn't come here with the intention of blowing up your life, but more people will be murdered if we don't get on with things. Just this morning we found a victim. A mother. Her son is in the hospital getting surgery right now. He'll never see his mother again. On Monday, a baby girl, not even five months old, lost her mother. Help us stop this killer."

He stopped pacing and nodded, almost to himself. Taking a steadying breath, he looked back and forth between them. "I don't know about no killer. All I know is some lady approached me."

"A woman?" Josie said.

"Yeah. I don't know her. I don't know her name."

"She's not a customer here?" asked Gretchen.

He shrugged. "Who knows? She could be. Probably, she is. How else would she know what we got on our lot? But I don't meet the customers. They got front desk guys for that."

And they were all charm, too. "You don't see any of the customers?" Josie asked.

"I mean, sometimes, yeah, if I'm in and out, but ninety-nine percent of the time, I'm back here. It's an endless line of cars and there's only three of us during the day. We barely even get a break for lunch. I stay back here. The boss and front desk jockeys handle the customers."

"Then where did this woman approach you?" asked Gretchen.

He looked at the floor and nudged the creeper with the toe of his boot. "At the playground. I was there with my daughter. She was running around the big jungle gym thing. This lady comes up to me, starts talking about how pretty my kid is—and she really is—and I don't give it too much thought 'cause women talk to me all the time at the playground. All of us parents and grandparents do, you know? Hell, that's how I found out about blue light and shit, and that I was giving my daughter screen time too close to bed. Really helped with her sleep cycle, you know?"

Josie kind of hated that Garcia's life was about to get blown up. She liked him, in spite of his underhanded dealings with the older cars. He probably knew more about parenting than she and Noah combined, and they were on the precipice of asking someone to give them their child to raise. "When was this?"

"About three weeks ago."

Gretchen said, "So, what? She just said hey, I know you work at this auto repair shop. I need access to some cars without GPS. Can you help me?"

He laughed mirthlessly. "Basically, yeah. I told her she was nuts and to get the fuck away from me and my daughter. Then she told me how much she was willing to pay."

"Which was?" Josie asked.

He told them.

Gretchen met Josie's eyes briefly. The unspoken agreement between them was that it was hard to blame Edgar for taking her up on her offer.

He continued, "But I told her I didn't want to know why. I didn't want to know her name or anything about her. I didn't want to know anything at all. Cash only. I'd leave her the padlock key in a hidden spot. The keys for the older cars would be in the consoles. All she had to do was not get caught and make sure the cars were always returned and the gate was always locked afterward. I can show you the key in case you want to try to get prints. Seems like something you would want to do."

Josie wasn't sure Hummel could pull a clear print from a key that had been handled by Edgar and this woman, but it was worth a shot. "Great. How did she pay you?"

"Cash in the glove compartments. I checked every morning 'cause I never knew when she was coming."

Gretchen arched a brow. "She wasn't caught on camera taking the cars and returning them?"

Edgar chuckled. "My boss got a padlock on the gate out there. You think he's springing for cameras? Please. One of the guys out front talked him into Ring cameras but the batteries ran out a month after he put them up and he didn't bother to recharge them. He said no one would know they were dead and just having them was a deterrent."

That happened more than people thought. Josie said, "What did this woman look like?"

Edgar sighed. "I don't know. Like someone's grandmother."

FORTY-THREE

"Someone's grandmother." Gretchen kept repeating Edgar Garcia's words as she and Josie got off the elevator on the sixth floor of Denton Memorial Hospital. The woman he'd gone on to describe could have been any woman over seventy with short white hair, slightly hunched shoulders and a little extra weight around her middle. At first, Josie thought Garcia had decided to lie to them. What kind of elderly woman stole classic cars in the middle of the night and used them to pick up a murderer at a remote location?

Then she realized that it was entirely possible that the 'grandmother' wasn't the one actually moving the cars. Maybe she was just the set-up person. She made the arrangement with Garcia, ensured that the key to the lot would be available, and then the killer was the one who took them off the lot, stashed them at the murder scenes ahead of time, and returned them when he was finished. Garcia had confirmed that since the classic cars didn't belong to clients, his boss hadn't noticed when a couple of them were missing from the lot during the day.

"What kind of grandmother would help a serial killer?" Gretchen said as they turned down the hallway toward Jared

Rowe's room. Almost all the patient doors were closed. Still, the muffled sounds of hospital machines, televisions, and conversations filtered through.

Josie didn't answer because they'd reached room 604. Noah and Turner had gone to the auto repair shop to oversee the impounding of the classic vehicles so that she and Gretchen could interview the boy. They had taken brief detours at both their homes to shower and change their clothes so as not to further traumatize him with the stench of his own mother's decomposition. Gretchen rapped lightly against the door and pushed it open when they heard a muffled, 'Come in.'

Jared Rowe's eyes were filled with a deadness that sent a shiver up Josie's spine. He was shut down, his emotions buried deep in a place he could not access. At least, not right now. Josie recognized the look. How many times had she done the same thing in her own life? Starting when she was a child, learning how to cut her psyche off from the trauma and pain being inflicted on her, until the habit became as natural as breathing. Whenever those excruciating emotions threatened to return, she drowned them with Wild Turkey, until it started affecting her relationship with Noah. She hadn't had a drink in years.

Looking at Jared Rowe, she really wanted one now.

Gretchen approached the bed, introducing them, and flashing her credentials. Jared's gaze flitted over them quickly and then focused on the ceiling above him. His face had regained some color. A blue hospital gown had replaced his bloodied clothing. Bandages covered his forearms. The hand that had been pierced through with the knife was wrapped in gauze. An IV fed fluids into a vein in his other hand.

Josie studied the vital signs on the monitor beside his bed. The numbers looked good considering what he had been through. "Jared, we need to ask you some questions."

Eyes still on the ceiling, he gave a small nod.

"Jared," Gretchen said. "I'm very sorry about your mom."

"Can you tell us her name?" asked Josie.

"Ev—" He cleared his throat. "Everly."

Gretchen jotted the name down on her notepad. "Is your dad at home?"

His tone was flat. "He doesn't live here. My parents are divorced. He lives in Jersey."

Josie glanced at his vitals again. Still stable. "Jared, can you tell us what happened? How did you and your mom end up in the church at Harper's Peak?"

He licked his lips. For a heartbeat, his eyes met Josie's and she knew, in spite of his flat affect, that he was only a hair's breadth from losing control of his emotions, to giving in to the terror she saw behind his mask.

There wasn't a damn thing anyone could do for him.

Josie knew that from experience. His heart rate ticked upward. She reached over the bedrail to the hand with the IV in it and covered his fingers with her palm. "Breathe."

Nodding, he tipped his head back and closed his eyes, drawing in deep breaths. Josie watched his heart rate return to its baseline. His fingers trembled under her touch. They waited. When he opened his eyes again, he said, "I don't know if I can do this."

Gretchen got closer, until her stomach pressed against the bedrail. "We can come back, Jared. If you can tell us anything at all now, it will help but we're not going to push."

He found Josie again and she felt something spark between them. Did he recognize his own grief and trauma in her? Despite all the work she'd done to process it? All the therapy? "How?" he murmured.

She knew what he was asking. How was he going to live now? Get through the days? The nights? How was he going to survive the loss of his mother? Josie said the only thing she could think of—the way she'd survived Lisette's death. "One minute at a time."

Gretchen said, "Who can we call for you, Jared? Someone in town? Other family? A friend or neighbor?"

He told her the name of his grandmother, but he didn't know her phone number. "It's in my cell phone. He took it."

Josie felt a brief stab of excitement. If the killer took Jared's cell phone, they might be able to track his movements. She looked at Gretchen, who was already on her phone, firing off a text to Noah.

"That's okay," Josie assured him. "We'll find it and get in touch with her."

As he kept eye contact with her, the shaking in his fingers began to subside. "My mom called me. It was late, real late. Like one in the morning. She wasn't, um, home. I work at Sandman's restaurant in the summer. I help close, so I don't get home till after midnight usually. That's the only reason I was still awake when she called. I saw her before I went to work. At, like, four. She works at a bank. She's usually coming home as I'm leaving."

Gretchen scribbled on her notepad as he spoke while Josie kept the interview going. "How did she seem? Was she stressed about anything lately?"

"No. She was her normal self," he said. "I mean, she's, uh, always stressed about the bills and stuff, but that was it."

"Was she having issues with anyone lately?" Josie asked. "Boyfriend, ex-boyfriend? Coworker? Neighbor? Anyone at all?"

He shook his head. "She doesn't have a boyfriend. Her ex just got married. He hasn't been around in a couple of years. I don't think she's having trouble with anyone else."

Josie didn't correct his use of the present tense. "Did she say anything to you about being followed or feeling like someone was watching her lately?"

"No, nothing."

"I assume you each have your own vehicle?"

"That's right," Jared said. "Hers was home when I got there

but then she wasn't and I thought it was weird. I started to get a little freaked out. I texted her but she didn't respond. I waited a half hour and called but it went to voicemail. I was wondering if I should, um, call the police or something, but then she called me."

Gretchen continued to take notes, documenting his account. Josie knew she was being quiet so as not to break the connection he obviously felt with her.

Under Josie's hand, his fingers began to shake again. "She called you from her phone?"

"Yes." He sucked in a deep breath and exhaled shakily. "I knew something was wrong from how, uh, high-pitched her voice sounded."

He stopped, his chest rising and falling rapidly. Josie lightly squeezed his fingers. "Take your time. Stop when you need to and remember, the moment you tell us you're done, we leave. Like Detective Palmer said, we can come back."

Nodding, he continued. "She said that she was in trouble and needed me to come get her. She wouldn't tell me what kind of trouble. She wouldn't say much at all. Wouldn't answer any of my questions. Just kept repeating herself. She was in trouble and needed me. It was really weird. I think—um—now I think that he made her call and that he was telling her what to say and what not to say because she would never ask me to come if he was there. She wouldn't put me in danger like that. I was so freaked out that I went. I just... went."

FORTY-FOUR

Josie squeezed his fingers again, putting more pressure on them until his shoulders relaxed slightly. "She told you where to find her."

He swallowed, Adam's apple bobbing. "Yes. She said to come by myself, that she didn't want anyone else to see her or know what was going on. I got really worried at that point but then she said she didn't need the police or an ambulance or anything. Just me. Then she started crying and just begging me to do what she said, and she'd explain everything when I got there. She told me to come to Harper's Peak. I was never there so she told me to park in any one of the lots and walk up to the church."

Gretchen's phone chirped. Quickly, she took it out and responded to a text before resuming her note-taking.

"Did she give you directions to the church?" asked Josie.

"Yeah. It was dark so I brought a flashlight. I kept expecting someone to stop me but no one did. There was some wedding going on in the one building and a concert happening outside some other building. No one even noticed me."

"Were the lights on inside the church?" The church wasn't visible from any of the resort buildings, as far as Josie knew. Even if it was, no guest would think anything of seeing lights in the windows of a building on the edge of the resort. Since the church was closed off, staff members might have found it suspicious but according to the owner and managing director, no reports concerning the church had been made recently.

"Yeah," said Jared. "She had told me to go in the back. The door was open. I called for her, but she didn't answer. I went inside and—and—"

He squeezed his eyes shut. The tremors went from his fingers up his arm. Soon, his entire body quivered. Josie hesitated. They were so close to finding out what happened, but she didn't want to send him over the edge. He was already so traumatized. "Jared," she said. "Breathe. That's all you need to do in this moment. Breathe. That's it."

He nodded, the movement jerky.

Gretchen mouthed, *Grandmother's on the way*.

Josie was glad. She didn't want to leave him alone. "We're going to stop now."

His eyes sprang open, searching for her as if he was afraid she'd already left. "Please," he said. "I want to—to finish telling you. If I do, it will help you catch him, right? Then he'll go to prison for what he did to my mom?"

"It will help," Josie agreed. "We're going to do everything we can to catch him and work with prosecutors so they can do their part."

It was the best she could do. There were no guarantees in her line of work. Killers eluded police. Investigations fell apart. Evidence sometimes wasn't plentiful or convincing enough to build an airtight case. Juries acquitted, sometimes in the face of mountains of evidence that the defendants had committed the crimes for which they were on trial. There were technicalities and any number of missteps that could occur and lead to a murderer going free. Right now, Jared Rowe didn't need to know any of that.

"I went inside the church. That's when I—I saw her. In the middle aisle. She was—she was already dead. I mean, I think. She had to be. There was so much blood. I got out my phone to call 911 and I started to run toward her, but then I don't know. He was there, just like this dark figure, almost like a shadow, and he was on me, stabbing and stabbing. For a second, I thought I was hallucinating him, like he was some kind of demon or something. I got my hands up. It went so fast. One second I was walking in and seeing my mom and the next second there was this huge knife straight through my whole hand! I think I passed out. The next thing I knew, I was on the floor and something heavy landed on my back. I couldn't breathe."

"You were under the pulpit," Josie told him. "It was tipped onto its side. It probably knocked the wind out of you when it landed."

"Yeah, yeah, that's how it felt except I didn't even think of that at the time. I just thought I was going to die. Right then. It felt like forever until I could breathe again. He was walking around. I saw his boots but that was it. I couldn't move. I tried to talk but it was hard. I begged him to let me go. He never said a word. He just... left."

Gretchen jumped in. "Did you ever hear or sense anyone else there with him?"

"No. I mean, it was dark and I didn't have a chance to look around or anything but I don't remember anyone but him."

"One last question," Josie said. "This may seem strange but, Jared, was or is anyone in your family in law enforcement? Retired police officer or assistant district attorney?"

His brow furrowed. "I, um, my grandfather was a cop. He

retired when I was in preschool, I think. He lives in the nursing home up on that big hill. Rockview or something?"

Josie's grandmother had lived there in her last years. "I know it. What's his name?"

"Hugh Weaver."

FORTY-FIVE

"Hugh Weaver was a drunk." Noah shaded his eyes, watching as the ERT loaded a second car onto the police department's flatbed tow truck. "He didn't retire. He was asked to resign."

Josie took a step backward, into the shade of the only tree on Schock's Auto Repair's back lot. Under it was a stone wall where Gretchen and Turner sat with three feet between them, sweaty and haggard. Turner had taken off his jacket and tossed it onto the wall beside him. It was nearing dinnertime and the ERT still had one more car to impound. Josie needed coffee, food, and more sleep. She wasn't the only one. The day's developments had them all on edge.

Turner fanned his face as the flatbed belched exhaust in their direction. "Hey, Palmer. You ever meet this Weaver guy?"

She didn't glance his way. "Before my time."

"Quinn?"

Josie hefted herself onto the wall beside Gretchen. Overhead, a blue jay swooped from branch to branch, shrieking. "I met him a few times. He was one of the crime scene techs. Noah's right. Every time I ever saw him, he reeked of alcohol."

Gretchen tilted her chin, watching the angry bird. "Was he active at the same time as Kellan Neal and James Lampson?"

"Yes," said Josie.

"But he wasn't part of the whole human trafficking thing?" Turner rifled inside his jacket pockets for his phone and began scrolling. "That's why he's in a nursing home and not in prison?"

Noah waved at the tow truck driver as he pulled away. "The only thing Hugh Weaver cared about was his next drink. If he was aware of the trafficking ring, no one could prove it. He wasn't implicated."

Josie mentally worked through the names of the men whose progeny had been killed as well as the years they were active working for the city. Kellan Neal, James Lampson, and now, Hugh Weaver. They overlapped by several years. They'd probably been involved in several cases together—Lampson as a detective, Weaver as one of the crime scene techs and Neal preparing them both to testify in court. Why these three? Lampson was corrupt. Weaver was incompetent and unprofessional, but Neal was beyond reproach, which meant these murders weren't about punishing bad actors.

What the hell was it about?

Noah stepped under the tree with them, using his forearm to wipe the sweat from his brow. "Gretchen, where did you get with those records searches?"

"The request I made to the DA's office for cases that involved both Neal and Lampson that were overturned after Lampson went to prison is still pending. In terms of stabbing cases that were not overturned involving both Lampson and Neal, I made a list. I emailed it to you guys this morning before Quinn called about Harper's Peak."

Josie and Noah each took out their phones. They'd been so busy, Josie hadn't even checked her email. Now she pulled up the list, taking a few minutes to scroll through it. Nothing sparked her memory, but most of the cases were over ten years old. She would have been on patrol. The extent of her involvement on any of those cases would have been limited to canvassing or guarding the perimeter of a scene—if she had any involvement at all. Some were from before she'd even started on the force.

Turner tossed his phone on top of his jacket and stood up, eyeing the blue jay screeching directly over his head. "But now we've got Weaver."

"I can narrow that list down more by adding him to the search parameters but it will take a while," Gretchen said.

"What the hell else do we have to do?" Turner complained. "Soon, there will be another name to add to our list, right? We've got another polaroid. This guy ain't stopping. Shit, he's probably two murders ahead of us already, so how in the hell could you narrow down any case? What if you find one involving the three guys we've already got and at the next scene, we find a victim related to someone who didn't work on that case? Then we're right back where we started."

She hated that he was probably right. Perhaps their most promising lead in Everly Rowe's murder were her and her son's cell phones, but they had been quickly located under an azalea bush near the church. The killer had taken them so that Jared couldn't use either of them to call for help. Not that he would have been able to do so, pinned under the pulpit. The geofence had turned up nothing. As usual.

"Hey," Turner continued. "Did anyone check with Remy Tate to see where he was last night?"

"Home in bed," Noah said. "Or so he claims. I sent Dougherty over to his place earlier."

After the last interview with Remy Tate, during which Noah broke the news that Stella had been murdered, he'd given consent for them to pull the GPS report from his car. It hadn't put him at the scenes where Cleo or Stella were found. He had also agreed to a search of his house. Nothing had been found to link him to Stella's murder although by then, he would have had plenty of time to dispose of any evidence.

"He's a dead end," Josie said. Giving up on the list, she opened her gallery and swiped to the photo of the new polaroid. She'd been racking her brain trying to figure out which of their cases that had been most widely covered in the press involved treetops or climbing trees. It was absurd. Was this guy just having fun at their expense now?

The blue jay hopped along the branch directly over Turner's jacket. A second later, a fat splatter of excrement landed on it. Gretchen howled with laughter.

"Son of a bitch!" Turner yelled.

Jumping up, Gretchen clapped her hands together. "On that high note, I'm going back to the stationhouse to search for stabbing cases in which Neal, Lampson, and now Weaver were all involved."

Turner was too intent on trying to wipe the shit from the shoulder of his jacket with a tissue he pulled from his pocket to notice her leaving. "That's piss, paint, glue and now bird shit all in one week."

Noah smirked, a rare show of amusement at Turner's expense, but quickly shuttered his expression when Turner plopped back onto the wall, shoulders slumped in defeat. "I know, I know," he mumbled. "Not important. Where were we? I guess it's too early for autopsy results, even for the doc. She's fast." The note of admiration in his voice while talking about Anya made Josie slightly queasy but a lecture about staying away from her was for another day.

"We won't know anything until tomorrow at the soonest." Noah walked over and sat beside Josie. "But I'm sure the findings will be in keeping with his MO. No sexual assault. Head injury. Multiple stab wounds. We're also waiting on Hummel to process Greg Downey's stolen car. He's going to run prints from that, the church, and the phones."

"He's not gonna find anything," Turner said. "This guy doesn't leave prints, remember?"

"No prints," Josie murmured. It still bothered her that the killer had managed not to leave prints anywhere. Hummel had pulled plenty of unknown sets of prints in the Cleo Tate and Stella Townsend cases but there was no single set of unknowns that appeared at both scenes. Yet, DNA had been left at the scenes. She didn't believe for a second that the killer hadn't managed to leave his own DNA behind. Locard's Exchange Principle dictated that he had to have left something at the scenes. It was a fundamental concept in forensic science. Every time a person made contact with another person, place, or thing, an exchange of physical materials took place. In terms of crime scenes, that meant that a criminal always left something behind.

"You know what else has been bothering me?" she said.

Turner found a loose pebble along the stone wall and tossed it up at the blue jay still lurking overhead. Luckily, his aim with pebbles was as good as his aim with foam basketballs. It went wide. The bird squawked again. "Enlighten us, swee— Quinn."

"There's no blood trail. All the blood from the stabbings is contained to where the victims are found."

"But if you stabbed someone as savagely as this guy did," Noah said, "you'd be covered in blood."

"Yes," Josie said.

"We should have found drops somewhere, at the very least," Turner said. "So what? Is he wearing some kind of suit? Like the ones we use at crime scenes? That would be ironic."

But it wasn't out of the question. It wasn't only law enforcement that wore them. Workers who did mold remediation or handled fiberglass wore them, just like painters and people who worked in food processing. They weren't that hard to come by.

Maybe that's what was in his cross-body bag. "But what does he do with them once he leaves the scene?"

"Burns them," Turner offered. He waved a hand at the lot full of cars. "Do they have a burn pit here? A barrel or something?"

"No," said Noah, standing as the police flatbed returned to the lot.

Even if the killer wore Tyvek suits when he did the actual stabbings, there was no way he hadn't left DNA behind on his victims before that. It was the middle of July. The heat and humidity were off the charts. Josie had no doubt that, at the very least, he'd left sweat behind. The DNA samples Hummel had collected surely contained the genetic material of the killer. If he wasn't in the DNA database, then it wouldn't help them identify or locate him but it would be on record. Why bother to avoid leaving fingerprints if your DNA was going to give you away sooner or later?

Unless he wasn't savvy enough to realize this. That seemed unlikely given all the planning that had gone into these killings. Josie was going round and round and getting nowhere.

A loud, high-pitched alarm sounded as the flatbed backed up to the final car. Soon they'd be back in the air-conditioned stationhouse. Josie thought about the three crime scenes. By the end of the evening, the photos of all three victims would be pinned to the corkboard in the great room. Not that Josie needed reminders. The scenes were still vivid in her mind. Like the killer's polaroids, their bodies told a story. Cleo clutching the edge of the boat, trying to climb out. Stella reaching for the edge of the helipad, trying to crawl away. Everly flat on her back, one arm flung outward, as if she was trying to grab something, but she'd been too badly stabbed to even turn on her side. A bloodied chef's knife lay at each one of their feet.

A few feet away, she heard the rapid tapping of Turner's fingers on his leg. "What are you working on, Quinn?"

"Nothing. Everything is a dead end right now." It was a waiting game. Processing evidence took time, and with three murders in a week, their in-house ERT was already overwhelmed. The state lab was perpetually backed up. They'd receive their expedited requests for DNA results sooner than normal but not soon enough.

Noah left them to confer with the tow truck driver.

"Come on, Quinn," Turner goaded. "You're the superstar around here. What's next?"

She shrugged. Her body begged for coffee. "Release the stills we have of the suspect from the parking lot at Stella Townsend's apartment complex and Griffin Hall to the press. You can't see his face well, but someone might recognize him."

Turner smiled. "I'll man the tip line."

"So you can stay in the air conditioning? I don't think so."

Josie heard him chuckle as he gathered his jacket and phone. "Fine. Let's get back to the stationhouse and see what kind of list Palmer's got for us now."

FORTY-SIX

Josie's body practically sang with relief when she finally sagged into her desk chair. Even the overtaxed air conditioning felt divine. Noah had stopped to get them all takeout and coffee. They ate in silence while Gretchen worked on the new list of old cases. Caffeine and nourishment gave them their second wind. No one talked about going home just yet. With two blonde lattes making her restless, Josie got up and walked over to the corkboard.

Behind her, she heard the telltale pop of the tab from one of Turner's energy drinks. A moment later, he was standing beside her, arm brushing hers as he tipped his head back and gulped down the entire can. When he finished, yellow drops clung to his beard. How had Trinity tolerated this guy over multiple lunches?

"I see your wheels turning over here, Quinn," he said.

Josie elbowed him. "You're standing too close."

With a heavy sigh, he dropped his gaze to her. "Listen, sweetheart... Ah, fuck."

Josie glanced over her shoulder in time to see Gretchen's grin. Turner produced a dollar. Josie shook her head. "I'm telling you that you stand too close to me—a lot. I don't like it. We don't know each other that well. If you think you're able to simply listen to me and stop doing it, you can keep that dollar."

Noah appeared behind them and plucked it out of Turner's hand. "No, he can't. He still called you sweetheart. This is going in the jar. But Josie's right."

Turner took an exaggerated step away from her, scowling. "All right, fine. I'm just trying to do this whole team thing. Listen to your opinion and shit."

Josie didn't know if that was progress or not. She traced a finger from one crime scene photo to another. "If you were going to kill people because you wanted revenge on some cops or an ADA who did you dirty, why would you target these women?"

Turner followed the path of her finger. "Why kill them when their dad or grandfathers are still alive?"

"Exactly."

Noah folded his arms across his chest. "Lampson's in prison. Pretty hard to get to him."

"LT, if you know the right people, you could make something fatal happen to a guy in prison," said Turner. "Stage it to look like a prison fight."

"But what would make them suffer more?" Josie said. "Killing them or killing the people they love?"

"I don't think Lampson loved anyone but himself," Noah said. "But I agree. This killer is getting revenge by killing family members."

"Then why didn't he kill the baby or the kid?" Turner asked. "Or is he one of these guys who thinks he's all noble and shit because he won't kill kids?"

It was possible that the killer had some reason for leaving Gracie Tate and Jared Rowe alive. After all, he'd lured Jared to the church and not killed him. Unless he thought the pulpit had killed him or would before the police arrived.

Josie said, "He's trying to recreate something. This isn't about some convict who just got out of prison and wants revenge on the people who put him away. This killer is recreating a crime scene. A specific crime scene."

The printer in the corner of the room belched to life. "Hang on," said Gretchen. "I've got the new list."

She brought it over to them. It was significantly shorter but still, Josie didn't immediately recognize any names. "We need to pull up the crime scene photos," she said. "That's how we'll know which case we're looking for."

Turner crumpled his can and threw it away. His phone appeared in his hand, thumb swiping rhythmically as he sauntered back to his desk. Clearly, he'd grown bored with their current topic. Josie sat at her desk while Noah and Gretchen crowded behind her. She started with the first case on the list, pulling up the crime scene photos from each one. After an hour, her shoulders ached and her eyes felt gritty and dry. Noah went to get another round of coffees. When he returned, he pushed his chair next to Josie's so he could view the slideshow of death from each file she reviewed. Gretchen went back to her own computer and started at the end of the list, searching from the last case and working toward the middle. Turner snoozed in his chair, his head tipped back, mouth open like a toddler. One of his hands still gripped his phone. Even in sleep he couldn't let it go.

Every time Josie thought about taking a break or calling it a night, she remembered Jared Rowe's deadened expression and it gave her the jolt she needed to continue. Then, she opened a new file, pulled up one of the crime scene photos and knew she'd found what they were looking for. A burst of energy surged through her body. Her senses sharpened. The fatigue she'd been fighting for the last hour evaporated.

"This is it!" she said. "This is it!"

Gretchen leapt from her chair and hurried over. Noah

leaned in closer. Josie picked up a pen from her desk and threw it at Turner, hitting him square in the chest. He bolted upright, phone tumbling to the floor. "What the hell?"

"Josie found the case," Gretchen told him.

He looked down at the pen in his lap. "Did you do this?"

"Shut the hell up and get over here. Come on."

Josie thought he was going to argue. Arguing with Gretchen was definitely his favorite thing next to scrolling on his phone. Instead, he stood, snatched his phone from the floor and walked around the desks, taking up position directly behind her.

"Look," Josie said, clicking through the crime scene photos.

Gretchen turned toward the corkboard briefly. "The positions of the bodies are pretty much identical."

"This is the one," Noah said.

"What case are we talking about?" asked Turner.

The more photos that flashed across the screen, the more Josie remembered about the case. She didn't need to check the reports to know she'd been the responding officer.

"The Cook family," she said. "The Cook family murders."

FORTY-SEVEN

They were at the motel again. Different room, same sheets made practically of sandpaper. She didn't care. He was more passionate this time. It was almost as if his feelings finally matched hers. When they were finished, she collapsed into a boneless heap next to him. Her chest heaved, perspiration covered her body, and the euphoria going off like fireworks in her head made her feel high.

He poured her a glass of wine from a bottle he'd brought with him. He'd remembered the opener but hadn't brought glasses so he used the small foam coffee cups the motel stocked in every room. Pretty fancy considering how seedy the place was on the outside.

They sat beside one another, backs leaning against the headboard. He held out his cup and she touched it with hers, giggling. "What are we toasting to?"

"To the beginning."

Heat rose to her cheeks. The beginning of them? But her hopes were dashed when he added, "Of the plan."

Stiffening, she refused to taste any more of the wine, even though he'd brought her favorite. Then she remembered how he'd confided in her and no one else. It didn't matter that she'd given him little choice, it only mattered that they were here now, talking about something sacred to him, and she was a part of it. A part of his life again, finally.

His eyes glazed over as he stared straight ahead, envisioning the havoc he'd wreak, no doubt. After a moment, he blinked and came back to her. "Did you find him? The monster?"

Abandoning her earlier disappointment, she sipped more wine. It was the only name on his list that he truly cared about. It meant everything to him, and he meant everything to her. She knew the bloodshed that could be avoided if she gave him what he wanted.

"I did." She placed her cup on the nightstand and turned so she could look deeply into his eyes. "I'm so sorry, my love. He died ten years ago. Car accident."

A vein in his temple throbbed. His features turned to stone.

"I truly am sorry. But it's not over. There are the others."

He said nothing.

Desperate to bring him back to her, she rattled off the names on the list. It was their mental list. She wasn't ever to put it in writing anywhere, so she'd committed it to memory. When she still got no response, she repeated it.

Finally, the life returned to his eyes. He recited the names after her, leaving three of them off.

"You forgot a few of them," she said. "Or have you changed your mind?"

The coldness in his eyes sent a chill over her entire body, despite the sweat still drying on her skin. "I've already taken care of two of them. The last..." he waved a hand in the air, "I changed my mind."

"You can't be serious."

His mood changed like the wind, again. She could barely keep up. Brow furrowed, he said, "I'm very serious. I have something different planned for her."

He told her because now he told her everything. It took all of her willpower not to leap out of the bed and stalk out of the room because once again, what was between them would end in unspeakable violence that left her utterly alone and him in the arms of another woman.

FORTY-EIGHT

Disjointed memories of the Cook family homicides flashed through Josie's mind. At the time, it felt like something she could never possibly forget but after so many years on the job, witnessing so much depravity and cruelty, it became harder to draw up memories from a scene she'd responded to when she was just a rookie. She'd been so inexperienced and stupid. She'd made many mistakes. Most of them were excusable and even expected. The seasoned field training officer they'd paired her with, Artie Peluso, often covered for the minor mishaps.

But there were some things she had to take accountability for whether he wanted to protect her or not. What happened on the Cook case was one of them.

"Shit," she muttered.

"The Cook family." Turner said, "LT, you remember this?"

Noah leaned forward to look at the dates on the photo that filled Josie's screen. "Before my time. I joined the department two years after Josie."

"I was a rookie," Josie said. "My field training officer, Artie Peluso, and I responded to a 911 call in the historic district."

Josie started clicking through reports, scanning them to

refresh her memory. "Evan and Amelia Cook had three children and they were hosting a student from Ireland through
some program. Not an exchange program, something else. They
were having extensive carpentry work done in their home. It
went on for months. They'd hired this guy named Roger Bell.
He had done work for a lot of families in that neighborhood. If I
recall, he came highly recommended by neighbors."

She clicked through more of the file until she found his mug
shot. Shaggy dark hair hung to his shoulders. A tattoo of a black
snake curled up one side of his neck. Only slivers of his brown
irises were visible thanks to his two black eyes. Most of his face
was swollen and bruised. A deep cut scored his lower lip. Back
then, a lot of the officers on the Denton PD weren't above
roughing up suspects who "resisted arrest." Those suspects, like
Roger Bell, were usually being arrested for heinous crimes. Not
that that made it right. Josie hadn't heard anything, but she'd bet
her paycheck that's what had happened based on the photo
filling the screen. She'd never met Roger Bell in person. After
being called to the initial scene, her involvement in the case was
over.

Gretchen went back to her desk. "I'm going to access the
file, too. Print out some stuff. This will go faster with both of us
going over it."

Josie skimmed over more of the reports, reading off the
pertinent information. "A witness reported that Roger Bell
became fixated on the foreign student, Miranda O'Malley. She
was sixteen."

"How old was Bell?" asked Noah.

Josie went back to his arrest information. "Twenty-two."

Gretchen continued searching the Cook file. "Let's see," she
mumbled under her breath. "Here we go. A witness reported
that Miranda became uncomfortable with the amount of attention Bell was giving her and the nature of it and told the Cooks.
They fired him. He kept coming back around though,

convinced that Miranda reciprocated his feelings. One day, Mr. Cook threatened to call the police. Bell left but he came back soon after and stabbed everyone in the house."

"Seems like Mr. Bell didn't take rejection very well," Turner said.

There was so much Josie didn't remember about the Cook case—things she had never known since she wasn't involved in the investigation—but she remembered, even now, how normal everything had seemed when she and Peluso pulled up to the sprawling Victorian. It was late afternoon, nearing dinner. Kids played and rode their bikes in the street. It was springtime. Warm. Some neighbors had their windows open. The smell of meals being cooked filled the air. A television in a nearby house played a talk show, its sound up high, the host discussing summer reads.

"Why this case?" asked Turner. "Why is the killer trying to recreate this scene?"

Josie pulled up the crime scene photos again and started clicking through them slowly. They'd been taken out of order and in the file, they were arranged haphazardly. Typically, photos of crime scenes located indoors were taken starting outside the building at the nearest intersection and then coming in closer until they moved to the interior. Then each room on each floor was photographed as well as the backyard and garage, if necessary. Crime scenes were documented that way so that when the case went to court, the prosecutor could more easily make jurors feel as though they'd been there. It also helped them to grasp the layout of the building.

The photos in the Cook file were shuffled around with the backyard first, then the street view, then the foyer. Josie remembered standing in that foyer, inhaling the coppery scent of blood even before they'd found the bodies. The next series of pictures were from the second floor. With each photo, more memories returned. The way her heart had thundered in her chest as she and Peluso cleared each room. How hard it had been to stay upright, to take every step carefully and methodically when she was dizzy from adrenaline. The phantom fingers of terror that crawled up the back of her neck, leaving her unsettled even after the house was cleared.

Shaking off the sensations of that day, Josie kept sifting through the photos of the second floor. The master bedroom, pristine with its bed made. The bathroom crammed with toiletries for six people. The bedroom shared by the youngest and eldest sister—each side markedly different, one outfitted for a toddler and the other for a young girl on the verge of being a teenager. Miranda O'Malley's bedroom, messy with clothes strewn across the bed and on the floor. A backpack overstuffed with makeup, clothes, and books sat next to the door. One of the night tables and her desk chair crowded the door as well. The small wooden desk had been pulled away from the wall. Josie hadn't really registered those details that day but now it looked like she'd been rearranging furniture. The final bedroom belonged to the Cooks' teenage son. It, too, was in the kind of disarray one would expect to see in a teen's inner sanctum. Discarded clothes on the floor around the bed. Empty soda cans on every available surface. On the bed was an overturned backpack with items spilling out of it: books, a magazine with a big-busted, scantily clad woman on the cover, pens, gum, chewing tobacco, an iPod, a slim brown leather case of some sort, and earphones.

It was all so normal. A bustling household. Snapshots of a family on any given day. But one floor down: bloody carnage.

Josie took a deep breath as the first pictures of the downstairs flashed across the screen. "Here," she said. "This is the scene he's recreating—well, the scenes. Look closely. What's missing?"

Twice they went through the relevant photos. Then Noah

said, "The knife. Our killer left it at each scene. There's no knife in the Cook family crime scene photos."

"I haven't gotten that far." Gretchen clicked her mouse furiously. "Bell took it with him?"

"No, it was there. I saw it with my own eyes." This part of the case Josie remembered more clearly because of the shit-storm that had followed. "It was in the kitchen. It just wasn't photographed."

Other than the blood pooling and streaking the tile floor and spattered across the cabinets and walls, the kitchen looked unre-markable. Dishes dried in the rack next to the sink. Lined up neatly on the countertop were appliances, a butcher block, and a utensil jar. Appointment cards and children's drawings covered the fridge. The normalcy cradling the horror always bothered Josie.

"The knife wasn't photographed?" Turner's fingers drummed against his thigh. "How is that even possible?"

Noah met Josie's eyes. "Hugh Weaver."

She held his gaze. "He was the crime scene tech that day. He was supposed to have help, but the other guys were late. He started anyway."

"He was drunk," Noah filled in.

"Yes," said Josie. "I thought he was. Peluso thought so, too."

Gretchen arched a brow. "Is that why he missed the knife? Because he was inebriated?"

"That's not the only reason." Josie pushed the rest of the story out before she lost her nerve. How Lampson had arrived on-scene and immediately zeroed in on a group of teenage girls. How he'd cornered one of them. How she'd looked like a defenseless rabbit staring into the gaping jaw of an apex preda-tor. "She was Miranda O'Malley's best friend. Lived nearby. Lampson maintained that was the only reason he needed to talk to her so badly. I found out later that he wanted her to get into the back of his car and wait for him so he could take her to the stationhouse to get her statement. She didn't want to get in."

"Knowing Frisk," said Noah, voice filled with disgust, "he would have made a stop on the way there."

Josie said, "I couldn't just stand by."

The rage that had filled her entire body that day was imprinted on her. Unimaginable carnage had waited inside the house, and Lampson couldn't care less. He was too busy doing what he always did. What he was never held accountable for—harassing teenage girls.

"Oh shit," Turner said, "You left your post, didn't you?"

Josie looked up at him. "I got another officer, Dusty Branson, to come up on the porch to take my place."

"So what was the problem?" Turner asked.

"I was a hothead back then."

It had taken her years to be able to control her anger.

Noah knew her better than anyone. "You went after Lampson."

FORTY-NINE

Josie sighed. She wanted to look anywhere but at her colleagues, but the one thing she would not do was try to escape accountability for her screw-ups. Raising her chin, she said, "Yeah. I ran down to the sidewalk. I pushed him. Hard. He fell. It wasn't pretty. I said a whole bunch of things I shouldn't have said."

"Bet it felt good, though," said Gretchen as her index finger kept hammering her computer mouse.

It had. Until the consequences of her actions came back to bite her in the ass.

"It was quite the commotion. Weaver came to the door, pushed Dusty right out of the way and came outside. Peluso left the back and came around to separate us. Bud Ernst was supposed to be covering the back for Peluso but then he came around, too. When additional units showed up, we were all out front, shouting at one another. Dusty left the front door when things got heated between Peluso and Lampson."

"Both entrances were unattended," Noah said. "Anyone could have gotten in and messed with things."

This part Josie remembered more vividly than the rest

because of all the blowback when it came time for Kellan Neal to put Roger Bell on trial. "That's exactly what the defense attorney argued in his motion to suppress evidence. When Hugh Weaver went back in, the knife wasn't there. He didn't even realize that it was gone. No one did. He took the rest of his photos. The other members of the ERT showed up to help but they didn't find the knife either. Later, Lampson went back and found it under a radiator. No one ever did figure out what happened, but the theory was that Weaver kicked it when he rushed outside to see what the commotion was about."

"Are you serious, Quinn?" Turner reached into his pocket and took his phone out but this time, he didn't scroll, just held it in his hand. "That can't be real shit. That is beyond incompetence. It's—I'm not sure I even believe you."

Josie hooked a thumb over her shoulder toward the computer screen. "It's all in there. Ernst was fired. Weaver was suspended for months. He was fired for something else several years later, although I'm pretty sure once the dust settled, he found work elsewhere."

"Still don't believe this horseshit," Turner said. "Although if you're right that these murders are about the Cook family, the polaroids make a hell of a lot of sense. But man, how the hell did anyone get away with that shit? It's not just incompetence. It's dereliction of duty. Negligence."

Noah crossed his arms over his chest, body turning slightly to face Turner. "I'm not saying this in anyone's defense, but we're talking fifteen years ago. The department was corrupt from top to bottom. How do you think that sex-trafficking ring survived and thrived for so long?"

Josie said, "The Chief back then, before Wayland Harris took the job, protected all of the officers involved. Peluso and I didn't get fired because we made sure someone took over our posts before we left them. Branson should have been fired but,

like Lampson, he was under the protection of the network of
men who needed to keep their crimes under wraps. Plus, the
girl—Miranda O'Malley's best friend—refused to file a
complaint against him. Wouldn't give us a statement. I don't
think her name is even in the file. Even if she had tried to report
him, like I said, he was protected."

"After Josie busted that sex-trafficking ring, there were only
a handful of us left," Noah said. "When she became interim
chief, it took months for her to fill all the vacancies."

Gretchen raised a hand. "I took one of them. It was a bit of a
shitshow when I got here, with the rebuild."

Turner's thumb brushed the side of his phone, like he was
itching to press the start button, log in, and start scrolling.
"Kellan Neal must have been apoplectic."

"He was," Josie said. "When he realized just how badly
things had been screwed up. He did his best to salvage the
case." Turning back to her computer, she read through more
documents, trying to recall exactly what had happened after the
debacle with the knife. She hadn't followed the rest of the case
that closely. She was too busy trying to obliterate her memories
of the scene and her screw-up with Wild Turkey.

Gretchen beat her to it, reading off the facts as she located
them. "There were witnesses who saw Roger Bell entering the
Cook residence. Other witnesses who saw him only a block
away after the murders, covered in blood. Unfortunately, his
clothes were never found. Once he was arrested, he refused to
talk."

"But Quinn saw the knife," Turner said. "That didn't
count?"

Josie sighed. "I saw it when I first went in. Peluso didn't
notice it, but I did. I was willing to testify to that, but the judge
ruled in favor of the defense and the knife was kept out."

The ancient printer sputtered to life. Gretchen stood up

and walked over to it, waiting for the pages to emerge in the output tray. Once she had what she needed, she walked to the corkboard. The rest of them watched as she pinned a photo from the Cook crime scene under a photo from their present-day scenes.

She narrated as she went. "Evan Cook was the father. The positioning of his body most closely resembles the way our killer staged Cleo Tate's body."

Evan Cook had been stabbed in the front parlor, just off the foyer. He had turned on his side after being attacked. He'd been found with one hand gripping the edge of a chair, as if he'd tried to pull himself up.

"Amelia Cook was his wife," Gretchen went on, pinning another photo over part of the map, nowhere near their present-day crime scene photos. "The mother. Her body position doesn't match up with any of our victims."

Although the pictures showed the individual victims, Josie remembered from just having perused the file that Amelia had been found in the hall that led from the foyer to the dining room, her body like a discarded marionette, rolled partially onto her shoulder, her arms twisted round one another.

Turner's fingertips beat out a rhythm on his thigh. "You mean any of the victims we've found *so far*."

Ignoring him, Gretchen took another photo and put it under Stella Townsend's crime scene picture. "Iris Cook. Thirteen years old. Daughter of Evan and Amelia. She was found in the breakfast room, on her stomach like she was trying to crawl away. Then there's the visiting student, Miranda O'Malley. She was found near Iris. Her positioning matches that of Everly Rowe."

Miranda's photo went beneath Everly's—both on their backs, one arm flung outward, each one bearing the most stab wounds because Miranda was Bell's main target. She'd been found in the corner of the room, behind the overturned table. Josie wondered if there would have been less bloodshed if Bell had found Miranda alone at the home, or had he always intended to kill them all?

Empty-handed, Gretchen turned toward them. "Then you've got another kid, Simon Cook, seventeen years old. Found in the kitchen, stabbed in the back. Finally, a toddler, Felicity Cook, three years old, also in the kitchen, stabbed once in the abdomen and once in the chest. No photos of them."

Josie's mouth was suddenly dry. The memory she'd worked so hard to bury for the last fifteen years came rushing back. Peluso dropping to his knees beside the boy, finding a pulse, rolling him over to find tiny Felicity Cook sheltered beneath her brother's body. Peluso had immediately started working on Simon while Josie did what she could to keep the life from draining out of the tiny girl's fragile body, at least until the EMTs arrived.

"There are no photos," Josie choked out. "Not from the scene. They were both alive when we got there."

Noah said, "Did they survive?"

Josie remembered getting the news from Peluso a week later that the girl had finally been upgraded to stable condition. He'd known how badly shaken Josie had been from trying to save her. "I'm pretty sure Felicity survived," Josie said. "But I don't know about Simon. I wasn't involved in anything more than the initial call and I didn't follow it. I was just trying to keep my head above water back then, being new, and after the disaster with the murder weapon, I didn't much want to think about it."

She didn't mention the way she'd spiraled into alcohol use.

Gretchen returned to her desk, clicking her mouse a few times. "They both survived, at least until trial. The charges against Bell for those two victims were attempted murder."

Turner went back to his desk, sitting and tossing his basketball at the net over and over, missing every time. "So what are we looking at here? It's obviously some kind of revenge tour, targeting everyone in law enforcement who screwed up the scene and got the knife kept out. But why?"

Josie spun her chair around to face him. "Because Roger Bell was acquitted of all charges. He went free."

FIFTY

"Are you kidding me, sweetheart?" Turner went perfectly still, which was weird since normally, he was in a perpetual state of motion. Then, with a groan, he took one of the two dollars in the jar on his desk and pushed it down into Josie's, which was already full to bursting. "Let me try this again. Are you fucking kidding me?"

Gretchen angled her computer screen so they could all see the court dockets. The not guiltys seemed to go on forever. "Josie's right."

Noah rubbed at his jaw. His five o'clock shadow had appeared while they were on shift. That was how long they'd been chasing the Polaroid Killer. "I don't remember this case."

Josie stood and leaned across her desk, peering at the documents Gretchen had pulled up. "The trial concluded two years after the murders. You would have just joined the department."

"How was this guy not convicted though?" asked Turner, picking up his basketball and squeezing it in his fist like a stress ball. "Two victims survived."

Josie vaguely remembered the grumblings in the department after Bell got off. Back then, the men she worked with were more concerned about the fact that Bell's acquittal made them all look stupid than with the reality that a mass murderer was walking the streets again. Only Peluso was well and truly stricken. She tried to call up the details of their conversations about the case or the news reports, but nothing came to her.

Taking her seat again, she opened her internet browser and searched for the case. A few minutes later, she had some answers. "Simon Cook testified at trial that he was upstairs in his bedroom when the stabbings occurred. He said he heard screams and ran downstairs where he found his entire family and Miranda O'Malley bleeding."

"He didn't see Bell?" asked Gretchen.

Josie kept reading. "He testified that when he entered the breakfast room, Bell was straddling Miranda, stabbing her. Felicity was near the doorway to the kitchen, making noises." She had to stop for a moment, remembering the gurgling in the tiny girl's throat.

Sensing her distress, Noah rolled his chair over and gently pushed her aside. He scrolled through the rest of the article she'd found. "Simon went on to testify that he picked up his little sister and fled toward the back door. Once inside the kitchen, he was stabbed from behind. On cross-examination, the defense attorney got him to admit that given his account and the position of the furniture in the breakfast room, there was no way he could have actually seen Bell's face. Apparently, his initial statements to police were inconsistent with his trial testimony.

"The prosecution argued that the inconsistencies were minor especially given that his family had just been slaughtered and he had just been stabbed three times, but I guess it was too damaging to his credibility. Evidently, Bell's defense was that someone else had been bothering Miranda, not him, and that he'd returned to the Cook house that day to check on her and found everyone stabbed. The 'it wasn't me' defense. I guess between that and the inconsistencies in Simon's testimony, it was enough to put reasonable doubt into the minds of the jurors."

Turner gave a low whistle. "And they let Bell walk. Damn."

Josie sighed. "Without the knife, which had Bell's DNA on it, there wasn't enough to convict."

A few moments passed in silence while they absorbed the information. Turner spoke first. "So we're looking for the kid, then. The brother. What's his name? Simon Cook?"

Gretchen sat back in her chair, causing it to creak. "It deeply, deeply pains me to say this but I think you're right."

Turner grinned so wide he looked almost feral. "I don't know what's more satisfying, Palmer. That you agree with me or that I've caused you to be, what was that? 'Deeply pained.'"

Before Gretchen could jab back at him, Noah said, "It makes sense. He's getting revenge on the people whose mistakes allowed Bell to go free by making them go through what he went through—losing a family member to violence. The knife at each scene and the polaroids are direct references to the screw-up."

"But why now?" Josie said. "It's been fifteen years since the murders. A little less since the trial. Why wait all this time? What triggered this?"

"Maybe he was just working up the nerve," Turner said. "Who cares? All that matters is that we find him. We got a picture of this kid?"

Josie found one in the Cook file that showed Simon's face. It had been taken in the hospital when the police were documenting his injuries. In it, his sandy hair was cut close to his scalp. He had a round, chubby face. Josie remembered how heavy he'd been when she and Peluso turned him over. How surprised she was when she realized his weight hadn't smothered his little sister. In the photo, his dark eyes were glassy. He looked almost high but then again, he was probably on a lot of pain medication while recovering from his wounds. She printed it and then hung it on the corkboard before taking a moment to study it again.

Turner said, "Look like anyone you've seen recently, Quinn?"

"No," she admitted. She tried to imagine Simon Cook's face fifteen years later. Had he lost weight? Had his features sharpened at all? Was his hair grown out?

Noah pushed his chair back to his own desk. "I'm going to find out where this kid is now—and his surviving sister. If we can find him, then we don't need to figure out where the last polaroid was taken."

It was the best lead they had. The best they'd had in days and yet, something told Josie that locating Simon Cook wasn't going to be as easy as it seemed.

"See if you can find his grandmother, too," Turner said. "Since she's paying guys to let her steal cars for this asshole."

The stairwell door whooshed open, sending all the crime scene photos pinned to the corkboard fluttering. Chief Chitwood strode in with Amber trailing behind him, her trusty tablet in hand. The two of them stopped next to the corkboard. "I need an update," said the Chief. "We're gonna have to put something together for the press or Kellan Neal's going to start tearing us a new one on television at four, five, six, eleven and whenever the hell else WYEP airs their news. Not to mention he called the Mayor, so now I got her breathing down my damn neck. So let's hear it, and make it good."

Josie brought him up to speed on everything they'd figured out in the last several hours. As she spoke, Amber took rapid notes on her tablet. When she finished, the Chief said, "Yeah. All right. Find that Cook kid, then. I'll hold off as long as I can on making any statements or releasing any information. But for godssake, do it fast."

Someone's cell phone rang. Everyone looked around. "Chief," Amber said. "It's you."

"Oh, right." He took his phone from his pocket and growled at it. "That's the damn Mayor again. Amber, you're with me. My office. Help me put this fire out."

They disappeared into the Chief's office, the door slamming shut behind them.

"You think this Cook kid took Bell out first?" asked Turner. "That's what I would have done."

Gretchen looked over at him, one brow severely arched. "You know that thing on your desk with the screen and the keyboard? It works. Try it out. Maybe you can find out what happened to Roger Bell and if he's still alive."

With a scowl, Turner placed his basketball onto his desk and pulled his keyboard toward him. Josie was surprised he even knew how to work the damn thing given how terrible his reports were and how long it took him to file them. Under his breath, he mumbled, "What are you gonna be doing?"

Gretchen plucked a dry-erase marker from her desk drawer and brandished it at him. "I'm going to try to figure out his next target."

"His next target is already dead," Turner said flatly.

"Not necessarily." Gretchen strode over to the corkboard and spun it so that the other side, a dry-erase board, faced their desks. "He left the polaroid for the church four days before he killed Everly Rowe, even though we didn't find it right away. There's still a chance his next victim hasn't been taken yet, which means there's a chance we can find them before the killer strikes again."

FIFTY-ONE

Along one side of the whiteboard, Gretchen scrawled the names of people who had been present at the Cook scene. Frisk Lampson, Hugh Weaver, Josie, Artie Peluso, Dusty Branson, Bud Ernst.

Josie joined Gretchen at the board. She held her hand out and Gretchen gave her the marker. "I've been thinking about this, but there's a problem. This guy is targeting children and grandchildren, right? I don't have children." She crossed off her name.

Over his shoulder, Noah said, "Branson's in prison. He never had kids."

Josie drew a line through his name. "Peluso has two sons. One is a gunnery sergeant in the Marine Corps and last I heard, he was stationed overseas. His other son is an FBI agent working out of the Minneapolis field office."

Gretchen frowned. "We should make sure they're still alive and accounted for, though."

Josie nodded but crossed off Peluso's name as well. Then she put a final line through the last name on the list. "Bud Ernst never had children."

"What if it's not just children?" Gretchen suggested. "What if it's any family member? A spouse? A sibling?"

A chill enveloped Josie's body as the faces of Noah and Trinity flashed through her mind. But Noah could more than handle himself and even though Trinity was still staying with them, so was Drake. She couldn't be safer.

"Neal wasn't there that day," Turner pointed out. "He was still targeted."

Josie shook off the fear needling her. "True."

"If he's not limiting himself to people who were at the scene," Gretchen said, "who's left? The Chief at the time? He covered for Lampson and Branson, too."

"He's dead," Josie said. "But I guess we could still check on his family."

"You girls—" Turner broke off when Josie and Gretchen turned to glower at him. "Ladies... no? Women?"

"Detectives," Josie said. "Just say detectives."

He shook his head and muttered, "Everything's gotta be so hard."

"Turner," Josie snapped.

"Okay, okay. You detectives should start making some phone calls."

Two hours later, they were still at their desks, exhausted, weary and with more questions than answers. In the past month, Artie Peluso's wife had been killed in a hit-and-run accident in the town where they lived in South Jersey. Dusty Branson's mother had fallen down the steps of her home in Maryland and broken her neck. Bud Ernst had been strangled to death in an apparent home invasion in the Poconos, where he'd retired. None of the crimes had occurred in Denton PD's jurisdiction. A call to the police department handling Ernst's homicide revealed that no polaroid had been found at the crime scene.

None of it seemed coincidental. All of it sent Josie's heart into overdrive. Hers was the only name left on the list, but another round of phone calls assured her that everyone she loved was safe and accounted for and now, all of them had been warned. Shannon, Christian, Patrick, and Brenna were going to spend the next few days in Callowhill, which was two hours away. Chief Chitwood had agreed to let Misty, Harris, and Cindy Quinn, Harris's grandmother, stay at his farmhouse. Drake and Trinity refused to leave. Josie didn't press the issue since she was confident her sister was safe with Drake.

The search for Simon and Felicity Cook, as well as Roger Bell, turned up nothing.

"Simon and Felicity stopped existing after the trial," Noah said. "There's nothing, although I found an old story on the WYEP website that said after the murders, they were separated and put into foster care. I guess there was no family nearby or willing to take them in. The articles don't reference any family members other than Miranda O'Malley's parents, who flew over from Ireland to attend the trial."

"So no grandmother?" said Turner.

"I searched Amelia and Evan Cooks' names to see if I could locate their parents," said Gretchen. "Amelia's parents were still alive at the time of the trial, but her mother died two years later and her father died shortly after. Maybe an aunt or something?"

Noah sighed. "Mapping out the Cook family tree could take some time."

Chief Chitwood's door flew open. He poked his head out and hollered, "Fraley!" even though Noah was right there. "Get in here. We need to talk about exactly what we're going to release to the press at this point."

As Noah disappeared into the Chief's office, Turner said, "Let's get the foster care records."

"We can try," said Josie. "But I doubt we'll be able to without anything connecting Simon Cook directly to any of the current murders. We don't have enough probable cause for a warrant. All we have is a theory that he's behind these killings."

Gretchen pushed a hand through her spiked hair. "Shit."

Apparently unconcerned, Turner went back to scrolling on his phone. "In case you were wondering, Bell existed for a couple of years after the trial and then poof! Gone. Nothing. No records."

"They changed their names," Josie suggested. "If Simon and Felicity were adopted, they might have taken on their adoptive families' names. It would make sense to do it, especially if they were worried that Bell might try to finish what he started."

"If I'm Roger Bell, and this whole city knows I'm a stone-cold killer," said Turner, "I'd change my name, too."

A headache started to pulse in Josie's temples. She fished through her desk drawers until she came up with a bottle of ibuprofen.

Gretchen said, "You can't look up name changes. The records are sealed by the courts."

Josie tossed two ibuprofen into her mouth and swallowed them dry. "Sealed records," she echoed. Is that what Stella Townsend had been after? Her grandfather's involvement in the Cook case? She would have been able to glean most of the details from public sources since the murders and the trial were covered widely in the local press. Was she trying to track down the Cook children for some reason? They'd searched Stella's laptop and found lots of notes pertaining to Frisk Lampson and her wide-ranging ideas for an exposé, but Josie didn't recall seeing any mention of the Cook case. Then again, up until the day she was murdered, she was still meeting with Remy Tate in hopes of getting the information she was after.

"We're back to the polaroid," Gretchen said. "Unless we can figure out a way to find Simon or Felicity Cook."

"There's no one left for this guy to kill," Turner said. "We're missing someone on the list."

Josie turned toward the dry-erase board and silently read off the names again. Her, Lampson, Weaver, Peluso, Branson, Ernst, and Neal. They'd been looking strictly at law enforcement and the prosecution, but the names on the list weren't the only people who'd contributed to Roger Bell going free.

The overwhelming fatigue Josie had been fighting all evening receded, replaced by a buzz of anxiety. "We overlooked someone. Someone major," she said. "Bell's defense attorney. He wrote and filed the motion that kept the knife out of evidence. He was just doing his job but he was good at it."

"He still live around here?" Turner asked. "Does he have kids?"

Quickly, Josie pulled up the dockets and found the name. The contents of her stomach curdled. "Yes and yes," she said.

"Who is it?" Turner's eyebrows knit with what looked like concern. "Quinn, you okay? You look sick or something."

"Bell's defense attorney was Andrew Bowen, and he *hates* me. I put his mother in prison for murder."

FIFTY-TWO

The ibuprofen Josie had taken at the stationhouse burned a hole in her gut. Just sitting outside Andrew Bowen's house in her parked car, in the dark, sent a coil of anxiety slithering up her spine. She tried to recall how many children there'd been in the framed family photo she'd seen the last time she was in his office. That was years ago, which meant the children would be teenagers by now. Two? Three? At least one girl.

"I should do this," Gretchen said from the passenger's seat. "He's fairly neutral when it comes to me."

Turner rapped against Josie's window. "Are we going to do this or what?"

"We should let Douchebag do it," Josie suggested.

"That's not a bad idea. I'm pretty sure he and Bowen speak the same language."

Under any other circumstances, Josie would have laughed but she couldn't stop thinking that the next victim could be a kid. They got out of the car, joining Turner in the driveway that meandered up to Bowen's palatial estate. This is what defending people had bought him. Josie had no doubt many of his clients were innocent, but he had also represented a man who'd slaughtered a family, a man whose DNA was on the murder weapon, and celebrated his acquittal.

Josie wondered if Andrew Bowen ever lost sleep over Roger Bell walking free.

Probably not.

They let Turner take the lead, ringing the doorbell in rapid fashion until Gretchen hissed at him to stop. It was after one in the morning. Lights blinked on inside. A surveillance camera affixed to the doorframe sent out a burst of static. Then Bowen's voice squawked through. "Can I help you?"

"Andrew Bowen?" Turner said.

"Yes, can I help you?"

Turner took out his ID and shoved it against the eye of the camera. "Denton PD. We need to talk. We think one of your kids might be in danger."

The door swung open. Andrew Bowen stood before them in a faded Duquesne T-shirt and gray sweatpants. Pushing a hand through his blond hair, he blinked. "Did you say one of my children is in danger?"

Gretchen stepped forward. "Yes. You have three children, correct?"

Bowen shook his head. "Wait, wait. Is this some kind of prank?"

"I'm afraid not," Turner said. "How old are your kids?"

"My kids are asleep in their beds," Bowen snapped. "I don't know where you're getting your information but it's incorrect. Now, I'd appreciate it if you left us alone."

A soft female voice called out from behind Bowen. "Andy? Is everything okay?"

"Yes, Evelyn. Just a case of mistaken identity."

"I promise you, it's not," said Gretchen.

"Good night, Detectives." Bowen started to close the door.

Josie muscled her way between Gretchen and Turner and wedged her foot between the door and its frame. "Bowen, please. Hear me out."

A pale face, framed by brown curls, glared at her from over Bowen's shoulder. "What is *she* doing here?"

"*She* works for the Denton Police Department," Turner said. "*She* is here doing her job. *You* are making it harder by not listening to us. Go check on your fucking kids."

"Turner," Gretchen admonished, but her tone was soft.

Josie kept her foot inside the door. She was grateful for the thickness of her boot because Andrew Bowen continued to try to close the door on it. Still, it smarted. Quashing her desire to pull it back, Josie tried to keep her tone reasonable, unemotional. There was a lot of history between the two of them, none of it good. If the Bowens weren't inclined to listen to Turner or Gretchen, then there was little to no chance of them entertaining Josie's explanation, but she had to try. There could be a girl out there, already dead, or at the mercy of a killer.

Josie wasn't leaving her post again.

"Please," she said. "Mr. and Mrs. Bowen. You know I would not be here unless it was critically important. You can keep hating me. Call me every name in the book. Spit on me." She inhaled sharply as Bowen increased pressure on her foot. "Crush my foot."

Turner's long arm reached around her and pushed the door, easily sending Bowen stumbling backward. He bumped into his wife, who cried out. "Are you crazy?"

Josie said, "The person who killed Cleo Tate, Stella Townsend, and Everly Rowe is targeting people involved in the Cook family murders. Do you remember that case, Bowen?"

He blinked again, paling. "Roger Bell was my client."

"I don't remember that," Evelyn said, wrapping a hand around his upper arm.

"I'd only been practicing a couple of years. Bell didn't have much money. He couldn't afford me, really, but I needed the work and no one else would take his case."

"Because he was a murderer," Gretchen said.

Turner scoffed. "I'm pretty sure that's not a problem for defense attorneys."

Evelyn stared at the side of her husband's face. "That's unusual, isn't it? That no one else wanted his case?"

Andrew blew out a breath. "Not because of guilt or innocence. Everyone is entitled to legal representation. It was because he was broke. He was acquitted."

Josie flexed her foot. "That doesn't mean he wasn't guilty."

"Andrew?" Evelyn said, a question in her voice.

Andrew Bowen remained impassive. Josie was certain Bell wasn't the only guilty person Bowen had successfully defended. Maybe the most violent, but not the only one.

"Someone is killing the children and grandchildren of everyone connected to the Cook case," Josie said. "Not just those of us who screwed up at the scene that day."

"Kellan Neal—Cleo Tate's father—was the prosecutor," Gretchen said. "He failed to keep the murder weapon in evidence."

Bowen swallowed. "I'm terribly sorry that Kellan's daughter was killed. He's a good man and he was an admirable opponent in the courtroom, but this has nothing to do with me or my family. I did my job. All of you did not."

"You're really thick, Counselor," Turner said. "It's because you did your job so well that we think you're the next target. Not you, specifically, but one of your kids. Probably the oldest girl. You've got daughters, right?"

Before Bowen could answer, Evelyn was gone. All Josie could see were the backs of her calves as she raced up the steps in the grand foyer behind her husband.

Bowen didn't react. Like Kellan Neal, he was a skilled litigator, a master at concealing his true emotions. "We have one daughter. Our oldest. Juliet. She's sixteen."

Evelyn's screams cut through the stillness of the house. Josie felt them like a thousand daggers piercing her heart. It didn't matter to her that the Bowens hated her or that Andrew had consistently proven himself to be morally questionable—his career as a defense attorney notwithstanding. At the end of the day, they were just parents whose lives would be irreparably shattered when they lost their child.

No. *If* they lost their child.

Josie knew her optimism was misguided and unrealistic but she couldn't help it.

"Andy! Andy!" Evelyn's feet slapped against the hardwood steps as she raced back toward them, clutching something against her nightgown. Her eyes were wide and terrified, gleaming with tears. "She's gone. Juliet's gone. Her bed is still made and... this... this was on top of her pillow."

The hand pressed to her chest unfurled, trembling so badly that Andrew grabbed her wrist to steady it. "I don't understand," he said.

Josie took a step forward, crossing the threshold even though they hadn't invited her inside. She felt Turner and Gretchen at her back, leaning in to see what was in Evelyn's palm.

"Is that..." Turner started.

"It is," Gretchen said.

"Shit," the two of them said in unison.

A polaroid danced in Evelyn's quivering palm. Blood smudged the pristine white edges.

Gretchen said, "Can you tell what it shows? Is it as blurry as the last ones?"

"What last ones?" Bowen said, voice sharper now.

Josie's lips worked to reply, to tell Gretchen that it wasn't blurred or distorted. This one was as crisp and clear as was possible for a polaroid. But she couldn't speak. A dizzying wave of pure terror threatened to crash over her and then suddenly, she was floating above the Bowens' front step, looking down on the five of them as they peered at a polaroid picture of the shelf in hers and Noah's living room where their wedding picture was displayed.

FIFTY-THREE

Gretchen was talking but Josie couldn't hear her over the roar of blood in her ears. She was vaguely aware of the odor of burning rubber. Her brain registered how white her knuckles were, wrapped around the steering wheel of her SUV, and how fast the city streets flew past the windows. Her brain told her there was pain in the ball of her right foot as it held the gas pedal against the floor of the vehicle, but she couldn't feel it. She couldn't feel her body at all. At least she was in it again. Mostly. Horns blared as she fishtailed through an intersection on a red light.

Gretchen's body snapped back and forth. Josie was pretty sure she was shouting something, but adrenaline had temporarily suspended her hearing. Her entire physical being had been pushed aside to make room for one driving thought.

Home. She had to get home.

She blasted through another intersection, this time almost hitting a car. The SUV lurched to the side. For a heartbeat, Josie thought it was going to tip onto its side. Then all four tires met asphalt again and in the rearview mirror, she saw smoke billowing from behind her as the SUV strained against its limits.

Home. She had to get home.

She wasn't operating on any conscious level but something in her told her she was close to her house. Close to finding them —Trout, Trinity, Drake. Alive or dead? Surely Simon Cook and his accomplice, assuming he had one, were no match for Drake.

Noah's voice cut through Josie's protective mental cocoon like it was made of air. Gretchen held her cell phone to Josie's ear, set to speaker. "Josie," he said, her name on his lips like an answer to all her prayers. She'd known he wasn't at home. She had left him at the stationhouse. But there had been some irrational part of her that still feared for his life. Josie tried to speak again, like she'd tried on the Bowens' threshold, but still, nothing came.

Gretchen said, "I don't think she can talk right now."

"Josie," Noah said. "I'm on my way there right now. I'll meet you."

There was some short exchange between him and Gretchen and then he hung up. Josie's mind was stuck on the fact that he hadn't told her that he'd called Drake and Trinity and that one of them had answered and told him they were fine. So was Trout. Noah would have just said that if he could. It was the only thing she needed to hear. Noah always knew what she needed.

"They're probably sleeping," Gretchen said. "Do they sleep with their phones turned off or the sound muted?"

She didn't know. Why didn't she know? That seemed like something she should know about her own sister and her fiancé.

As the more rational part of her brain started coming back online, it tried to soothe her by reminding her that their surveillance cameras would have sent notifications to their phones if someone had broken in.

Except someone had broken in to take the photo and no notifications were received, the panicked part of her shouted back. They didn't have cameras covering every angle outside of the house.

Another drifting turn, tires squealing, Gretchen crying out, and they were on Josie's street. Noah was there, his vehicle parked diagonally across the driveway, driver's side door slung open. Josie took the curb next to the driveway, slamming on the brakes so hard, her forehead almost hit the steering wheel. Then she was pounding up her own front steps, closing the distance to Noah as he fumbled with the lock.

Before he could unlock it, the door opened. Noah fell forward, staggering to stay upright. Josie followed, clutching at his waist to stay on her feet. The sounds of Trout's barks brought her hysteria level down a notch. His nails clicked against the hardwood as he came down the stairs but Josie couldn't see him because Trinity and Drake stood in the middle of the foyer, both their faces foggy with sleep. Trinity held her phone, blinking as she looked from its glowing screen to them. Behind her, Drake rubbed his bare chest. Half his hair stuck straight up. "What the hell is going on?" he said, voice thick with sleep.

Trout's body brushed against Josie's legs, his barks now whimpers.

"Did something happen?" Trinity asked, sounding more alert than Drake. "Is everyone okay?"

FIFTY-FOUR

Josie squinted against the sunlight peeking around the corner of her house, its shafts stretching across her backyard. At her feet, Trout sniffed, nose never leaving the ground. It was almost as if he knew she was trying to figure something out and he wanted to help. Even though thoroughly smelling every blade of grass was not going to get them any closer to figuring out how the killer had gotten into their house to take the polaroid. She didn't hear Noah approach, but she felt his chest against her back and sagged into it. He wrapped her up in his arms, pressing a kiss to the top of her head.

"Drake and I both think he got in through the side window in the kitchen. It looks like it was messed with from the outside. He could easily have approached the house from that direction and slipped around the side without being caught on camera."

Josie sighed. "But how did he manage it? We've had nonstop guests. Even when no one is here, Trout—" She broke off. She couldn't stop thinking about Trout being in the house with a killer. He barked at people he didn't know when they came to the house, but he was not a ferocious guard dog by any means. Clearly, he wasn't even a deterrent.

"We think he was here the night of Trinity's proposal. The house was empty. Trout was with us."

In a twisted way, that eased some of Josie's anxiety. At least her sweet Trout hadn't been alone with that bastard.

"Did you talk to Turner?" she asked.

"The Bowens' house was clean. No major signs of a struggle. No evidence of a break-in and nothing on the security cameras. Turner said there were a few weak points where he could have gotten in though. An unlocked kitchen window around back. No cameras there. Other than the blood around the edges of the polaroid, there were six additional drops—four in the bedroom near the door and two in the hall. The ones in the bedroom were smeared. Anyway, Hummel typed them. They match Juliet's blood type."

Josie suppressed a shudder, imagining the Bowens finding out that the blood in their daughter's room belonged to her. It didn't matter if it was a little or a lot. Someone had broken into their home, made their child bleed, and taken her.

"Josie," Noah said. "We haven't found her."

We haven't found her body, was what he really meant. He was trying to give her hope. Not finding Juliet Bowen's body was a blessing and a curse. So far, they hadn't found a polaroid that wasn't with a body. Josie had half expected them to find Juliet's corpse somewhere inside their house. It was a relief that they hadn't but it didn't mean they wouldn't find it in another place, once they figured out that location. She was convinced that the polaroid of treetops found at the Everly Rowe scene would lead them to Juliet.

"Geofence? LPRs?" Josie said. "How did he get there? Did someone drop him off? How did he transport her?"

"We don't know how he got there but he left in one of the Bowens' cars. Drove it right out of the garage," Noah said against her temple. "There's footage of the car pulling out but it's not clear enough to see his face, only the brim of his hat.

Turner called the infotainment company. They located the car near West Denton Elementary school. We've got units searching now. Gretchen got someone from the university to bring drones. Luke and Blue are on their way."

Trout circled back to Josie's feet and pressed his nose against her boot. "She won't be there, Noah. That's not how this game is played."

And yet, the killer had changed the rules by leaving a polaroid with no body before they'd even figured out the last one.

Trout lifted his snout and pressed it against her other boot, taking short inhales. "What about Juliet's phone?"

Noah said, "It was in her room. Josie, I promise you, everything that can be done is being done."

Apparently satisfied that her boots were not of concern, Trout went back to scenting the grass. Josie turned in Noah's arms, basking in the warmth of his hazel eyes. "I don't understand what's going on. Two polaroids, no body yet. The one in Juliet's bed is so obvious. With the others, it took so long to figure out where he was leading us. Why is he changing things up now? I feel like if I could just figure out—"

His hands cupped her face. "Josie, we need to get some rest. You need to get some sleep or you won't be figuring anything out."

"But the house," she said, realizing for the first time that she was, in fact, so tired that it was getting hard to form a coherent sentence.

Noah smiled and brushed his lips over her forehead. "We'll have a unit stationed here. Trinity and Drake are getting a hotel room."

"They're not going home?"

"You know your sister. She's not going anywhere until she knows you're safe, and Drake's not going anywhere without her. At least until their bosses start complaining."

Josie managed a half-hearted laugh.

"The three of us are going to stay with Gretchen and Paula. Gretchen promised to keep her cat away from Trout." He pulled her closer until her cheek was pressed against his beating heart. "We'll figure out everything else later, after we've had some rest. While we sleep, the investigation will grind on. The Chief is on so Gretchen can sleep as well. Turner said he can work straight through until one of us comes back."

"But Juliet Bowen…" Josie said.

"No one will stop looking for her," Noah promised. "Maybe by the time we wake up, there will be some developments."

FIFTY-FIVE

She'd chosen to jog over the South Bridge this time. Alone. Tight black yoga pants hugged her curves. A matching sports bra did little to cover the way her breasts jiggled as she ran. When she had emerged from her apartment building looking like a fantasy and dressed in the same clothes she'd worn the day she'd lured him to the city park, he knew today was the day. Finally, she was ready to give herself to him. Why else would she have chosen this area of the city? It bordered farmland the next county over. Few businesses or homes had been built in this area. It didn't even look like it belonged in a city. There wasn't a lot of foot traffic or even cars. Everyone always used the East Bridge instead.

He'd followed her slowly in his car until he could predict her path. If she wanted to get him alone, she'd cross the South Bridge and wait near the little shoulder on the other side that dipped toward the riverbank below. It was shaded. Cozy. Private. Now, he stood in that very spot, his hard-on straining painfully against his pants, and waited for her. As she passed, he darted out and grabbed her, looping an arm around her slender waist and pulling her into the little alcove. She let out a scream that sent lust spiraling through his body.

"You son of a bitch! Let me go!" She scratched at his forearms and when he didn't release her, she clenched her fists and hit his arms.

He put her down and pressed her into the wall of the nearest bridge support, covering her body with his and burying his face in her neck. Her small frame went rigid. She was completely turned on.

"Why did you make me wait so long?" he asked, hands roaming her body. "Nobody likes a tease."

She slapped at his chest, pushing against him with all her might. "I'm not teasing you. There's been a misunderstanding."

He took a step back, narrowing his eyes at her. "Oh, like the last time?"

She bent to tie her shoe. "I don't want to talk about last time. In fact, we should never talk about it. To anyone."

A grin spread across his face. "You don't want me to tell your secrets."

She straightened and said nothing. That was all the confirmation he needed. He had something over her. It was surprising how good it felt. How hard it made him. This was going to be very, very fun. A tiny yelp burst through her parted lips when he lunged forward and collared her throat with one of his hands. Adorable.

He licked the side of her face, tasting the salt and sweat from her jog. "If you want me to keep your secrets, you need to give me something."

Her breath smelled like Cherry Coke. "Oh, I'll give you something," she said, only seconds before he felt a sharp, stinging pain near his belly button. He glanced down between their bodies, his brain unable to process what he was seeing. "What the hell...?"

The handle of a knife protruded from his abdomen. He

stumbled back, away from her. Both hands curled around the handle. She watched him with an unnerving grin on her face. He tried to pull it out. Were you supposed to pull a knife out, or leave it in? Why would she invite him here and then stab him? Unwilling to let her watch him, he put his back to her and focused on the river rushing along the bank thirty feet below. He hoped the blade wasn't long. Blood stained his hands.

Her feet crunched over rocks as she drew nearer. "What I really want you to do with my secrets is take them to the grave."

Something slammed into his back. His body pitched forward and fell, tumbling down the embankment, a knife inside him, until he plunged into the churning water.

FIFTY-SIX

Eight hours later, freshly showered and caffeinated, Josie shouldered her way into Hummel's inner sanctum with Noah in tow. The ERT worked out of the police impound lot. It was tucked away on a winding mountain road in North Denton, far from any significant residential developments. The lot itself was surrounded by chain-link fence and guarded by an officer in a small booth. The only building was the one they now stood inside, a flat, nondescript cinderblock structure with two garage bays on one side and two small rooms on the other: an office and the evidence processing room.

Hummel sat at the stainless-steel table in the center of the room, a laptop open in front of him. Dark circles smudged the skin under his eyes. Even with his small staff working around the clock, Josie was certain he'd gotten less sleep than anyone in the last week. Offering them a subdued smile, he said, "Welcome to hell. Have a seat."

Noah laughed and pulled out a chair for Josie before settling in next to her. "I hope you've got something for us because there weren't any miracles while we slept."

Josie didn't know what she'd expected but the news they'd

received upon waking was downright demoralizing. Even with Juliet Bowen's face plastered all over the news and social media, together with the still photos they'd gathered of the killer from previous scenes, there were no viable leads. Andrew and Evelyn Bowen had given a press conference, begging for any information that would lead to the return of their daughter. In an unusual show of solidarity, Kellan Neal had joined them. Now the press knew that there was a serial killer loose in Denton. They still hadn't gotten wind of the polaroids. Without some sort of distinct element to exploit, they hadn't been able to come up with a clever name for him, which was just fine by Josie.

There had been questions about whether the killer was targeting the children of attorneys or whether there was some connection to law enforcement generally. No one had dug up Stella's connection to Frisk Lampson or Everly Rowe's connection to Hugh Weaver, but Josie knew it was only a matter of hours before that happened. Her money was on Dallas Jones to break those stories and then start digging for more connections. In the meantime, Turner had spent some time trying to track down any living relatives of the Cook children, but the ones he'd located didn't live in Denton and were too distant to know anything that could help.

Hummel's long sigh drew her out of her thoughts. "If you're looking for miracles, a police impound lot is generally not the best place to start. I couldn't get prints from any of the keys you gave me. I got a couple of low-quality partials, but they didn't match up to anything in AFIS. I don't know what the hell this guy is doing, but I printed every vehicle you brought me, and no single set of unknown prints turns up across the board. I also didn't find any prints that match grandmotherly types in AFIS. Are you sure it's just one guy?"

"We're not sure of anything," Josie admitted. "Still trying to piece everything together. Is there anything you can tell us? Even if it doesn't seem helpful?"

Hummel laughed and stood up. "Oh, I've got tons of unhelpful things I can tell you. But only one that's new. Come on."

He led them out to the garage. Each bay held one of the classic cars they'd impounded from the back lot of Schock's Auto Repair. A blue 1990 Ford Taurus and a 1997 Chevrolet Corvette that needed a new paint job. White and gray patches dotted its faded yellow finish. "I already processed these," Hummel said, edging around to the driver's side of the Taurus. "So you can get right in, touch them, whatever."

He opened the door and gestured for one of them to get inside. Josie was closest so she climbed in. Cracks spider-legged across the dash. The singed black circle of a cigarette burn scarred the passenger's seat. There was a hole where the radio had been, two frayed wires now dangling limply from its mouth. A crusty gray ring lined the bottom of the center console cupholder.

"First of all," Hummel said, resting an arm atop the open door. "No visible blood. I did pull some latent bloodstains from all the cars we impounded. On the driver's side of the vehicle."

"How much?" Noah asked.

"You can look at the photos. It wasn't much. More in the Corvette than the other two cars but it wasn't a crazy amount. He clearly tried to clean it up."

If the latent blood was found on the driver's side, that meant the killer had driven the vehicles. Or at least, he'd driven them away from the murders. The grandmother type was looking more and more like a set-up person.

"I swabbed for DNA. Got some short dark hairs. Everything's out to the lab. Oh, and this was the only weird thing. I found it in these two vehicles, not the '92 Ford Sierra." Leaning into the car, he pointed to the lever to the right of the steering wheel responsible for shifting gears. "I took samples but you can see some still clinging there. Clear little flakes of something. I don't know what it's from but since it was in these two cars and around the shifters, I figure maybe the killer left it behind."

Hummel backed out so Noah could poke his head inside. Josie leaned to the right to give him room and get a better look at the flecks that adhered to the lever. Something in the back of her mind stirred. Memories of the past week swirled around. The way her heart rate ticked up told her that this was important, that some part of her knew why, she just had to get there.

Noah extricated himself while Josie reached out and touched one of the tiny flakes with her finger. It came off the lever and attached to her skin.

"No idea what it is?" Noah asked Hummel.

"I don't know. Some kind of glue maybe? The lab will analyze it."

She gets this shit everywhere. Everywhere.

Josie's heart did a double-tap. The killer had been right under their nose from day one. He'd offered himself up as their very first lead.

"Noah," she said. "I know where we can find Simon Cook."

FIFTY-SEVEN

The Hampton home looked almost exactly as it had when Josie and Turner arrived there the day that Cleo Tate was abducted except that this time, their remaining car was no longer in the driveway. Noah ran a search for the tag number and got it out to all their patrol units. They'd made two stops on their way, one at WYEP for a brief and fruitless conversation with Vicky Platt, who then tried to get information from them to run on their next newscast. The second stop was at Remy Tate's house. That interview had proven only marginally more useful, though Josie was still trying to fit all the pieces together in her head as she and Noah got out of their SUV.

As they walked up the front steps, Noah said, "You sure about this?"

Josie's pulse ticked upward. "As sure as I can be."

He'd already tried to find whatever information he could about the Hamptons on the drive over. They'd lived in Philadelphia until four years ago when they moved to Denton. Sheila had lived in Denton previously, but Isaac's prior addresses were all in Philadelphia, at least as far back as they were able to check. He seemed to magically come into existence twelve years ago.

His vital information didn't match up exactly with Simon Cook's but it was close. Josie wondered if Simon Cook had stolen an identity all those years ago rather than simply changing his name. Jenna Hampton had turned eighteen a few months before her death. There was no way to prove that Isaac and Jenna were really Simon and Felicity Cook without an admission from Isaac or DNA testing. There was also not enough probable cause at this juncture to arrest Isaac Hampton even if they did locate him.

Although Isaac's industrial engineer wife used glue in her prototypes and they'd found what they believed to be glue in the classic cars the killer drove from the crime scenes, it wasn't enough of a connection. If they could get samples of the glue Sheila used and the state lab could match it up with the glue found in the vehicles, that would be a start but still not enough to arrest Isaac. Which was why they hadn't brought the full force of the police department with them. All they could hope for now was to bring him into the stationhouse for a talk and hope any statement he gave was enough for them to investigate him further.

Josie rang the doorbell. When no one answered, she rang it a second time. Moments later, Sheila Hampton opened the door. Her eyes were bloodshot, face red and blotchy from crying. She barely looked at them before taking a step backward. The door began to close. "This isn't a good time."

"Please, Mrs. Hampton," Noah said. "We wouldn't bother you if it wasn't vitally important."

"It's about your husband," Josie added.

Sheila hesitated. One of her hands was curled tightly around the edge of the door. "He's not here, so maybe come back later."

"Do you know where we can find him?" asked Noah.

She shook her head. Maybe it was grief over the loss of her daughter. It wasn't out of the realm of possibility. Josie knew better than anyone the way it could catch you off guard months or even years after the loss. Yet, she suspected something else was at play. There was a strange tension rolling off Sheila Hampton that put all of Josie's senses on high alert.

"When was the last time you saw him?" Noah pressed.

"Um, earlier today. This morning, I guess. I don't remember the exact time."

"We'd like to ask you some questions," Josie said. "While we're here."

Sheila's grip on the door tightened until her knuckles blanched. Josie didn't have to look at Noah to know he, too, noticed something was off. Years of working together and being married left them uniquely attuned to one another.

Was Isaac inside, hiding? If so, where was their other vehicle?

"Mrs. Hampton," Noah said gently. "Is everything all right? Is there anything we can help you with?"

Shaking her head vigorously, she loosened her grip on the door and stepped back, as if to allow them entry. "No, no. Everything is fine. You can come in and see for yourself."

Noah stepped over the threshold first. Behind him, Josie's fingers twitched over the holster of her Glock.

The house had the same heavy air of tragedy inside it. Sorrow was a thick cloud enveloping them as they entered the living room. Nothing looked different. No signs of a struggle. There were no discernible threats and yet, Josie couldn't ignore the low thrum of anxiety coursing through her body. Sheila panned their surroundings and then looked up at them as if to say, "See? Nothing amiss here."

Noah said, "Is anyone here with you?"

"No one's here. It's just me." She turned her back and walked toward the kitchen. They passed through a short hallway. On one side was a door—a closet or possibly the door to the garage—and on the other, stairs to the second floor. A rolling suitcase sat at the bottom of the steps.

The kitchen was small but brighter than the living room. The cabinets were all white, the countertops speckled gray. A large window overlooked the backyard. Hemmed in by a white vinyl privacy fence, it was empty except for a barbecue grill. The grass was cut short and the garden beds running along the base of the fence were filled with the yellow, wilted leaves of long-dead tulips. A light brown hazmat suit—similar to the Tyvek suits they wore at crime scenes—hung from a clothesline.

Forcing her gaze from the hazmat suit, Josie noticed the kitchen table was covered with Sheila's work materials. Goggles, earplugs, headphones—some intact and others broken apart into smaller pieces. Tubes of glue littered the table. An open duffel bag was in the center of it all. Brown and white fabric, the texture of the hazmat suit out back, poked from its opening.

It was all the equipment one might need to stab a woman to death without getting soaked in her blood. All available right here at home. How much did Sheila know about her husband's activities? Was she involved at all?

This had become more than a fact-finding visit. Sheila Hampton needed to come to the stationhouse with them for an interview.

Noticing Josie's interest in the materials on the table, she quickly began throwing the rest of the items into the duffel bag. "I was packing to go back to New York. I've got a rideshare coming to take me to the rental car company in South Denton."

Noah positioned himself near the hall, keeping an eye on the front entrance and the stairs.

Josie said, "You and Isaac haven't patched things up?"

Stuffing the last of the goggles into the bag, she struggled to zip it closed. "No. It's not going to work out. Besides, I think he's been seeing someone else."

"What makes you say that?" Noah asked.

The last few inches of the zipper failed to close. Abandoning it, Sheila smiled weakly. "Just, um, a wife's intuition. He gets a text, which he's secretive about, and then he has to leave abruptly. When he returns, he's... more relaxed than when he left."

Josie wondered if he was more relaxed because he'd just slaughtered someone, but then who was he communicating with in secret? The grandmother figure who helped him gain access to vehicles without GPS?

"Any idea who he's been seeing?" Josie asked.

A tear slid down her cheek. "Does it matter? I just—I need to get back to New York. My rideshare will be here really soon, so if you don't mind..."

Noah motioned toward the window, where the hazmat suit was visible, swinging gently in the breeze. "Does your husband ever use any of your equipment?"

Sheila's head swiveled toward the window. "Oh, right. I need to take that one down—um, take it back with me."

Quickly, she bustled past Josie. Her shaking hands made it difficult to get the back door open.

"Mrs. Hampton," Josie said. "I think you should cancel the rideshare. You're going to need to come to the police station with us to answer some questions."

"Just, um, just a minute. I'll just take this down. I mean, it might rain."

Though the humidity seemed at an all-time high and thick clouds filled the summer sky, rain wasn't in the day's forecast. Sheila slipped out the back door. Josie followed. Noah stood in the doorway, body turned so he could also monitor the inside of the house. As Sheila pinched the clothespins, releasing the suit from the line, Josie said, "Mrs. Hampton, if you know where your husband is, now is the time to tell us."

Sheila paused, fisting the brown material. She was wearing a tank top again and the muscles of her shoulders tensed. A

palpable wave of trepidation rolled off her, reminding Josie of
prey when cornered. Josie's fingers grazed the snap of her
holster even though her logical mind couldn't pinpoint a threat.
Then Sheila lunged forward and threw the hazmat suit over
Josie's head. Everything happened in a matter of heartbeats.
The fabric scratched Josie's cheek as she fought to toss it aside.
Footsteps drummed a staccato beat away from her—soft at first
and then louder. Sheila's sandals slapping the concrete. Noah
shouted something. She heard what she thought was the back
door banging open. There was a tug around her head and the
suit dropped. "She went down the alley," Noah said, taking off
after Sheila.

Josie's heart revved in her chest as she got her bearings.
Then she raced back through the house and burst out of the
front door. Noah was headed east in pursuit of Sheila Hampton
as she sprinted along the sidewalk past her neighbors' houses. A
few of them were on their porches and shouted to one another
as the foot chase continued. Josie grimaced as Sheila narrowly
avoided a splash pool in one driveway with two toddlers in it.

Taking the steps two at a time, Josie rushed to the sidewalk
and crossed the street. Ahead, Sheila took a hard left, bolting
into the path of a minivan. The van lurched to a stop, the driver
leaning on the horn. Sheila didn't slow down. She was now
directly in Josie's path but before Josie could reach her, she
disappeared between two houses.

Sweat poured from Josie's scalp, burning her eyes. Mentally,
she called up a map of the development. Then she cut through
the nearest alleyway, moving parallel to Sheila. Many of the
backyards on this side of the street were sectioned off by bushes
or chain-link fences no more than four feet high. Josie hopped
one of them, landing in the adjacent yard, and spied Sheila four
houses to her right just as she disappeared again, threading her
way between another two houses. Seconds later, Noah
followed, shouting after her to stop running.

Josie stayed on her own path. The next street curved into a crescent shape, circling back to where the Hamptons lived. Opposite the last row of houses was a playground and pond and, more importantly, a much taller fence meant to discourage anyone from plunging into the ravine on the other side of it.

Sheila Hampton would be cornered.

Josie was in good shape but running full speed in this oppressive heat set her lungs on fire. Fighting a wave of dizziness, she emerged from the final row of houses to see Sheila running in her direction to avoid Noah. Her arms and legs flailed—the uncoordinated run of a desperate person whose limbic system had chosen flight over fight. Even if Josie wasn't closing in, Sheila would have exhausted herself within minutes. As it was, her face was flushed a deep red. Her mouth hung open and her chest heaved, trying to draw in the thick air.

Noah shouted after her, ordering her to stop, but she kept moving, zigzagging between a swing set and a jungle gym. Luckily, it was too hot for children to use the playground, so they were alone except for a gentleman walking his dog. Startled by the commotion, he took out his cell phone and held it up. Recording them, most likely.

He was going to get a show.

"Stop!" Josie hollered as she stepped out from behind a slide and into Sheila's path. With a yelp, Sheila swerved, kicking up mulch. One of Josie's hands clutched her bare shoulder, but her skin was so slick from perspiration that she slipped away. Josie spun to pursue her, but she was already several steps ahead. A surge of hope flooded Josie's system as she watched Sheila fall to her knees. Josie gained a few feet. Sheila staggered back up. Vomit poured from her mouth, but she kept going, Josie at her heels.

"Stop!" Josie demanded again. This time her fingers seized on the back of Sheila's tank top only to have it slide out of her grasp, too. The pond was only feet away now. It was maybe forty feet in diameter, but Josie had no idea how deep it went. She really didn't want to find out.

"Mrs. Hampton! Stop running!"

Finally, Josie caught hold of the waistband of her shorts. Yanking Sheila back, Josie reached around to capture one of her wrists, but the woman started lashing out blindly, hitting and kicking at anything she could make contact with. Josie grunted as a heel slammed into her shin, sending a streak of pain up her leg. She narrowly avoided a backhand fist to the face. Sheila was like a wild animal, snarling and raging against Josie's attempts to subdue her. Vomit and sweat stained her clothes, the pungent odors combining to make Josie's eyes water. The struggle felt like it lasted an eternity when in reality only seconds had passed. Over Sheila's shrieks and the blood rushing in her own head, Josie was vaguely aware of Noah's boots pounding behind them. She did her best to keep Sheila in her clutches, but the ground gave way beneath their feet, the soft lip of grass that surrounded the pond disintegrating under the weight of their thrashing bodies.

FIFTY-EIGHT

The water hit Josie like a slap. It was shockingly warm. She sank fast, her heavy boots dragging her to the brackish depths. Something hard punched against her hip. There was pressure and then a push. Sheila using Josie's body to kick away. The pond was pitch-black, the only murky light coming from over Josie's head. Forcing air through her nose to discharge the sludge that had found its way into her nostrils when they fell in, she swam toward the glow. The muscles of her arms and legs screamed as she forced her body through the thick water, her feet like two cinderblocks.

Breaking the surface, she took a deep breath and then coughed out a slurry of oily brown-green liquid. The taste nearly made her gag. She used the heel of one hand to brush water and debris from her eyes while her legs worked to keep her afloat.

"Josie!" Noah was on the bank, tugging his own boots off. The dog walker was just behind him, taking even more video.

Turning away from Noah, Josie saw Sheila splashing jerkily toward the opposite bank. Josie went after her. Pain seared through her muscles as she swam. As she predicted, overexertion and exhaustion kicked in, impeding Sheila's progress. A loud splash sounded behind them. Noah jumping in. As Josie's fingers brushed some part of Sheila's body beneath the water, the woman started to sob. Her writhing slowed, and she plunged under the surface. Josie dove after her, fighting against Sheila's floundering limbs. Drowning people were never still or calm. Their bodies panicked, battling to stay alive, to find air. Sheila was no different. Josie took several punches and kicks to her arms, torso and face before she was able to feel her way around Sheila's midsection. Hooking one arm under the woman's armpit, Josie used the other to aid her in getting them back to the surface.

"Stop struggling," Josie told her once their heads were above water. "I'm trying to keep you from dying."

A long wail erupted from Sheila's throat. She kept moving, warring with Josie, dragging them both down. Noah's approach drew her attention. "Please," Josie said. "Stop fighting. We're going to get you out of here."

Whether it was the fatigue or the realization that she might be able to escape from Josie but not from them both, Sheila went limp in Josie's arms. Noah swam up and took her from Josie's grip. Immediately, the strain on her body, from her lungs to her legs, eased. Noah pulled Sheila along and Josie followed. He hefted her onto the bank and then helped Josie before getting out himself.

Josie and Sheila lay side by side trying to catch their breath. Turning her head, Josie coughed up more water. Noah's hand grazed her back. Through burning eyes, she finally looked at him. He leaned over her but kept his eyes on Sheila, although the woman made no more attempts to elude them. He wore nothing but his boxer briefs and socks. It had made it easier for him to navigate the water. Josie might have been annoyed that he'd taken the time to strip down before jumping in after her, but she knew firsthand how quickly he could remove his clothes when something was at stake. That something was usually much more appealing than a dirty pond. The dog walker rushed toward them, one arm full of Noah's things.

Sheila lay flat on her back, tears running down the sides of her dirt-streaked face. "I didn't know," she cried. "I didn't know."

"Didn't know what?" Josie asked.

Noah took his things from the dog walker and started getting dressed. "Did you call 911?"

The man nodded solemnly. It was clear he wanted to stay as close to the action as possible, but Noah smoothly and patiently got him to move along, tasking him with waiting down the road to direct emergency vehicles their way.

"I didn't know who he really was," Sheila said. "I never would have married him if I knew."

Josie sat upright, trying to shake off the dizziness that still assailed her. "You adopted Felicity Cook."

Sheila gave a jerky nod. "Yes. It was after the trial. I had her name changed. Took her to Philadelphia to live. Then I met Isaac. How could I have known?"

Josie's mind whirred to life, momentarily clearing the fog caused by the intense strain on her body's resources. A glimmer of doubt flickered deep in her brain. She worked to rearrange the facts as she knew them. "Your husband never told you his true identity?"

"No. Of course not."

Noah dropped down beside Josie. She could see from his expression that he, too, was trying to fit the puzzle pieces together. If Isaac Hampton was Simon Cook—the older brother of Sheila's adopted daughter, why wouldn't he tell her? Why hide that fact?

"He was so good," Sheila went on. "A good father. A good husband. Most of the time. He always had some anger issues. I called the police a few times but he never actually hurt us, so I never pressed charges. If I had known the truth, I would have taken Jenna and run."

Felicity and Simon Cook had been separated after their family was slaughtered and put into foster care. Simon would have aged out soon after that. He, too, had changed his name. Likely to avoid Roger Bell. With him free, there was no guarantee that he wouldn't try to finish what he started.

Noah swiped a hand through his wet hair. "You didn't recognize him? When you first met?"

Sheila sniffed. Her face crumpled as a fresh sob shook her frame. "No."

When they spoke with Vicky Platt earlier, she maintained that Stella Townsend had never disclosed what she was looking for in the sealed court records. Josie had been certain she knew exactly what Townsend was searching for, and Remy Tate had confirmed it when they paid him a visit only an hour ago. He hadn't been aware of Stella's ulterior motives. She'd never asked him to search sealed records, but she had visited him at his office a few times after Dallas wrapped his story, ostensibly to clarify some of the things Remy had said during his interview. During one of those visits, Remy had left her alone in his office. By his account, once he returned, Stella had come on to him, hinting that she was interested in him sexually. He'd gotten distracted. After she left, he'd noticed that he'd left the records database open on his computer. Among the searches he'd done that day were two names he didn't recognize. Simon Cook and Roger Bell.

He hadn't confronted Stella because, well, he was more interested in trying to coax her into an affair. Josie and Noah had asked him to access those files, but he reminded them that they needed a warrant.

Noah kept going as sirens wailed in the distance. "Did you watch any of the trial coverage?"

The warrant was still tricky without proof that Simon

Cook was involved in the murders of Cleo Tate, Stella Townsend, and Everly Rowe. If any of the DNA samples came back as a match then they'd have no problem getting a judge to sign off on it. But right now, all they had were loose bits of information that refused to coalesce into a complete picture.

"Of course I watched the trial coverage," Sheila said, finally pushing herself into a sitting position. "Everyone in the city watched it! But it was years later, and he looked completely different. Isaac didn't have a tattoo! I didn't even realize back then you could get them removed. It never even crossed my mind. Why would it?"

Tattoo? Josie met Noah's eyes and saw her own confusion mirrored there.

"He told me today," Sheila said, lower lip trembling. "He hasn't been himself. Like I said, I was sure he was having an affair. We had a fight. I don't even know—I can't even—I'm not sure how it came up but he told me. He said now that Jenna was dead, it didn't matter. Nothing mattered. As if he could just gloss over his betrayal using her death. Screw him. I threw him out and started packing."

Josie thought back to the discrepancy in age between Simon Cook and Isaac Hampton, trying to remember precisely how many years separated them.

Sheila's fingers twisted in her lap. Her voice was quiet when she next spoke. "Um, before he left, he told me something."

Josie wondered if Isaac had confessed to the murders. Was that why Sheila had run? Had she really not known? Not had any involvement? Not even suspected?

"What did he tell you?" Noah asked, glancing over Sheila's head as an ambulance and two police cruisers pulled up nearby.

She looked at Josie. "He said you would come."

"The police?" Josie asked.

"No. You. Detective Quinn."

Noah's brow knit with concern. "Did he say why Detective Quinn would show up?"

"No, and I didn't ask. I was already—already in such shock. I couldn't process anything more."

In spite of the heat still smothering them, Josie felt a chill along the nape of her neck. "What else did he say?"

"It makes no sense but here it is: he said to tell you, 'Don't overlook it.'"

Josie exchanged another look with Noah. Don't overlook what?

Sheila lurched toward Josie and dug her fingers into Josie's forearm. "Now that I told you everything, you can let me go, right? I didn't do anything wrong. I'm sorry I ran, but when he told me that you were going to come to the house, I got scared. I thought I knew him, but I didn't know him at all. How would he know you were going to come looking for him? Unless he's gotten caught up in something bad? I just lost my daughter and now my husband. My entire life has been a lie. When you came to the house and then you wanted to question me even though he wasn't there, I just... I panicked. Whatever he's done, I wasn't a part of it. You have to believe me. I told you everything. I just want to go back to New York."

Noah sighed. "I'm afraid you'll still have to come down to the station to give a statement."

Don't overlook it. Josie's mind spun the loose bits round and round, hoping if it whirled them just so, she'd see what she was missing. Townsend's illegal records searches. Sheila's assertions that she never would have married Isaac if she knew his true identity. The gap in age between Simon Cook and his new identity, Isaac Hampton. It was five years, she remembered now. Five years. Then there was the tattoo.

That was it. The tattoo. Josie's heart did a double tap. Nausea churned in her stomach. It couldn't be. It didn't make sense. At the same time, given the little they did know, especially now with Sheila's confessions, it was the only thing that made sense.

Josie swallowed, tasting the scummy pondwater again. "Mrs. Hampton, what did your husband say his real name was?"

She knew the answer—as insane as it seemed—but she needed to hear Sheila say it out loud.

From behind them, the heavy feet of emergency responders sounded. Noah held up a hand to signal for them to pause. "Mrs. Hampton," he said. "Your husband's real name."

She released Josie's arm and wiped away another tear. "I—I thought you knew. Roger Bell. My husband's original name, before he changed it, was Roger Bell."

FIFTY-NINE

"Let me get this straight." Turner trailed behind Josie, stepping over debris on the first floor of the abandoned textile mill near Denton East High School. "Isaac Hampton isn't Simon Cook. He's Roger Bell. The killer—of the Cook family, that is—and you think he's also the Polaroid Killer."

Josie sighed and tugged at the collar of her polo shirt. It was only marginally cooler inside the cavernous building, but she was still sweating. It was almost nine p.m. but the temperature hadn't let up. So much for the long shower she'd taken after her dip in the pond. "How many times do I have to go over this with you before you understand it?" she asked irritably.

"I don't know, swee— Quinn. I'm just saying that everything about this case is shady as hell. Hey, do you think this guy shit himself when the ERT came to his house to get elimination prints from him?"

"I don't know." Since the ERT was only looking to eliminate which prints belonged to the Hampton couple when they processed the stolen car, they hadn't run them through AFIS, which would have immediately flagged Isaac Hampton's prints as belonging to Roger Bell. Instead, Officer Chan, who'd just completed her Level II latent print certification, did the print comparisons herself. Then she'd taken the prints found in the car that didn't match the Hamptons' and run those through AFIS. It wasn't against protocol not to use AFIS when processing elimination prints. Certainly, neither of the Hamptons had been suspect at that time so there was no reason to enter their prints into AFIS.

But hindsight was a bitch.

They had run Isaac Hampton's prints through AFIS after the confrontation with Sheila and they matched to Roger Bell.

Turner kicked at a cluster of vines that had snaked in through one of the broken windows and crept across the dirty wooden floor. "He really got lucky that Chan didn't use AFIS. Pretty risky to put himself in the crosshairs like that by stealing his own damn car, don't you think?"

"I don't think it mattered to him." Josie aimed her flashlight at a pile of garbage. A rat scurried out from under it, racing away from her. "It would have made things more difficult for him to keep killing and playing this sick game he's dragged us into, but I'm pretty sure his endgame was always for us to find out he was the Polaroid Killer."

They stopped in front of a tall window. Most of its panes had been smashed out long ago. Outside, halogen lights blazed. Josie could see the ERT processing Isaac Hampton's car. The one he'd left in this morning after revealing to his wife that he was the man who slaughtered her adopted daughter's family. The same man a jury acquitted. Once Sheila had been taken back to the stationhouse, Turner had called the infotainment company associated with the Hamptons' remaining vehicle and gotten them to give up its location—without a warrant. It had taken some time and a lot of needling on his part, but he'd finally succeeded.

It was the only reason Josie was letting him follow her around the mill for a second pass. That, and if she left him and

Gretchen alone for any length of time, she was afraid of what would happen. Denton PD had arrived at the mill to find the car empty, save for Isaac Hampton's cell phone which he'd smashed to bits. It had taken over an hour for the bevy of officers to clear the five-story building. Hampton, or Roger Bell, was not inside, nor was Juliet Bowen, but Josie had insisted on searching the premises again, though she couldn't say why. All she knew was that finding Juliet was the priority and right now, they had nothing else to go on.

Gretchen and Noah were following other leads, including a search of the Hampton house. Sheila had granted them permission.

Glass crunched under Josie's feet as she moved away from the window and deeper into the large room. She swept her flashlight over heaps of twisted metal, large rollers, and wooden pallets. Turner's beam joined hers, pausing on the remnants of a tall metal apparatus that took up half the room and stretched almost to the ceiling. Shredded fabric hung from one of the metal bars. More rats skittered away from the light.

Turner made a noise of disgust. "How do you think Bell avoided leaving his prints in the other cars—Stella Townsend's, that Downey guy's, and the classic cars? Gloves? Bet his wife's got a shit-ton of different disposable gloves."

But the witness to Cleo Tate's abduction hadn't seen him wearing gloves, and he didn't appear to have gloves on in the surveillance footage they'd pulled of him. "No," said Josie. "Not gloves. The glue. That industrial-strength glue his wife was using for her prototypes. It would have only been temporary, but it would have prevented his prints from being left behind."

Yet, the DNA samples Hummel had taken from each victim would surely be a match to Roger Bell. It was just a matter of time before the state lab returned results. The temporary alteration of his prints had only bought him time.

"Do you really think this broad—I mean, Sheila Hampton— had no idea what her hubby was up to?"

"It's hard to say." Josie stepped over a pile of broken beer bottles. "If she did, I doubt she'd admit it. I'm not sure we could prove it anyway. I think she knew that he was involved in something illegal because he asked her to pass that message along to me, but I don't think she suspected him of murdering three Denton women in the last week."

If Sheila Hampton was telling the truth, then Josie believed the shock of finding out her husband's true identity had been enough to send her brain into survival mode. In those first hours after his revelation, she might not have been mentally and emotionally able to face the possibility that he was behind the recent murders.

Josie had done some of the initial questioning once they arrived at the stationhouse—before she went home to bathe. Sheila Hampton had admitted Isaac could easily have come and gone from the house without her realizing it since they slept in separate bedrooms, and he rarely came out of his except to eat. The tension in the household was high, given their daughter's death and the fact that Sheila suspected him of cheating on her.

In terms of her work equipment, the most recent prototypes she'd created hadn't been disturbed or gone missing, but she claimed that in the garage were several boxes of safety equipment from previous jobs. She kept everything in case she needed it later. According to her, it drove Isaac crazy that she didn't just throw the boxes away, especially after she left to take the job in New York City.

Turner stopped to study some graffiti lining one of the cinderblock walls. "You think this Sheila could be the grandmother that paid Edgar Garcia for access to the old cars?"

"Brennan ran a photo of Sheila over to Garcia. He said it's not her." Sheila hadn't been able to identify anyone they knew who might fit the bill of a grandmotherly type. Her husband had always told her he had no living family. A quick background check on Roger Bell confirmed this was true.

Josie found the stairwell door and motioned Turner toward it. With a heavy sigh, he trudged up the steps after her, taking his sweet time. His voice faded as he fell behind. "What exactly are we looking for again?"

"Not sure," Josie called over her shoulder. "I'll know it when I see it."

"You've got to be kidding me," came his distant mutter.

"Turner, hurry up!"

He didn't answer. She wouldn't put it past him to have gone back downstairs to wait for her. Cursing under her breath, she kept climbing to the next floor.

As she reached the landing, concrete crumbled beneath her boots. Her body pitched forward at first, her forearms slamming painfully against the floor. The flashlight rolled out of her hand, plunging everything into near-total darkness. Light bounced above and below but it wasn't enough for her to get her bearings. Her feet scrabbled for purchase. Just as she managed to pull herself upright, more of the ground beneath her gave way. Flailing, her center of gravity shifted. Her upper body tipped back. The metal railing disintegrated in her hand as she tried to stop herself from toppling. For a heartbeat, she teetered, suspended in the air. There was no time to call out, to get her bearings, to react at all. Her stomach dropped as she tumbled into blackness.

SIXTY

Josie's head glanced off something hard—a step or maybe part of the railing, she couldn't be sure. Bracing herself for a painful descent, she let her limbs go slack. The air whooshed out of her lungs when her body hit something solid enough to break her fall but soft enough not to inflict pain. Turner's chest. His flashlight clattered down the shaft, the beam of light dancing as it receded. Clutching her shoulders, he steadied her. Together, they froze.

"Shit." His breath skated past the shell of her ear. "I can't see a damn thing. I lost my flashlight. Where's yours?"

Josie pointed up the steps where a dim yellow glow struggled to cut through the darkness. "On the landing. But the steps broke apart right under me. That's why I fell."

His hands were still on her shoulders. "This place is dangerous as hell. I can't believe no one got hurt when we came through here the first time. I'm pretty sure my light fell down toward the first floor."

"We should go back down then," Josie said. "There's another staircase on the opposite side of the building. We can try that one."

Turner gently turned her body so they could proceed back to the first floor. He kept one hand clamped around her bicep. "I know you don't like me touching you, but I figured you'd make an exception this time. I'll let go when we're all the way down."

For once, Josie didn't mind. Turner had probably just saved her from a broken neck, although she'd be damned if she admitted it to him. He had a lot of flaws, but he'd proven himself to be strong and quick on his feet. It was, perhaps, his only redeeming quality. On a previous case, to save her from being mauled by a dog, he'd picked her up and tossed her over a six-foot fence like she weighed nothing. He'd called her 'Paper Airplane' for weeks after that.

True to his word, once they emerged from the stairwell onto the first floor, Turner released her. He went back into the stairwell to find his flashlight. The harsh glow of the halogens pierced some nearby windows, saving her from complete darkness. Josie took the time to assess herself for injuries. Scraped forearms. Slight bump on her head. Nothing serious. As she rubbed her scalp, a memory hit her like a slap. Her mouth went dry. She hadn't forgotten what happened at this old mill all those years ago, but she hadn't exactly been keyed in on the details during the initial search for Isaac Hampton.

Turner said something to her. She was too lost in the past to focus on his words.

Light pierced her eyes. She threw a hand up to cover them. "Turner, what the hell?"

"Something's wrong," he said. "I can tell."

Josie blinked as he lowered his torch. "How can you tell?"

"Because you didn't answer me when I called your name. You just looked, I don't know, frozen. Then I called you 'sweetheart' and you didn't even respond. I'm not giving you a dollar for that one, by the way, since I was just testing you. Did you hear something? There are a lot of rats in this place."

Josie shook her head and walked toward him. "Andrew

Bowen's mother brought me here once. I was working a case. I went to question her. She brought me here to show me something and then she tried to kill me. In one of the stairwells."

Turner tapped his fingers against his thigh. "So what you're saying is you were a lot dumber back then."

Josie put her hands on her hips. "Now for that, I want a dollar."

"No way. That's not how the system works. You got a problem with it, talk to your hub— the LT. So this bitch tried to kill you and now we're looking for her granddaughter in the same place. You think Roger Bell left his car here on purpose?"

Trying not to let her irritation get to her, Josie let him lead the way to the other stairwell. "No. No one would have known that. It wasn't in news reports or anything."

They passed more badly damaged decaying machines. What used to be different types of looms. "Why did this Isaac guy—or Bell—leave his car here then?" Turner asked. "Because it's so remote, or was there some other case that involved this shithole?"

"The mill, specifically?" she said. "Off the top of my head, I'm not sure."

Slowly, they worked their way up the steps, this time without incident. Turner gave Josie his flashlight and he used the app on his phone so that they could maneuver through the decrepit ghosts of textile machines past. Then Turner's beam fell away, and she realized he had stopped moving. Turning back, she saw his face bathed in light from his phone screen. "Are you kidding me right now? You can't stay off that thing for five minutes?"

He didn't even look at her. His thumb moved at warp speed. "Don't get your panties in a bunch, Quinn. It's the LT. They just finished the search of the Hampton house. No obvious stuff like bloody clothes or hazmat suits or whatever. There was a polaroid camera in the kid's old room though. That'll get taken into evidence. Oh, and they took a couple of tubes of glue so they can compare it to the stuff in the old cars."

Still nothing that was going to help them find Juliet Bowen.

"Come on," Josie said. "There's nothing here. Let's go up to the third floor."

Turner groaned but switched back to his flashlight app and let her take the lead. They made it to the next floor safely. Inside the doors, Josie accidentally kicked a cluster of dry-rotted spools of thread, sending them careening in every direction. As they worked their way through more debris, Turner's light lingered on a roller that was as big as him. "What I wanna know is why is Bell on a revenge tour? He got off!"

It was a question that Josie had been obsessing over all day.

"Not to mention, what kind of sick bastard tracks down and seduces the woman raising the child he nearly stabbed to death?" Turner continued. "How did he find them? What was he trying to do? I'm telling you, Quinn. I've seen some crazy shit in my day but nothing this twisted."

Skirting a pile of what looked like dried-up wool but could possibly be the remains of a fluffy rodent, Josie merely nodded. They were missing more puzzle pieces than she thought. She'd never say it out loud, but Turner was right. Bell's behavior made no sense. He should have been celebrating his freedom for the last fifteen years, not raising the girl he almost killed and plotting to kill the family members of the people whose actions had kept him out of prison.

It didn't make sense.

Josie heard the sound of tiny feet scratching along the floor. Turner's light went wild as he jumped and bobbled his phone. "Goddamn rodents! This place is seriously giving me the creeps, Quinn."

She swept her light in his direction. Dust had gathered in his thick curls. His eyes bulged as he searched the floor around his feet. With his free hand, he tugged at his beard. Like he had the night he'd brought Amber to her house. This was his nervous tic, Josie realized. She, too, hated being in dark spaces but she could take them if they were big enough. It was small, confined dark spaces that undid her. Another gift from the woman who'd abducted her and pretended to be her mother.

"Turner," Josie said, wanting to distract him. "Why do you think Bell waited all this time to do this?"

He took one last scan around his feet and started walking again. "Hell if I know."

Shaking her head, Josie kept moving, sweeping her light along the floor to look for any holes or rotted areas. "Think."

"Why do I have to do the thinking?" he complained.

A massive structure loomed ahead. Josie's heart did a little flutter. Her body remembered it before her mind got there. "It's kind of your job," she replied.

"I don't know. When people go off the deep end, there's usually a triggering event. The death of his daughter. It made him snap. I mean, if you don't have your kids, what's the point in living, right?"

Freezing in place, Josie swiveled her head in his direction. Was this another inexplicable glimpse of his humanity? What did he know about having kids? Josie certainly couldn't imagine him as a dad. In the low light, his face was just visible. "What?" he said. "You don't think I'm right? Oh, you think Bell didn't have feelings like that, don't you? 'Cause he's a stone-cold killer?"

The memory of Felicity Cook—Jenna Hampton—bleeding out under her hands still made Josie sick to her stomach. What kind of person could do such a thing to a child? Not someone who had any type of parental instincts. She didn't believe anyone was capable of that much change. "I think Jenna's death was the trigger." She wouldn't go as far as saying the words 'you're right.' He'd be insufferable for days. "I'm just not sure why. Come on, there's somewhere I want to check up ahead."

SIXTY-ONE

Silently, Turner picked his way through more dirt and debris alongside her until the huge machine came into relief. He tipped his head back to take it all in, waving his light around like a conductor to try to get a full picture of it. "What the hell is this?"

The words caught in Josie's throat as the memory of the last time she'd stood before it came flooding back. Clearing her throat, she tried again. Her voice sounded choked. "It's a soft-flow dye machine."

The metal beast was comprised of an immense, complex system of pumps, nozzles, and pipes, all surrounding a cylinder so enormous that a ladder was necessary to reach the top of it. The metal chamber was infected with rust. The last time Josie had seen it, a long fissure left a gaping, jagged hole in the center of it. Now, the wound was so large, it had split the chamber into two. One side sagged to the ground, the framing beneath it having crumbled. The other held straight. Despite her thrashing heart, Josie stepped closer and tried to see inside the two cavities. She was too short.

"Turner," she said, trying to keep her voice steady. "Can you see inside either of those?"

"These were cleared. If you think Isaac—or Bell—is hiding in there, forget it."

"I know they were cleared. I still want to see if there's anything inside."

He pointed his phone's flashlight under his chin, giving his visage a creepy, disembodied vibe. "Rats. Rats are inside. Happy? If you want to look inside, climb up and look."

The last thing she wanted to do was climb into the hulls of the dye machine, but her gut—or maybe it was past experience —told her that if there was any place in this building where they might find something useful, it was there. Her tongue felt like sandpaper. She could keep trying to coax him or she could just tell him the truth. The second option was about as appealing as a colonoscopy. Then again, the last time she'd asked something of him—to treat their K-9 handler, Luke, with respect and not mention his scarred hands—Turner had done it.

With a sigh, Josie said, "I can't. I can't go inside of that thing. I mean, I can, but—" She'd need Noah there with her, or Gretchen. Or she could just white-knuckle it and hope she didn't pass out. "When Sophia Bowen didn't succeed in killing me in the stairwell, she forced me into that thing and... I just don't do well in dark, confined spaces, okay? If there was someone in there who needed rescuing, I'd jump right in and pray that my adrenaline was stronger than my panic attack, but like you said, there's not. So... I'm asking you to do it. Please."

God, she hated saying please to him. She hated talking about this with anyone besides Noah, Gretchen, and her therapist. She waited for his laughter, for some cutting remark, for a teasing comment, but nothing came. Instead, he asked, "You don't do well in dark, confined spaces because of the Bowen bitch or because of something else?"

Her eyes found his in the semi-dark of their lights. For once, the mischievous gleam she usually saw there was absent. He tugged at his beard again.

"Does it matter?" she said.

There was a beat of silence. Then he shook his head. "No, no. It doesn't matter at all. I'll check the one on the left first. Can you just keep your light on the opening?"

Shocked at his non-reaction, Josie mumbled a yes and did as he asked. It was an easy climb for him with his large frame and rangy limbs. He disappeared inside one half, the light from his phone bouncing wildly as he looked around. When he emerged, his upper lip was curled in disgust. "For future reference," he said, "I don't do well with rats and it's because of this experience."

A laugh burst unexpectedly from her throat. She'd never laughed at anything Turner said before. She laughed at his expense quite often but never at his jokes. What was the world coming to?

His voice echoed from inside the other half of the cylinder. "I think we're getting along now, Quinn."

"No, we're not."

Moments later, he climbed out, one hand extended over his head. Something shiny dangled from his fingers. "I got something. A necklace."

He jumped down from the dye machine and held it in front of her face. The necklace was in pristine condition. A glittering gold chain with a matching charm in the shape of the letter J.

J for Juliet.

The chain was broken, like someone had torn it from her neck. Had she managed to do it so she could leave them a clue? Or had it merely come off when Bell struggled to get her out of the tube?

"Is there any blood in there?"

"I couldn't see any," Turner answered.

"Bell kept her here," Josie said, excitement overtaking her

anxiety. "He took her from her house last night around midnight, less than twenty-four hours ago, in one of the Bowens' cars."

Turner let the charm dangle, glinting in the beams from their flashlights. "But he went home afterward to ruin his wife's life and ask her to give you some dumb, cryptic message."

"Then he left in his own vehicle and came here."

"Because the girl was here," Turner said, waving his phone toward the dye machine. "In there. We still got a car problem, Quinn. This guy doesn't have access to the classic cars from the auto shop. But he drove the Bowens' car to that school in West Denton and left it there."

"But he had Juliet with him, and he brought her here." Josie picked up the thread. "They couldn't have made it on foot, which means he had to have driven her here. We can check the GPS history on the car outside to see if he used that to stash her here last night."

"He still would have needed to keep a car here," Turner said. "To leave in. What are you thinking? The grandmother type? She has a car? Or maybe there's a car from the Schock's Auto Repair lot that isn't accounted for?"

"I don't know," Josie said. "But right now it doesn't matter. What matters is that there's a very good chance that Juliet Bowen is still alive and if she is, we might be able to find her before he kills her."

Turner put the necklace into his pocket. He should have left it in place and called the ERT in but it was too late now. Josie was too buzzed on the idea that Juliet Bowen might still be alive to give him shit about it—though she certainly would later.

"I'm all for big heroics," he said. "But we don't have any damn way to find her."

"He left me a message," Josie said. "'Don't overlook it.'"

"What the hell does that mean?"

"I don't know but we have to be able to figure it out. We

have to! He made us play this game. He wouldn't give us... game pieces if he didn't want us to keep playing. There's the message and the polaroid—"

"Fuck that polaroid, Quinn. A bunch of fucking treetops? In the middle of Central Pennsylvania? Come on."

Josie arched a brow. "Do you have a better suggestion?"

Turner jumped and made a satisfyingly childlike shriek as two rats climbed over his loafers. A stream of expletives shot out of his mouth. He nearly dropped his phone. "Can we get the hell out of here?"

Josie turned to walk back to the stairwell. "Boots. You need boots to work in Denton."

He grumbled something under his breath. In the stairwell, Turner started talking again. "This guy doesn't do anything randomly, right? Except maybe the classic cars, but those had a purpose. Other than that, everything he's done has had some connection to previous cases or the people who screwed up at the Cook crime scene."

Josie trod carefully. She couldn't shake the remnants of panic she'd felt free-falling into darkness when the steps in the other stairwell gave way. "True."

"He's kind of going out of his way even when it doesn't help him out," Turner added. "Like now that he can't get the cars from that lot, he's still got one here, one there, dragging this kid all over creation. It only increases his chances of getting caught, so why bother?"

"You're saying him using this mill does mean something," she said.

"Yeah, and him leaving the Bowens' car at that school in West Denton. Come on, Quinn. Aren't there any big cases you can think of that involved this mill and that school?"

Her brain worked through the most memorable cases she'd solved. They reached the first floor and headed toward the exit. The Sophia Bowen connection to this mill wasn't widely known and it hadn't been reported in the press. It was a bizarre coincidence. What about the mill and West Denton Elementary School? Something sparked in the back of her mind. It was the school. A memory flickered. She chased it but couldn't catch it. Once outside again, Turner took a deep breath and started brushing off his suit. He didn't think the polaroid or the message were helpful but what if they were in combination with the other things?

The mill.

West Denton Elementary School.

Treetops.

Don't overlook it.

Josie glanced around the weed-strewn gravel lot where the members of the ERT still worked. Turner went over and spoke with Hummel, gesturing toward the building. He took out the necklace again. Beyond the halogen lights was only night.

Treetops. The mill.

Josie spun around until she was facing the direction of her old high school. A small mountain separated the mill from the school. From the summit, you could see the treetops and the mill in all its decaying glory. Was Juliet Bowen there? It overlooked the trees. Maybe that was the message. But the polaroid didn't show the mill. The treetops were unbroken. Plus, that summit wasn't an easy place to access. The last time Josie was up there, she'd been shot—in the vest—and it had taken an eternity to get back down.

"Oh my God," she blurted out.

Turner and Hummel were arguing now. Oblivious.

She'd been shot on the summit overlooking the mill while working the case of Lucy Ross, a seven-year-old girl abducted from the city park.

Josie stalked over to Turner and Hummel. "Hey!"

They were shouting too loudly at one another to hear her.

Lucy Ross had gone to West Denton Elementary. The case

had sent them all over the city, including a very distinct place a mile into the woods in Northern Denton, only accessible by hiking trail. Now that she figured it out, she felt stupid for not realizing it sooner just from the polaroid and Bell's message. Don't overlook it. He'd literally spelled it out for her.

"Hey!" Josie tried again, raising her voice. When they didn't respond, she shouted loudly enough to be heard by every person on the premises. "I know where to find Juliet Bowen!"

Turner and Hummel froze. Their heads swiveled toward her. "Where?" said Turner.

"The Overlook."

SIXTY-TWO

One of the many unusual rock formations in and around Denton, the Overlook most closely resembled a tree-sized monolith, flat and narrow on top, except that one side of it was angled, making it possible for people to walk up to the top. It wasn't easy but it could be done. If you made it to the top, you usually slid back down on your ass. Noah always said it was like a giant slide. Locals called it the Overlook because the top of it was level with the trees surrounding it.

Josie stared at it as she kneaded her lower back with a fist. She kept her body hidden behind an oak tree. They were in the middle of the forest. Even with all the flashlights she and the other officers had brought, together with some powerful spotlights, the top of the Overlook wasn't visible from the ground. It was too dark. Her colleagues bustled around her, keeping cover behind trees while they set up a perimeter. A search of the immediate area hadn't turned up Bell, but they were still taking every precaution. He hadn't given any indication that he had a gun or that he'd used a gun in any of his crimes, but they still had to consider him armed. He was a threat. If he was at the top of the Overlook, that put him in an elevated position. Tactically, it was very bad for Denton PD.

A burning sensation filled Josie's stomach. On the way from the mill to the Overlook, she'd choked down an expired granola bar she'd found in her glove compartment. Now it churned uncomfortably in her gut. A heaviness settled in her limbs. Her feet ached. Rest wasn't even on the radar.

She smelled Noah's aftershave before she felt the heat of his body at her back. "The drone shows two figures up top."

"Two?" said Josie. "Can you get a clean shot of them?"

He shook his head. "The university sent a thermal drone this time. It looks at heat signatures."

Two heat signatures meant that Juliet Bowen was still alive.

"The Chief's here," Noah said. "We're trying to figure out how to approach this. I don't think we can get a crane out here. We can't even get vehicles close to this thing. The hiking trail is too narrow."

"Let me go up," Josie said. "I can climb to the top. I've done it before. In the dark."

"Too dangerous."

"If we do nothing, he's going to stab Juliet Bowen to death."

"You don't know that." Noah glanced around them. His face was visible in the glow cast by dozens of different types of lights. Tension lined his face. "We don't know what he's going to do. He changed his protocol. We can't predict his behavior at this point."

Noah was right. All along, Bell's MO had been the same. Abduct a woman. Take her to a remote location. Hit her over the head to disorient her. Don his hazmat suit and stab her to death. Leave a polaroid of the location of his next victim. Then he walked away, stripped off the bloodied suit, and got into a car he'd "borrowed" from Schock's Auto Repair. Whether he'd stashed it near the scene ahead of time or the mysterious grandmother figure—or someone else—was waiting for him, she still couldn't figure out. Regardless, with the minor variation of luring Jared Rowe to Harper's Peak and letting him live, Bell's actions had been consistent.

Until Juliet Bowen.

Instead of killing her and leaving a polaroid with her body, he'd left one in her bed when he abducted her. Josie wasn't surprised that the polaroid pointed to her. She was the last person on his revenge list. Though they couldn't prove it, Josie firmly believed he'd killed Artie Peluso's wife; Dusty Branson's mother; and Bud Ernst. They had all lived outside of Denton's jurisdiction. They weren't a part of what he was doing now, here in Denton, and yet they were connected. Practice kills, maybe. Except Roger Bell wouldn't have needed practice.

Footsteps sounded behind them. Gretchen trudged over, Turner trailing behind her. "Well," she said. "He didn't shoot at the drone or throw anything at it. I guess that's something."

Josie still couldn't wrap her mind around why Bell was bent on getting revenge on everyone involved in the Cook case. If anyone had cause to seek vengeance, it was Simon Cook. They hadn't been able to access his new name yet, which meant they couldn't locate him. Even if Bell's claim that he'd walked in on the stabbings after the fact was true, he'd gone free. There had been irreparable damage to his reputation, but he'd managed to change his name and start over. By all accounts, he'd lived a happy life with Sheila Hampton and her daughter.

Josie was convinced that Jenna Hampton's death had triggered his rampage. It was one of the few things about this insane case that made sense. If she was right, that meant he'd truly loved the girl, even if it didn't line up with what she'd seen in the Cook house. If Bell was going to go on a killing spree provoked by grief, why seek revenge on the people whose mistakes and incompetence had allowed him to go free—to become Jenna's father? Or, in the case of Andrew Bowen, why try to hurt the man who did his job well enough to ensure that Bell was acquitted? It was almost like he was angry that he hadn't gone to prison, even though he'd maintained his innocence throughout the trial.

Maybe she was looking at this the wrong way. Maybe instead of trying to fit a thousand malformed puzzle pieces together, she needed instead to focus on only one thing. The Cook case—and this revenge tour—had always turned on one thing. The murder weapon. The knife that wasn't photographed and that Andrew Bowen managed to keep out of evidence. What if the knife had come in during the trial?

What was she missing?

Turner's fingers tapped a beat against his thigh. "What's this guy's deal? He made himself a sitting duck."

Noah sighed. "He did, and there are only two ways he's getting off that rock: in police custody or in a body bag."

Josie took out her phone and tapped out a text to Sergeant Dan Lamay. She didn't think he was still on shift, but she knew he'd get her what she needed right away, no questions asked. If he was awake.

"This dickhead was on a pretty good run," Turner said. "Why change his pattern now?"

"Because that's what psychotic killers do," Gretchen said. She, too, looked at her phone. "The other drones are here. I think we can get some light up there. We're trying to find someone who's proficient at rock-climbing. Maybe they can give one of us a crash course and we can get someone up there to try to talk to this guy."

"One of you can take a crash course," Turner said. "I'm not rock-climbing. Definitely not in the middle of the night. Let that bastard sit up there. Eventually he'll get hungry or tired and he'll have to come down. If he decides to do it by throwing himself over, I'm not gonna be upset."

Josie glared at him. "There's a sixteen-year-old girl up there."

"And he hasn't killed her," Turner pointed out.

"Yet," Josie said.

A twig snapped. All four of them searched for the source of the noise. Weaving through tree trunks was Dr. Chris McAllister, a Denton University professor. He acted as a consultant whenever they had need of drones. In his hands was a large controller with a screen in the center of it. As he got closer, Josie saw the neon-pink and -purple colors of the top of the Overlook. Two blurred yellow figures were visible along one of the edges. McAllister paused, thumbs working the knobs and buttons on either side of the screen. Noah left them, walking over to the professor to confer with him.

"What about one of those rescue helicopters?" Turner said. "With the baskets."

"Maybe," Josie said. "But the top of that rock isn't very big. The air might be too much. Plus, you'd have to get Bell to cooperate and actually put Juliet into the basket."

"This qualifies as a hostage situation." Gretchen took out her cell phone. "We should call SERT."

SERT, or Special Emergency Response Team, was a highly trained unit within the state police. They responded to high-risk situations, assisting Pennsylvania police departments that didn't have their own SWAT teams. They had both a tactical unit and a negotiations unit.

Josie didn't protest, although even with SERT on the scene, there was still the issue of getting safely to the top of the Overlook. Her cell phone vibrated. A text from Lamay. He must have been at the station after all. She opened the attachment she'd asked for, eyes skimming it. The sweat caused by the thick July air dried on her skin. It felt as though someone was trailing cold fingers up her spine.

Turner said, "What's up with you, Quinn?"

Before she could answer, the report she was reading disappeared, replaced by an incoming call. She didn't recognize the number, but she answered anyway.

At the sound of Roger Bell's voice, the acid already raging in her stomach flared hotter. "Detective Quinn. I knew you'd find me."

Josie waved frantically to the others to gather around and put her phone on speaker. Noah and Dr. McAllister rushed over. Everyone crowded near her, straining to hear the other end of the conversation. "What do you want, Roger?"

"Oh, so you did figure it out. Or did Sheila tell you?"

McAllister turned his screen toward them. On it, one of the figures dragged the other one toward the edge of the plateau. Juliet's body appeared to be limp, but it still had a heat signature.

"Let me talk to Juliet," Josie said.

"Talk to her when you get up here."

"We're trying to find a way up there. Unless you want to end this and bring her down yourself."

"That's not the ending I had in mind," he said. "You owe me at least one conversation, Detective. You and me, alone."

Josie's pulse raced. She looked at her colleagues. Turner and Gretchen were focused on McAllister's screen. Only Noah was locked in on her.

"Send Juliet down," Josie said. "And I'll come up there."

Bell's chuckle was like sandpaper dragging over her skin. "If you want a chance at saving this little bitch, you'll come up here."

Dr. McAllister gasped. For a moment, the controller bobbled in his hands. Then he brought the figures back into the middle of the screen.

"Shit," said Turner. "He's holding her over."

Bell pushed Juliet's upper body past the edge of the cliff. He knelt with one of his legs across her calves, holding her in place. Her body wriggled but Josie didn't see any of her limbs thrashing. Bell must have restrained her arms and legs. She was helpless up there, at his mercy. Even if she had it in her to fight back or escape and take the stone slide to the bottom, she couldn't. Through her phone, Josie heard the girl scream. Bell said, "Stop moving or you'll die sooner than I intended. Detective, I know you can see me. I hear your drone."

Josie heard the girl whimpering softly. On the screen, her body went still.

"Come on, Detective," Bell needled. "I'm getting impatient."

"Stop," Josie said. "Pull her back! I'm coming."

She turned to run to the base of the rock, but Noah caught her wrist.

Turner whispered, "Quinn, this kid is his only bargaining chip. If he throws her over, he doesn't get what he wants. He's not going to kill her just to get you up there."

Turner was wrong. Bell would get exactly what he wanted. Revenge on his old defense attorney, the next-to-last name on his revenge roll. In doing so, he'd force Josie to live with an unconscionable choice—a decision far worse than the one she'd made at the Cook residence fifteen years ago.

"I'm not comfortable taking that chance," Josie said, but Noah's grip was firm and unyielding.

"Josie," he said, managing to infuse a myriad of emotions into her name. The tortured look in his hazel eyes told her he wasn't comfortable risking the life of an innocent teenage girl either.

"I can do it," she said. "I've climbed it in the dark before. I climbed it with Ray tons of times in high school."

Bell's voice rose to a shout in Josie's ear. "You don't believe me? Let me give you a little more incentive, then. Her death doesn't have to be fast."

They watched in horror as Bell yanked Juliet back from the edge. He straddled her prone body. One of his arms reached for something at his side. The video wasn't crisp enough for them to see what it was but as his hand rose up over his head and then swooped down toward the girl, Josie knew exactly what he was doing.

One stab. Bell's voice vibrated with anger. "If you're not up here in five minutes, I'll keep going."

"I'm coming. Right now." Josie hung up and ripped her wrist away from Noah. She sprinted toward the base of the Overlook. Just as her feet touched stone, strong hands wrapped around her upper arms. She fought against them but it was useless. Noah spun her to face him.

"Josie, you promised to always come home to me."

His reference to their wedding vows sent a little stab of fear right into her heart. Still, her body strained against his grip. Every inch of her skin heated with adrenaline and panic. What was he doing? He knew her. Better than any person alive. He knew she wouldn't be able to live with herself if she didn't try to save Juliet Bowen, even if it meant losing her job, her entire career, maybe even her life. "You promised to always run toward the danger with me," she said.

He nodded. "I did."

Then he let her go, giving her a short lead before scrambling up after her.

SIXTY-THREE

There was a flashlight on her belt, but Josie needed her hands and feet to maneuver the narrow incline in the dark. As a teenager, Josie and her late husband Ray had become acquainted with almost all the rock formations in Denton, particularly the ones in remote areas. No adults to tell them what to do or not do. There was a weird sort of privacy being alone in the middle of the woods on top of a stone formation, especially the Overlook. It hadn't taken long for them to become adept at climbing it. It was one of their favorites because not many kids their age could climb it or had the courage to climb it —at least not more than once. Josie and Ray had lived childhoods that stamped the fear of death out of them—at least back then. They'd been invincible, never once considering how dangerous it was to repeatedly visit the top of the Overlook.

Now, muscle memory took over, just as it had when Josie climbed to the top for the Lucy Ross case. Her feet moved nimbly, staying in the center of the path. As they got closer to the summit, it got steeper. She leaned into it, walking with her hands and feet, concentrating on the feel of the cool stone under her palms so she didn't think about how high they were or the fact that any movement too far to the left or too far to the right would send her plummeting to her death. She focused on the sound of Noah's breathing just behind her. He'd also grown up in Denton. Had gone to the same high school as her and Ray. He'd likely climbed this thing at least once before.

As confident as she was in her ability to handle the Overlook, her body still reacted to the threat of falling. Her palms were clammy. An uncomfortable pressure built in her chest as she labored to draw breath. Blood rushed in her ears. Her scalp prickled.

"Drones," Noah said.

As they came within a few feet of the top, two small devices covered in lights whizzed over their heads. They hovered in the sky, casting an eerie glow. "Thank God," she mumbled. Finally, they reached the top. Josie threw herself over the lip of the plateau, landing on her knees. "I'm here! I'm here!"

Staggering to her feet, she drew her Glock. Bell stood less than twenty feet away. He had dragged Juliet upright and wrapped an arm around her neck. Josie could see the strain it took to keep her on her feet in the way the muscles of his forearm corded. Juliet's wrists and feet were bound with zip ties. Bell pressed the tip of the stained knife blade against her side. Blood spread across her white T-shirt. The wound was to her abdomen. She would still bleed out without medical attention, but a chest wound would have been much worse. If the blade had nicked her heart, she'd have a lot less time. Her eyes were closed but Josie could see the tear stains on her cheeks. Her long, dark hair was matted with dirt and leaves.

Over the buzz of the drones above them and her own labored breathing, Josie heard Noah moving just below her. He stayed out of sight, but she knew he was there, at the ready. Keeping her pistol in a low ready position, Josie sidestepped, trying to get a better angle on Bell, one that would give her the best chance of not hitting Juliet in the event that she needed to shoot him. In response, he backed up, tugging Juliet's sagging body along with him, closer to the edge.

"Please," the girl whispered. "Get me out of here."

Josie took a step toward him, trying to block out the fear that scattered goosebumps all over her skin. Even with her feet planted solidly on the ground, it was hard to fight the feeling of vertigo. The hovering drones gave off a fair amount of light. It was the pitch-black beyond the dome of that light that threatened Josie's sense of balance. Free fall in every direction. "Put her down, Roger."

He shuffled closer to the edge. Juliet moaned in pain. Her body tried to curl in on itself, but Bell wrenched her upward.

"I thought you wanted to talk, Roger." Josie tried to keep track of where her body was in relation to the drop-off, but looking away from Bell and Juliet for even a second felt dizzying. "Put Juliet down."

"So you can shoot me before we've had a chance to get things straight? I don't think so."

Her arms ached. "I'll put my gun away if you lower Juliet to the ground."

"I'm not stupid, Detective. You'll have to go first."

Noah was still hidden. He might have a shot if Josie could get Bell away from Juliet. Slowly, Josie holstered her weapon. Bell loosened his grip on the girl and lowered her to the ground. She curled onto her side, the edge of the cliff only inches from her knees. Roger stood nearby, knife still dangling from his hand. He was still close enough to push or even kick her over. Josie considered negotiating further to get Juliet into a less precarious position, but Bell was too smart to make himself vulnerable, not while she had a gun.

"You don't have to do this," Josie said. "You don't have to hurt Juliet—any more than you already have."

"Oh, but I do. There's really no choice at this point, is there?"

The pale skin of his face was shiny with sweat. His blond hair glistened. Josie wondered if he'd dyed it all these years. Faint silvery lines striped his neck where the snake tattoo had been. There was a strange gleam in his eyes, excited and predatory. His body remained still and relaxed, other than his white-knuckle grip on the knife. He was trapped. Out of options. He knew it. He'd gone to great lengths to create this very situation and yet, he seemed oddly happy.

Anticipation. That's what Josie saw in his eyes.

Dread clutched at her heart, squeezing painfully. All around them, the abyss of blackness pulsed against the glow of the drone lights.

If he'd just wanted to kill the girl, he would have done so already.

"What do you want, Roger?"

His fingers flexed around the handle of the knife. "What do you think I want, Detective Quinn?"

"You want people to pay. You've accomplished that. You don't need to kill Juliet. You've already made your point. All over this city—and beyond—you've made families suffer. Just like you and Sheila are suffering now that Jenna's gone. It's over. You got what you wanted."

He lurched toward her, knife spearing the air. In spite of the jolt of sheer terror that rattled her body, Josie held firm.

"If you think that I got what I wanted, then you weren't paying attention. I thought you got my message. I thought you understood."

She thought about the report Lamay had sent over just before she got Bell's call. No one had been paying attention fifteen years ago, or if they were, they hadn't cared. Her mind worked frantically to put together the bigger picture—to see what had led them here to this moment, but she did understand one thing. Roger Bell wasn't just after revenge. He could have gotten that without all the dramatics, without offering himself up to police on a silver platter.

He wanted his story told. These murders had been about getting the attention of the people who'd failed him, who'd failed the Cook family, as much as they'd been about retribution.

"Roger, I get it," Josie said quickly.

Roger dropped to his knees, hovering over Juliet. "I picked you. I spared you! Because I thought you were better than them. I thought you saw things that other people don't. You saw the girl on the street that day, didn't you? Do you remember her name?"

"No." She'd scoured the Cook file, but the girl had declined to make a statement, much less file a complaint against Lampson.

"Tory," Bell said.

Josie didn't know where he was going with this, but it didn't matter because he lowered his free hand to Juliet's hip. Josie stumbled forward, boot catching on a divot in the stone. Her body wobbled and flailed as she tried to regain her footing. "Stop!" she cried, thinking Roger was going to roll Juliet off the side and into oblivion.

Instead, he held Juliet's body in place and lifted the knife high above his head. Josie reacted without thought, closing the distance between them, and wrapping her hands around his wrist. His back was to her, so he wasn't prepared for her attack. As he struggled against her grip, still trying to bring the knife down into Juliet's side, Josie had a sudden moment of perfect clarity. Snapshots of the Cook crime scene photos flitted through her mind, like a deck of cards being shuffled.

Simon Cook in the hospital, three stab wounds to his back. The kitchen. The butcher block. The bag in Miranda O'Malley's bedroom, packed full to bursting. The furniture pushed almost up to her door. Simon Cook's overturned backpack, its contents scattered across his bed. The leather case too large for an iPod. Another image came—not from photos but from memory. Little Felicity Cook's chest flayed wide open. Being trapped under her big brother had probably saved her life, in an ironic twist. Then loose bits of information Josie had gathered in the last week from interviews and a review of the Cook file coalesced. The witness who had said that Bell was unnaturally fixated on Miranda O'Malley. Jenna Hampton dying of cardiac issues. Bell's message. Don't overlook it.

Josie tried to control the knife, yanking back on his wrist, trying to pull him away from Juliet. "Stop, Roger! Stop! You don't need to do this. I know! Okay? I know!"

He hadn't just been leading her here. He'd been asking her to see what everyone else had overlooked—intentionally or not, including the DNA results from the knife that didn't make it into evidence at trial.

A shadow moved at her back, Noah approaching from the side, his pistol aimed at Bell's rib cage. "Put the knife down! Put it down now!"

It wasn't a good shot. One look down over Bell's shoulder told Josie that Juliet's position was more precarious than ever. He no longer grasped her hip, instead using his other hand to try and pry Josie's fingers from his wrist. His upper body twisted. Their fight to control the knife caused Bell's body to nudge Juliet closer to the edge. Her head lolled over it, hair fluttering into the abyss.

Josie shouted more loudly. "I know, Roger! I know! Please, stop."

Noah holstered his weapon and joined Josie, taking hold of Bell's free hand and whipping it down and behind his back. The motion stunned him long enough for Josie to pry the knife from his grip. She tossed it away and wrenched his arm behind his back as Noah had done. Both she and Noah slid hands under his armpits and dragged him backward. His legs kicked out, hitting Juliet's back. Her body teetered for a brief, frozen moment. Around Josie, the entire world went silent and still. Even the air in her lungs froze. Then Noah let go of Bell and dove for Juliet, just as she rolled into the darkness.

SIXTY-FOUR

"No!" Josie pushed Bell aside and scrambled toward Noah. He was on his stomach, arms hanging from the edge. She dropped to her knees and leaned her head over as far as she dared. A long breath gushed from her lungs as she saw Noah's hands looped through one of Juliet's elbows. The zip ties binding her wrists gave him more traction, but Josie could see from the veins bulging in his forehead and the way he bared his teeth that he wasn't going to be able to hold her for long. Juliet was completely limp, dead weight. Josie sprawled onto her stomach beside Noah and reached for the girl. Her arms weren't as long as Noah's. With a groan, he tried to lightly swing Juliet toward Josie. It cost him a few inches, his body sliding forward. Josie was too focused on grabbing onto Juliet's shoulder to register the panic building inside her. With a hand hooked into Juliet's armpit, she pulled with all her might. Sweat poured down her face. The toes of her boots dug into the stone and her knees pressed against it. Her abs pulled taut, using every ounce of strength she had to help Noah bring the girl back to safety.

They managed to raise Juliet's body upward, pulling her arms across the stone floor so that the ledge was tucked under her armpits. Her chin dipped to her chest, almost touching the rocky surface. Then a large hand gripped the back of Josie's neck and dragged her upright. Bell held her against his chest. The blade of the knife bit into her throat. Then came the warm trickle of blood. It pooled in the hollow of her throat. With both hands, she yanked at Bell's forearm but he was too strong and she was too worried about Noah at their feet, trying to hold Juliet in place. There was no way he'd be able to pull her up entirely. Not without help.

Bell's hot, rancid breath skated down her jaw. "What do you think you know?"

"Everything," Josie said.

Noah's legs trembled with the effort of keeping his body from sliding. The muscles of his forearms twitched as he tried to keep Juliet's arms pinned in place. Josie's heart was going so fast, it felt like there was no time at all between beats. Under normal circumstances, she would fight back against Bell, but hand-to-hand combat was messy and unpredictable. Josie couldn't afford a single misstep. It could get one or all of them killed.

"Tell me," Bell said.

Josie tried to steady her breath, willing her pulse to slow. She needed to think clearly over the adrenaline barreling through her veins, setting every cell on fire. "Let me help them," she said.

The knife pinched the tender skin of her throat again. "No. You talk first. Maybe if you're right, I'll let one of them live."

Josie nearly choked on the gasp that bubbled up from her throat. One of them. She'd cross that bridge when she came to it. Right now, Noah had mere minutes before he either lost his grip on Juliet Bowen or went over the side with her. Mentally, she gathered up all the panic running wild in her brain and stuffed it into a box. A very sturdy box. Then she shoved that box into the impenetrable vault inside her where she sent all the things that were too horrible for her mind and body to contain.

Good God, she hoped her theory was right.

"You didn't kill the Cooks."

A small bit of tension drained from Bell's entire body. Josie could feel it from the loosening of the knife against her skin to the momentary weakening of his knees where they dug into the backs of her thighs.

Noah's breathing was heavy and loud. Guttural noises rose from his throat. Not wanting to waste any more time, Josie forced out the narrative she'd constructed in her head only moments ago as fast as she could. "You didn't kill them. You—you worked there more than at any other home in the neighborhood. They were like your family. You loved little Fel—Felicity and Miranda, too. Even though she was underage."

Bell pushed against her back, shuffling their fused bodies closer to Noah and Juliet. His foot shot out, making contact with Noah's side, just below the kidney. His body jerked. His grip on Juliet faltered. Josie screamed involuntarily, hating the desperate sound. She'd gotten that part wrong.

Trying again, she said, "No, no. You cared for Miranda. Like a sister. You weren't the one bothering her. You only wanted to protect her. Something was happening in that house. Maybe you saw it or maybe she just told you, but Miranda was in danger. Her—her room. She was putting the furniture up against the door at night, wasn't she? To keep someone out."

Bell watched Noah squirm near his feet. Juliet's body slid another couple of inches. "Who?"

"Simon," Josie breathed. "It was Simon. He was the one obsessed with Miranda. There was only one witness who stated that you were the one with an unnatural fixation on her, making her uncomfortable. That witness was Simon. When you tried to tell the Cooks what was going on, he turned it around on you. They believed him over you because he was their son."

A sheen of sweat covered Noah's forearms. More unintelligible noises came from deep in his chest. Every part of his body shook. Juliet's forehead rested against the ledge.

"The Cooks fired you because of what Simon said. Miranda corroborated your story, but they didn't believe her."

Bell kicked out at Noah again, this time making contact with his hip. Noah was too deep in concentration, trying to keep Juliet from plummeting to her death, to even register it.

"Okay, okay," Josie said. "She wanted to corroborate your story, but she was too afraid of Simon. He—he threatened her. There was a bag in her room on the day of the murders. It was packed full of clothes and makeup. She was going to leave. You came back that day. First you tried again to convince the Cooks that Simon was a danger to Miranda. They still didn't listen. You left and came back later, not to hurt anyone. You came back for Miranda. You were going to take her away from the house, but when you got there, everyone was already... dead."

Bell's arm was like a vise across her chest, almost cutting off her air. Panting, Josie forged ahead. "Except Simon. You went into the kitchen and found him stabbing little Felicity. His back was to you. He didn't see you. You took the knife from him and stabbed him three times from behind. He—he fell onto Felicity. You thought she was already dead. You were—you were in shock. Scared. No one believed you when you told them the truth about Simon. Why would they believe you when it came to the murders? So you ran."

His grip tightened on her, but she no longer felt the knife against her throat. Shoving her forward, he lifted a foot in Noah's direction. Josie yanked at his forearm. "Please," she screamed. "Please. Don't."

Instead of kicking, Bell planted his foot across one of Noah's quaking calves and applied pressure. Noah hissed in pain.

"The knife! The knife!" Hysteria sent her voice up an octave. "The butcher block on the countertop was full. There

weren't any knives missing. Simon was a minor. He wouldn't
have been able to buy a hunting knife or anything like that, but
no one would have stopped him from buying a kitchen knife. It
had a sheath. A brown leather sheath. It was on his bed that day
but no one noticed it. It was next to his iPod. It was way too big
to be a cover for an iPod but no one ever bothered to look that
closely. But most importantly, the knife itself—the DNA of all
the Cooks and Miranda was found on the blade but only two
people left DNA on the handle. You and Simon."

Bell ground his heel into the back of Noah's calf. Josie realized that he wasn't struggling quite as much. He had gotten a
better grip on Juliet. Was Bell still trying to hurt him or keep
him in place?

"Why didn't you tell everyone it was Simon?" That was the
part that Josie couldn't figure out. Why hadn't Bell simply
pointed a finger at Simon?

Against her back, she felt a low growl vibrate inside Bell's
chest. His foot came off Noah's calf. He started to slide. Josie
racked her brain, trying not to give in to the screaming, swirling
tornado of panic bumping against the limits of her
consciousness.

"Please," she begged, watching as Juliet's forehead slipped
beneath the ledge. Words rushed from her mouth, so fast, she
could barely keep them in order. "Wait. I know. I can think of it.
Your—your mug shot! You tried to tell the police when you were
arrested but they beat the shit out of you. It was Lampson,
wasn't it? He refused to take a statement where you named
Simon Cook. You were his suspect. It was a slam dunk. He was
—he was lazy like that and then Bowen! Bowen! He—he didn't
believe you. He said no one else would. You could use the 'I
walked in after the fact' defense but accusing a boy whose
family had just been slaughtered and admitting you'd stabbed
him would be too damaging. Nobody would buy it, especially
because you ran."

As a defense attorney, Andrew Bowen was required to present whatever defense his client offered, regardless of its merit. Instead, he'd bullied a scared and vulnerable Bell, insisting he not accuse Simon at all.

"Bowen didn't need much of a defense anyway because he could get the knife thrown out," Josie continued.

Bell put his foot back on Noah's leg. Josie's entire body went weak with momentary relief. "If Bowen had believed you, presented the defense you gave him, and let the knife come into evidence, maybe Simon could have been charged. But he didn't care about Simon or even who killed the Cooks. All he cared about was getting you acquitted because that was his job."

She strongly doubted her colleagues at the time would have gone back and reviewed the evidence with a view toward developing Simon as a suspect, but there was enough there to have supported Roger's claims, had Bowen let him testify to them. Had the knife been admissible.

"Jo—Josie," Noah choked.

She tugged at Bell's forearm again. "Please. Help them. Or let me help them."

"You forgot the most important part," Bell whispered in her ear. "The reason we're here."

Josie didn't want to expend any more mental energy playing Roger Bell's game. She wanted to beg for the lives of her husband and Juliet Bowen but knew it would do no good. "Felicity. No, Jenna. You tracked her down to protect her."

The arm around her chest let up, allowing her to draw a full breath, finally. She kept going. "You were afraid Simon would find her and probably you, too, and finish what he started. You felt obligated to watch over her since he was still out there. You fell in love with Sheila and Jenna."

Bell's arm fell to Josie's waist, holding her so loosely now. She wondered if she could lunge forward, slip out of his grasp, and dive onto Noah's quivering body in time. Bell's voice was scratchy. "Jenna was everything to me. Everything that was good and pure and beautiful in the world. She was my second chance. My silver lining. A miracle. Then she died. A murder that took fifteen years to claim its victim."

"Yes," Josie said. "Her cardiac issues were from the stab wounds Simon inflicted, weren't they? The heart muscle was too damaged, too weakened to survive long-term."

Josie felt something hot and wet against her temple and realized that Bell was weeping. "Sheila tried to get her on the transplant list, but the wait was too long. I would rather have served a half dozen life terms in prison than watch my little girl waste away and die. He took her from me that day and every single person who showed up afterward let him."

He released her, pushing her toward Noah as he lifted his foot. The knife clattered to the ground. Bell strode away from them, toward the opposite side of the plateau. Josie had no time to see what he would do next. She threw herself onto her stomach and started to haul Juliet Bowen back up onto the Overlook. Noah's grip was weak, his arms shaking so badly, it was hard to believe he had any strength left in them. Once they'd pulled Juliet's upper body to safety, Josie gently pushed Noah aside and dragged her the rest of the way.

Noah flipped onto his back and stared at the drone floating overhead, chest heaving. Josie pressed two fingers to Juliet's throat, relieved to find a thready pulse. It was then that she noticed Roger staring at her from across the stone floor, his back to the darkness, heels kissing the abyss beyond.

"Roger, wait."

A sad smile touched his lips. "Detective Quinn. Do you know how it feels to lose everything?"

Josie stood up, advancing on him. "I know what it feels like to lose someone you love."

She should have known this was how he would end things. Deep down, she had known it.

He held up a hand, stopping her in her tracks. "You want to protect the innocent? Then protect the innocent. Don't come after me."

There was nothing she could do. In the time it would take to reach him, he'd be gone. "But..." she spluttered. "The last polaroid. You can't—the plan, your game—it's unfinished."

"You found this place," Bell said, a peace so palpable spreading across his face, Josie could feel its wave where she stood. Dammit. No matter what he'd lost, he should be held accountable for his crimes.

"No," she said. "The polaroid you left in Juliet's bed. The one taken inside my home."

His calm expression faltered. Confusion flickered in his eyes. "I didn't take a polaroid from inside your home."

The fine hairs on Josie's arms and the back of her neck rose. "Then who did?"

He shook his head.

"The older woman helping you," Josie blurted. "Her?"

Again, that slow, morose shake of his head. "She's innocent in all this. She just wanted to help me. She had no idea what I was doing."

"Then who took the last polaroid?" Josie demanded. Her voice was getting high-pitched again.

He mumbled something to himself, but Josie couldn't make it out. She stepped closer, now tempted to go after him, to try to drag him back to the center of the perch they were on and do whatever she had to do to get an answer. She opened her mouth to interrogate him further, but he spoke before she could get a word out.

"Losing everything you love feels like falling," he said. "From a very great height."

Then he crossed his arms over his chest and let his body fall.

SIXTY-FIVE
TWO WEEKS LATER

"What are we doing here, Quinn?" Turner pushed his curly mop away from his forehead. A sheen of sweat covered his face. He was wearing his suit jacket even though it was almost one hundred degrees.

Josie kept walking down one of the tree-lined streets of the oldest residential neighborhood in the city. Stately Victorian homes rose up on either side, their manicured lawns stretched out like emerald carpets. Her friend Misty lived only a couple of blocks away. If Turner wasn't with her, she'd stop by and have lunch. The pleasant thought of Misty and Harris was pushed to the back of her mind as the old Cook residence came into view.

"This is it," Josie said, stopping in front of the home.

Turner sighed. "We're still on this. Quinn, you have to let this shit go. The Polaroid Killer is dead. The girl survived. We have no leads on the mysterious grandmother but hey, I don't think Granny is going to go on a stabbing spree, so case closed."

Except it wasn't closed. Not for Josie. She couldn't stop thinking about the grandmotherly woman who'd bought Bell access to the classic cars on Schock's Auto Repair lot. She couldn't sleep at night wondering about the final polaroid, taken inside her house. The rest of the team was more or less convinced that Bell had lied about not taking it. Noah said it was just another way to screw with her mind. Gretchen thought he'd denied taking it because he knew it would have this effect on her. Slowly drive her out of her mind. Who could trust a man who'd lied to his wife for over a decade and slaughtered so many innocent people?

Bell had been looney tunes, as Turner put it.

But Josie had read everything else correctly. She'd been able to figure out that Isaac Hampton was really Roger Bell, not Simon Cook. She'd figured out what Bell wanted her to see—the story he wanted to come out—just from the small, infinitesimal details in the case file and news reports. Her guesses had saved the lives of her husband and Juliet Bowen. When everything was said and done, Kellan Neal had admitted to her that after Bell's acquittal, Andrew Bowen had come to him, suggesting that Simon Cook was the actual killer, and imploring him to look into charges. Neal wouldn't even entertain it.

When Josie spoke with Andrew Bowen at his daughter's bedside in the hospital, he confirmed Neal's recollection. He hadn't believed Bell's version of events. He hadn't even believed in his innocence, but he had a job to do. He was young and hungry, bent on proving himself as a defense attorney. His only interest was in an acquittal, and he did what he had to do in order to get it, including completely dismissing Bell's claims that Simon Cook was the killer. Bell's story didn't matter because Bowen was able to keep the knife out. Then, after being acquitted of four counts of first-degree homicide and two counts of attempted homicide, Bell was a broken man. That got Bowen to thinking that maybe he had been telling the truth. It ate at him, even after Bell disappeared from the area. To ease his own guilt, Bowen had broached the subject with Neal, and even Lampson.

Nothing ever came of it.

"Did you hear me, Quinn?" Turner's voice broke through her ruminations.

Josie touched the picket fence surrounding the Cook property. It was vacant. A For Rent sign hung crookedly on the front door. A developer had bought it after the trial but when he realized that the home was on the historical register and therefore, he couldn't knock it down and build an apartment building in its place, he sold it to someone else, who'd been trying to rent it out ever since. There had been a few tenants over the years, but most people didn't want to live in a house where so much violence had occurred.

"I heard you," Josie muttered.

It had been painted since then. A new roof had been installed. The flowers Amelia Cook had planted in the front yard were long gone.

"Can we eat after this walk down memory lane?" Turner took out his phone and started scrolling. "I'm starving."

"I'm not having lunch with you."

"Come on, Quinn. Buy me lunch. Somewhere nice. You're flush with cash. Hell, I don't think I can fit one more dollar into your jar."

"I'll get another jar."

"You won't need one if you spend some of it taking me to lunch. If you think about it, it's really me buying you lunch since that's my money."

She rolled her eyes and pushed the gate open. As she walked up to the porch, sense memories crashed over her. The overpowering scent of blood. Little Felicity Cook's fragile, cracked sternum under Josie's fingers. The odor of her own vomit. The bile burning the back of her throat. Blood sticky on her forearms and wet against her kneecaps where it had soaked through her pants. Peluso's hand at her back. The unbridled rage consuming her as she watched Lampson harass a teenage girl.

Turning to face the street, Josie saw Turner standing in almost the same place the girl had been that day.

Tory.

Why had Roger Bell known her name? Because she was Miranda O'Malley's best friend? It made sense given how much time he'd spent at the Cook family home. Enough time to bond with Felicity and feel protective of Miranda. What didn't make sense was why no one had ever interviewed Tory to corroborate the events that led to the murders. Surely, Miranda would have told her that it was Simon making her uncomfortable and not Bell. Then again, it would have been Lampson's job to get her statement. Josie doubted the girl had been willing to make herself available after what happened.

"Quinn," Turner called without looking up from his phone. "Revisiting this house of horrors is a waste of time."

Roger Bell had visited this house multiple times after the death of his daughter, Jenna Hampton. They'd received the GPS report from his vehicle yesterday. It showed that he had driven here, to the old Cook house, over two dozen times in the last two months. He'd started coming here long before the murders. Sometimes his car was parked in front of the house for hours and other times for no longer than fifteen minutes.

Josie wondered if Sheila Hampton had been right about her husband having an affair. When Josie first examined the GPS records, she wondered if his mistress lived here, in one of these houses. Why else would he be here so often? But then she had seen all his visits to the Patio Motel. Just off the interstate, it was the very definition of seedy. The building was practically falling down. The room numbers on the exterior doors were written in Sharpie. An old in-ground pool sat out front, filled with garbage. The owner rented by the hour and only took cash. No credit cards, no records. He didn't check IDs so his guest log was unreliable. The names she'd found in it that matched the times Bell had been there were listed as Daffy and Daisy Duck.

The owner claimed he had never seen Roger Bell there. When Josie showed him the GPS records, he said he didn't remember. It was a dead end. As was Bell's phone. They'd managed to get records of his text messages. There were several that referenced meeting at "PM", a clear reference to the Patio Motel, but the phone number he was communicating with was a burner.

Turner pocketed his phone and sauntered up the path, stopping at the bottom of the steps. "Quinn, really. I know someone helped this guy. We all know it. But we can't prove it. All the evidence that came back processed, all the records, only point to him. Clearly, he made sure we wouldn't be able to identify his accomplice. We can't find that person without some sort of lead, and we're fresh out of those."

He was right. They were at an impasse. Frustration knotted the muscles in her shoulder blades. Slowly, she scanned the houses all around them. There were only two people she knew personally in this area. Misty and Margaret Bonitz. Josie walked the length of the wraparound porch until she could see between two houses across the street.

Turner said, "Whaddya wanna do? Start knocking on doors? See if anyone remembers seeing him hanging around? Ask if they remember whether or not he was with someone else?"

Margaret Bonitz lived one block over. She was the longest-tenured resident in the neighborhood. Long before the Cook murders, Margaret and her husband had moved into their home. They'd raised their children and seen them off to their adult lives in other parts of the country. Then Mr. Bonitz passed away, leaving Margaret alone in their big old house. Every time Josie visited, it was like a time capsule, everything just as it was in the late nineties after she was widowed. In fact, she still kept his '95 Lincoln Continental in the garage.

"Son of a bitch," Josie said.

Turner squinted up at her. "What's that?"

"Remember when you spoke with Margaret Bonitz a few weeks ago?"

"Oh, the lady whose dog you let piss on me? Yeah."

"What was her complaint? Why did she call?"

Turner shook his head, looking at her like she was nuts. "I don't know. Something about a neighbor putting their garbage into her bins on trash day. Who cares?"

Josie moved down the steps, stopping in front of him. "Did you look in her garbage bin?"

"You really are losing your mind."

"Did you?"

He said nothing. The way he pursed his lips told her he was seconds away from being finished with this entire conversation.

"Turner!" Josie snapped.

"Of course I did!" He threw his hands in the air and let them fall to his sides. "I know you think every day is my first day on the job but it's not. You think I'm careless and lazy and that I'm only here to do the least amount of work in order to get my paycheck, but—"

"What was in it?"

"What?"

Josie put a hand on her hip. "What was in Mrs. Bonitz's trash bin?"

"Trash, Quinn. Trash."

The urge to throat punch him was very, very strong. He must have figured that out because he took a step back from her and said, "I don't know. I just opened the bag and peeked inside. I didn't go through it. There was just some old exterminator suit or something. Wait."

Josie left him standing there, his mouth agape, and strode

back to her SUV. By the time she started the ignition, Turner was folding himself into the passenger's seat. "You think Bell came here to dispose of the hazmat suits he took from his wife's work supplies and wore to murder people so he could put them into Mrs. Bonitz's trash?"

"I don't know," Josie said, pulling away from the curb.

"There wasn't any blood on the suit I saw," Turner pointed out. "And she called us before the murders started."

Josie swung the SUV around the corner and onto Margaret Bonitz's street. "Before the murders in Denton started. Bud Ernst was strangled shortly before the first murder in our jurisdiction. He lived in the Poconos. Not far from here. It's entirely possible that Bell was responsible. Maybe he wore the suit so he could avoid leaving DNA. Then he brought the suit back with him and threw it out in her garbage. No one would ever think of searching Margaret Bonitz's garbage for evidence of a murder."

They never had figured out what Bell did with the hazmat suits when he finished with them.

Turner eyed the house as they pulled up in front of it. "You think Margaret Bonitz is the grandmother?"

Josie threw the SUV in park and turned it off. "Let's go find out."

SIXTY-SIX

The Jack Russell terrier was sunning on its back in the middle of the yard. It didn't move when Josie and Turner walked past it, but it did turn its head and give a perfunctory growl. Mrs. Bonitz took a few minutes to answer the doorbell. She greeted Josie with a smile. "So good to see you, young lady."

Then she looked behind Josie, where Turner's huge frame blocked all the light from the door. Scowling, she said, "You again."

Turner didn't respond.

"May we come in?" Josie asked.

Mrs. Bonitz looked behind her where the foyer narrowed into a hallway leading to the kitchen. Wringing her hands, she said, "Well, if you don't mind company. An old neighbor stopped by to chat. Haven't seen her since she was headed off to college." The deep lines around her eyes crinkled as her expression darkened. "We were just talking about Roger since we both knew him from way back when. It's a shock, I'll tell you. Those poor women. I had no idea what he was up to, you know. No idea it was even him until I saw the news."

A fluttering sensation filled Josie's chest. Briefly, she looked

over her shoulder at Turner. Surprise flickered in his eyes. Then
his features turned stony. "Mrs. Bonitz," he said. "We're sorry to
interrupt your reunion but we'd like you to come down to the
stationhouse. There are some questions we need to ask you."

Mrs. Bonitz swayed as she stepped backward. She rested a
hand on the circular table in the center of the foyer to steady
herself, sending the Tiffany-style lamp bobbling. Josie followed,
catching it before it toppled to the floor. For the first time, she
noticed that the molding and the wainscoting looked new. Even
the pine floor looked level and freshly lacquered. In fact, all of
the woodwork and flooring in the foyer as well as the stairs and
entryway into the parlor looked newly restored. The last time
she'd been inside, the house had been shabby and neglected,
much of the woodwork warped, splintered, or rotted. Mrs.
Bonitz was on a fixed income. She didn't have the budget for
major repairs.

"You want me to come to the police station? I don't think I—
well, I'm not really dressed for it, and I... I think there's been a
misunderstanding."

Turner crossed the threshold. "A misunderstanding we can
discuss at the station. Why don't you let your guest know you're
coming with us, and we'll give you a ride?"

Mrs. Bonitz didn't budge. Her fingers stroked the lace doily
on the table nervously. It was only marginally cooler in the
house than outside. A small air conditioner hummed in one of
the front windows, doing little to bring the temperature down.
"I told you, I didn't know that young man was Roger Bell. I
didn't recognize him. He came and offered to do work for me.
Didn't want a cent from me. Just asked me to help him with
something. I never would have helped him if I thought he was a
murderer, although I never did think Roger Bell was a killer. He
worked for me before the Cooks. Did you know that?"

"Mrs. Bonitz," Josie said. "Why don't we find your purse so

we can get down to the station. Anything you need to tell us can wait until we get there."

She seemed not to hear Josie. "Back then, Roger was a lovely young man. Sweet and kind. A gentleman. I knew he didn't hurt the Cooks. I never believed it. He stayed with me, you know? After the trial. He had no one. The whole city hated him. Except me. That was the last time I saw him. Then a couple of months ago this other man shows up. Wanted to work for me. Fix up all the—" She gestured around them. "Wood, like Roger did before on the second floor. I offered to pay him but all he wanted was a favor. Give a man some money so he could have access to some cars. Pick him up from places. The middle of damn nowhere."

Josie touched Mrs. Bonitz's shoulder. "We can talk about that at the station. Where's your purse?"

Mrs. Bonitz pulled away from Josie, planting both hands against the table. "I just told you I didn't do anything wrong, and I have company—"

Turner's fingers drummed against his leg. "Listen, lady—"

A female voice cut him off. "Are you really going to drag a woman in her nineties down to the police station like some kind of criminal?"

Vicky Platt stood in the doorway of the kitchen. In heels, a fitted black skirt, and a sleeveless silk blouse, she looked every bit the powerful television producer. One hand rested on her hip while the other hung at her side, clutching her cell phone.

"We're doing our jobs." Turner appraised her. "I suggest you gather your things and get out of here."

Vicky returned his slow perusal, unimpressed. "I liked you better the last time we spoke."

"Yeah, well, most women don't like me at all." Turner muscled past Josie and gently placed a hand on Mrs. Bonitz's back, ushering her across the foyer toward a closet. His careful movements were at odds with his bad attitude. Fishing around inside the closet, he came up with a purse and a cane.

Josie was frozen in place, watching as Vicky bent her head to her phone, thumbs tapping wildly. Mrs. Bonitz had called her an old neighbor. Not a producer from WYEP. Not the press. They'd both known Roger Bell. Finished with her text, Vicky looked up and locked eyes with Josie. The eyes. Why hadn't she noticed before? Then again, why would she have noticed? She'd spoken to Vicky before they knew about the Cook case.

"Quinn," Turner said as he and Mrs. Bonitz shuffled toward the front door.

"Just a minute," Josie said. "I want to talk to Tory."

He huffed. "Fine. Whatever. We'll wait in the car. Give me your keys."

Without breaking eye contact with Vicky, Josie got them out of her pocket and dropped them into his waiting palm.

Once the door closed behind Turner and Mrs. Bonitz, Vicky smiled. "I didn't think you remembered."

"I didn't," Josie said. "Your name isn't in the police file. Roger was the one who told me. Right before he died."

Pain rippled across Vicky's face. For a moment, Josie thought she was going to cry.

"He called you Tory. I didn't make the connection until just now. Victoria. You went by Tory then."

Vicky's eyes watered. "I started going by Vicky when I got married. Vicky Platt sounded better than Tory Platt. At least, my husband thought so. We got divorced after two years but I just stayed Vicky Platt. You were... you were with Roger when he died?"

Josie nodded.

A tear rolled down Vicky's cheek. She used the heel of her palm to wipe it away. "He talked about me?"

A tingle began at the base of Josie's spine. Things started to shift in the shadowy place in the back of her mind. The place

where her brain dumped little facts and loose pieces of information that didn't seem important. Random floating particles
connected to nothing. Meaningless without context.

"You were in love with Roger Bell."

Vicky didn't answer, instead palming away more tears. She
was a producer for WYEP. According to Dallas Jones, she was
aggressive in pursuing stories, almost to the point of harassment.
Yet, in the aftermath of Roger Bell's dramatic death and the
resurfacing of the Cook family murders, she hadn't used her
connection to him at all to further her career.

From outside, Josie heard Mrs. Bonitz admonishing her dog.
Turner complaining loudly. "You were having an affair with
him."

Sniffling, Vicky said, "It's not illegal. We only... started
recently. Only found one another again in the last year. Roger
was separated from his wife. If you're thinking that I knew he
was planning to go on a murder spree, I didn't. If you want me
to come to your station to tell you that, on the record, I will."

She did want to take Vicky down to the station because she
didn't believe her. But her gut told her that the ride to the
station would only give her time to compose herself and
rehearse her denials. "If you're prepared to come down to the
station," Josie said, "you won't mind if I Mirandize you."

Vicky gave her a wobbly smile and wiped at her nose. "Can
you do it in the kitchen?"

Josie nodded and followed her into Mrs. Bonitz's kitchen.
Apparently, Roger Bell's work hadn't extended to this room.
The floorboards were dull and warped in some places. The
wooden cabinets were a faded sea-moss green, some of their
knobs gone. The heavy oak table in the center of the room
canted to the side. Two unfinished coffee cups sat atop it. A
massive box air conditioner sat in a window next to the back
door, the frame sagging under its weight. An uneven glugging
noise sputtered from its vents as it labored to push cold air into

the room. While Josie recited her Miranda rights, Vicky tore a paper towel from the roll suspended over the sink and dabbed at her face. Once she acknowledged that she understood her rights, Josie resumed her questions.

"You were Miranda O'Malley's best friend. Yet you fell in love with the man everyone thought killed her. Did you know Roger didn't kill the Cooks, or did he convince you of that when you reconnected?"

Vicky leaned her hip against the edge of the sink. The light was better in here and Josie spied faint fingerprint bruises on her throat, mostly covered with foundation. "I knew he didn't kill anyone. He was far too sweet and kind and caring to do anything like that. I mean, he was obsessed with getting Miranda out of the house."

There was a hint of petulance in her voice when she said Miranda's name. Her eyes lifted up and to the left, as if she was about to roll them but then she caught herself.

He was obsessed with getting Miranda out of the house.

She didn't sound like someone who was grateful that an adult was taking charge and trying to help her best friend out of a dangerous situation. She sounded like a girlfriend who was annoyed that her man was paying attention to someone else.

Josie moved out of the doorway to the head of the table, now only a few feet from Vicky. "Were you and Roger seeing one another then?"

Vicky crumpled the paper towel in her fist. On the back of her hand was another bruise, dark and angry. "I was a minor."

"That never stopped a man before."

Vicky laughed and Josie could hear the undertone of bitterness. "Right. Well, it stopped Roger. He wouldn't touch me."

"Did he touch Miranda?"

Vicky picked at an imaginary piece of lint on her blouse. "No, but sometimes I thought he wanted to."

"And Miranda?" Josie coaxed. "What did she think?"

Vicky's upper lip curled in an almost-sneer. It was disconcerting considering they were talking about a girl who'd been brutally slain, a girl who was supposed to be her best friend. "She thought he was a knight in shining armor. Her savior. The day before... it happened, she told me she thought she was in love with him. He'd offered to come get her and take her to his place until she could be reunited with her parents. She didn't say, but I thought she was going to try something once they were alone in his apartment."

"But if Roger wouldn't touch you because you were underage, why would he become physical with Miranda?"

Vicky shrugged and for a heartbeat, she looked like the teenage girl Josie had seen standing on the sidewalk, watching police go in and out of her best friend's house. "I don't know. Probably the same reason Simon was obsessed with her. All I ever wanted was Roger. I was in love with him first. I had his attention first. She knew that! She just didn't care. All she cared about was him being her personal hero and getting him alone in his apartment."

"You've always been in love with him, haven't you?" Josie watched her face carefully. "In fact, you would do anything for him, wouldn't you? Even try to access sealed court records."

Vicky went very still. The corners of her mouth twitched. "I didn't need to access court records to find Roger. He saw me on television. We did a behind-the-scenes, meet-the-producers piece. He recognized me and tracked me down."

"And asked you to help him locate Simon?"

Vicky said nothing.

"You used Stella's desire to do a big story on her grandfather to manipulate her into accessing Simon's new identity."

Vicky sighed. Something in her eyes shifted. Her face hardened. A mask slipping off to reveal something very different beneath it. "I suggested that she should start with the Cook file. I might have told her that her grandfather royally screwed up the case and got away with it, to properly motivate her. We just needed to find Simon and Roger so we could interview them. I had already found Roger, but she didn't need to know that."

Denton PD had gotten access to Simon Cook's new identity but hadn't been able to locate him. He lived in a rundown house on the outskirts of Bellewood, forty miles away, and worked under the table for a roofing company. His boss hadn't seen him in weeks. "Did you pass Simon's information on to Roger?"

"I couldn't," Vicky whispered.

Over the gurgling of the air conditioner, Josie thought she heard heavy footsteps.

"Why couldn't you tell Roger where to find Simon?"

Vicky's head swiveled toward the back door. Josie followed her gaze but saw nothing. The footsteps had stopped. Tension hung in the air like an electric charge. The phantom fingers of fear skittered across Josie's scalp. Her hand went to her holster as the lizard part of her brain registered a threat before she could actually see it.

Josie heard Vicky's next words as if from a great distance. "I couldn't let Roger find Simon because I created a monster."

SIXTY-SEVEN

A shadow appeared at the back door. It creaked open and a man squeezed through it. He was as tall as Turner but thick, round, and wide. A moving wall that swallowed up all the space in the room. Beady eyes glimmered from his round face, aglow with hunger. An apex predator about to pounce on its next meal. Josie recognized him from the day at the Cooks' house and the photos from the case file that had been taken in the hospital.

Simon Cook.

Without thought, her fingers unsnapped her holster. Her palm wrapped around the pistol grip. He sidestepped the table and advanced on the two of them. From her periphery, Josie saw Vicky visibly tense. Her fingers scratched at the bruises on her throat.

Simon stopped a few feet from them. He wore long pants and a white T-shirt. On the side of his abdomen, a strip of red bled through, staining his shirt. He looked sick, feral. His fingers twitched at his sides. Eyeing Josie, he addressed Vicky. "Why did you text me?"

What the hell was happening? Josie's palm tightened

around the handle of her gun. She wanted to see Vicky's face, but she dared not take her eyes off Simon.

"You know," Vicky said quietly.

Simon licked his lips. Josie's stomach roiled. He wasn't armed, as far as she could tell. He wasn't wanted in connection with any crimes. Not yet. The DA's office was still reviewing the Cook file to see if there was enough to charge him with his family's deaths. He was, however, wanted for questioning. "Mr. Cook, I'm Detective Josie Quinn. Denton PD. We've been trying to locate you. We need you to come to the police station to answer some questions."

Simon's expression darkened. "Is she serious?"

Vicky's voice cracked. "Yes."

"I am serious, Mr. Cook," Josie said firmly. Slowly, she angled her body so that she had a full view of him and Vicky. "My colleague is outside. We're prepared to give you a ride to the station now."

She would be annoyed that Turner hadn't come back in, but he had no reason to think Vicky Platt was a threat and he wouldn't have seen Simon enter through the back door.

Simon's fists flexed at his sides. "You didn't tell me she was a cop. You tricked me."

Every cell in Josie's body screamed danger even though Simon hadn't done anything to pose a threat to her—no matter that his words implied otherwise. She couldn't pull her weapon on him without reason. Still her fingers twitched, desperate to have her Glock in her hands.

There was a tremor in Vicky's voice. "I didn't."

He pointed a finger at Vicky, and she flinched. Josie had no doubt the bruises on her throat and hand had come from Simon Cook. Fresh blood leaked from the wound under his shirt, spreading across the fabric. It seemed to have no effect on him. "What are you trying to do? What is this?"

Vicky rubbed at her throat. "You know what this is. We made a deal."

Simon fingered the blood on his shirt. "The deal was that I take care of some bitch—not a cop—and you give me what I want. Whenever I want it. Not just once."

Vicky visibly shuddered. Her thighs clenched.

"Both of you need to come down to the station to talk with us," Josie said.

Simon edged closer to Vicky. "Oh what? You didn't like it? Give me a break. You came looking for me. I know you liked it. Besides, it was the least you could do after you tried to kill me. Maybe I should tell your friend here about that, huh?"

"Maybe I should tell her what you did to your own family."

Simon took another step, crowding Vicky. "Maybe I should tell her what really happened that day. How you told me Roger was coming to take Miranda away from me. How you said she lied about not wanting to be with me and I hadn't misread all the signals she'd been sending. Remember? You said she just didn't want to do things while we were in my parents' house. You told me I would lose her to Roger if I didn't do something."

Vicky pressed her body against the edge of the sink, recoiling from him. "I meant you should talk to your parents to make sure Roger didn't have access to her. I didn't tell you to kill Miranda and your whole damn family, you sicko."

Josie wasn't sure she believed Vicky. She'd wanted Roger for herself. Her infatuation with him had lasted fifteen years, through her own marriage to someone else. She'd manipulated Stella Townsend into getting Simon's new name because Roger wanted revenge. There was no way in hell Vicky didn't know what he was planning. Obviously, Simon had had issues back when his family and Miranda were still alive. He'd frightened Miranda so badly she'd pushed furniture against her bedroom door to keep him out. She'd been willing to run off with an older man to escape him.

Simon clearly wasn't living in the same reality as the people around him—then or now. Vicky had used that to drive a wedge between Miranda and Roger. Maybe she hadn't understood how unstable Simon had been or that he was capable of unspeakable violence, but she had manipulated him, nonetheless.

That was why she couldn't tell Roger where to find him.

Roger was already haunted by what happened to the Cooks. She couldn't risk the man she loved finding out that she'd had a role in it. But she'd made contact with Simon again, and clearly things hadn't gone as planned.

What was Vicky's endgame right now?

She had to know Josie would shoot Simon if he tried to attack her. Even Simon had figured that out. She'd try to manipulate him again. Make a deal with him she had no intention of keeping. Summoning him here while the two of them were alone. He must have been stalking her to arrive so quickly. She'd banked on him being crazy enough to try to kill Josie even though she was armed. Death by cop. Vicky would be free of him. Her secrets would be safe.

"You lied to me again," Simon snarled.

"And you just ran your mouth, you stupid shit. What are you going to do now?"

As every process in Josie's body went into overdrive, time slowed. Simon lunged for Vicky, wrapping his meaty hands around her throat and driving her backward until her body slammed into a freestanding glass china cabinet. One of the panes shattered as the back of Vicky's skull smashed into it. Simon lifted her until both her feet dangled off the floor, kicking wildly. One of her heels flew off. Her eyes bulged and her nails dug into his forearms, scratching deeply enough to draw blood. Josie moved in on him, pistol aimed at his side, the pad of her index finger already on the trigger. She was a good shot, but it was still a risk to Vicky in close quarters. She shouted commands at Simon. When he didn't obey any of them, Josie took the shot.

The concussive boom echoed through the small room. Simon's body jerked and then froze before falling to his knees and then his back. Blood bloomed along the side of his shirt, under his rib cage, spreading fast. As Vicky fell onto her hands and knees, wheezing, Josie holstered her Glock and squatted to flip Simon onto his stomach. It was no easy task, given his weight. She was out of breath by the time she secured his wrists with zip ties.

She sensed Vicky lurching to her feet. Then something flashed. Before Josie could process what was happening, her arm flew up, blocking her face. Pain seared through her forearm. Some part of her brain registered the large shard of glass embedded in her skin as Vicky Platt tried to pull it back out to stab again. A savage anger twisted her features.

Josie managed to get to her feet as Vicky tore the shard away. Blood poured from the gash, but her body felt nothing. Adrenaline blocked out everything after the initial pain, including the wild, uneven beat of her heart. It blotted out any shock or fear she might have felt, narrowing her focus to one thing: survival.

She reached for her pistol again. Vicky raised the bloody shard over her head and flew at Josie. A shot rang out. The deafening blast rang in Josie's ears, making it temporarily impossible to hear. The glass dropped from Vicky's hand. Blood, hers and Josie's, dripped from her fingers as she placed them on her abdomen, probing the hole in the waistline of her skirt. Turner appeared, forcing Vicky facedown on the floor next to Simon. His mouth moved as he zip-tied her wrists.

Turner tore paper towels from the roll over the sink and then stepped over Vicky and Simon. He thrust them at Josie. His voice was faint as her hearing began to return. "I already called additional units and a medic. Pressure on that wound, Quinn." When she didn't take the towels immediately, he took her arm and pressed them against the gash. Pushing her elbow up, he said, "Keep this above your heart."

As her hearing improved, she became aware of Vicky, cheek pressed to the floor, crying and screaming with everything she had left in her body. "You bitch! I hate you! I hate you! You ruined everything."

Turner squatted down and let his head hang so it was almost level with hers. "Hey, sweetheart, you have the right to remain silent—"

"She's already been Mirandized," Josie said.

Vicky's eyes were glazed over with rage. "You were on the list! My Roger was supposed to kill you and then come back to me. You were the last one! The last one! We were going to run away together. Instead, he decided to spare you if you could figure out what happened. He's dead because of you! You ruined my life!"

Turner shook his head. He pulled a pair of vinyl gloves from his inner jacket pocket and snapped them on. Kneeling next to Simon, he rolled him over easily and checked the wound.

"The last polaroid," Josie said when Vicky paused for breath. "That was you."

"Yes, it was me!" Vicky's voice started to lose steam. "Who do you think drove him to that house? I snuck in after he left with that girl. If Roger wasn't going to kill you, then I would! This sick bastard was supposed to do it for me but then you came here, and we were alone. I could have gotten rid of you both."

Turner pressed two fingers to Simon's neck and then shook his head. He was already gone. Moving over to Vicky, he flipped her, too, and put pressure on her abdomen. "Let me guess. Quinn kills him. You kill her. Then you come running outside to me like some kind of damsel in distress with a convenient story about how they killed one another. Quick thinking, I gotta say. You know who'll be real interested in this little story of yours? Your prison roommate."

SIXTY-EIGHT

A MONTH LATER

Josie sprawled on her couch, her feet resting in Noah's lap, while they watched Trinity flit around their living room, moving things around and then putting them back in place. So far, she'd rearranged the photos and other things on their entertainment center three times. She'd emptied the toy box they kept for Harris, spreading the toys around the room strategically. Lived-in but not too messy. Then she'd put them back. After that, she picked up Trout's toys, depositing them into the bin with his name on it, and moved that from one end of the room to the other and back. From his spot curled against Josie's side, Trout watched, only lifting his head when Trinity touched his beloved hedgehog. He cast a worried look in Josie's direction and she scratched his head in reassurance.

Noah laughed. "I know we said you could help us create our profile key for the adoption agency, but I think it would be faster if we did it ourselves."

Trinity stopped in the center of the room and put her hands on her hips, glaring at him. "After the mess with that crazy polaroid lady getting in here, don't you think it's even more important to put your best foot forward with this profile?"

Josie's gut tightened. They'd installed extra cameras and security since the close of the Polaroid Killer case, but they'd felt compelled to report it to the agency. She'd been certain it would be the death knell for their adoption hopes, but after some consideration and promises from Josie and Noah to add additional safety measures, they'd been given a second chance.

Still, Josie wondered if any birth parent would hand over an infant to two law enforcement officers.

Noah, sensing her distress, squeezed her feet in his large hands. They'd had many conversations about it since Vicky Platt's arrest. Not just about her violating their home but about the fact that they both could have died on the Overlook. It wasn't something they'd discussed with their case manager, and it wasn't something birth parents would find out because it was all in a day's work. But it bothered both of them. What if they'd had a baby waiting for them at home? Would they have rushed up to save Juliet Bowen so easily? Would one of them have wanted to stay on the ground so that their child might keep one parent? How would they have decided which?

"Josie," Noah whispered. "Remember what we talked about."

They'd decided that, despite all these worries and fears, they were going to move ahead. Ever since their colleague, Mett, died, they'd tried to live by his motto. No regrets.

It was a hell of a lot harder than Josie ever anticipated.

"What is it?" Trinity narrowed her eyes. "You're still worried about this whole thing being authentically 'you,' aren't you?"

Josie was glad that Trinity's psychic twin skills couldn't pick up on the true source of her trepidation.

Trinity threw her arms in the air. "Fine. We don't have to use my producer or the camera person if you're really that uncomfortable."

Noah lifted Josie's feet off his lap and went over to the toy box, rifling through it until he found the remote-control monster truck he and Harris played with obsessively. Then he fished out its controller and put them both on one of the lower shelves of the entertainment center. Long ago, he'd threaded an extension cord through the back so he could plug the charger in. Satisfied, Noah dug Trout's hedgehog from the basket and put it in the dog bed. Trout gave a sigh of approval. "We're not uncomfortable," Noah said. "We're grateful for the help."

"It's true," Josie reassured her sister. "We tried doing the video a few times and… well, I think Harris would have done a better job. If someone else is filming and directing us a little, we won't be as worried about how awkward it feels, and we can just be us."

"But," Noah said, "I don't think we need to stage this place. It should look like it always does."

Trinity scoffed. "Like you have a hundred houseguests a week and your dog runs your household?"

Josie stifled a laugh.

"Yes." Noah grinned. "Because that's us. Authentically us."

A LETTER FROM LISA

Thank you so much for choosing to read *Remember Her Name*. If you enjoyed the book and want to keep up to date with all my latest releases, just sign up at the following link. Your email address will never be shared, and you can unsubscribe at any time.

www.bookouture.com/lisa-regan

This book was a lot of fun to write especially because, in a way, it revisited Josie's greatest hits. As always, this is fiction and it's intended to give you fabulous readers a few hours of thrilling entertainment. I worked with my law enforcement consultants to make the police procedure as authentic as possible. Technology is always improving, and procedures sometimes change with time, but I have tried to incorporate current practices as accurately as possible, such as the way elimination prints are handled in the event that a department has an in-house latent print examiner (with Level II certification). Any mistakes are entirely my own.

Again, thank you so much for reading. I love writing this series. I'm so grateful that readers are still so invested in Josie. I love hearing from readers. You can get in touch with me through my website or any of the social media outlets below, as well as my Goodreads page. Also, I'd really appreciate it if you'd leave a review and recommend *Remember Her Name*, or perhaps other books in the series, to other readers. Reviews and word-of-mouth recommendations go such a long way toward helping new readers discover my books. Thank you so much for your relentless enthusiasm for this series. Josie and I remain ever grateful, and we hope to see you next time!

Thanks,

Lisa Regan

www.lisaregan.com

 facebook.com/LisaReganCrimeAuthor

 x.com/LisaIRegan

ACKNOWLEDGMENTS

Fantastic readers: As always, I am indebted to you for your loyalty to this series. I've said this before, but I'll say it again: it truly is my privilege and pleasure to write these stories for all of you. You are the greatest readers in the world. I am so grateful to all of you, and in awe of your passion for all things Josie Quinn. I love hearing from you, and even if I'm deep in the process of a first draft or a round of edits and cannot be on social media as much as I'd like to, I'm always reading your messages, comments, and emails. I am here for everything you have to say! Thank you to the members of my Reader Lounge. You are such a special group of readers. I'm astounded by the way you continue to make the Lounge a group filled with respect, kindness, lots and lots of laughs, and passion for reading. You are my people and I adore you.

Thank you, as always, to my husband, Fred, for keeping everything in our lives running smoothly so I can fully devote my attention to Denton when needed. Thank you for knowing when I need to get out of my head so I can recharge my creative batteries. Thank you, my love, for protecting the peace and space I need to write at my best (and bringing me tea late at night). As always, thank you for helping me work out plot issues and brainstorm, whether it's in the car, over dinner, or late at night in my office. Thank you for answering every inane research question I ask, no matter how bizarre. Your expertise knows no bounds. Thank you to my daughter, Morgan, for sacrificing so much time with me and also being so wonderfully supportive. You are so caring and thoughtful, and it means more than you know.

Thank you to my superstar multimedia coordinator, friend and first reader, Maureen Downey, for juggling so many things while I write; always knowing what to do; and keeping me motivated. Thank you for reading such an early draft to let me know if I was on the right track. Thank you to my first readers and friends: Katie Mettner, Dana Mason, Nancy S. Thompson, and Torese Hummel. As always, your thoughts, suggestions, critiques, and "catches" are essential to making the book the best it can be! Thank you to Matty Dalrymple and Jane Kelly for always making yourselves available for brainstorming!

Thank you to my grandmothers: Helen Conlen and Marilyn House; my parents: Donna House, Joyce Regan, the late Billy Regan, Rusty House, and Julie House; my brothers and sisters-in-law: Sean and Cassie House, Kevin and Christine Brock and Andy Brock; as well as my lovely sisters: Ava McKittrick and Melissia McKittrick. Thank you as well to all of the people who continue to spread the word about my books even after twenty-five of them (total)—Debbie Tralies, Jean and Dennis Regan, Tracy Dauphin, Jeanne Cassidy, the Regans, the Conlens, and the Houses. I see you out there still telling people about my work, and I appreciate it! I am incredibly grateful to all the lovely reviewers and bloggers who take the time to read and review each and every book. I'm also very grateful to the reviewers and bloggers who have just read this as their first Josie Quinn story. Thank you for giving Josie a chance!

Thank you, as always, to Lt. Jason Jay for all your amazing and detailed help and for answering each and every one of my questions, which are endless! I can never thank you enough for the way you get back to me so quickly even when you're in the middle of something fun or it's late at night. I don't know what I would do without you! Thank you to Stephanie Kelley, my fabulous law enforcement consultant, for all your very thoughtful and detailed assistance, and for understanding the high-wire act that is making these books authentic while still providing entertainment value. I love that you're so patient and kind. Thank you to Leanne Kale Sparks for answering so many of my defense attorney questions. You are so kind and generous. Thank you to Michelle Mordan for your lovely assistance with all things EMS.

Thank you to Jessie Botterill for your insight, brilliance, endless patience and for believing in this book! Thank you for not balking at my crazy, eleventh-hour ideas. Also, thank you for teaching me the word "stonker." You are the best! Finally, thank you to Noelle Holten, Kim Nash, Liz Hatherell, and Jenny Page, as well as the entire team at Bookouture.

PUBLISHING TEAM

Turning a manuscript into a book requires the efforts of many people. The publishing team at Bookouture would like to acknowledge everyone who contributed to this publication.

Audio
Alba Proko
Sinead O'Connor
Melissa Tran

Commercial
Lauren Morrissette
Hannah Richmond
Imogen Allport

Cover design
The Brewster Project

Data and analysis
Mark Alder
Mohamed Bussuri

Editorial
Jessie Botterill
Ria Clare

Copyeditor
Liz Hatherell

Proofreader
Jenny Page

Marketing
Alex Crow
Melanie Price
Occy Carr
Ciara Rosney
Martyna Młynarska

Operations and distribution
Marina Valles
Stephanie Straub

Production
Hannah Snetsinger
Mandy Kullar
Jen Shannon

Publicity
Kim Nash
Noelle Holten
Jess Readett
Sarah Hardy

Rights and contracts
Peta Nightingale
Richard King
Saidah Graham

Made in the USA
Monee, IL
14 September 2024

65802020R00225